Rimworld

-Into the Green-

JL Curtis

Books by JL Curtis

The Grey Man- Vignettes

The Grey Man- Payback

The Grey Man- Changes

The Grey Man- Partners

Short Stories by JL Curtis

Rimworld- Stranded

(Kindle only)

Author's Note: This is a work of fiction. Names, characters, places, and incidents are a product of the author's imagination. Locales and public names are sometimes used for atmospheric purposes. Any resemblance to actual people, living or dead, or to businesses, companies, events, institutions, or locales is completely coincidental.

Published by JLC&A. Available from Amazon.com in Kindle format or soft cover book, printed by CreateSpace.

Rimworld- Into the Green/ JL Curtis. -- 1st ed.
ISBN-13:978-1545474211
ISBN-10: 1545474214

DEDICATION

Blame this one on Peter and Ian!

Dedicated to those that toil in the dungeons in the R&D/S&T worlds, and the aliens in the basement. They make the impossible possible. Medicine, communications, space travel, lasers, science and technology advances...

ACKNOWLEDGMENTS

Thanks to the usual suspects.

Special thanks to my editor Stephanie Martin, and to Holly Chism.

Cover art by Tina Garceau.

Table of Contents

Prologue

The Hundred Years War was supposedly over, or at so said the powers that be. The Dragons or Dragoons, as they had come to be called, came out of the Coma Berenices Nebula and contacted the expanding Galactic Empire and the Galactic Patrol three hundred years ago, either in 2550, or 2560 depending on who one believed. There was always some question since the Consolidated Union War had finally wound down, and no one was really sure whether the Dragoons first contacted the disparate CU entities, or the Galactic Empire.

***

GalPat Colonel Nan Randall wanted to scream, or alternatively, drag a few politicians out here without armor, and let them *negotiate* with the Dragoons. She saw Captain McNeil go down and his telltale go red on her HUD meaning this negotiation had taken another one of her soldiers. Cursing, she keyed her comm, saying calmly, "Garibaldi, swing your company left, get that ridgeline between you and the Goon's line. Culverhouse, you're no longer reserve. Right flank is all yours."

Randall thought, *Damn, what I wouldn't give to have some bots to send forward, but the freakin' stores ship lost her starboard drive before the last transition and she's still at least two days out. We don't have two days to wait. Need to put this one to bed now...*

Quickly scanning her armor status, she cued her AI, "Okay Ethan, let's go to war. Combat retention now." Feeling the suit's gel tighten, she squirmed into a more comfortable position and keyed her comm, "Charlie, on me. We're going up the gut. Bounding advance by platoon, use the boulder field to your advantage. Let's go dig those bastards out and blow their asses away."

She started forward and commanded the AI, "Ethan, auto evade around bearing two-niner-three." The AI immediately started jinking both the altitude and heading of the bounding run until she and the company got to the first line of rocks. Chief McQuerry and his platoon bounded forward under Charlie platoon's covering fire, and Randall winced as she saw two red personnel telltales pop up, indicating two more troops had been killed.

Lieutenant Moore's platoon was next, as the two platoons laid down covering fire. Randall got a carat on one of the Dragoons that thought it was not visible and put a Stinger missile on it, smiling to herself as the Goon and part of a boulder disappeared. Moore's platoon made it with no losses, but a couple of telltales were yellow and she heard the call, "Medic up."

Carating another rock pile, she pushed it to Charlie Company and keyed up, "Okay Charlie, one more time, now!" She jumped and started firing as she moved forward. First one, then a second red suit status telltales popped up as she slid to a stop behind the rock pile. Ammo was yellow, down to sixty percent, but she blinked that alert away.

Sergeant Obergon keyed up. "Lost Pop and Guest on that one. Mac, you've got first squad .now." She heard a "Roger" and nodded to herself that Mac was stepping up.

Just as she went to call Chief McQuerry forward, Captain Garibaldi keyed up, "Got the ridgeline. Good IR sight line into their camp, and I think we've got the fusion plant located. We're not taking any fire. Don't think they know we're here."

Captain Culverhouse keyed in, "Got them occupied on this side. Take 'em Bob."

Colonel Randall said, "Take the fusion plant with everything you have on my count." Keying company wide, she continued, "Listen up, going to take the fusion plant on my count. At three, everyone go to ground and eat dirt. Garibaldi take it in one, two, three…"

The sky lit with actinic fire, and the blast bounced the armor around like marbles on a table top. Randall rolled over with a groan, shook her head, and finally got her camera clear of dust. Looking toward the Dragoon's line, all she saw was a glassine surface. Even the rock pile she'd been behind was melted over halfway down. She quickly took inventory of the company and saw Culverhouse with a yellow telltale. Keying the command channel, she asked, "Culverhouse, what happened?"

An abashed Culverhouse, obviously in pain, replied, "I forgot to duck. Took a pretty good sized boulder upside the head."

Randall snickered to herself, and keyed the uplink to the strike group in orbit, "Colonel Randall here, we're ready for pickup. Dragoon outpost is gone, another mud ball has been saved for the empire."

***

In the first twenty years of the possibly ended Hundred Years War, the Galactic Patrol had pushed the Dragoons back to the forty light year range, but the Goons' cooperation with the Traders, who were inside Galactic space, had given them better ships and weapons, allowing them to regain ground and planets through their all-out attacks. The next eighty years were a constant back and forth conflict across space, with the Dragoons getting within ten light years of Earth at one point, and actually getting one strike through that made landfall. After years of battle grinding on and pulverizing both ships and personnel, with over one million troops and spacers dead, and an estimated fifty million colonists lost on various planets, there was the infamous meeting at Vega that set the cease fire in 2606.

From one of the countless briefs: *Dragons, (common usage term Dragoons or Goons)- Patriarchal society. Air breathers. Six to seven feet tall. Two to three hundred pounds. Bipedal, opposable thumbs, three fingered clawed forelegs, three toed clawed feet. Vestigial tails, vestigial wings. Prominent fangs. Multiple colorations, do not tie to specific clans or patriarchal lines. Rudimentary space activity, warrior ruling class. Expansionist, using slave labor, cultural values include capture of worlds, minerals, battle to advance within society.*

Subnote 23- Carnivorous, eat prisoners and dead, including their own.

Subnote 31- Males start training as warriors at three years or age. Females mainly breeders, administrators. Can live to four hundred years of age.

Subnote 56- Partnered with or subsumed humans and Consolidated Unions worlds (hereafter known as 'Traders') in the outlying star clusters before/during the Hundred Years War. Gained access to then-current galactic space technology and weapons through CU shipyards and manufactories.

Subnote 133- Demilitarized Zone (DMZ) established after Galactic Patrol cease fire in 2606 at the 28 light year demarcation line when three separate battles (See Hundred Year War, Appendix 48) stopped the incursions. Numerous smaller incursions continue to this day, with Dragoons claiming worlds based on establishment of outposts: establishment of patriarchal Dragoon enclaves include minimum of ten Dragoons including 5 male and 5 female (Reference GALPAT REPORT 8745 (Cluster Skirmish 2790-2793) Section 3-A-35-c) .

Subnote 204- Cooperation between CU Traders and Dragoons continues. Traders used to move material/Dragoons between various locations within Dragoon Sphere of Influence (SOI).

GALPAT TACNOTE 601- 'Traders' move freely between Dragoon SOI and Galactic Empire as couriers moving Dragoons between embassies. Unconfirmed reports Traders are acting as raiders to steal new tech in raids against soft targets/engineering complexes/limited incursions into shipyards.

BOLO: Any suspicious traffic as reported by GalPat controllers. Be advised, basic ship data similar to generic galactic ship set. If vectored for intercept, assume defense posture 3Delta. Check transponder beacon and data plate against current GalPat library. No definitive differences in physical appearance, primary language is Spanglish, but also speak Galactic with no noticeable accent; run standard datachip citizen checks against current GalPat database.

Confirmed reports (See GalPat Incident Report subset 281) Traders also conducting pirate operations throughout known space. Primary prey includes- Unescorted Military transports, liners, and colony ships (outside 20 light year range gate). Kidnapping/ransom primarily pointed at high value targets. Shipset used includes Consolidated Union Destroyer (CUDDS) class vessels, Cruiser (CUCRU) class vessels from Hundred Year War. If encountered, authorized weapons Red/Tight unless fired on. If fired on, weapons Green.

Incursions continue in Rimworld clusters: Dragoons/Traders continue to attempt to claim additional worlds within the 28 light year boundary, including worlds currently settled by Galactic Empire settlers. All GalPat patrols are encouraged to make full planetary scans when making contact with colony worlds, or when transiting any empty quadrant containing potentially habitable worlds (See GALPAT INTEL NOTE 321 for scan procedures).

***

The Galactic Scout teams didn't really worry about the big picture. One new system or planet at a time was their mission. Between the space telescopes, the Scout research ships that located and plotted various spatial phenomena including wormholes, jump points and black holes, and their core mission of certifying worlds as habitable for settlers, they were busy enough.

Sergeant Ethan Fargo, eighty-four and in his prime, Earth native and team lead, was outwardly unremarkable in every way. He had medium brown hair, brown eyes and a smooth expression that belied the sense of inner strength you only see if you looked him in the eye. He'd been genied for athletics and hand/eye coordination as a child, and it continued to serve him well. His additional duties as empath and intel kept him hopping, along with herding the 'cats' of his team.

Pop, resembling nothing less than a five foot tall bipedal weasel, showing a little gray around :the muzzle, hailing from Kepler 62E, scout and primary security, seemingly lazy, he was anything but sloth-like in the field. Hardt: thickset, blond haired, blue eyed and taciturn, born of German Earth stock from Waldron-Antares 4, science lead and primary pilot for the small drop shuttle they had been using. DenAfr, the huge Taurasian symbiote pair that looked like a :headless elephant, sifter and primary medic, checking the air, water and soil for composition. DenAfr was always playing tricks with his ability to extrude pseudopods, tapping people, moving things behind one's back and other little annoyances. In addition, it was the back up security with Pop. Diez: stout with black hair and dark brown eyes, of Hispanic descent with a carefully cultured little moustache, also Earth native, linguist, backup medic, and a level five psi. Diez also maintained their armored suits and comm software and hardware that they used in the field.

Fargo called the team meeting to order, "Okay, we're the go team. Lynx Galaxy this time." Slewing the holovid, he brought up the location of planet X423W. Glancing at Hardt, he continued, "Standard routing takes us through jump points Charlie, Echo Six and Bravo Three. I talked to the colonel earlier and he promised they'd get us within a seventy-two div track to the planet."

Hardt rolled his eyes, "Sure, sure. I'll believe *that* when I see the planet. After that last cluster…"

Fargo held up his hand, "Over and done. Moving on," he flipped the holo to the specifications from the first-in scans, "Looks like some potential here. They only got three probes back, but looks like good O2, and from the pictures it's got some good atmosphere. Unknowns are the plant life, other life forms, and composition."

DenAfr's GalTrans squeaked, "So we know nothing of the actual composition of the planet?"

Fargo sighed, "No, we don't know anything…"

DenAfr squealed, "So it is possible I will get a discovery, *so* excited." It extruded multiple pseudopods which waved like grass before the wind.

Pop asked, "Weaps?"

"As always, White/Tight unless we get hit. We'll be in field armor until we finish the base survey and make the follow-on determination from there." Pop nodded and slumped back down.

Fargo turned to Diez, who said, "I know. Check all armor, check that the medical telltales on the soft suits are working and are actually talking to the armor this time. And yes, I've already checked that the tissue cans are correctly auto-arming whenever we are in the field. That last cluster was a software error when they pushed an update to us while we were in the field."

Fargo nodded, "And deity forbid, if one of us had gone down, there wouldn't have been a self-destruct and tissue retrieval for burial."

Hardt asked, "Why didn't it work? Just curious."

Diez took control of the holo, popping up a display of the grey tissue can, 1 ½ inches by 3 inches with a flashing code string on the end. "See this code string? That's your numbers. When you put the skinsuit on, it's supposed to automatically read your chip and pull those numbers. Without that, no French fried Hardt, since it can't activate without those numbers."

Hardt shivered, "Never did like a system that's going to automatically fry me if I die, but…"

Everyone else chorused, "It beats getting eaten by a Goon!"

Fargo finished the standard brief, everyone gave their positional briefs and planned actions, and they lined up the landing spots for the two months long planeting.

Chief Sergeant Williamson came in and started the Dragoon briefing, much to the dismay of Pop and Diaz. Pop asked, "Is this really necessary Chief? It's the same brief as…"

Williamson interrupted, "You know it is. There is always a slim chance of encounters anywhere in space."

Diez chimed in, "If it's in space, we're useless…"

Fargo finally said, "Alright, enough. Just shut up and listen. The sooner you do, the sooner we're out of here."

Planeting

It was supposed to be easy. They'd done this twenty-four times before… This one would get them a silver star for their insignia.

The scout team had been landed on X423W two days earlier to perform the second-in scouting of the T-2.C class planet. As a team, they'd been together for twenty-five years, and settled into their roles like an old, comfortable, polygamous marriage.

What they hadn't expected was encountering Traders or a Dragoon, even after the briefing…

Pop was the first one down, just after he yelled the warning and fired the first rounds from the top of the karst ridge. Hardt had recovered Pop's can after he'd fallen down the ridge. Hardt was hit just as he made it to the cover of a stand of something resembling trees, dying before anyone could get to him. Fargo had finally managed to dodge through the field of boulders to get to Hardt, confirmed the red tattletale, and keyed the destruct code.

Fargo picked up Hardt's can, then Pop's as Diez came over common saying the Traders were targeting them remotely. *Gotta remember to report that, I wonder if that targeting works on battle armor too,* Fargo thought.

Diez said, "Dump armor", and carated a location a half mile away. Fargo, Diez and DenAfr made runs for it from their locations and jumped into a ravine a hundred or so feet deep on anti-grav, giving them momentary cover. They'd climbed quickly from their suits, with DenAfr, having a few problems extracting itself from the armor, but that wasn't unusual for it.

Diez ran an override code, repowered the armor, and commanded autonomous recovery mode. The code sent the armor climbing toward the upper end of the ravine enroute to the drop shuttle. The three of them, now in skinsuits and masks headed in the opposite direction going down the ravine as it shallowed out. Fargo remembered looking up at the twin red suns, and being thankful the temps were manageable by the skinsuit, and the air was marginally breathable as they moved quickly to put distance between themselves and their armor.

Fargo missed the armament, including the heavy pulse rifle, but his implicit trust in Diez and his intel expertise overrode the desire to keep it. At least he had his 6mm bead pistol and 16mm bead rifle that he'd recovered from the suit's locker, as did Diez. DenAfr, due to its size, was able to detach the 20mm pulse rifle from its armor, and carried the one hundred pound rifle with ease in the pseudopods it had extruded. The other thing Fargo carried was a bandoleer with the two recovery cans containing the remains of Pop and Hardt.

They'd made it about 10 klicks down the brush-choked ravine when DenAfr rounded a blind corner, and ran head on into four Traders. It shot two and bludgeoned one, but wasn't fast enough to get the fourth one. Neither Fargo nor Diez had a shot until they'd cleared DenAfr's bulk, but by then it was too late.

That they had killed the last of the four Traders wasn't much comfort, as the loss of DenAfr meant they were really in the hurt locker. Without DenAfr, they would have no warning if the Traders decided to throw a Biowep at them. Fargo remembered checking the telltale on their skinsuit, confirming it was red, then keying the suit and turning away as it burned down into a can. Surprising Fargo, it was exactly the same size as the cans for Pop and Hardt. He added it to the 40mm bandoleer he'd grabbed out of his armor. He ran his thumb over the tabs on the ends of the can and watched as each lit with the GalScout personnel code for the individual's remains.

He and Diez had made it another seven, maybe eight klicks, circling back toward their camp through the waist high bluish colored brush toward the drop shuttle homing beacon before they'd been caught in the open by another group of Traders in light armor coming over a distant ridge line. They took cover in a wallow about fifteen feet across, six feet deep at the edge, ten or more feet deep in the middle, muddy and filled with what looked like bone fragments. It stank with a rank scent he could smell even through the filters and Fargo saw what looked like deep claw marks in the sides. Thankfully it was empty and deep enough to protect them from direct fire, but it was also hard to target the Traders without their armor. Instead they had to physically climb up to the top of the wallow using the claw marks like steps, shoot and slide back down before the incoming fire took their heads off.

Diez had psi-linked with Fargo and confirmed he'd triggered the emergency beacon before they evacuated the camp and he'd also sent out a blind broadcast while they were on the run, hoping there was some friendly ship that might hear it.

Fargo had thought, *Well, that'll be a fat chance in hell, the scout ship isn't due back for another ten day, and we're so damn far out in the boonies I doubt there is anybody else in this star system.*

Fargo knew he was at the end of his rope physically, but noted that even though Diez was as tired as he was, there wasn't any indication of that in the telepathic link, which earned a chuckle from Diez. "See, as long as I'm breathing, telepathy works. I stop breathing, it doesn't work. File that one away Fargo."

Fargo thought back, "Yeah, breathing is good. Getting out of here is going to be a problem."

Diez crept up to the lip of the wallow, fired and slid back down to the bottom projecting, "Well, I *think* we've cut them down a few. I see three out there and I think I got a hit on one of them. The most you sensed was nine, right?"

Fargo thought back, "I screwed up, I wasn't open enough. I was trying to sense if there were any animals, and I was blocking higher order in our band. But yeah, nine. And something else, probably a Dragoon. At least that's all I could sense on the higher levels when I opened up."

Fargo climbed up to the lip, stuck his head up slowly, and surveyed the plain to the east of their camp and the drop shuttle. Looking slowly and opening his mind to any empathic sources again, he was jarred to feel someone behind him with a sense of gloating. As he started to turn, Diez had both projected and screamed, "Opposite lip! Drop!"

Cursing himself, Fargo was half way through turning loose of the edge and sliding down, but couldn't disengage his feet in time. He felt a blow to his leg as he dropped back to the bottom of the wallow, firing on the way down. Diez had fired on full pulse at the one weak point they knew on the Trader's light armor, the connection plate between the body and helmet. From an upward angle it was actually fairly easy to kill them if you put enough beads on the seam. Diez was in the process of reloading when two more heads popped over the edge of the wallow. Fargo yelled at Diez as he fired at the one he thought was aiming into the wallow and took him out, but the second shot down into Diez before Fargo could shift his aim.

Diez reared up, screamed both verbally and telepathically as he was hit across the chest and hips, but fired on pulse again and chewed up the side of the wallow, then the lip, and finally the second Trader as Fargo also fired. Fargo felt a blow on his left arm, and lost his rifle. He watched in horror as the arm and rifle cartwheeled away from him; then the pain hit.

Fargo looked down and realized most of his left arm was gone, just as the pharmacope hit him with another dose of pain killers. Fargo's mind was a little fuzzy, but he realized he'd already had one dose, and wondered why. He started to get up to go to Diez, but fell over. Rolling over, he looked down and saw that his right leg ended at the knee. *Oh, that's where the other dose came from, damn good thing these skins have smart tech built in*, he thought.

Diez had slumped to his knees, and his pain came hammering through the link hitting Fargo until his pharmacope dumped pain killers into him as well. Crawling over, Fargo managed to get to Diez, and propped himself against the side of the wallow as he pulled Diez across his lap. Panting, Diez thought, *"Damn, this shit is not good! Well, hate to say this Fargo, but I think they stuck a fork in us."*

Fargo thought back, *"Stuck a fork in us?"*

Diez coughed and pulled his breathing mask to the side, spat a mouthful of bright red blood, then left his mask hanging. *"Old Earth term. We're done Fargo. Well done. It's been a good twenty-five years. Had more fun than the law allowed. Got to see more shit than I ever thought I would. Proud to serve with you. Couldn't ask for…"*

Fargo said, "Diez, you gotta hang on man. You can't leave me now. Your pharmacope is as good as mine and mine's keeping my ass alive. Diez. Diez!" Fargo leaned over and looked Diez in the eyes, then saw more blood dribble from his mouth.

Diez seemed to focus on Fargo, a half smile forming on his lips and one last thought came across the link. *"Fargo, you'll never believe what you missed."* Diez shook his head, almost in sadness and continued, *"You'll never believe…"*

Fargo screamed as he felt Diez die, and thought his head was going to explode. He blacked out briefly, then slowly came back around, staring up at the yellow-green sky. Something was wrong with his head, it was like he had double vision, except that it was in his mind. He slowly reached down and checked Diez's telltale. It was blood red.

Sliding Diez off his lap, he keyed the destruct code and rolled away as Diez was consumed inside the suit and it shrunk into another can. He picked it up and placed it in the bandoleer with the other four, running his thumb across the tops of each can and getting the ID codes for the remains encased in the can. Pulling his bead pistol, Fargo leaned back against the side of the wallow awaiting the inevitable on planet X423W as he dictated an updated status to his skin suit's memory.

After a couple of minutes, Fargo decided to climb to the lip of the wallow and get it over with, rather than sitting in the bottom of a hole waiting to die. He was a former Terran Marine dammit, and Marines go out on their feet, not on their asses. Holstering his pistol, he started slowly scrabbling up the side of the wallow, every bump of his leg or arm sending shooting pain throughout his body. Rather than give in to the pain, it pissed him off even more and he redoubled his efforts. After what seemed like an eternity, he made it all the way to the lip of the wallow, and rolled slowly over.

As he lay there, he wondered if anyone would ever find them, or even care if they did. He wasn't much of a praying man, but he said a prayer for his team members, and hoped there was an afterlife so he'd see Cindy and Ike one more time. Levering himself up on the body of the Trader he'd shot, he looked across the flat, sensing, and then seeing two more Traders accompanied by one Dragoon coming out of the forest in armor.

His thoughts turned to the last stanza of Fiddler's Green he'd learned in The Basic School on Earth.

And so when man and horse go down
Beneath a saber keen,
Or in a roaring charge of fierce melee
You stop a bullet clean,
And the hostiles come to get your scalp,
Just empty your canteen,
And put your pistol to your head
And go to Fiddlers' Green..

He checked his pistol, settled down behind the Trader's armored body and waited for them to get in range. Then the world turned black.

Alive

Fargo was in and out of consciousness as his body slowly healed; memories and reality seemed to be one and the same, at times. He wasn't sure if he was alive or dead. If these visions were dreams or was his life passing slowly in front of his eyes.

The original planning for what was Planet Z43F5 consisted of reviews of the first contact team's probes. The fact that there appeared to be some structures, possibly ancient terraformers, and other objects grouped near them had been an exciting twist for Fargo and his team, especially since the world had been classified as a T-1, B which was about as close to Earth as one got. They'd never drawn one of the 'lost' worlds, and the probes showed good O2 saturation, breathable air and the presence of water, but there was no sign of higher level intelligent life or sentient beings.

Fargo and his team had planeted near one of the terraformer structures in the southern temperate zone and found a rudimentary landing pad, around a thousand empty containers, and the remains of what might have been a small shuttle, but per SOP they'd stayed in their armor for the initial sweeps, and didn't investigate it any further as the whole area was overgrown and slowly deteriorating in the moist, tropical conditions.

Fargo's thoughts were interrupted by a strange conversation that seemed to be taking place in his mind. He didn't know who it was, but they were discussing his body for some reason. Fargo wanted to remember to tell them that whatever they were using tickled, but he dropped back into unconsciousness.

Sometime later, Fargo's thoughts segued back to what he now knew as Hunter's world, but how did he know that? Why did he think of it as home? He had a mental image of shaking his head, and another memory drifted to the surface. *At the fourth and last planeting on Z43F5, they'd discovered a more complete landing pad and another thousand containers, with one major difference. Two of the containers had been opened, set up, powered up and lived in for an extended period of time. And the containers were still connected to the terraformer's power, so the sonics field around them was intact.*

It was a basic Hab unit and inside they'd discovered a written log and other documents.

According to the documents, the SierraSafari Club had the rights to Z43F5 in the first great colonization expansion from Earth in 2250, and had dedicated the world to a hunt preserve. They had put down terraformers to complete the transition to mimic global areas based on their historic documents and had started shipping first-landing equipment and a few hundred set up personnel, along with arks of flora and fauna, and apparently even arachnids, insects, and worms from Earth just before the great war.

Apparently there had been a total of four terraformers, offset ninety degrees from each other, two in the southern hemisphere, and two in the northern hemisphere. Diez had recognized them as being an old de Perez design, and joked they were guaranteed for a thousand years.

Fargo's thoughts were again interrupted by an overwhelming need to scratch his arm and his leg, and he 'heard' voices in his head much more plainly, *"Look at the spike in Neuro. I believe he's itching like seven hells of a Dragoon's lair. That tells me the nerve and bio interfaces in his arm and leg are starting to connect."*

A second disembodied voice said, *"We agree. We will increase the pain blocker to eight milligrams per milliliter. That should be sufficient."*

Moments later Fargo felt something like a cool breeze and the need to scratch stopped. As he puzzled over that, he once again dropped into unconsciousness, catching one last comment from the disembodied voice, *"We wonder if Fargo is truly under. His brain and lace activity are higher than they should be in the tank. We must ponder on this. This is not possible."*

MKwerts! a Kepleran and also named Pop, pointed to the cranial scan, "OneSvel, look at this, his neural lace is not a standard GalScout lace. He's got extra chips in the frontal, parietal, *all* of his nodes and the neocortex!"

"We missed that." OneSvel dug back through Fargo's medical records, finally finding a cranial scan from his induction physical thirty years earlier. Putting the holograms up simultaneously, they slowly overlaid them. "This is unusual. We must research this. He apparently had a…"

OneSvel waved another terminal to life and accessed Fargo's personnel record after the system verified his need to know. "Ah, Marine. He has what I believe is an independent command lace."

Pop asked, "Marine? Independent command lace?"

OneSvel brought up another hologram, merging it slowly with the other two. It overlaid almost perfectly. "See how they overlay? Need to know information here, Fargo was a Terran Marine prior to GalScouts; we are not supposed to know that. They insert command modules into officers that will have any kind of combat commands. But the Marines should have nulled those modules when he left. Based on what we are seeing, I believe they are active. That would explain his heightened activity and resistance... no, never mind."

Pop shrugged, "Do we need to remove them? I can set up the autosurg to do that in about ten minutes."

"No! They have an autodestruct program. Any attempt to remove them will cause them to self-destruct and kill Fargo." OneSvel muttered to itself, *Marines, Terran Marines... What were they known for? Ah, recovery of their own. They even recovered their dead. One wonders if that caused Fargo's problem on the ship.* OneSvel filed that thought away for later contemplation, but didn't make any official entries in Fargo's medical record.

***

Fargo surfaced once again, this time the memories were much older. *Home leave, walking hand in hand with Cindy along a tree shaded path on the front range of the Rockies, smelling the freshness of pines and clean air. A freshly minted second lieutenant in the Terran Marines, he remembered his pride in finishing The Basic School at the top of the class. Proposing marriage, and their agreement to get married as soon as he'd finished space training on Luna.*

***

Fargo walked from the meadow into the nearpine forest, and stared up at the old growth in amazement. There were few limbs below thirty feet, and the pine straw was like walking on a mattress. He inhaled the scent of the pines as he listened to the roar of the waterfall a hundred meters away. *I could live here. Reminds me a lot of home, but there's nothing there for me now, and I'll never get back there any time soon, anyway.*

He continued through the forest to the waterfall, noting the location of the creek bed and how it ran in almost a perfect perpendicular to the bench, then fell in another waterfall into the canyon below. Pacing beside the creek bed, his Marine background kicked in and he noted the gradual slope for about seventy yards, then a flattening for another hundred yards before the bench ended. The sight lines were excellent in the meadow, and the bench extended another three hundred yards to the west, which meant lots of evening light from the sun. He marked the location on his datacomp without conscious thought. *Yeah, I could definitely live here. Prefab cabin, plenty of water, thirty-fifty div flight to the strip. Shit, I must be dreaming.*

He could see DenAfr trudging back up the slight slope to the shuttle and he picked up his pace, extending his senses. Other than some low level awareness, he picked up nothing else, and nothing threatening. They met at the ramp and DenAfr said, "We found what appears to be an excellent concentration of ore, and hard rock structures. These trees appear to be another overseed of an Earth variant-"

Fargo interrupted, "Long leaf pine. It is what is called old growth on Earth. I think this is probably like what we've seen at the other sites and matches what was in that log."

DenAfr inclined the pseudopod carrying the recorder, "We agree. Very little of the original vegetation here seems to have been of anything other than bush size. I have found nothing to indicate larger cover. Examination of mulch shows that, prior to the terraformers, there does appear to have been a stable atmosphere, but containing less oxygen than now, and a much higher concentration of argon. We are concerned however, about what is knocking out the flyers. We are down to only thirty left."

Fargo shrugged, "I'm guessing some native airborne species that we haven't seen. Maybe like that fuzzy thing we saw from the shuttle last ten day. We lift in two days to meet the ship, and frankly, getting back with any of them is good."

***

Fargo realized he was awake, and sniffed the air softly. *Hospital smell, now the question is where.* Subtly testing his muscles, he realized he was strapped down. And he was itching. Both his left arm and right leg were itching like hell. *Must be in the tank again.*

Yeah, I remember losing the arm, and I guess I lost the leg too. Letting his empathic sense expand, he didn't sense anyone or anything close, but his mind was *hearing* a babble of thoughts, emotions, *something.*

He slowly opened his eyes, and picked out what he recognized as a typical Gal hospital room, and he sighed. Somehow he'd made it back, but of that, he had no memory. The last thing he remembered was Diez dying in his arms and…

Locking his mind down, he thought, *the cans! Where were the cans? Did I make it back with the cans of his teammates? Why the fuck can't I remember? And what the hell is going on in my head? Am I truly crazy now?*

As these thoughts flickered through his mind, the door dilated and OneSvel, the Taurasian doctor symbiote, trundled through the opening squeaking a greeting which his Galtrans parsed into, "Fargo, you live. I saw your brain activity pick up as you regained natural consciousness and I knew you would spike momentarily."

As OneSvel bustled around it continued, "In answer to your questions, you are the sole survivor of your team. You brought all their remains back. Your emergency signal was picked up by a GalPat destroyer that was transiting the star system looking for a pirate they believed had dropped into that system. They arrived in time to take out the remaining Traders, two Dragoons and their ship, and got you aboard."

Fargo interrupted, "How long?" and coughed. OneSvel extruded a pseudopod, picked up a bulb and straw and held it for Fargo to drink. Fargo dropped his head back, "Thanks. How long have I been out?"

OneSvel chittered again, "Almost three weeks, Fargo. There were *problems* when you were taken aboard the destroyer. And that's not counting the 45 day transit."

Fargo rolled his head and looked at him, "Doc what are you talking about? Over two months? I…That's not…"

OneSvel continued, "Gently, Fargo. We are not sure what happened to you, but your brain scans are completely different. Also, it appears you would not go into cryo or stasis. Every time the ship's doctor tried to take away the cans and put you under, apparently your mind refused to shut down, and you went into physical spasms fighting to hold onto the band with the cans attached. He said your response was unlike anything he'd ever seen. They put you in the medbox with the cans around your torso, but that also meant they couldn't do any reconstructive work. They could only maintain you at the state you were recovered in. Unconscious and barely alive."

A grizzled Kepleran, showing white on his muzzle and barely five feet tall, came in and salaamed Fargo, his GalTrans saying, "I am MKwerts!. Thanks of the clan for the return of VMtersz! to us. The honor of the clan is awaiting the details of his death." He gently released the straps holding Fargo on the hospital bed, and helped Fargo to sit up, holding him gently as Fargo's equilibrium swam into a different alignment. Fargo once again marveled at the strength the little Kepleran had, as they all seemed to have. Fargo had called VMtersz! Pop, but thinking back, it seemed like *all* the Keplerans from 62E were called Pop. He filed that away and vowed to research where that naming convention came from.

Once Fargo had his balance, the old Kepleran released him and Fargo rolled his shoulders, leaning back on his arms to stay stable. He turned to him and replied, "Pop, my Pop, died with valor, he was the first to see the Traders, and the first to fire. He gave his life to protect us, and he will be recommended for a Star award as soon as I can do that."

The old Kepleran salaamed again saying, "Then he fulfilled his duty to you and to the clan. Your word is enough." Bustling around, he provided Fargo with a clean uniform, shined boots, his beret, and his personal data cube, which meant they'd accessed his billeting to get them. "The fresher is here," the Kepleran said, sliding a panel aside.

Fargo managed to stand after two attempts, and with Pop's assistance made it to the fresher, realizing he *really* needed to go. As he sat in the fresher, he opened his mind and realized he was 'hearing' what might be fragments of thoughts from both Pop and OneSvel, but neither made any real sense. It seemed that OneSvel was conflicted as to whether to report the changes in Fargo's brain pattern, and Pop seemed to be mentally composing a song about VMtersz!. Fargo tried and finally succeeded in tamping down his mind so that he was alone in his head, but it wasn't easy. If he let his concentration slip, well, it wasn't pretty.

Duty Calls

Fargo, cleaned up and feeling considerably better, stepped from the fresher and put on his uniform. OneSvel then directed him to lie back down as Pop scuttled out of the room with the old bedding and the hospital gown he'd worn. Fargo asked, "When am I going to debrief?"

OneSvel answered, "You were brought out of rehab long enough to debrief the lieutenant, the captain, and the colonel right after the GalPat ship dropped you here. The colonel made the death notifications, but did not provide any details. Your personal debrief is complete, but the final team rites have not been completed, awaiting your return to life or death."

Fargo sagged back on the bed at this, hoping that the lieutenant had already done it, but knowing it really was his responsibility as team leader. Looking up at OneSvel, Fargo said, "If it needs doing, let's get it done."

OneSvel replied, "We have a hover chair coming. You cannot manage the rites in your condition, but we must say we honor your desire to complete them." Moments later a hover chair floated into the room, and OneSvel helped Fargo into it, saying, "Please do not hesitate to stop if your condition deteriorates. We do not want to lose you after all the work."

Fargo navigated the hover chair out of the hospital with OneSvel trailing behind him, and floated across to the team spaces. Entering their space brought tears to Fargo's eyes as he looked at the familiar area and truly understood that he was the only survivor from his team. Moving slowly to the safe, he opened it and extracted the cookies containing each of the team members' final wishes. As he turned back, he realized a number of people had crowded into the spaces, including the lieutenant, the captain, Pop and other team leaders that were on planet.

Fargo levered himself out of the chair, determined to do this standing on his own two feet. He stepped to the data reader in the center of the room and said, "Before we start, I believe a prayer for the dead is in order. I will say the Christian prayer, please say a prayer to your own deity as I do this." He bowed his head and continued,

"Remember, O Deity,
those whom we are remembering today,
men of the true faith;
do thou thyself give these men rest there in the land of the living,
in thy kingdom,
in the delight of your Paradise,
where the light of thy countenance visiteth them and always shineth upon them.
Let them know peace and honor in your house,
Amen."

Breaking open the first cookie, he slipped VMtersz! final wishes into the reader. Fargo stood at attention as his wishes were played, then followed with the cookies of the other team members. Each had given 10% of their funds for a team party, with the exception of Diez, who'd said to take his shirts to Lee Fong's laundry in sector D and spend that money on a party. All the rest had made the usual bequests, to their crèche, to their family in Hardt's case, and to ship passage in VMtersz! case. Fargo remembered Pop talking about how the goal of *all* young Kepleran from 62E was to get off planet and go elsewhere due to crowding. Diez had also made a specific bequest to Fargo of what Diez called artifacts. Fargo figured he'd worry about that later.

Lieutenant Walters and Captain Zmicas stepped over to Fargo as he sank back into the hover chair and OneSvel extruded a pseudopod to check Fargo's condition. Captain Zmicas said, "Sergeant Fargo, I appreciate your prompt action on this. You know tradition is important and Walters and I will see that the monies are directed as specified. Where do you want the party money to go?"

Fargo leaned back and looked up at the captain, "Just put it in the general fund sir. I'm not going to have a party. I might have a drink to them, but not a party. I'll have to chase down Diez's stuff but I'll get that to you as soon as I can."

"Roger that Sergeant. You've got two weeks of rehab coming before you report back to us. I'd appreciate it if you can get that done by the time you report back in."

Fargo nodded, "Will do sir."

OneSvel interrupted, "Sorry Captain, but we are concerned that Sergeant Fargo's vitals are spiking and we need to return him to the hospital now, if you please."

Walters and Zmicas stepped back hurriedly saying, "Do what you need to Doc. Remember sergeant, we're only a comm link away if you need anything."

Fargo replied, "Yes sir," as OneSvel keyed the chair into action.

Back in the room, OneSvel and Pop fussed around getting Fargo back in the bed and Fargo reached over to his data cube, keyed it and said, "Home." A holo of his cabin on Hunter popped into existence, and he drifted off to sleep staring at it. After a half hour, it automatically shut down and OneSvel noted it in the log in its office. *Home*, what a novel concept.

***

A week later, Fargo had progressed to the point that OneSvel felt comfortable letting him out on liberty. Fargo took the opportunity to take the keycard Diez left, and went to his apartment off base, surprised to find it was actually over Lee Fong's laundry. When Fargo inserted the card, rather than the door dilating, a speaker said, "State name and reason for entry."

Fargo shrugged and said, "Sergeant Ethan Fargo, final rites execution."

The speaker said, "Insert card again."

Fargo did so and the door dilated this time. Fargo looked around curiously as he entered, realizing he'd never seen how Diez lived off base. The rooms were small, tastefully furnished, and clean. Diez had a small desk and work center in the corner, but no e-tainment suite in the main room, nor was there one in the bedroom. Just the normal comm link and nothing else.

Fargo looked in the closet and saw the synsilk shirts Diez was so proud of hanging separately at the end of the closet and guessed these were the shirts Diez had been talking about. Loud and garish, they were Diez' one eccentricity. *Well, the one I know about anyway.* Fargo sat on the bed thinking, *I didn't really know Diez, or Pop, or Hardt, or DenAfr. Twenty-five years, and other than work, and a party once a year, I didn't really know a damn one of them outside of work. Shit.* Tears rolled down Fargo's face as he sat sobbing. He vowed to visit all the families somehow, some way. It wasn't like he had any other place to go.

Getting himself back under control, he used the fresher to wash his face, and picked up the shirts as he left the room. Locking the door, he went downstairs to Lee Fong's and asked for Mr. Fong. An elderly ethnically Asian man came slowly from the back of the laundry. Seeing the shirts he visibly wilted asking, "Is this what I think it is?"

Fargo replied, "Yes sir. Diez is dead, died on our last mission, and I'm fulfilling his final bequests. He asked that these be brought to you. He said you would know their value and…"

Lee Fong took the shirts gingerly, rubbing his fingers over each of them, "Thirty thousand credit. You want now?"

Fargo rocked back, "*Thirty thousand*? How?"

Fong continued, "Not synsilk, real Earth silk, mebbe six hundred years old. Cannot be faked. These Thai silk. Hawaii party shirts from back before Great War. Only ones I ever see are in museums. They real. I clean for Mr. Diez for twenty-five year myself. Nobody else touch. How you want credit?"

Fargo stuttered, "Ah, credit chip is fine. What do I do with the rest of the items?"

Fong cut him off, "I own building, I will dispose of rest of belongings. All clothes and data module donated to help poor. All other Diez had on deposit at GalScout work." Fong laid the shirts gently on the counter and ran a credit chip, then handed it to Fargo, "You go now. I would grieve in peace, please."

Fargo could only nod and leave. Returning to base, he stopped by Captain Zmicas' office and dropped the credit chip on his desk. "Here is the remainder from Diez sir. Have the personnel trunks been cleared?"

Zmicas looked up, "Sit. All except Diez: apparently, he left the contents of his trunk to you. So his and yours are still in the team space. Oh, while I'm thinking of it, be aware you are going before a med board when you get back."

"Sir?"

"Your cryo and stasis fail, or whatever it was, and the ongoing nightmares you're apparently experiencing."

"So what you're telling me is I'm…"

Zmicas nodded slightly, "You're probably going to be retired. It's not the end of the world. At least you survived it. Even if no one can explain what happened."

Fargo leaned back in the chair, "So for my good job of recovering the cans, bringing them back and surviving, I'm getting booted?"

Well, better that than being a lab rat for the next ten years while the docs keep trying to discover what happened and trying to induce the failure again."

Fargo shuddered, "Out it is. Thank you sir."

Zmicas looked directly at him, "You *will* be missed, but it's better for your sanity."

***

Fargo waited until everyone had left for the day before he drug the trunks out. He knew what his contained, but had no idea what was in Diez' trunk. With some trepidation, he keyed the code in and heard the locks release. He sat staring at the trunk for a couple of minutes before he finally pushed the lid open.

The first thing he saw was another of Diez's garish synsilk shirts. Moving it, there were two more that Fargo had never seen Diez wear. Moving them, he saw five cases and a newer standalone datacomp. Pulling out one of the cases, he opened it and saw an antique knife. Searching his memory, he finally came up with the name: Bowie.

Turning it over, he didn't see any marks on it, but it had obviously been well used. The bone handle was comfortable in his hand, but he was surprised at the weight. Underneath it was a dark leather sheath, again well used, with what looked like small beads worked into it. Sliding the knife into the sheath, it fit like a glove. He turned the sheath over and saw de Perez carved roughly into it and the number eighteen, but the last two numbers were worn off.

Setting it aside, he opened the next small case, and found an antique chemical pistol. He was surprised again by the weight of it. He looked at the side and it had a line of patent dates, then a graphic he guessed represented a horse, followed by Colt and Hartford, CT. Turning the pistol over, he saw Model of 1911 US Army. It was obviously an old steel chemical pistol, from his history lessons he came up with World War One or Two. That made this pistol over 800 years old!

The third case was longer and heavier. Opening it, it found another antique, this one was an 1894 Winchester, again well used. Fargo placed it gently back in the case and wondered what Diez' background had been, to have all these weapons that were that old. The other two cases were actual ammunition for the two guns, although Fargo wasn't sure he'd actually shoot either one.

He picked up the 1911 again, noticing how well it fit his hand, but the only thing that appeared to be a sight was a little bump by the muzzle and a notch on the back of the gun. He slipped it back in the case, vowing to research both of them to see how they actually operated.

The trunk didn't contain anything else, but it was almost brand new. Fargo shrugged and opened his battered trunk, moving everything he had into Diez' newer one. There were the picture cubes of Cindy and Ike, his Terran Marine records, a few picture cubes from his childhood and his mess dress uniform from the Marines. At least they hadn't taken that away from him.

Sitting back he sighed, combining the contents of the two trunks didn't even fill one. He figured he'd have room for all his shipsuits and probably

everything else out of his room with no problem.
Changing the codes, he pushed the new trunk back
into a slot and moved the old trunk over to the door.

Paying the Piper

Fargo had finally been medically cleared by OneSvel and moved back into his quarters after three weeks. He awoke at the usual time, and started to put on his class one uniform, then stopped. Punching his wrist comp, he checked the plan of the day and saw it was number two or utility uniform for other than official business.

Fargo walked into the morning meeting fifteen minutes early as usual, coffee bulb in hand and datacomp under his arm. Sliding into his usual seat, he stopped suddenly. *Crap, I don't even know what to do. I don't have a team anymore. Am I even supposed to be here? Ah damn, maybe I should...*

He sensed Lieutenant Lewis and Captain Zmicas coming down the hall, but sensed nothing unusual as they walked through the door. Zmicas said, "Morning Fargo, glad to see you up and about. Since your team is gone, I'm going to put you on training support for a bit until we get the results of the medical board."

Fargo replied, "Yes, sir. You want me to help NasTess?"

Zmicas shook his head, "No, you're going to be his boss. Ah shit, forget for now that I said that."

Fargo nodded, "Okay captain, whatever you say." Fargo thought, *that's strange. NasTess ranks me.*

Unless he got busted, but if he did, that would be all over camp. Maybe I'm just jumpy.

The room filled slowly, as other team leaders, officers, and support managers trickled in. Finally Colonel Zhang stumped through the door, and the meeting got underway. Two hours later it wrapped up, and Colonel Zhang said, "Fargo, front and center please."

Fargo got up gingerly and walked to the front, coming to attention in front of the Colonel and saluted, "Reporting as ordered, sir."

"NasTass, if you please."

Sergeant NasTess cleared his throat, or at least that's what Fargo thought he did, then his GalTrans started the litany, "By orders from General Fox, as confirmed by HQ Galactic Scouts, eleven, twenty, Earth year twenty-eight twenty-three, Ethan NMN Fargo is promoted to the rank of lieutenant, Galactic Scouts. This promotion comes with the responsibilities, privileges and accoutrements of rank. Given this day, in accordance with GalScout Directive two-one-three-two, by Colonel Ching Zhang."

Colonel Zhang picked up a single silver bar and proceeded to remove Fargo's sergeant emblem, replacing it with the bar. Stepping back he said, "Congratulations, Lieutenant. It is well deserved." Sotto voice, he continued, "Sorry this is a bit late. Report to me at thirteen, my office."

Fargo, somewhat overwhelmed, saluted again, "Thank you, sir."

The colonel looked up, "That's it folks, dismissed."

An impromptu receiving line formed as one of the support techs wheeled in a cake and a carafe of drinks. Everyone congratulated Fargo, then proceeded to the food and drink. His hand hurting from all the congratulatory handshakes, he finally got a chance to get one of the last pieces of cake, but nothing was left in the carafe. He hit the autochef for a bulb of coffee, and retreated to his room.

***

The colonel waved Fargo, now dressed in Class A's into his office, "Take a seat Lieutenant. Drink?"

Fargo sat gingerly in front of the desk as Zhang walked around behind the desk, sat and brought up a holo, "No thank you, sir. I'm still recovering and alcohol isn't a good idea right now." He shifted his feet and blurted, "It feels strange to be called lieutenant!"

The colonel nodded, as his hands moved in GalPat sign language, telling Fargo to play dumb. "You were actually promoted while you were in the field, and we didn't have a way to communicate that to you. With your previous service, you should have been a lieutenant long before this. Having said that, we hate to lose you, but you understand the issue we're facing with your condition, don't you?" At the same time the colonel thought, *Don't show surprise. OneSvel told me your psi is now off the charts. Do you think you can carry on a conversation in link?*

Fargo sat back to cover his surprise and signed he would play dumb saying, "I guess I understand, sir. But I was hoping that I could be of some use here. I figure I've got at least another forty years of productivity. But I don't ever want to lead men again. Lost my entire team." *Yes sir, I think I can.*

Ignoring the last statement, Zhang continued, "If we were back at Earth four or Earth prime, we certainly would use you. The problem is we're out on the pointy end and space and billets are limited. You're being medically retired with seventy-five percent of your salary and full medical benefits." *We have other things we would like for you to do. As a level five psi that no one knows about, and as a retired GalScout, you can move around freely, especially if you go out to the Rimworld Cluster, where your home is.* The colonel passed Fargo a new data chip, "Here's your retired chip. That and twenty credits will buy you a bulb of coffee at most places." *Rub your right thumb over the retired notation from right to left.*

Fargo took the chip saying, "That's not even for good coffee, Colonel." He surreptitiously moved his thumb as directed and saw the chip change from gray/retired to blue/active. *What is this sir?*

The colonel reached back and punched the autochef, "Kona black, right?" *As I said, we have other work for you. You were a damn good combat commander in the Marines, yes we do run background checks. I know you lost most of your command there, but it wasn't your fault. It was bad intel and you got the shitty end of the stick on that. I also understand why you didn't want any more command opportunities as it were.* He passed Fargo his bulb of coffee as the colonel tweaked his to his particular taste.

"Thank you, sir." Fargo said. *I can't seem to keep people that I'm responsible for alive, that's my problem. But what do you want me to do? My place on Hunter is remote, and the only people I know there are my sister and her husband. I chose it to get away from people and not deal with anyone except by choice.*

Zhang said, "I hear you've got a place on Hunter. You took your service credits and made that move a few years ago, didn't you? If I remember correctly, you were second in on it when it was still Z43F5. What prompted you to jump on it if I may ask?" *Your sister's husband is the Tight Beam Tech rep for the entire planet, and is also on the steering group for the entire star cluster. It's all about freedom of movement, especially if you're providing 'security' for him.*

Fargo shifted in his chair as he took a sip of coffee, "It reminded me of home, sir. I grew up on the front range of the Rockies on Earth, and when I saw that bench among the trees, well, I just jumped at the chance. I don't have any family other than my sister now." *What kind of freedom of movement? It's not like I would have a reason to travel within the star cluster. And what would I be looking for?*

The colonel nodded, "One has to grab those moments when you get the chance. I'm from Earth four and I inherited the family home in Charles Town. It's where I grew up, and my wife and children live there now. It's where I'll retire to in my dotage." *At a much higher level, there are some Traders and their Dragoon masters that are believed to be holed up or basing out of the Rimworld Cluster. Also, somewhere in that region there is hydrocarbon and ice mining going on. We will send you an encrypted data chip with the information once you are in place. GalPat*

Intel thinks the cluster may be a jumping off point for the next series of incursions into the DMZ.

Zhang asked, "Are you ready to go through the ceremony? I think yours will be the second retirement I've ever done, so I hope I don't screw it up!" *We're not asking you to charge around like a, what was the old saying, bull in a china shop? We need eyes and ears in that cluster. We and GalPat Intel believe you can help us by reporting what you see and hear. That potentially will save lives if we can stay step ahead of the Dragoons and Traders.*

Fargo nodded solemnly, "I guess so, sir. The sooner we get it over with, the sooner I can go home." *I'll do what I can sir. But I can't promise anything.*

The colonel finished his bulb and flipped it at the disposal unit, "Okay, let's go do this." Rising from behind the desk, he led Fargo out to the parade ground where the formation of GalScouts and a few civilians waited.

As they cleared the entry, the band started playing the GalScout anthem as the colonel marched to the podium. Fargo waited at attention until the anthem had completed and Captain Zmicas acting as master of ceremonies said, "Lieutenant Ethan Fargo, front and center!"

Fargo marched to his assigned position exactly two yards in front of the podium, saluted and said, "Lieutenant Fargo, reporting as ordered sir."

Colonel Zhang replied, "At ease, Lieutenant. Company, at ease!" Looking down at his notes, which Fargo realized were actually hand written, the colonel continued, "We are here today to retire one of our own. But before we do that, I want to say a few words. Contrary to what the scuttlebutt says, Lieutenant Fargo is *not* being retired because he lost his team. The first sumbitch I hear say that, I *will* courts martial them. Lieutenant Fargo has a previously undiagnosed medical condition that prevents him from being put in stasis. As you know, this is a medical disqualifier for service in the GalScouts. I have known Lieutenant Fargo for over fifteen years and never seen other than exemplary performance from him. Captain?"

Zmicas cleared his throat and read, "Attention to orders." The entire company popped to attention as Zmicas continued, "The Galactic Scouts present to Lieutenant Ethan NMN Fargo the Galactic Scout Battle Star with planet cluster for his exemplary actions on planet X423W in the face of overwhelming odds against a Trader incursion on twelve, twenty-one, Earth year twenty-eight twenty-three. His actions to attempt to save his men and subsequent actions during the hours-long running firefight reflect the highest traditions of the Galactic Scouts. While his entire team was lost, Lieutenant, then Sergeant, Fargo managed to recover the remains of each of his team mates, and return their remains to their respective planets. The Lieutenant was intent on going down fighting when he was rescued by a GalPat destroyer who responded to the team's emergency beacon. Let us always remember the courage of Lieutenant Fargo, as evidenced by this suitcam footage of the last minutes of the fight."

As the colonel stepped forward to attach the GalScout Battle Star, Fargo stood frozen as the last moments of the climb up the side of the wallow played holographically above his head. He was stunned to realize he'd been saying the words, not just thinking them, as he heard *Dum Vivimus, Vivamus[1]*, over and over as he climbed the side of the wallow. Saluting the colonel, Fargo felt a tear run slowly down his cheek.

---

[1] While we live, let us live.

Going Home

Ethan Fargo, GalScout lieutenant (newly retired, kinda, sorta) walked slowly down the space station passageway to the gate assigned to the merchant ship *Hyderabad*. His trunks dutifully trailed him by two yards electronically tethered to the pinger he wore on his shipsuit.

His thoughts veered wildly through time, space and a range of emotions; from childhood, through twenty years with the Terran Marines, the death of Cindy and Ike while he fought in the Cluster Skirmish, as they called the battle for Vega system and now thirty years of Galactic Scout service. All gone in one fell swoop, just because he'd had some kind of cryo/stasis nightmare and the problems coming back from X423W; or at least that's what the docs had said at the medical board.

Fargo was glad he was alone, or as alone as one ever could be on a space station, since the other issues he was dealing with were the nightmares and trying to learn how to shield his thoughts and psi talent. Shaking his head in frustration, he tried to damp down the circles his mind was running in.

A trained level four empath for forty years he was now all of a sudden a level five psi. All because of Diez dying in his arms while they were linked.

Something had *broken* in his head, and now the flood gates were open. It had been truly scary coming out of the Med-Comp to find those dreams really weren't dreams... *He'd been the thoughts of the medics and docs that had worked on him...*

Stopping at the boarding tube, he handed his data chip to the helmeted, armed and obviously bored watch at the head of the transfer tube saying, "Fargo, Ethan pax for *Hyderabad*. Terminal planet Hunter, Rim World cluster."

The watch took his data chip, plugged it into a hand reader and quickly scanned it replying, "Go on aboard, you're in compartment three, looks like you're the only pax for at least this leg. Captain Jace is already aboard and we're just waiting on one more dip pouch. As soon as it's aboard, we drop tubes and blast from here. Ship diagram is on the bulkhead directly across from the boarding tube."

Fargo nodded his thanks and asked, "Trunk storage?"

The watch looked the trunks over, "Both in storage? Any personal? We're programmed for about fifty two days enroute. Also, all personal weapons go to the armory."

Reaching up, Fargo grabbed the duffle pack off the top of the first trunk and set it to the side; opening the trunk, he picked out his personal electronics bag. Closing the trunk he cocked his head, finally saying, "This should be all I need. Tracking code for the trunks is three two five, if your extensionals handle standard mil-freq systems." Unbuckling his pistol belt, he clipped his vibro knife to it and handed it to the watch.

The watch took them, nodded, and stepped aside, allowing Fargo to enter the boarding tube. As he stepped across the zero-G threshold, he heard the watch speaking into his communicator, "Pax Fargo, Ethan coming aboard. Weapons collected and will be placed in armory. Still waiting on dip pouch."

Floating down the boarding tube, Fargo relaxed for the first time today. He was actually on his way to the green hills he'd wanted to call home since he'd first seen them on the planetary survey twenty years earlier. He wondered what this old freighter was carrying that was going to Hunter, and wondered if it was something his sister had ordered.

As he swung across the threshold, he noted the hatch seemed to be extremely thick, but he was distracted by a blue tinged Kepleran from 62F with, as usual, a pinched expression who said, "Keldar, I am the purser. Your chits are in order. Compartment three forward. Standard meal schedule."

Fargo nodded, thinking, *what is it with the Keplerans from F? I don't think I've ever seen one smile. But then most money people don't smile, come to think of it. And that seems to be the area they all end up in.* Turning forward, he glanced at the ship diagram and snapped a picture with his wrist comp then selected his compartment on the diagram. Seconds later his comp pinged and gave him directions to the compartment. Up one ladder, down a cross passage, through an open lock and he finally found the compartment.

He noticed while the passageway was clean, with nothing laying around, this was obviously a working freighter not a luxury liner. Dilating the entry, he stepped through into what turned out to be a two person compartment, with a small fresher stuffed in the back center of the compartment. Looking at the two bunks, he decided to take the one on the left, that way if he was sitting at the fold out desk he saw, he would have his strong side protected. *Stop it! You're frikken acting like everybody in the world is your enemy. Just because the purser... Keldar? Yeah, Keldar was being his normal frustrated self, it don't mean shit.*

Unpacking his meager belongings, he plopped the electronics bag on the fold out desk, then thought better of that, and placed it in the cubby above the desk. Looking at his wrist comp, he decided to go find what passed for a lounge or mess before they got underway. It looked like there was both a lounge *and* a mess on board, but he didn't know which he would be allowed to use. Following his wrist comp, he located the lounge and was surprised to find almost the exact autochef he'd had on the GalScout ships. Curious, he punched up his favorite coffee blend, and lo and behold, it spit out a bulb moments later. Jiggling it between his hands, he carried it to the table and sat down watching the external monitor showing on the wall screen. Taking a cautious sip, he smiled as he tasted *his* coffee.

Suddenly the [2]IC blared, "All hands, last package aboard, secure all loose equipment, prep for space.

Engineering, fifteen minute warning. Launch crew fifteen minute warning. Drop tube and disconnect three zero minutes. Mr. Fargo, please make your way to the lounge for safety brief and procedures."

Fargo mumbled, "I'm here already."

Seconds later, a bluff, bearded man in a shipsuit came into the lounge, radiating confidence and authority. He moved to the autochef and dialed a drink of some type, then came over to the table. "Mister Fargo, I'm Captain Jace. Welcome aboard, and I'd like to take a few minutes of your time for the safety brief, and emergency procedures if we may. Since you're our only passenger for at least the next leg or two, this shouldn't take long."

Fargo stood and shook the outstretched hand, "Thank you Captain, I'd appreciate it. Most of my experience is on GalScout ships so I'm sure there are differences."

Jace chuckled, "Less than you might think Mister Fargo. You're familiar with Ganymede Corp escape pods, correct?"

Fargo nodded, "Yep, and it's Ethan or Fargo, no mister. We had Ganymedes on the GalScout ships, thankfully I never had to use one other than in sims."

"Trust me, we're not planning on using any of them this trip either," the captain said. Changing the wall display, he brought up a soft EVA suit. "These are available in every space, and they're one size fits all. If you get an alarm, you've got about a minute depending on which space you're in to don one."

---

[2] Intercom

Blowing up the display, he continued, "Standard step in model, auto-closure tabs, and attached soft helmet. Sixty minute standalone air supply," rotating the display, he pointed to a plug set on the side of the suit. "O-two hookup, comms hookup, battery charger. Each compartment has a double hose connection in the overhead and one by the hatch." Spinning the diagram around, he showed the pouch on the other side of the suit, "Sixty feet of collapsible hose. Run it around the front or back, hook up the length needed and leave the rest in the pouch. Any questions?"

Fargo shook his head, "No, I've trained on these a time or two also. What about hard suits?"

"Three in each suit locker port and starboard. Eng, myself and the cargomaster have our custom hard suits," Jace said; noted the wrist comp and asked, "You wear it all the time?"

Fargo replied, "All day every day. Sixty-ish years I've had one, feel naked without one. I've already downloaded the schematic of the ship into it."

"Okay good. If you want, I can put you on the command push for updates too. This would allow you to keep up with where we are, and time enroute, other than when we're in hyper."

Fargo said, "That's fine. I'd appreciate it, not that it will help much. I'm not a spacer."

Jace spoke to the air, "AI, match Mister Fargo's wrist comp and add him to command push if you would."

A pleasant female voice responded out of the speaker, "Done captain, Mister Fargo, please check your comp in three, two-"

Fargo's wrist comp beeped an alert and he glanced at it. It showed an alert in red that said 'SHIP PUSH TEST', it also started a count in the female voice: "One, two, three, four, five, four, three, two, one. Please confirm by voice and touch receipt of alert."

Looking at Captain Jace, Fargo cocked his head, Jace mimed pushing the alert acknowledgement, then talking. Fargo punched the acknowledgement saying out loud, "AI Ser... er... Fargo, copied all audio and visual alerts."

The AI responded, "Thank you."

"Okay, that does it Fargo. Since you're the only pax, you're welcome on the bridge when we depart, which is in about ten minutes," Captain Jace said.

Fargo thought for a second, then said, "Sure, why not. Usually I'm not in a position to get to watch, and GalScout bridges are real small." Following the captain up ladders and through hatches, they finally arrived at the bridge, which, Fargo noted in amazement, actually had clear armorplast panels in front and to the sides of the pilot's seat in addition to the normal piloting and navigation panels. Motioning to them he asked, "Isn't that kinda unusual? I mean one doesn't expect to see clear panels up here."

The pilot turned around and replied, "Not really sir. This old tub is capable of planeting, and to do that, one needs to be able to actually see the environment real time."

The captain said, "Mister Fargo, Evie is our pilot and we're damn lucky to have her. Best touch I've ever seen, and even better than me."

Fargo looked, trying not to stare; Evie was a Hilbornite, an inner world known for their medical care systems and doctors. She was beautiful, even with the golden cat's eyes and softly furred features, "How do you do, Miss."

Evie trilled a laugh, "So-so. I'm a free space pilot, being the only woman on board is not fun. But this beats the hell out of the options. I guess that's why I'm known as the Ice Bitch."

Confused Fargo said, "Options?"

Evie replied, "Oh, my folks wanted me to marry and go into the family business. But doctoring isn't my strong suit. This is a lot more fun, and I'm one of only a hundred or so female free space pilots in the known universe," glancing up she continued, "Time to blow and go Captain. Two minutes." With that she nodded, spun her chair around and concentrated on getting the ship off the station.

The captain motioned Fargo to the observer's chair and Fargo strapped in as the crew started dropping umbilical connections and finally the docking tube. Pressers kicked the ship out of the dock at a couple of feet per second, and Evie gently brought thrusters on line backing away from the station. Rolling into the vertical, she nudged the ship into forward motion saying, "All systems nominal, half an hour to fifty-G limit Captain, then seven hours to hyper."

Captain Jace said, "Roger all, we are go for hyper. Any questions Mister Fargo?"

Pointing to the two empty stations he asked, "You don't use a communicator or navigator?"

Jace replied, "Nope, not unless we're on a complicated departure or approach, or going into a mil-system. We've got an upgraded nav-comm suite and the AI handles it most of the time. If I really need navigation or communications manned, I'd just bring number two and number three on. They are both qualified. But since this one is really easy; I mean we're just five AUs into the grav well, so it's easy to get out to Harbison's World from this side. We're aiming at the hyper limit directly on course; if we'd been deeper in-system or on the other side of the system- Well, it'd be like going around our elbow to get to our asshole, rather than a direct shot, and this would be about a fifty hour trip."

Fargo pointed toward the stern, "Is that rumbling noise normal? I'm not used to hearing that on the Gal ships I've been on."

The captain shrugged, "Slight out of balance situation between the EM engines. These old ships need tuning on a pretty regular basis, but it's hard to find parts sometimes. Eng does a pretty good job with what he has. I'll mention it to him to see if he can get them a bit closer together. Once we hit the hyper limit, the Alcubierre metric is pretty smooth."

Fargo thanked him and left the bridge, realizing it was basically boring, just watching the screens and monitoring the AI was not something he wanted to do. Looking up the mess on his wrist comp, he decided to find it now, rather than later as he realized it was eighteen. He might as well know if he could eat there or not.

As it turned out, the mess was adjacent to the lounge and he found it with no trouble. Entering, he noted the purser at one table, who only nodded at him and continued eating. He went to the autochef and punched up a 1200 calorie meal and another coffee as a bulky, hulking Arcturian humanoid came in.

Arcturus was a heavy world, with 1.6 gravities as the normal, and was one of the primary spice worlds due to the hardy plants grown in the acidic soil there. The Arcturian squeaked a greeting that his Galtrans projected to Fargo's implant as, "Ho, passenger of the ship, autochef you understand? I am Klang, cargomaster."

Fargo thought for a few seconds untangled the syntax and answered, "Ho Klang, Fargo I am. Understand the autochef I do. Thank you for the question and care of my trunks."

The autochef dinged and pushed out Fargo's tray with his meal and coffee. Using it as an excuse, he picked up the tray, nodded to Klang and went to another table. Sitting down, he ate quickly, as was his wont after years in the service. Going back to his compartment, he finished his coffee bulb and lay down to get some sleep.

Six hours later, the IC blared, "Secure all loose gear, strap in, prepare for hyper transition in ten."

Grumbling, Fargo reached down and pulled the net and straps up over the bunk and secured them, then rolled over. Knowing there would be a five minute and a one minute call, he just laid there. As soon as the *Hyderabad* transitioned, strangely, the rumbling went away. Fargo's muzzy thought was that shouldn't have happened, it should have gotten louder with the additional stresses of hyper flight.

By the third day of the transit, Fargo was starting to go stir crazy and took to prowling the decks, learning the ship as a way to stave off boredom. In the process of doing that, he found a full gym in a small compartment on the upper level. Deciding he could at least get back in shape, he started working out daily. He also discovered a mil-grade VR sim in an adjacent compartment. He started a weight regimen his docs had prescribed and also began running training sims, gradually using more and more advanced ones as he got back in shape. He'd met the remaining crew and decided they were some of the least communicative folks he'd ever seen.

Knowing *Hyderabad* was small at just 200 yards long, he was still struck by the low level of manning; there were less than twenty 'people' onboard if he didn't count planets of origin. Subconsciously, he also became aware of a rather strange layout for the ship, and what seemed to be a lot of restricted or closed areas. The most talkative of the crew was the engineer, known simply as Eng. He claimed to be from Scotland on old Earth, and definitely spoke with a brogue.

Another strange thing was that although he could empathically sense responses from the various crewmembers, he didn't pick up a single stray thought. He was beginning to wonder if he'd lost his telepathic ability, and actually was hoping he had.

The other thing he'd done was start on the hypno-dumps for Hunter, learning everything he could about it since he'd surveyed it. Since he hadn't physically set foot there in twenty years, it helped to learn what the colonists had discovered and had done. One of the more interesting facts was that less than ten percent of the planet was actually colonized and that the population was centered in the plains north and south of the equator in the temperate zone. One major spaceport, less than a half million colonists, and farming and hunting were the two main income producers. Some manufacturing was starting, but that was all it was: starting. Still four operating terraformers on the planet, but they were currently in idle /environmental maintenance mode.

Revelation

Fargo pulled a bulb of coffee from the autochef and walked back to his compartment slowly. Entering he pulled down the desk and dug out his electronics bag, deciding to finally look at Diez' final holo. Setting up the reader willed to him by Diez, he fed the data chip in and slouched back in the chair, watching Diez form above the reader. Rather than starting into the "If you're watching this spiel," the reader said, "Unconnected, standalone mode confirmed." The reader then asked, "Do you have numbers?"

Fargo looked at it, wondering what was going on when the reader again said, "Do you have numbers?"

Fargo heard, "Eighteen ninety-four Winchester," come out of his mouth and he sat up in surprise thinking *where the fuck did that come from.*

A sad looking Diez formed above the reader and said, "Ethan, I hope you're alone. If not… Well you might want to shut me down till later.

Not knowing why, Fargo said, "I'm alone."

Diez started back up and said, "What I'm about to tell you is going to change your life Ethan. More than you can possibly know. Matter of fact, if I wasn't dead, you'd probably be wanting to kill me after you hear this. And yes, I did add some things to your hypno when we were mission prepping. I hope someday you'll forgive me."

Diez wiped his hand across his face in a gesture Fargo had never seen. It was almost as if Diez was in pain. Finally the face looked straight out, "Ethan, I'm not who you and everybody else thought I was. You know how the GalScouts are pretty picky on selection and *starting over*, never going back past the day folks join GalScouts. Well I kinda cheated to get in. My full name is Roberto de Perez the tenth. Roberto Diez was just what I used to get into the Scouts. You asked me more than once how I knew so much about communications and systems, but you never pushed it. Well, the truth is I am, or was, a genie polymath. Yes, I'm *that* de Perez. I am- was the last de Perez and single stockholder of de Perez Galactic."

Fargo slumped back stunned as the holo continued, "You wondered why I laughed at the goings on and comments about de Perez back in the Los San Diego enclave. Simply put, that was a simulacrum properly aged and presentable that stood in for me since ninety-one. In eighty-seven the Consolidated Union tried to wipe out the entire de Perez corporate hierarchy by nuking our family gathering at the Los Alamos Albuquerque plant. They did get everybody but me, because I was late leaving the deep lab. As it was, I spent almost three years in chemo and radiation treatment in addition to trying to rebuild the company. Since I'd set up remotes due to my hospitalization that allowed me to connect with management, I just continued that after I recovered to the point I could actually interact with people again. It was nice to not have to actually interact with people, partially due to paranoia, and partly due to the damnable security requirements they put me under."

Fargo fumbled for the coffee bulb as Diez continued, "I also decided I didn't want to live in a fancy prison, which is what the compound in Los San Diego became. Due to my treatments, I cannot have children, either by natural means or by artificial. Something in the treatments has made my sperm and DNA toxic. We were developing simulacra for GalPatrol to use for training and I just slipped another one into the line. When it was ready, I did a nano pack change, and smuggled myself out of Los San Diego and out to Altair Four as a low-level lab manager on a routine personnel exchange."

Diez looked down as if he was remembering, "At the lab, I was free to do what I wished. I continued my electronics developments, including the FTL and Wave Rider communications systems and we also did the first autonomous scout ships there. Probably the best was the self-aware AI we developed for those ships, but that was outlawed by the Galactic Counsel in ninety-seven. By then I had built comms tunnels that allowed me to push my inventions back to Los San Diego, and have the simulacrum make selected appearances announcing another *great invention*."

Diez chuckled, "Had 'em all fooled. But I was stagnating. Then I saw a recruiting pitch for the GalScouts and how they needed comms types. I built a resume, inserted it into all the requisite databases, and went down and applied as Roberto Diez. You know the rest. I was assigned to your team out of training, and up till now you kept my ass alive. Which I really appreciated."

Diez looked down again, "Why am I dumping this on you Ethan? Because you're the last person in the world to want this. I've seen what you did to help others, and I know your background. Forgive me for that, but I tracked you all the way back to your birth in the Denco enclave. I know about the Marines, and what happened there. I know how you took care of your team, and how you interacted with all the support personnel. You lead by example, which is something I could never have done.

Fargo reached out blindly and shut off the reader, not wanting to believe what he was hearing. He paced his compartment for a few minutes, then went back to the lounge, hoping somebody was there that he could talk to. The lounge was empty, so he got another bulb of coffee and went to the mess. It was also empty, and he continued up to the bridge. The captain and Evie were on duty, and he asked permission to enter. The captain said, "Sure, come on in Fargo. Going stir crazy yet?"

Fargo chuckled ruefully, not willing to admit how close to the truth that remark was just now. "Yeah, pretty much. This is the first time since I went to boot at Paris Island and then up to Luna for the space training that I had to spend any time doing absolutely nothing."

The captain said, "Well, I'd offer to put you in stasis, but apparently you can't do that. There are some entertainment vids on the system if you want, or I can loan you some of my data chips of stuff from old Earth."

Fargo waved that off saying, "No thanks, I'll go dig around on the system and see what's there."

Evie turned around from the pilot's position saying, "Hey, bright spot is only one more day to Harbison's World. We'll have a day, maybe two, at the station while the goods get transshipped, and we see if there are any loads that match our transits. That will at least get you off here!"

Fargo nodded, "Yeah, I guess I could do that. Can I stay aboard at night, or do I need to clear the ship?"

The captain replied, "Nope, you can stay aboard, not an issue. You can draw your weapon and carry it on station, but it will have to be locked up when you're aboard. I know you're legal anywhere, but..."

Fargo said, "Oh I know, rules are rules. Not that I disagree, but it's like I'm missing a part of me."

Evie smiled, "And it's fifth day, ship time, so fish special tonight from the autochef, yum!"

Fargo and the captain both laughed as the captain said, "Evie, I swear, you got more than cat's eyes, you got cat's love of fish. If you start purring..."

Evie arched an eyebrow, "I'll have you know I *only* purr in certain circumstances."

Fargo shook his head, "I'm leaving before it gets any deeper up here," nodding to them both, he left and ended up in the VR sim. Looking for anything to take his mind off what was on the data chip, he dialed up a Silverback hunt from Hunter. Silverbacks, six legged and something like a cross between a pre-historic saber-toothed tiger and lion were the most dangerous animal on Hunter. They were notorious for traveling in pairs, with one teasing the hunter while the other tracked the hunter, and killed them in very grisly fashion. The real irony was their fur was highly sought after, and worth a month's tech pay, if one survived the hunt and brought one in. Fargo geared up and tried three hunts, only to be killed each time. Racking the equipment in disgust, he drank the last of the cold coffee, and went to the mess.

Klang was eating when Fargo came in and squeaked a greeting, "Ho, Fargo passenger. Workout in the sims you do. Spar you like?"

Ruefully Fargo shook his head, "Ho Klang, spar I cannot, weakling I am. Light gravity world. Broken bones I need not."

Klang nodded, "Bored if you are, not to injure promise I."

Fargo replied, "Ho Klang, consider will I," he grabbed his food from the autochef and sat eating, trying to wrap his head around what he'd heard from Diez and trying to decide if he actually believed it. Dawdling over his food, he finally decided to go listen to the rest of the data chip and then try to figure out what to do. Getting up he took his tray back to the autochef, and got another coffee bulb.

Back in his compartment, he sat staring at the reader, finally hitting the start button again. The reader said, "Unconnected, standalone mode confirmed." The reader then asked, "Do you have numbers?"

Fargo said, "Eighteen ninety-four Winchester."

A sad looking Diez formed above the reader and said, "Ethan, I hope you're alone. If not- Well you might want to shut me down till later.

Fargo said, "I'm alone."

Diez said, "Continue from last position?"

"Yeah."

Diez said, "I hope you took my knife and guns I bequeathed to you. Not only were they special to me, the Bowie knife was one that the original Ignacio de Perez himself carried over a thousand years ago. The eighteen ninety-four Winchester was also carried by a member of the family, and the nineteen-eleven was carried by another ancestor in the Second World War on old Earth. Hidden in the grip of the nineteen-eleven is a data chip that when plugged into this reader, this reader only, and verified by your DNA will allow you to connect to the corporation via FTL and do things."

The holo looked down, then back up, "I know you're probably struggling with this, wondering if I'm pulling a practical joke on you. Ethan I will tell you that I am not. You can verify this by contacting your sister. She will have received a one million credit grant from de Perez Galactic within thirty days of my death. And yes, I cheated there too. One more thing you can check, there was a fire in my apartment within twenty-four hours of your fulfilling the final request. This was set up to destroy certain things there that people did not need to know about. It will have been written off as an electrical fire from an overheated autochef. Again easy to check."

Fargo sat back even more stunned. He'd remembered the fire, and being thankful he hadn't waited another day to visit Diez' apartment. Hitting pause on the reader, he started wondering what else Diez had done to him under hypno, and what was going to pop out next. Thinking back, some of the things Diez had done, or had been able to do now started to make sense. And that scared Fargo even more. The thing that truly petrified Fargo was that *there was not a single damn person he could tell.*

***

Captain Jace leaned back in the captain's chair on the bridge as Fargo closed the hologram down, his eyes moving around the bridge as his chipset calculated what he'd just seen. So Fargo was his new owner. He wondered if de Perez ever planned to tell Fargo he also owned this ship and everything in it.

He quickly composed an FTL message to send to his various molycirc banks scattered throughout the known universe containing backups of himself with this new information, and added a query for additional data on Hunter, Fargo's sister and family, and possible options for the star system.

In less than a second, the message was transmitted via a separate secure FTL transmitter hidden in the myriad wiring of the *Hyderabad*. Jace's chipset wondered if Fargo even knew what *Hyderabad* stood for, much less if he'd even guessed the secret of the ship. What was it de Perez had always said, "All things in their own time." Yeah, that was it.

***

Fargo's comp dinged, "Hyper Alert. 30 minutes to standard space return. Secure all loose items, prepare for down transition. Acknowledge."

Fargo touched his comp, "Fargo, acknowledge."

Fifteen hours later, *Hyderabad* was docked at the space station orbiting Harbison's World. Fargo had decided to go aboard the station, if only for a quick pass through, to smell air that was *less* canned, and to get something other than an autochef meal.

Picking up his personal weapons from Klang, he slipped the gun belt and knife on, and took a deep breath. *Better or worse, let's see what there is here...* Stepping out of the boarding tube he turned to Khalil, "Permission to go ashore?"

Khalil smiled, "Enjoy, sir. Just remember we cast off in nine hours. With or without you."

Fargo laughed, "Oh, I'll be back, probably long before then." Sniffing the air he said, "Well, it doesn't smell like the ship anyway."

Khalil laughed, "Depending on where you go, it gets considerably worse on here."

Fargo held up his hands defensively, "Don't want to know. Nope, not a bit!" With that, he headed for the central section of the station, looking around curiously. It had been at least five years since he'd seen a civilian station, and marveled at some of the styles in evidence.

Passing the section with the maintenance shops, he saw an arrow saying Central Core. Turning he followed that passageway, and gradually felt the decrease in g-forces as he walked. The central core turned out to be a four level open area, with a variety of shops, restaurants, outfitters, bars, and the ever present bordellos.

Looking into one bar that was fairly well lit, he saw a number of humanoids, and figured it would be fairly safe. As he stepped into the bar, he saw a couple of tables of spacers back in one corner, with all of them wearing their party suits. Mixed in with them were a few military pilots, and from the holos and patterns on their suits, he guessed they were F-288 pilots, probably from the detachment that maintained space superiority in this cluster.

Ordering a bulb of supposedly *guaranteed* old Earth scotch, Fargo slipped into a booth with his back to the wall and just watched the action. The spacers and pilots were getting rowdier and rowdier, as their party suits became more and more garish. Finishing his bulb, Fargo decided this might be a good time to find somewhere else to be, and he slipped quietly out the hatch.

Strolling further along the central core, he saw restaurants, and finally a strip of bordellos. Checking his datacomp, he decided to get his ashes hauled, then eat. Picking the cleanest looking bordello, he took the quick pick with a simulacrum, and twenty minutes later was back on the core walk, five hundred credits poorer, but feeling much better.

He sniffed, smelled Italian food, and his stomach rumbled in response. He opened his senses to try to narrow down the location, and felt like he'd been hit with a thousand voices, as a maelstrom of emotions bombarded his mind. He quickly locked his empathic sense back down, built a mind block on his psi sense and kept walking until he saw a holo of a baker throwing a pizza, and an air unit outflow valve about the hatch.

Slipping through the curtain, he noted wryly that they were pumping the scent of their cooking into the central core. But it worked, and here he was. Sitting at a table facing the door, he quickly ordered from the tabletop automenu, and a real waiter came by with a water bulb and asked if he'd like a wine or other liquor.

Fargo leaned back and thought, "Red wine. Mid-price. Deliver with the food please."

The waiter nodded and slipped silently away. Minutes later, the waiter reappeared with his order, and deftly placed the dishes on the table, followed by a real carafe and wine glass. Pouring the wine the waiter asked, "Is the wine suitable, sir?"

Fargo sipped appreciatively, "This is actually very good. Yes, definitely suitable." Digging into the plate of pasta, Fargo was surprised at the quality of the meal, and reminded himself that it'd been a long time since he'd actually had a real meal anywhere other than the base, or on a ship.

After finishing the meal, he dialed a dessert, and watched as it popped out of the table in front of him. Figuring he was pushing his luck, he finished it, paid his bill, and headed back to the ship.

Transit

Back aboard *Hyderabad*, Fargo resigned himself to a long, boring transit, since Klang had told him they had no cargo for Star Center, and would go direct to Hunter's space station. He started working out more and more, and using the VR sim to practice firing his weapons.

He'd also started sparring with Khalil, one of the crew from Earth 4. He started trying to use his senses to try to anticipate movements, but Khalil apparently had a pretty good mind block, as Fargo never was able to read anything other than low empathic levels of emotion. As Fargo improved, he was able to beat Khalil two out of three, then three out of four bouts.

His ego got the best of him and he challenged Klang to spar, with Klang promising to go easy. That lasted about twenty seconds, as he attempted to leg sweep Klang, and it was like kicking a tree. Klang may have been big, and muscular, but he was also snake quick, and he grabbed Fargo's upper arm and threw him into the side wall of the gym, knocking Fargo unconscious.

Fargo woke up in the medbox, in traction and with a dry mouth. Looking out, he saw a worried Klang, and Captain Jace staring back at him. Captain Jace asked, "Can you talk? How many fingers am I holding up."

Fargo wondered why that question and as he went to answer, his whole jaw creaked, "Uh, two. What happened?"

Jace slapped Klang on the shoulder, "You were sparring with Klang, always a bad idea, and he threw you."

"Into what?"

"Um, the far bulkhead. He forgot he wasn't sparring with one of his Arcturian loaders."

Klang squeaked and he GalTrans said, "Lieutenant of the Scouts, Klang bad. Harm not meant. Klang sorry to cause injury."

Fargo said ruefully, "Klang, understand I do. Ego my mistake. Human cannot beat Arcturian, Fargo should better know. Fault is mine."

Klang ducked his head and squeaked, "Damage you, I did not?"

Fargo looked at Captain Jace, "Nothing serious, Captain can verify?"

Jace replied, "Nothing major broken. Concussed, broken jaw and left orbital. Both will be repaired by tomorrow. Concussion may take a day or two."

Fargo sighed, "Another night in the box. Oh well. I guess I'm paying for my stupidity."

Jace laughed, "Awake or asleep?"

Fargo said, "Put me out. I've spent so damn much time in these boxes I'm starting to get claustrophobic." The last thing he remembered was the captain reaching for the medbox controls.

***

As the IC blared the hyper warning, Fargo closed the reader, and slipped it back into its slot in the desk.

Forty-five days of boredom had allowed Fargo to get more familiar with the entire Rimworld cluster than he ever wanted to be. He'd read all the articles, reports, and watched all the vids and newsies from Hunter, and the other habitable worlds in the cluster.

He'd also seen his sister, Luann, and her husband Mikhail in a couple of the vids, since Mikhail was the Tight Beam Technology manager for Hunter, responsible for all the power beams and communication riders that went to every building on the planet. He and his team had built the system off the four existing terraformers, placed the subfeeder beams, and ensured each building had power and communications available. He had been featured pretty much any time there were TBT issues, or expansions on Hunter, or anywhere else in the cluster.

Mikhail and Luann had also taken on a secondary colony skill as general merchandise providers, and their trading post at Rushing River was apparently doing well. He'd also found birth notices for their two children, so apparently he was an uncle, with both a nephew and a niece.

Hunter's population was approaching a half million, with the larger settlements centered near the four terraformers that were still working in what was considered maintenance modes. The diversity of plant and animal life were also of interest to scientists, zoologists, xenophiles, and xenobiologists, who visited the planet regularly.

As a colony world, they didn't have a lot of weather support or satellites up, since TBT provided not only power but communications and e-tainment over the same fused beam. There were two comms satellites in geo-synchronous polar orbits, and they fed communications to the TBT stations at the terraformers.

The *Hyderabad* eased into the docking clamps at Hunter's space station with a slight bump, and the IC clicked on, "Docked. Landing party prep for connection. Passengers are free to unstrap and gather belongings. Estimated fifteen minutes to complete connections. Customs, Immigration and Pest Control aboard in twenty. Passengers may depart after C and I are finished."

Fargo unstrapped, grabbed his already packed bags, and slipped over to the mess. Punching the autochef for one more cup of coffee, he sat thinking, *I'll be seeing Luann for the first time in almost fifteen years. She's going to let me stay with them for a while, whatever that is, till I get my feet on the ground. What I really want is to get to the cabin and get away from people.* The autochef dinged and spit out his coffee bulb, and he juggled it as he sat back down. *What will she say? What, how... How are they doing? Mikhail seems successful, and from the pictures Luann seems to be doing okay. I wonder if I owe them any money... Am I doing the right thing? What am I going to do? What...*

The IC clicked on, "Passengers are now authorized to depart the ship. Luggage will be at the station side of the boarding tube. Thank you for flying with us!"

Fargo picked up his meager bags, and headed for the boarding tube. Keldar was standing there and said dismissively, "Your bill is paid. You may go." Fargo started to snap back at him, then decided it just wasn't worth it. Floating through the boarding tube, he hit the grav line at the space station side of the tube, and stepped quickly forward. Klang was standing there as the guard, and had both Fargo's trunks and his weapons.

Placing his bags in the first trunk, he slipped the gun belt and vibro knife on, turned to Klang and said, "Master of the cargo, pleasure it has been to fly with you. Wishes for a continued good life, I offer."

Klang bowed his head, and his GalTrans spit out, "Lieutenant of the retired, pleasure was mine. Education you did give me. Enjoyment in your life I wish." Fargo nodded and keyed his trunks into action as he walked slowly down the sterile passageway. Finding the passage to the core, he turned down it, and found the scheduler board. A shuttle was departing in two hours for Rushing River Spaceport.

Inserting his data cube into the automated scheduler, he confirmed his seat, and the size and weight of his trunks. A panel slid aside and he was directed to place his trunks on the belt inside. He did so, wondering if he'd ever see them again, then laughed at himself for the thought.

Finally, the small atmospheric capable shuttle undocked from the space station, and Fargo, along with six other passengers, felt the pressure of g-forces as the small shuttle dropped away from the station. Ninety-three divs and one re-entry later, the shuttle landed at Rushing River Spaceport.

Auto loaders were unloading the shuttle as Fargo and the others walked stiffly down the boarding ramp.

Fargo twisted and bent, trying to get the kink out of his back from almost four hours strapped in a seat, and took the time to look around. It had been almost three months since he'd actually smelled unfiltered air, and he took a deep breath, reveling in not only the scent of the burnt hypergolic fuel, but the hint of wood smoke and a tiny hint of near pine in the air.

Fargo walked toward the administration building with some trepidation, not sure if Luann or Mikhail would even be there. His fears were put to rest when he was fifty yards from the building. Luann burst out the door and started running toward him. He recognized the blonde hair and small figure immediately, and without thinking he started jogging toward her, then scooped her up in his arms.

He was shocked when his psi talent kicked in as he touched her and he got Luann's jumbled thoughts of love, worry, a reverent prayer of thanks and worry over what he would think of the cabin she and Mikhail had bought and installed for him. He hugged her back, and set her gently on the ramp. Seeing tears running down her face, he asked, "Lu, what's wrong?"

Luann hit him in the chest, "I didn't know if you were alive or dead, you bastard! I had to find out from the Patrol that you'd actually survived! Six fucking months without a word! Damn you!"

Stunned, Fargo stepped back, "What. Do. You. Mean?"

Luann smacked him again, "The last message I got from you was that you were going out for a month or two. Then nothing! Nothing! How could you do this to your little sister?"

"Lu, I was out for over two months between the trip back and the time in the Med-Comp. I wasn't even conscious! How the hell did you…"

She hugged him fiercely, laughing and crying, "You should have figured out some way to contact me, even if you were unconscious!" Grabbing him by the hand she said, "Come on. Mikhail is with the kids and I'm afraid he's going to burn dinner if we don't get back quick. Where are your bags?"

Fargo was jolted again as Luann's thoughts flooded his mind, now centered on dinner, worry about how Ian and Inga would react and the hope that he'd like his room. Disengaging from Luann, he got his trunks and asked, "How do we get back to your place?"

Luann laughed, "Oh, we've got a runabout. Stay here and I'll go get it." She disappeared around the corner of the building, and came back with what looked to Fargo like an ancient Jeep. Using the anti-grav built into the trunks, he got them in the back, and hopped in as Luann drove them quickly back to the Town of Rushing River.

***

Luann and Mikhail had taken a homesteading contract to Hunter back in '07, after Fargo had made one of his very infrequent trips back to Earth and told them what he'd seen on this Earth analog. Earth normal, 1.05 standard gravities, terraformed over 400 years ago, then lost and never colonized other than a SierraSafari outpost when the Great War started. Abundant life forms, many imported from Earth by the SierraSafari group. The group included trees, edible plants, animals, birds, and even insects in their imports. Best of all, it turned out to be only two jumps from Kepler 62.

Luann chattered about how they'd been selected as primary members, due to Mikhail's Tight Beam Technology position, and his willingness to be the planetary manager for the systems in the sector as they were installed. She complained about the year in training and putting together the supplies for the trading post. But she reserved her real bitching for the year in stasis coming out here, "My God Ethan, how do you stand that stuff? I mean, going under and not knowing if I was going to wake up, or I would and Mikhail wouldn't or he would and I wouldn't, I mean…" She skipped over the ten years they had managed to not only survive, but actually make a little credit by trading with the hunters for the pelts and supplies for those that ventured into the Green, as the mountainous, heavily forested outback was called. She also talked about having Ian and Inga, the pains, and joys the kids brought and how much time they took. Fargo never got a word in edgewise, and wondered how they'd had the time and energy to have kids. That is, if Luann was to be believed.

***

The entire family sat down at the kitchen table in the back of the trading post to a steak dinner with all the trimmings, and a pie from a fruit that tasted like a strawberry, except it was the size of a person's fist.

Fargo pushed back from the table and groaned, "Oh, that was delicious, Luann. You don't know how long it's been since I had an actual home cooked meal!" He glanced over at Ian, who was squirming in his seat, "You want to ask me something Ian?"

Ian grinned, "How long since you had a home cooked meal, Unka?"

Fargo cocked his head, "Probably fifteen years, Ian. At least that long, maybe longer!"

Inga, eyes huge, said, "Longer than I am old? I am…" Inga surreptitiously counted on her fingers, tongue sticking out, "I am seben!"

Fargo smiled at her, "Almost three times as long as you are old, Inga."

Luann smiled and Mikhail laughed at that as Luann said, "Okay kids, plates in the sonic, and you can watch e-tainment for thirty minutes, then it's your bedtime!"

The kids quickly put their dishes away and hurried upstairs to the e-tainment center in the living room. Mikhail stood and stretched, "Ethan, let's get out of here and let Luann get the kitchen cleaned up. She's particular where things go, and neither of us need to get on her bad side."

Fargo laughed as Luann swatted at Mikhail with a kitchen towel, "Out, out! Get your coffee and go! I'll be there in a few minutes."

***

Mikhail, tall and lean with a dark European complexion, was the diametric opposite of Luann. Almost silent by comparison, Fargo's handshake with him had given Fargo a taste of an ordered mind, a loving husband and father, logical and planning new ventures well beyond tonight's meal.

Fargo smiled at the thought of Ian with Luann's personality and Inga with Mikhail's. They each took a bulb of coffee, and went into the main room. Luann came into the room as Mikhail brought Fargo up to speed on his proposed job and finished by saying, "So, that's the deal. You can work as little or as much as you want. It's all within the star system, so no going into stasis. You'd be providing security for TBT expansions. I do about two months a year on the road doing mods, expansions and cut overs. You'd be officially an employee of TBT, authorized weapons on any world as security, and any native species killed would be yours for whatever you'd want to do with them."

Fargo threw back the last of the coffee bulb, "That sounds great Mikhail, but let me think on it for one night."

Mikhail smiled, "No problem. Tomorrow, we'll drag out the liteflyer, and I'll take you up to your cabin. We can get a grav sled to tow your stuff up there in a couple of days."

Fargo nodded as Luann said to him, "Enough already. I'm tired. I know you're tiredfrom your trip, and I'm not sure what the kids are into upstairs."

After getting good night kisses from the kids, Fargo undressed and stretched out on the bed in the guest room. *My God. I'm really here. The deal with Mikhail is almost too good to be true, but it would generate some income, and the colonel wants me to get around the star cluster. Seems like a good way to do it.*

Fargo dropped off to sleep with a smile on his face.

First Sight

Mikhail and Fargo sat at the table, holograph live in front of them as Mikhail explained the TBT configuration and the nature of the lines crisscrossing Hunter. Zooming in, Mikhail continued, "See, here is the terraformer, the white line is the e-comm coming down from the satellite to ride the beams. That's where we're drawing all the power for this region from," pointing to the terraformer on the expanded holograph, he said, "The terraformer provides a little over three quarter million volts to these repeaters," pointing to the six main lines radiating from the terraformer, he continued, "The repeaters each get about one hundred thousand volts, due to transmission loss. The e-comm and e-tainment systems have a two way ride on each of those beams with the entire world's data and provide the feeds for the rest of the region. They are all at higher altitudes on the edge of the Green."

Rotating the view to a vertical slice, he continued, "See the altitude differences?"

Fargo nodded, "Yep, you're going up to get range, then coming back down. Subfeeders on the highest building or structure, right?"

Mikhail replied, "Yes. The subfeeders take power and the data from them, and also balance power requirements for the individual locations, whether they are houses or businesses. It's all based on kilowatt hours, but it's fairly cheap too. Each location picks off its particular e-comm and e-tainment based on the data address for that location and allow the data to flow back 'upstream' to the satellite."

Switching displays, Mikhail brought up a flight plan route, "Okay, here is how you will have to fly to and from your place. There is a ten mile ring around the spaceport that is TBT free. We feed it underground from this substation, here." Tracing the route he said, "By eight miles, you need to be five hundred feet AGL or better, which clears everything except the main feed beams here, here and here. For those, you need to be under two thousand, or above five thousand feet AGL."

Fargo asked, "AGL? Above… Above ground level?"

Mikhail nodded, "That's it. Now, this flight plan route will automatically display on your nav panel in the liteflyer, and it will automatically deviate to a safe altitude unless you physically override it. Flying into *any* beam isn't good, much less flying into a subfeeder or repeater beam."

Fargo smiled, "Good! I'm not the greatest flyer. I can fly, but not well."

Mikhail finished the briefing and they loaded up the runabout with Fargo's trunks and trundled out to the spaceport. Off to one side were small pads with little hangars constructed out of leftover containers. Going to one at the end of the second row, Mikhail thumbed the hatch open, and pointed to the yellow liteflyer on the right, "That's yours. It's a convertible, either four place or two place and cargo hold."

They pulled it out and Mikhail walked Fargo through the configuration sequence, helped him load the trunks in the back, and ran Fargo through the BIT check.

Mikhail asked, "You want me to fly the route and show you, or do you want to do it?"

Fargo smiled, "I'll bow to your experience, and your local course knowledge. Lead on, kind sir!"

Mikhail laughed and jumped in the left seat. Fargo gingerly got into the right seat, and closed the hatch as Mikhail powered up the liteflyer, "Tower, LF four-six-one, NE departure, destination as filed in the Green."

Tower replied in a bored electronic voice, "LF four-six-one, cleared for departure. No ship ops scheduled for the next twelve hours."

Fargo glanced over, "Automated tower and local control?

Mikhail grinned, "It is, until it isn't, then the fall back is one of the GalPat controllers having to do actual work. That happens, they are grumpy!" Lifting off smoothly, Mikhail selected the autopilot and crossed his arms. Looking at the groundspeed readout, he said, "About an hour at two-ninety-five indicated. You can do it faster, if you push up to high cruise or emergency power. Just be aware if you go to emergency power, it also sets off an alert, and starts sending tracking information to anybody that will listen."

Fargo nodded, "Okay. So speed runs are emergency only." Pointing to the control panel and a red line paralleling their line of flight he asked, "Main feed?"

"Yep, actually that's the one that feeds your cabin. It goes up to a repeater that was a PITA to install, but it's up almost seven thousand feet, and covers a pretty large area. Your place is only about three thousand feet up, so we'll stay under that feed."

For the next hour, Mikhail explained the ins and outs of the community, and their interaction with White Beach, which was technically the world capital. Mikhail was very happy that White Beach was over four thousand miles away, and the administrators didn't like going 'out in the field,' so to speak. Fargo listened with one ear, and drank in the rugged beauty of the Green as it rose in front and to the side of the liteflyer.

Roughly an hour later, Mikhail pointed, "Off your side, two o'clock. That is your one hundred-sixty acres. It encompasses the falls as you wanted, and the plateau all the way down to the tree line. The edge of the ridge is basically the eastern edge, so you'll get some nice sunsets and moon rises with Celeste and George."

Momentarily distracted, Fargo said, "What? Celeste and…"

Mikhail said, "They were the first two that died out of the original settlers. So the first white moon is Celeste, and the second or blue moon is George." Shrugging he continued, "Not my circus, not my monkeys on the naming conventions out here, but I did agree with the naming in these cases."

Fargo snorted, "Okay. Can we make a low pass?"

Mikhail brought the liteflyer down to fifty feet over the trees, coming in just inside the edge of the ridge, "This is your runway, if you will. At max gross weight, you can take off going downhill from the house and still clear the trees."

Fargo got his first good look at the cabin and whistled, "Wow, this is much nicer than I expected! It looks like it's been there for years!"

Mikhail grinned, "Well, you said Ranger cabin, you didn't specify which one. There were enough funds for the upgraded version, and that's what we got." Mikhail circled the property, flying as close to the falls as he dared, then came in for a landing over a field of blue flowers, taxiing the liteflyer to the pad just outside the storage container next to the house.

Fargo stepped out of the liteflyer and inhaled the scent of pines and a sweetish smell of the flowers wafting on the light breeze. *This is where I'll die, God willing.* He could dimly hear the waterfall in the distance, and marveled at the small rainbow visible in the bright sunlight. He did a slow walk around of the cabin, noting the sprayed brown plascrete walls, the green roof, and the porch extending across the front of the cabin. Going up the three steps, Fargo stopped and looked at Mikhail, sensing his apprehension.

Smiling Mikhail said, "Go ahead, it's keyed to you."

Fargo reached out tentatively and palmed the access panel, heard the door lock click, and opened the door. He stepped inside, and was amazed at how well decorated and finished the interior was. Walking slowly through the cabin, he saw the two bedrooms, the two freshers, and a small office with a desk, chair, and small e-tainment center. Coming back into the living room, he went through to the kitchen, seeing both an autochef and a real stove/oven/microwave combination. Shaking his head, he laughed out loud.

Looking around, he didn't see Mikhail and went back to the front door, "Come in, come in."

Mikhail came up the steps, "I figured you wanted to see it by yourself first."

Fargo laughed, "I know Luann had to have had a hand in selecting the kitchen. She got a stove put in, when I have *no* clue of how to actually use one."

Mikhail rolled his eyes, "Yeah, that was all her. The autochef is stocked, and she made sure there was some coffee in there."

Fargo punched up a coffee and looked questioningly at Mikhail, who nodded. While they waited, Mikhail said, "The other upgrades are that the living room loungers are conforming, and the bed in the master bedroom is conformal too. I took the liberty of putting you on as a TBT security employee, so your power and e-tainment are free. Also, you'll have access to all the TBT comms and alerts."

Fargo nodded, gingerly handing a coffee bulb to Mikhail, "Thanks. I do need to talk with you about what I can do to help out." Walking into the living room, he sank into one of the lounges, sighing as it formed to his body. The e-tainment center on the far wall automatically came to life. He continued, "Looking at what was available on the ship and the newsies, it looks like you've got a good number of maintenance folks, but little to no security."

Mikhail sighed, "That's correct. GalPat is supposed to provide security when I request it, but the colonel down in White Beach usually has an excuse to not provide anybody. What I usually end up doing is hiring some of the off duty troopers and paying them under the table."

"Politics? Or..."

"I'm not sure. Colonel Cameron, the nominal CO, doesn't like his troops out of his control. Colonel Keads, his number two, is a good guy, though. Cameron and I have disagreed on placement of some of the subfeeders. He wanted them in, so called, *easier* to guard locations, and I wanted them in the best feed locations, which usually meant rugged or higher elevations. Since TBT has override, I usually got what I wanted."

Fargo felt Mikhail's anger building and chuckled, "Pissed you off, did he?"

Mikhail ducked his head, "Well, it *might* have had something to do with it. He and Governor Klynton wanted the first service, basic settlers be damned, even if the settlers needed the service more for sonic fences than basic lighting. I only put half the team on their work, and prioritized the areas needing sonics first."

"And they found out?"

"Klynton had a hissy fit when she found out through one of her toadies that was out joy riding in one of the shuttles and saw lights and a feed line on the autopilot. Demanded I stop all other work until she got her service."

"Lemme guess, you refused?" Fargo asked.

Mikhail faced him squarely, "Of course I did. That's how we lost George and Celeste. Their homestead was up against the river, running off a hydro-generator while they waited for an installation. A pair of Silverbacks got inside the fence they had up, and got in the security door, killed them, and killed and ate most of the stock they'd penned up. George and Celeste were compartment mates coming out here."

Fargo said, "I'm sorry. It's never easy to lose someone you knew."

Mikhail looked at Fargo, "How do you deal with it, I mean..."

Fargo shrugged, "I try to remember the good. At least now I won't ever have to command troops in any kind of battle. I can't lose anyone else. I've lost too many..."

Mikhail said, "Well, whenever you can, deal with Colonel Keads," changing the subject, he said, "There is a small settlement of Ghorkas on Hunter. I've been thinking about contracting them for additional security, the ones that come down to Rushing River seem to be in shape and look and act like retired military. I've heard there are maybe two-three hundred of them back in the Green somewhere. Maybe you could look into that for me."

Fargo nodded, "What time to do we need to be back?"

Mikhail checked his wrist comp, "We should probably leave now. Why don't you fly the route back, and you can come back up here tomorrow and start settling in?"

***

Fargo gingerly piloted the liteflyer in for a landing on the strip at the cabin, taxied up to the storage building, and climbed slowly out. The first thing that struck him was the quiet. Only the winds sighing through the trees up slope from the house and an occasional birdsong heard. He inhaled deeply, smelling the nearpines and smiled. *Home. This is where I wanted to be and now I'm here. Can't ask for anything else as an old military man.* Looking around, he quickly unloaded the liteflyer, stacking the boxes, trunks and bags by the front door.

Once he'd done that, he opened the storage building, reached in and reconfigured the liteflyer for storage. It automatically folded the wings and tail into a compact package, and he rolled it easily into the building, closing the door after it.

Stepping up on the porch, he took in the sweep of the field, and canyon beyond it, greens shading to blues, with the occasional red rock protruding from the far wall of the canyon. With a sigh, he opened the cabin door and carried the packages in to their respective places. Unpacking his trunks, he laughed out loud, "Not a lot of clothes, not a lot of anything to show for eighty plus years. Guess I better be glad I won't be getting a lot of guests either."

Taking the Winchester, 1911 and the Bowie knife from the bottom of the trunk, he lined them up on the mantle. *I'll treat them right Diez, and I'll always take care of them for you.* He unpacked the kitchen box last, taking out two pounds of real Earth coffee, a grinder, and an electric pot. Setting them up, he ground enough beans for one cup of coffee, loaded the pot, and waited until it had boiled.

Taking his one cup of coffee, he went out and sat on the front steps as darkness fell. Something yipped further up the canyon as the winds died, and he watched the stars come out. Unfamiliar patterns, but he had time to learn the constellations here and he knew he'd do that, just for self-protection, if nothing else.

Coffee finished, he got up slowly, walked back into the cabin and shut the door softly. After a quick trip through the fresher, he fell into bed, and a deep, dreamless sleep.

Home

Fargo fell into the habit of rising early, fixing a bulb of coffee, and sitting on the porch in a chair he'd fashioned from leftover parts in the storage area. He'd marked off a shooting range toward the waterfall, and started practicing weekly.

He'd gotten the 16mm rifle sighted in, and also had gotten used to the holosight on it, since it was a lot simpler than he was used to. So far, he'd killed one neardeer with it, and added the best cuts to the autochef. He still hadn't attempted to use the stove or anything else after his fight with the fancy autochef over meals. Calories, basic recipe number and done was what he was used to, but no, not *this* autochef. It had so damn many selections it was driving him nuts, and to make it even worse, it didn't recognize standard GalScout menu numbers.

The one thing he hadn't overcome was the nightmares, not every night, but a couple of nights a week, they roiled his sleep. These were new ones, primarily revolving around his team. The worst one was Diez asking him why he'd let him die.

He'd done some minor maintenance on the storage area/ hangar for the liteflyer, and had taken to flying at least once a week, learning the area from the air. He'd gone back and read six months' worth of TBT email and trouble calls, reviewed Mikhail's files on TBT equipment locations and used the holo to familiarize himself with each feeder and subfeeder, along with the rough power requirements at all four of the existing terraformers and the subfeeders as well as how the power receptors and antennas worked on each building. He hadn't realized that every building got the entire comm feed, and only picked off what was addressed to that particular e-tainment center.

He was amazed that Mikhail's design covered the entire world from just those four locations. Equally amazing was the amount of power that was being consumed by White Beach. But considering it had almost one hundred thousand people in the immediate area, it was understandable.

Leaning back in his chair, Fargo expanded his empathic sense, while trying to block his psi sense. He thought he was finally getting the hang of it, but he did sense some low level activity, and *something* or *somethings* that might want to do harm, but he'd never sighted whatever it was.

At least twice a week, he walked the perimeter of his property, not only for the exercise, but to see if anything was moving across his land. He'd seen tracks that were probably a nearwolf, and a big one, some cat or predator tracks, and something with six legs and large paws that he thought might be a Silverback. That set of tracks, he'd only seen once.

The pool at the bottom of the falls was obviously a known watering hole for a number of species, and apparently some version of birds with claws. The field of blue flowers attracted some mutation of earth bees; they were almost as large as his thumb, and he gave them a wide birth.

Fargo checked the newsies on a daily basis, always looking for articles on the GalScouts and GalPat, along with articles on the worlds in the star cluster. He'd also continued to study the history of Hunter itself, getting smart on the world he was now calling home.

Evenings were taken up with e-tainment chats with Mikhail and Luann, so he was kept up to speed on what was happening in Rushing River, and the antics of Ian and Inga.

Fargo was usually in bed by 2100, and generally dropped off to sleep quickly. This night was different. He was awakened after midnight by barking, yowling and huffing. As he came awake, he let his empathic sense expand; he felt anger, pain, fear and determination, and an overpowering desire to kill.

That brought Fargo fully awake, and without thinking, he dressed, pulled his pistol belt on, grabbed his go bag, and took the 16mm Keel rifle down from the rack. Cautiously opening the door, his senses told him the fight was moving toward the waterfall.

Reaching back in the house, he picked up his NVG goggles and slipped them on. Easing to the corner of the house, he didn't see anything moving close to him, so he carefully started up the dim trail toward the waterfall. As he got closer, the same feelings were still there, if not stronger.

As he closed within a hundred yards, he started to see movement, but it was all close to the ground and very quick. He couldn't pick out what was moving, but there appeared to be three, maybe four different sizes of *things* moving. He cautiously moved a little closer, and suddenly the barking changed to howling, and he saw something big rear up at the base of the falls. Whatever it was, that was the source of the desire to kill.

Fargo made an almost unconscious decision that whatever it was, it needed to die before it killed anything else. He moved in another few yards, and it reared again. Without even thinking, the rifle rose, he got a good holosight picture of something with six limbs and fired just as it twisted.

The roar cut off with a huff, and the entire tableau froze as the animal dropped. He started forward and sensed something in extreme pain directly in front of him. Glancing down, he saw a large wolf like form that was bleeding badly from a slash in its hip.

He projected friendship and calm as he glanced quickly at the falls, but the thing at the base of the falls hadn't moved, so he knelt as close as he dared to the wolf and slipped off his go bag. Reaching in, he pulled out a clotting spray and said a quick prayer as he leaned closer.

The wolf bared its teeth at him and gave a half-hearted growl, but didn't move. Fargo quickly sprayed the area with the clotting and antiseptic spray, and touched the wolf lightly, trying to see if there were other injuries. He almost jerked his hand back when he sensed more wolves. This was a female with pups, and she was near term.

He cursed under his breath and racked his brain for what else he could do. Remembering he had a tube of surgiseal, he reached back and got it, pulled the wolf's pelt closed and applied the surgiseal to hold the wound closed. Lastly, he pulled out an auto injector and injected the wolf with enough nanos to hopefully keep her alive.

She sniffed the spray, and roughly licked his hand as he sank back on his knees. Looking up, he stiffened, he was surrounded by wolves, and what looked like mountain lions, with at least two bear-like beings sitting on the outside of the circle. *Oh shit, what have I got myself into now? I'm dead meat. Shit... I can't shoot them all. Hope they leave enough for Mikhail to...* The circle parted and a huge mountain lion stalked toward the wolf, nuzzled her and licked the wound. It turned to Fargo and stared at him, then licked his face with a tongue that felt like rough sandpaper. Fargo was shocked to feel that the lion was also a female, and also had kits almost ready to be born.

Afraid to move, and projecting calm as hard as he could, he continued to sit there as one of the bears came through the circle of animals, and did the same thing. It also licked Fargo, knocking his NVG goggles off and whuffing as she breathed in his scent. The wolf got up slowly, and limped toward the object at the base of the falls, giving Fargo time to recover his NVG goggles and slip them back on.

He was amazed at what he saw. The limping wolf peed on the carcass, followed by the female mountain lion and the female bear. The three of them sat in a row and howled, yowled and roared together, and the others did the same almost in answer. Fargo slumped back in the grass, not sure what had happened, and not sure anyone would believe it if he told them.

The three groups intermixed as they departed, with each one pacing slowly by Fargo and catching his scent. Fargo continued to sit in the grass until the last animal had been gone at least five minutes. Getting slowly to his feet, he repacked the go bag, slung it over his shoulder, and retrieved his rifle.

Pacing slowly forward, he saw the shape of the monster he killed resolve into a Silverback, and the hair on the back of his neck stood up. Extending his senses, he couldn't sense any other animals within range, and he quickly poked it in the eye with the barrel of his rifle, with his finger on the firing stud, just in case. Confirming the Silverback was dead, he suddenly realized he needed to piss, and decided he'd rather do that in the privacy of his cabin rather than add his scent to the carcass like the others.

Walking quickly and carefully back, he was soon safely inside the cabin with the door sealed. Stepping into the fresher, he realized his hands were shaking, and he was getting an adrenal dump. Finishing up, he stripped off the shipsuit, and made a quick pass through the fresher, then collapsed on the bed.

***

Fargo leaned back on his haunches, marveling once again at the luck of his shot from the night before. He cut away more tissue, exposing the twin hearts, and the fact that his one round had burst both of them. After skinning the beast, he finally got the skull cracked, and saw a lesion of some kind on the brain. He took more pictures of it, and measured the thickness of the frontal skull plate at almost a half an inch. He shuddered, realizing there was no way a

16mm bead was going to get through that much armor to kill it via a brain shot.

He peeled the meat away, exposing the forward set of shoulders, and measured the thickness, then decided to do an experiment. Getting a large sheet of plastic, he managed to load the remains of the Silverback on the gravsled, and carried it down to the range he'd set up. Putting the top half of the skull on one target, he propped the skeleton of the Silverback up on a couple of logs so that the joints were extended as if it were standing. He packed what he thought was roughly the right amount of meat around each shoulder, and went back to the one hundred yard line.

Firing two rounds at the skull, he shifted and fired one round at each front shoulder. Walking back to the target, he whistled as he looked at the skull. There was a crack, but, as he expected, neither bead had penetrated it. The beads penetrated the front shoulders, but not the back ones. A chill ran down Fargo's back as he looked at it. He repacked the meat, and put the two hearts back in their original positions.

Walking slowly back, he went to the line and fired two more rounds. They both got through the back shoulders, but didn't penetrate either heart or lungs. One more trip back to the line, and he fired three more rounds, one at each heart and one at the lungs. Tramping back to the target, he confirmed the two hearts and lungs were penetrated. He leaned against the gravsled thinking, *No frikkin wonder I never killed one in the sim on the ship. I never thought about having to make it through all that damn bone structure. I'm glad I've got a fifty round mag, because if I ever encounter two of these damn things, having to change mags would literally be the death of me.*

Checking the wind, Fargo made a pile of the meat, offal and bones of the Silverback, popped a mini-thermite grenade on a thirty-second delay and quickly rode the gravsled back up to the cabin. He saw the reflection of the glow in the gravsled's mirror and made a note to himself to make sure to scatter the ashes later.

Back at the cabin, he looked around for something to use on the Silverback's hide. He remembered watching an info-newsie on tanning hides and he thought back. *Gotta get all the flesh off the hide. Flensing? No, fleshing the hide. Need some kind of scraper.* Looking through the tools in the storage container, the only thing he could come up with was a rotary grinder. *Oh well, maybe this will work.*

Four hours later, covered in sweat and bits of Silverback flesh, Fargo stepped back from the now cleaned hide. *At least I got it this far. I'll make a run to Rushing River tomorrow. Hopefully Mikhail knows somebody that can finish it off.* Stripping off his coveralls, He sniffed and wadded them up and inserted them in the incinerator. Walking butt naked into the cabin, he stepped into the fresher, setting it on the refresh setting. Twenty minutes later, feeling a lot better, he slipped on his old shipsuit, and punched up a twelve hundred calorie dinner.

***

Fargo landed the liteflyer, glad to be on terra firma again. The flight down had been bumpy at best, even with the anti-grav stabilization. Parking on the pad, he hefted the Silverback hide out of the cargo compartment, and started walking toward the gate. Doc Grant, the retired GalPat surgeon that ran the local clinic, pulled up in a runabout, "Need a ride?"

"It would be appreciated. I'm going to Mikhail and Luann's store."

"Hop in." Fargo slid the Silverback hide in the back and Doc asked, "Where did you get that?"

Fargo buckled in as he replied, "Killed it on my place yesterday morning."

Doc whistled, "Impressive. And from what I've heard, you're one lucky man."

"There was only one. Don't know where the mate was. This one was a male. Speaking of which, I've got a picture of the brain, it looks like there was a lesion on it. Can you take a look at it?"

Doc nodded, "Yep. Let's get to the store and I'll be happy to look at it."

***

Luann fussed around, putting some cookies on the table, and shuffling the kids out of the kitchen as Fargo loaded the pictures into the holo. Bringing them up one by one, he explained each as Mikhail and Doc looked on in amazement. Doc finally said, "Yep, he looks like he was incapacitated in some form. Glad you were able to take him out before he came down here and rampaged around. The seven shots worry me though. I don't know too many people that could or would stand in there to shoot seven times at a charging Silverback. I still wonder what happened to the female."

Fargo nodded, "No idea on the mate, I got extremely lucky. If he'd been charging me, I wouldn't be here, because I would have shot once and expected him to go down." Turning to Mikhail he asked, "You know anyone that can finish the hide? I got the flesh off, but I don't have the right stuff to finish the tanning."

Mikhail thought for a second and hit his comm unit, moments later they heard, "Hey, Mikhail. What can I do for you?"

Mikhail smiled, "Kelly, can you come over to the store? I've got something I want you to look at and see if you can tan it."

"On the way."

Mikhail turned to Fargo, "Kelly is our local gunsmith and expert in planetary species. I know he's done some tanning before. I'm betting he'll know what to do with it, and how to do it."

***

After a quiet dinner, Luann got the kids in bed and the three of them sat around the table in the kitchen with bulbs of coffee, Luann finally asked, "Ethan, why are you not coming to town more? It's like you don't…"

Fargo sighed, "Luann, it's not that I don't want to see y'all, it's just… Well, I'm more comfortable up there. I've got peace and quiet, I can sleep in when I want, and nobody bothers me."

Mikhail cocked his head, but didn't say anything as Luann looked searchingly at Fargo, "But we're family."

"I know. It's not like I don't talk to you a couple of times a week if not more. I just like my peace and quiet." *And I'll be damned if I want to get wrapped up in a bunch of crap down here. I'm still trying to get my psi sense under control, but I'm not sharing that either!*

Mikhail finally said, "Don't know about you, but I'm tired. Tomorrow is going to be a long day." He finished his coffee and got up, "Night all."

Fargo took the hint and did the same, giving Luann a quick hug, "Night. See you in the morning." He sensed her worry and discontent at his answers, and quickly let go of her.

As Mikhail and Luann lay in bed later, she turned to him, "Why didn't you help me? I'm worried about Ethan, he's not the same. He's... He's *changed*."

Mikhail pulled her close, "Lu, Ethan is different now for a lot of reasons. Sixty years in the military, being a leader, and losing people is always life changing. He just lost a team he'd been with for over twenty years. He's dealing with his grief in his own way. And his way is solitude."

"But he's my brother! He should... I mean... You didn't change!"

"You met me after my service, you didn't know me before. I'd changed too, but you never saw that. You just need to give him some room, Lu."

"Room is one thing, but this Silverback hunting... People don't do that and survive. It's like he's trying to kill himself."

Mikhail said softly, "No, that's called adrenalin rush. It's him against nature. It is him proving his right to survive. I'll keep him busy, okay?"

Luann snuggled into his shoulder, "Alright, but I still worry about him."

"As you should. Now go to sleep, Love."

Back to Work

About a month after the set-to with the Silverback, Mikhail messaged Fargo about working a site during the installation of a new subfeeder. Picking him up early one morning in the small shuttle that TBT owned, they'd travelled four hours to a site near the White Beach terraformer, chatting about family, and what had been going on in Rushing River.

As they started their descent to the site, Mikhail turned businesslike, "You're going to be the new guy, and also in charge of site security. Any problem with that?"

"Nope, I think I'm pretty much up to speed on the operation, and I've read your previous reports on installations. Fargo stretched and parroted, "Basically, we have to provide twenty-four hour security until the sonic fence is up and operating, which is the last thing done. Four security people, four installation technicians, one combo work/Hab module, and two built out RCA buildings for equipment, and one tower, right?"

Mikhail nodded, "That's it. Site prep is already done, sonic saw and laser have leveled the site. Module is dropping in this morning, along with the crew. Heavy lift shuttle will bring the RCAs tomorrow, and the tower in three days. I've got to attend a meeting in White Beach tomorrow, so you basically get sixteen hours to get up to speed."

Fargo chuckled, "Nothing like a little pressure."

Mikhail handed him an actual file, "Here's the people on site. It's not for public consumption. Read it and give it back before we land."

Fargo scanned quickly through the folder, noting that there were four Ghorkas, three men and one woman, for security. One Arcturian technician, one from Earth four, and a Kepleran from 62E. As usual, the Kepleran's name was unpronounceable, and Fargo idly wondered if he went by Pop. "I thought there were normally four techs?"

Mikhail sighed, "There are, but I've got one on the far side of Hunter, so I'm the fourth for this install. I needed to get back in the field anyway. And after the meeting tomorrow, I'm sure I'll be needing to work off some frustrations!"

"That bad, huh?"

"It's Klynton and her crowd: always demand, never request, and always the highest priority…"

"Nuff said."

Mikhail brought the shuttle in for a smooth landing at the subfeeder site, as Fargo took in the area and the site itself. Stepping off the shuttle, Fargo extended his empathic senses as far as he could, but other than the TBT team, he didn't detect anything but a few lower level species, most of which were cowering in fear after the shuttle landing.

Mikhail came down the ramp saying, "We make the site bigger than is actually required, that way if we ever have to come do maintenance, we can drop the shuttle and parts right next to the installation. This is the shuttle pad," swinging his arm to the right, "That area over there will be the RCAs and over there." Pointing straight ahead, he finished, "The antenna will be up on that little rise back there. We do that at all of the sites."

Fargo nodded, "About three acres then. What's the height on this one?"

"Four hundred thirty-one actual, total with ground rise is eleven sixty-six. That will yield about a forty-two mile direct path, which covers the both existing and all of the planned additional habs in this area for the next ten years," Mikhail replied.

***

The Hab module was placed and the sensor sticks elevated as Mikhail finished the introductions, "Mankajiri is the lead, goes by Jiri."

Fargo shook his hand, "Nice to meet you Jiri. Former CSM for Third Corps? How the hell did you put up with those dirtballs?"

Jiri laughed, "I hear the Marine in that tone, and they were *my* dirtballs. They did pretty good." Turning to the lone female of the group, he said, "Kamala is our sensors expert. She can also go combat if required."

Fargo could only stare for a moment. Kamala was a beautiful woman, dark shining hair, green eyes and sparkling teeth sat atop a body even the bulky fieldsuit couldn't hide. Fargo nodded, "Kamala."

A tinkling laugh answered him, "My name means Goddess, but these guys say it should be she-devil. I didn't see as much combat as they did, but I can handle myself."

Jiri chuckled, "This is Adhit, he and Daman are the *outside* guys, so to speak."

Fargo shook hands with them both, and got nothing but calmness and curiosity from their minds. Noting the necklace of large claws Daman wore around his neck, he asked, "Uh, Daman, what the hell are those claws from?"

Daman smiled, sending chills up Fargo's back, "Oh, these? Slashgator."

Fargo thought back to the tapes he'd reviewed: *Slashgator. Water and dry land predator. Fourteen to eighteen feet in length fully grown, double set of teeth, claws on all four legs. Runs at twenty MPH for short distances. Armored body with overlapping scales, upper and lower body both. Double lungs, double hearts. Native to Hunter. No known predators. Located in tropical/semi-tropical environments surrounding equator.* "Okay, I've got to ask, how did you put it down?"

Daman's smile deepened, "Oh, we had a slight disagreement over my campsite. I stuck the stove in its mouth, and got behind it. I used this," patting his kukri at his belt. "And it lost, once I figured out the overlap pattern on the scales." Flicking the necklace, he added, "This is just one claw. The others are at home, along with his shell."

Fargo shook his head in wonder, "Just another day in the field, eh?"

All the Ghorkas laughed as Daman said, "Pretty much. We're not real good at backing up, or backing away from trouble."

Fargo flashed back to his dead team. *Shit, I swore I wasn't going to lead anybody again, and I get Ghorkas. I've never worked with them, but there are plenty of stories.* Smiling he replied, "So I've heard. Well, I'm a former Terran Marine, retired GalScout. I'm the newbie, so y'all tell me what I need to know, and how I can fit in."

Glancing up, he saw Mikhail smiling and guessed he'd taken the right approach. "Kamala, can you give me an overview brief on the sensor package?"

She smiled, "More than happy to. What should we call you?"

"Ethan or Fargo, I'll answer to both."

***

Fargo eased out of the Hab module and met Jiri at the far end as he climbed down from the overwatch chair on top, "All's quiet, Fargo. Nothing moving that I could see. NVGs are giving about three hundred yards of vis. You sure you're good for the entire twelve hours?"

Fargo took the goggles as he replied, "Yep, good to go. I want to get a full night to try to get an empathic baseline of area, and doing the overnight should give me any night animals that might be in the area, but outside the NVGs range."

Climbing to the top of the module, he sat in the chair mounted under the sensor head, and was surprised at how comfortable it was. Checking his fields of fire, he snapped the rifle to his shoulder and spun the chair 360 degrees. Satisfied that he had plenty of clearance, he dropped the rifle back to his lap and slowly scanned the full 360 degrees, taking his time to register features that he knew would look different at night. Sniffing the air, he was disappointed to find no scent of pines, only the scent of dusty grass, sand, and the residual burned smell from the lasers.

Near the middle of the watch, his radio buzzed, and Kamala said, "Something large at eight thirty from the Hab. Acoustics only, no visual."

Fargo clicked his mic twice and spun to look in that direction. Scanning back and forth to prevent a blind spot, he spent fifteen minutes staring down the bearing and extending his empathic sense, but nothing showed, or popped into his mind.

With an hour to go, he saw movement, and swiveled to honor the threat. It was low to the ground, moving in a jerky manner, and almost seemed to be running an *evasive* approach for lack of a better word. Fargo pulled the rifle to his shoulder, got a good sight picture and waited.

Ten minutes later, Fargo dropped the rifle back in his lap. *Fucking Trashpanda, sixty pounds of a cross species breeding way too smart for its own good, and gets into everything... Geez... I wonder if that is why Kamala never said anything. Programmed to ignore?* He heard rattling at the end of the Hab and hopped up, walked to the ladder, and sure enough, the Trashpanda was trying to get a grip on the next rung of the ladder. Fargo tried shooing it off by waving his arms, but that didn't work.

He hissed, "Go away you little mooch!" but that didn't work either. The panda finally got a grip on the next rung and started scrambling up the ladder. Fargo debated whether to try to poke it off the ladder with his rifle, take out the pistol and shoot it, or take the knife to it.

Deciding not to shoot it, *Can't wake the sleepers needlessly,* he pulled out the vibro knife and flicked it on. The Trashpanda froze, then dropped quickly to the ground and scuttled away from the Hab as fast as it could go. Fargo smiled in relief as he safed the knife and returned it to its holster.

***

Two days later, the antenna was up, the RCAs in, and the techs were making their final connections. The power feed from the terraformer was online, and one tech was in the process of balancing the power and e-tainment riding it as the support shuttle landed.

Mikhail returned in a foul mood, grumbling about Klynton and Cameron's demands for more power and more control over the e-tainment that rode the power beam. He'd disappeared into the RCA as soon as he grabbed a bulb of coffee and checked with Fargo, mumbling something about getting done and getting home.

The security team were doing the final checks on the sonic fence modules, pending putting power on them and Fargo had volunteered to take the last watch, so he could see how the modules were connected and worked.

Fargo felt the sonic fence come up, that tingling feeling that said 'something' was running, but not in a range that the human ear was capable of hearing. It was different from the 'sizzle' of the power running into the subfeeder. Figuring he was done, he headed for the ladder but Mikhail climbed on top and stood next to him, "Now it gets interesting. This is the first *firing* of the subfeeder, so we should be able to see it go out as a heat beam as it burns through the air. And I want to make sure nothing goes up in smoke up here either."

Fargo looked up at the multi-headed subfeeder and hoped they'd actually gotten the alignments all correct. As he glanced back, he saw something flash out of the corner of his eye, "Did you see that?"

"See what?"

As he brought his rifle up Fargo said, "I thought I saw a flash down where that band of green is."

He felt the first sizzle in the air as he dimly heard Mikhail yelling, "Abort, abort, abort!"

Commanding the holosight to max, he quickly scanned the area where he saw the flash, then saw another flash. It was a liteflyer, swooping and diving in and out of one of the canyons. "It's a liteflyer, I can barely make it out," Fargo yelled, as Mikhail scrambled down the ladder. Keeping the liteflyer in his sights, he saw a sudden flare and it disappeared into the canyon.

Fargo scrambled down the ladder as he felt the sizzling buzz stop moments later. He met Mikhail at the base of the ladder, "The flyer is down. I've got a mark…"

Mikhail grabbed him, "Let's go. We can take the shuttle." As the Ghorka boiled out of the Hab, he continued, "Jiri, Adhit with us. Kamala, check the sensors! See if you got anything on a liteflyer down the hill. I think we just burned one down."

***

Mikhail cursed long and loud when he couldn't find a place to land the shuttle, and Fargo finally said, "Dammit, just stop. We'll rope down, and see if anyone is alive. Get the authorities on the way as soon as you can. We'll make sure we document everything so that any evidence isn't compromised."

Fargo went off the aft ramp first, and as soon as he hit the ground and cleared the downdraft, smelt a smell he'd hoped to never encounter again, that of a burned body. Jiri and Adhit came down moments later and the shuttle peeled off and accelerated away, rope still dangling. They cautiously made their way down the side of the canyon, guided by the smell. Adhit finally said, "Ah, long pig for dinner again."

Jiri and Fargo both laughed, knowing it was Adhit's way of handling what he was pretty sure they were going to find. They finally saw the crashed liteflyer about forty feet ahead, and Fargo said, "Adhit, can you bring up the rear and put your datacomp on record? We're going to need documentation for all of this. Jiri, you're security backing us up..."

Jiri and Adhit both agreed, and they moved slowly forward. Fargo slung his rifle and used his vibro knife to cut away the vines. The smell grew stronger, and Fargo wished for a cigar or nose plugs, when he felt a tap on the shoulder. Turning he saw Jiri offering a small twisted smokestick. Taking it, he struck it on his pant leg, and inhaled, then coughed.

"Oh my God, Jiri, what the hell is this? Dried yak turds?"

Everyone laughed as Jiri said, "Only the finest Yeti turds, straight from the Himalayas!"

Fargo took another drag, coughed and said, "Okay, let's do this." They carefully approached the remnants of the flyer, noting the wings sheared off and stuck higher in the trees, but the main fuselage was pancaked into the floor of the canyon.

There were two cooked bodies in the cockpit, one apparently female in the pilot's seat, and one probably male in the passenger's seat. Fargo reached in to confirm there was no pulse, knowing there wouldn't be, but following procedure for the datacomp. He said, "No pulse, no respiration on either person. Reaching in and shutting the power switch off for safety purposes. No sound from the anti-grav at this time."

As he started to step away, he saw a small pack in the back seat. Picking it up, he opened it and found the female's ID chip. Flashing it to the datacomp he read, "Jill Gann, age twenty-three, White Beach. We will hold for the authorities."

Investigation

After he'd reported the one name they'd found to Mikhail, which brought a brief round of cussing from him, before the mic had cut off. After a quick consult, they'd spread out with Fargo leaned against a tree upwind of the crash, rifle in a hunter's carry, Jiri and Adhit were spread about thirty yards either side of him as they all swept the surrounding area for any threats. Suddenly, Fargo sensed something moving toward the crash from deeper in the canyon, "Jiri, Adhit, something coming from deeper in the canyon. It's hungry."

Jiri and Adhit had a quick conversation in their own language, then Adhit said mournfully, "I'm betting it's not one of the *normal* predators. Not our lucky day."

Unconsciously, they'd moved closer together, and moved around the crash site to take up a position between whatever Fargo was sensing and the site, odor be damned. After a couple of minutes, they heard intermittent noises but couldn't pick up any movement. Jiri said, "Not good. If we're not seeing anything it's low to the ground."

Adhit added, "Probably a Slashgator. Oh joy, oh joy."

Fargo turned sharply, "If it is, how to we kill it?"

Adhit laughed, "Feed it a stove?"

Jiri replied, "My rifle won't penetrate the scales," glancing at Fargo's rifle, he continued, "Don't think yours will either. The only way to kill it is to flip it over, or somehow get an upward angle to shoot it in the belly."

"Movement!" Adhit said quietly.

"Damn, it is a Slashgator," Jiri said.

Fargo finally saw it and cocked his head, "Why isn't it attacking us?"

Adhit replied, "We're no threat to it. It'll get around to us after it finishes lunch."

Fargo, dropped slowly to his knees, then prone, bringing the rifle to his shoulder. He looked up at Jiri, "See if you can get it to raise its head."

Jiri said softly, "It's too fast. It will be on you before you can shoot."

Fargo said, "Guess I better be pretty accurate, then."

They heard the moan of a shuttle overhead, but none of them took the chance of looking up, not wanting to take their eyes off the Slashgator for a second. It had finally sensed them, and turned, lifting its snout slightly. Fargo commanded the holoscope to medium magnification and could see a little bit of a gap between the rows of teeth. *Fifty yards, way too fucking close. Do I try it, or...* "Target," Fargo said aloud.

The hiss/crack of the 16mm rifle was almost drowned out by the shuttle as it settled lower in the canyon, causing the trees to sway. The wings of the flyer were blown out of the trees, and fluttered to the ground and dust and dirt sent flying, but Fargo never broke his concentration. He saw the 'gator snap, as if trying to bite whatever had hit it, then it opened its mouth in a roar as it started charging them.

Fargo's shots were metronomic, a half second apart, centered on the charging 'gator's mouth. Somehow he was able to keep track of the rounds fired and after ten, he was beginning to despair of ever stopping the beast. At fifteen shots, Fargo resigned himself. *Well, at least I got to see Luann, Ian and Inga...*

After two more shots, he realized Jiri and Adhit were screaming at him, and the 'gator had stopped. Its head was still moving, but the body wasn't. Getting up wearily, he was blown back to his knees by the shuttle that was hovering overhead. It finally moved off toward the side of the canyon, and Fargo could hear again. Jiri and Adhit were saying, "You got it, you got it. It's all but done." He noted both of them had dropped their weapons and pulled their kukris, meaning they were ready to fight to the death.

Picking up his rifle, he saw the Slashgator was only five feet from him, and he shuddered. *One second, maybe... That's what I had left.* As he watched it, the head dropped slowly, and the greenish blood stopped flowing from the mouth.

Adhit handed his kukri to Fargo, "You need to finish it. I think you broke his spine with those shots, but you need to cut its hearts."

With Adhit's advice, he finally managed to get the kukri between the plates and press it deep into the Slashgator's body. When he finally pierced the hearts, he felt the beast shudder once more, then go totally limp.

***

Twenty minutes later, the three of them heard crashing through the woods coming from the direction of the shuttle's landing. As the noises came closer, they moved back to the initial point where they had entered the accident scene and waited. Finally, a group of people appeared, some GalPat soldiers in uniform, a few men in civilian clothes, and one hysterical female, already screaming and sobbing.

A GalPat major stepped to the front saying belligerently, "What happened here? And who are you?"

Fargo saw both Ghorkas tense out of the corner of his eye, and he shifted his rifle to a hunter's carry, "Name's Fargo. We were first on scene. Saw the liteflyer go down. We have records of scene approach and checks we ran. Both pax DOA, master power is off. Backpack in the back seat where we…"

The hysterical woman burst by the major and Fargo screaming, "You bastards let my baby die!" as she ran toward the remnants of the fuselage. The wind shifted suddenly, and the woman caught a whiff of the dead bodies, went to her knees and began puking, screaming and crying at the tail of the wreckage.

The major sneered, "I'm the investigating officer. I will make the determination of what happened here. Don't need any of you *civilian security experts* telling me what happened. I'll need to confiscate all your weapons and datacomps. I saw you down there shooting into the brush when we came in. *If, big if,* we determine you didn't physically shoot the flyer down, you might get your guns back if you're polite."

Fargo started to retort when Mikhail pushed by the GalPat troops to stand by Fargo, "Don't say a word Fargo. Major Palette, you have no right to take anyone's weapons, nor do you have a right to confiscate any datacomps. I have already provided HQ with the tapes we've pulled from the sensor suite, and it proves Ms. Gann was in this area illegally."

Glaring at the major he continued, "There were air/flight notices posted, along with notifications on e-tainment systems throughout the area to *not* fly in this area over these three days. Also the autopilot should have automatically exited the area, or grounded the flyer for the duration of the notice. You know that as well as I do. That it didn't is suspect, to put it mildly."

The woman had recovered enough to approach the cockpit, and let out a blood curdling scream, then collapsed as she got a look at what was left of her daughter. That broke the tableau up, with the major and others moving forward. One slight, mousy civilian stopped, "Uh, Mr. Fargo, I'm Allan. I'm one of the liteflyer examiners. I'd appreciate any data you might have. I can accept a feed right here," he said, holding up a sealed case.

Fargo nodded, "Works for me. Jiri? Adhit? Adhit was the primary recorder, but you're welcome to all of our datacomps info." Allan set the case down, opened it, powered it up and pulled out a cable.

"How long have y'all been out here," Allan asked.

"About a week, total."

"Mind if I pull the entire week?"

Fargo glanced at Jiri and Adhit, "Nope, fine by me.

Allan diddled with a screen, and attached the magnetic cable to each datacomp in turn, verifying there was data being collected. Glancing at Fargo's rifle, he asked, "Did you use the rifle and have you cleared the memory on the holoscope?"

Fargo shook his head, "That's how I saw enough detail to see that it was a liteflyer and no, I haven't cleared it. Do you want that too?"

Allan said, "It might help." Allan attached the cable to the holoscope and the data blipped across.

A shaken, pale Mikhail came up, "My God. I hope I never see that again. Cooked in their own juices. Thankfully, the control panel is in good enough shape that there shouldn't be any issues over this. It's plain the autopilot emergency disconnect was pulled. Watch out for *Major* Palette, he's an ass kisser, head of palace guard, oh did I say that; governor's office security, and bucking for promotion."

"Who's the hysterical woman? And who the hell let her out here?"

Mikhail rolled his eyes, "Probably my fault. I passed the name. That's Gann's mother. She's Klynton's number two, that's how they got out here so quick. They jumped on the governor's shuttle with whomever was standing there, I think. Allan is a good guy, he works with us to put up notices, and he runs all accident investigations on Hunter. I think the rest of the GalPat troops are part of the palace guard. I don't really know who the others are."

"Lovely. We've already turned over our datacomp and holoscope data to Allan."

"Good! At least he got them before the major had a chance to muddle everything up. He's a grunt, doesn't know the first thing about flyers or flying."

Allan came puffing back, almost as pale as Mikhail, "Well, that wasn't pleasant. I almost wish I could use those pictures to show people what happens when you don't obey the rules. I'm going to have to pull the records from the e-comm to find out when Ms. Gann actually updated the autopilot." Turning to Mikhail he asked curiously, "How many volts to you think hit them?"

Mikhail shrugged, "Minimum of ten thousand. Maybe more, depending on which beam actually got them. There is one farm complex out here that draws about seventeen thousand."

They heard yells from the other side of the crash scene, and Jiri said, "Hmm, bet they found the Slashgator."

Mikhail and Allan both looked nervously over their shoulders, "Slashgator?"

Adhit replied, "Dead. Thanks to Ekavir."

"Ekavir?"

Jiri nodded, "Fargo earned his Ghorka name today, Ekavir."

Mikhail asked, "What?"

Adhit replied, "Bravest of the brave. Fifteen shots prone with a Slashgator charging him from fifty yards. He stopped it five feet from him. Ekavir never flinched."

Major Palette came stomping across the crash scene, followed by Mrs. Gann, "Why did you kill the Slashgator? Bored? Or do you just like killing things?"

Fargo bristled, "Should I have let it eat the two victims? That's where it was headed." Turning to Mrs. Gann he said softly, "I'm sorry for your loss. I will offer up a prayer for…"

Mrs. Gann interrupted with a screech, "Shut up! You killed my daughter! You murdering bast…" Palette grabbed her before she could physically attack Fargo, mumbled something in her ear, and led her back toward the shuttle.

Jiri broke the tension saying, "We better go get the 'gator's belly skin before somebody else does."

Fargo looked at him curiously, "Why?"

Adhit rolled his eyes, and covered what sounded suspiciously like a laugh with a cough, "You don't know? If you don't, I'll take it. No problem," he said with a smile.

Mikhail laughed, "Ethan, that belly skin is worth somewhere in the neighborhood of forty to sixty thousand credits. It's so rare, you can almost name your price. It makes some of the most beautiful iridescent leather you've ever seen!"

Fargo shook his head, and the group started toward the 'gator's body. As they walked through the crash scene, Allan and two others were removing the bodies from the liteflyer and putting them in body bags. They stood solemnly until that duty had been performed before continuing.

Once they got to the 'gator, they were met by the remaining GalPat soldiers, oohing and aahing over the carcass. With their help, they flipped the 'gator onto its back, and Fargo saw what they meant. The belly skin was as beautiful as the armored scales of the back were ugly. And this belly skin was almost unmarked. As he walked around it, he noted how the colors shifted in the light, and whistled at the beauty of it.

Handing his rifle to Jiri, he took out his vibro knife and carefully cut away the belly skin, getting as little meat as possible. Once that was done, he carved away as much meat as he could and confirmed he had in fact broken the spine with one or more shots. Peeling away the upper armor was fairly easy, and he popped out the eye, probing the skull to see if there was a way to get to the brain pan. It appeared there was a tiny opening, and he filed that away for future reference.

As he got to his feet, Adhit reminded him to cut one paw off, as he would need to make a necklace of the claws. *Not that I'll ever wear it, but if it makes them happy, I'll do it. Damn, I was just flat lucky on this one!*

Mikhail trotted over as he got up, "Allan says we can go, he's got all he needs from us, but we're stuck here one more night at least. He's going to send a crew out to retrieve the flyer tomorrow morning."

***

Two days later, with the new site up and fully operational they made it back to Rushing River, Mikhail took the belly skin from the Slashgator, promising to get it to the taxidermist to get it processed, and said, "Ethan, I wasn't going to say anything, but you know you've made an enemy, probably two of them, right?"

Fargo shrugged, "Not the first, won't be the last. I'll be glad to get back to the Green, and the peace and quiet. As long as they leave me alone, it's not a problem.

Mikhail just shook his head as Fargo climbed into his liteflyer.

Green Sweet Green

Fargo juggled the bulb of coffee as he settled into his chair on the front porch. He'd taken the liteflyer exploring a few times in the last month, killed a pair of Silverbacks about sixty miles north of the cabin, and cleaned and prepped the hides. Nothing had happened since the incident down at White Beach, but the niggling thought that kept recurring was Mikhail's comment about enemies, but he figured he was too far away and down the food chain for it to really be a problem. He owned what he had, didn't have any bills per se, and wasn't beholden to anyone on Hunter. His retired pay was enough for him to live on, even if he never worked for TBT again.

Suddenly his empathic sense alerted him to multiple *things* coming at the cabin. Fargo started up out of his chair, and saw probably thirty nearwolves, some mountain lions, and four bears intermingling as they came up from the flower field. Torn, Fargo extended his sense as far as he could, but didn't sense any anger or hunger in any of them, and sank slowly back into his chair, afraid to make any sudden movements. He did his best to remain calm and project harmlessness through his empathy.

The nearwolf female and mountain lion female, he finally realized, were carrying things in their mouths that were moving. They both paced up on the steps and stopped directly in front of Fargo, with the near wolf dropping the pup she had in her mouth in his lap. The mountain lion did the same thing with her cub. One of the bears swatted at her cub, sending it scrambling up the steps and it sat next to Fargo's chair, and squalled. Fargo was afraid to move, then had to grab both the wolf pup and mountain lion cub them as they pounced on the squalling bear cub. All three females howled, yowled, and roared together and stalked off the porch, leaving him holding the cub and pup. The bear cub, scared by the noise was doing its best to climb into his lap, and he finally reached with one hand and picked it up to save his leg from being clawed. Now all three of them were filling his lap, and he was afraid to move.

To his further amazement, a huge bear carried a full grown and obviously dead neardeer to the foot of the steps and dropped it there, earning it a lick from the female nearbear who had swatted the cub. His mind whirling with what he had just witnessed, he thought back to the night four months ago, when he'd shot the Silverback at the falls. He'd wondered then about the species fighting together, having never seen anything like that anywhere.

Now it was obvious there was at least some level of communication between the species, and he wondered if they had been genetically mutated by SierraSafari on purpose, or whether this was an outgrowth of some genetic strain that happened on Hunter in the intervening four hundred years.

As he thought about it, all the animals dispersed as quietly as they'd come. A sudden pain in his hand caused him to focus and he found the lion cub cheerfully trying to chew on his finger. Pulling his hand away, he saw the cub had drawn blood. Looking at the neardeer, he guess that was the food offering, and, based on the cub's nibbling him, they were probably hungry.

Projecting at the cubs and pup, he set them on the porch and grabbed the neardeer by a hind leg, dragging it over to his shed. He'd rigged a pulley after he'd killed the first deer, and quickly strapped this one into the spreader. Taking out his vibro knife, he quickly made the cuts and dropped the offal on the ground, planning to carry that off as soon as he'd finished getting the meat off the deer. The cubs and pup had other ideas, diving into the offal as if it were the finest steak in town.

Fargo just shook his head as all three of them, growling, hissing, and swatting at each other, while they set about devouring what was on the ground. He stepped away, washing his hands on the outside bench, leaning against it as the three of them went at it. He stepped quickly back in the house, picked up his datacomp, and sat down on the steps as he watched them eat. Doing a quick data search, he didn't find anything more than that the species had been introduced as mating pairs by SierraSafari as 'stocking' animals. Nothing about any genetic engineering, nothing about intraspecies or interspecies communications.

He rocked back against the steps. *What the fuck do I do now? Surely the xenos would go bat shit crazy over this, especially since it appears there are multiple modes of communication at some level, probably fairly*

high for the three groups... What if it's not just these three? Shit...
If I tell anybody, they'll take these cubs and the pup, probably try trapping the adults. Picking up the datacomp again, he quickly pulled up what was known about all three species on Hunter. All of them were labeled as dangerous to approach, with warnings against hunting them alone or in small groups. All of them were considered *game* species according to the data, but were far down on the list of trophy animals.

Lupus or Canis, Cattus, Urso. The ancient Latin roots for the three species stuck in his head, and Fargo rolled them around in his mind, inadvertently naming the pup and the cubs as he did so. He glanced back up as it got quiet to see the three of them in a pile, all sound asleep.

Shaking his head, he put the datacomp down and finished skinning out and getting the meat off the deer. Since the skin was in good shape, other than the ripped neck, he spent some time cleaning it as well as he could, setting it in the shed on top of the storage rack.

***

A month later, Fargo huffed his breath out in frustration as he found another chewed up boot, and Canis, tongue lolling with it firmly between his paws, with Cattus sprawled on his bed. If there was a bright spot, it was Urso. She didn't like being inside, preferring to loll on the porch instead.

The only good news, if you could say that, was that the autochef actually had a setting for *pet* food. He laughed to himself, remembering one meal from the autochef that he ended up feeding to the animals, something called kimchee, all three of them had refused to eat. Cattus had actually pawed at her nose for a good ten divs after sniffing it. He'd ended up putting it back the autochef, expecting it to burp like the one Diez had modified once.

The downside was that Fargo was having to hunt twice a week for neardeer to keep the three of them in food. Grumbling, he said, "You two are going to be the death of me yet. And do you know how hard it is to find a damn pair of boots that fit?" Turning on Cattus, he continued, "And you. You, and your damn claws. At least you're only shredding tree limbs, and not the furniture, except for the end table. Agghhhh..."

Fargo clicked the e-tainment off and stood in the middle of the room, "Now what the hell do I do with y'all," he asked the air as he stared down at Canis and Cattus, lying in the middle of the floor. "I've got to go to Rushing River, and I'll be dipped if I'm going to leave you inside. You'd tear the whole damn place down before I could get back."

Walking in the kitchen, he picked up their bowls, carried them to the porch and came back for the water dishes. As he carried them out, they followed him curiously. Urso was sprawled in front of the steps, sound asleep in a patch of sunshine, and they both pounced on her in glee. Fargo quickly grabbed what he needed, sealed the door, and projected *stay* at the three as he headed for the shed.

Dragging the liteflyer out, he quickly configured it, loaded the eight neardeer hides in the storage, and maneuvered it carefully past the three still playing.

Launching down his runway, he settled back for the ride to the spaceport.

**

Mikhail leaned back from the holographic presentation, "Any questions?"

A chorus of, "Nope, not really," were heard around the table as the techs, and Fargo digested the latest update on Hunter's TBT status, and the plans for the next month.

Finally Jergens, the lead for Adelaide, near the fourth transformer in the southern hemisphere asked, "Mate, what are the plans for the expansion down in our area? We're growing with every ship, hearing rumors of another couple of thousand Aussies coming in on the next colony run."

Mikhail grimaced, "Yes, I've heard the rumors, Jergens, but nothing firm that actually says we are actually getting the folks. I've pinged White Beach every other week, but trying to get any plascrete information out of them is like getting blood out of a GalPat administrator."

Everyone chuckled at that, and Mikhail continued, "I've got a set of contingency plans I'd like you and Fargo to review. Your area is a bit of a problem, with very little actual high ground. One of the easy ways to fix that is Geosync'ed sats, but I haven't heard back from Earth on approval, or any of those sats even being allocated to this sector." Turning to the others he said, "Why don't you take a lunch break while they look over the security details? We'll reconvene at thirteen."

Luann brought in sandwiches as Fargo and Jergens poured over the plans and security arrangements, with a number of discussions on procedures, time frames, and standard work schedules. Fargo finally stood up, arching his back and sighing in relief when it finally popped. "Fresher break, then we'll hit Mikhail with what we've come up with. Fair enough?"

Jergens stood, stretched and groaned, "Sounds good to me, mate."

***

Fargo finished presenting the changes he and Jergens had come up with, and Mikhail looked at Jergens, "You agree with this?"

Jergens nodded, "Sure do. There isn't any other way to get that much power moving that quickly. Your plan would drag it out too long."

Mikhail glanced at Fargo, "Security costs?"

Fargo shrugged, "It's going to go up, instead of one site, we'll need security for four sites simultaneously. Realistically, we're going to need a second shuttle, too. And possibly additional large caliber weapons too. I don't want to try one of those nearelephants with a sixteen. I'd say at least a twenty mil, if not thirty."

Mikhail winced at that, "Really? One, no, *four* thirty millimeters on a *maybe* need them?"

"Well, maybe you can borrow a couple from the GalPat det. I know they've got tripod mounted ones. I'll comm Jiri about getting extra personnel from him, so that's not an issue. They'll all know how to use one."

Mikhail mumbled, "I'll talk to the sergeant."

***

After an early dinner, Fargo loaded up the liteflyer with the things he'd gotten from Luann, including a new pair of boots. He wasn't looking forward to breaking them in, but he needed to do it before the next job started.

Pushing the speed up to just under what would classify as emergency, he was gliding in for a landing forty-five minutes after taking off from the spaceport. As he came in on short final, he noted a number of nearwolves and nearmountain lions surrounding the house. As he rolled out, he saw Canis, Cattus and Urso all sitting on the porch, watching the liteflyer come up to the shed. Stretching his empathic sense, he could *feel* a number of animals out to quite a distance from the house. *I really need to figure out a way to measure that. Never did that in the Scouts.*

He unloaded it, pushed the button to configure it for storage, pushed it into the shed, and carried the first load to the cabin. As he rounded the corner, he was met by what he'd termed the three matriarchs, wolf, mountain lion and bear. They were grooming their respective pup or cub, and watched him as he continued onto the porch and into the cabin. He couldn't help but wonder if the matriarchs were watching over the cubs from afar.

Coming back out for the second load, he stopped and knelt, filming them as they sat side by side, muttering, "Nobody is going to believe this, nope, I'm gonna be the crazy old man back in the Green." Getting up, he retrieved the last of the supplies, including his new boots. Loading everything in the cabin, he eased back onto the porch with a coffee bulb in hand, watching the interactions.

The more he thought about it, he was glad that he'd had the presence of mind to keep a video diary of the growth and interactions of the three. As he picked up the camera again, he saw the three matriarchs look at each other, then at their children. Canis, Cattus and Urso immediately came bounding up on the porch, jumping on him as he juggled the camera and coffee bulb to protect them and not burn the animals. When he looked back up, the front yard was empty.

After he'd petted and scratched all three of them, he got up, stretched and looked at the sky. The stars and George and Celeste were up, lighting the area with a brightness he'd never have believed back on Earth. With a sigh, he opened the door, and Canis and Cattus scooted by. With a pat and a scratch for Urso, he followed them in.

Flopping down on the lounge chair, he called up the e-tainment and the research link he'd been going through. Something really strange was going on with the animals on Hunter. According to the research papers he'd been working through, all three species were normally patriarchal, not matriarchal. They had been known to share territory, but that was up by Yosemite. It didn't explain, oh wait. *This is very similar to Yosemite, the altitude, remoteness, lack of people. Yeah, maybe those SierraSafari folks were smarter than I thought. What if they stocked all the regions on Hunter that were equivalents of places on Earth? Damn, we didn't do a full scale flora/fauna mapping when we did the second in. I wonder...*

Three hours later, he groaned and stretched. It looked like the settlement types had sent an advanced party to select sites and they at least had done a full mapping of those areas. But nothing had been done in the Green or any of the more rugged parts of Hunter.

With another groan, he got up, promptly tripped over Canis and almost went facedown. Canis yelped, startling Cattus who came up snarling and spitting as she turned to face a stumbling Fargo. He finally caught himself on the wall, cussed, and stumbled off to bed.

About 0300, he was awakened by Canis whining and Cattus' rumbling growl. He sat up and said grumpily, "Now what the hell do y'all want?" They both went out of the bedroom and Fargo followed them into the kitchen. He realized the food bowls were still outside. Cussing himself, he opened the front door, only to find Urso was blocking it. Stepping over her, he picked up the two food bowls and brought them inside, filled them from the autochef, pulled a leg bone out of the chiller and went back for the water bowls, giving the leg bone to Urso as he stepped out.

Shutting the door gently, he walked slowly back to his bedroom, scratching as he listened to Canis and Cattus eating nosily and Urso cracking the bone outside. He shivered as he thought of what they could do to him, or any human. Finally dropping off to sleep, he was visited by one of his many nightmares, this time with the sound of jaws tearing flesh.

Tick Tock

Fargo sat in the eating nook, staring out the plas-steel window at the striations of rock, nearpine, and nearoak on the far side of the canyon. Without realizing it, he was idly thumbing his ID chip from active to retired and back to active, his thoughts in turmoil as he sipped one of the few cups of real coffee he allowed himself on a monthly basis. Being this far out on a rim world like Hunter, a pound of coffee often cost more than five thousand credits, if it was even available; hence the few times he let himself actually enjoy, nay savor, a cup of real coffee. He even went so far as to brew it himself, rather than using the installed autochef.

Canis lay at his feet, growling at the chew toy Fargo had filled with a treat as she tried to figure out how to extract the treat, radiating frustration. Cattus padded slowly in from wherever she'd been dozing, stretched and yawned as only a cat can, and put a paw on the sill, raising her head slowly to see what held Fargo's interest. Not sighting any prey, she dropped back to the floor, slapped at Canis, and padded out of the room, radiating contentment.

Fargo sighed and took another sip of coffee, not willing to admit to himself he was bored, bored, bored. He'd been planning for this retirement the last ten years, and now after six months, he felt like he was slowly going nuts. After all, he was physically *only* eighty-five years old, according to the Barycentric Coordinate Time that had been adopted almost eight hundred years ago, so with his basic longevity treatments, he knew he was good for probably another fifty-sixty productive years. Due to his service in the Terran Marines, and now his enforced semi-retirement from the GalScouts, he'd spent a number of years in relativistic space and was almost nine years younger than his sister, now. That wasn't helping his mood either, as he needed to drag the liteflyer out and go down to the spaceport-cum-village at Rushing River and pick up supplies.

Even though he loved her, Luann's perpetual bossiness always grated on Fargo's empathic sense, along with the occasionally high pitched voice. But she *was* the only family he had in the entire universe, so he put up with it. Well, that, and she'd managed to get his land claim filed, this ranger cabin prefab assembled, and basic furnishing completed with the credits he'd sent her for the last twenty years.

Finishing the last of the coffee, Fargo slid the cup across to the autochef, which swallowed the cup without a sound. Fargo always expected the autochef to burp, but that never happened. He wished he'd known how Diez had programmed it, idly wondering if someone on Hunter could duplicate it. Pushing himself up, he walked to the front door and strapped on his 6mm pistol, checking to make sure he had a full charge, and that the safety was on.

Slapping his pockets, he verified he had his vibro knife, light, and locator in their usual places. He grabbed a medium weight jacket and put it on over his faded GalScout coverall; pulling the door open, he called calling, "Canis, Cattus, out." Grabbing the toy from Canis he said, "No, not taking the toy out. House only."

Canis looked up at him and rolled her lips, radiating frustration as Cattus slipped silently out. Projecting calmness Fargo said, "You can finish playing with it when I get back, dummy." Canis wagged her tail and stalked to the edge of the porch, saw Cattus sitting at the base of the steps licking a paw, and promptly launched herself at Cattus, knocking her tail over teakettle. Cattus came up yowling, and the fight was on. Fargo just shook his head at the two nine month old animals, and stepped around the two as they rolled, yowled, barked and generally tried to pin each other down.

Fargo went to the storage shed, thumbed the door open, and pulled the liteflyer out by its tail. Reaching in, he keyed the cargo configuration sequence and let the liteflyer unfold itself and complete the Built in Test (BIT) checks as he mentally cataloged additional things he might need. He pulled two rolled up Silverback pelts and a nearelk pelt from the stack on the bench, and dumped them in the back of the liteflyer. Thumbing the gun rack open, he pulled a scoped 16mm rifle from the rack, checked the load and power pack, safed it, and carried it to the liteflyer placing it in the rack he'd built for it. Closing the storage, he said into his wrist comp, "Lock, secure house and perimeter."

The house AI responded, "All buildings locked, perimeter secure standby for liteflyer departure. Winds nominal, turbulence at canyon mid-point above nine thousand feet. No spacecraft arrivals or departures in the next twenty-two hours. Spaceport security is at bravo."

He turned back to the animals now laying side by side and panting; he projected, "Visit pack, guard, protect." His empathy allowed him to get a pretty good feeling for their mental states, and a fuzzy kind of feedback, but he still wasn't sure what good if any his trying to project commands to them did. Of course he was still trying to come to grips with his new telepathic capabilities which was another reason he didn't like dealing with Luann. When he touched her, she sprayed thoughts like a damn water hose, and some of them he *really* didn't want to know. He'd always known, *intellectually*, that women were different, but damn… At least up here, he didn't have to worry about that.

Canis and Cattus both trotted out of the clearing toward their respective pack's ranges, and he heaved a sigh of relief. He didn't sense Urso, but she was a roamer anyway, she might already be with her sibs. Turning the liteflyer around, he climbed in and quickly checked the BIT again, confirming everything was green. Closing the canopy, he fired it up, and launched down the little runway and over the edge of the canyon, exhilarating in the feel of flight, smiling for the first time today. A niggling thought in the back of his mind was why he now enjoyed flying, since he'd always hated it before. *Was this Diez again*, he wondered.

An hour later safely on the ground at the field adjacent to the spaceport. He reached in the back, pulled out the three pelts, and thumbed the lock on the liteflyer, then started walking toward the village.

Omar, as he was known due to his large bulk, the Arcturian sergeant of the space port guards rattled to a stop in his patrol vehicle and squeaked a greeting that his Galtrans projected to Fargo's implant as, "Ho, lieutenant of the retired, ride to the village you would like?"

Fargo nodded, replying, "Ho Omar, appreciated is the ride," as he hopped into the cab.

Omar spared one eyestalk from the road to look at the pelts and asked, "For trade, pelts? Much credit your family gains with hunter prowess? Danger to self without reward is not health."

Fargo untangled that translation in his mind and thought for a minute on how to respond. He finally decided truth was the easiest saying, "Hunting to put food on the table and fuel in the flyer is good. Stopping predators," pointing to the Silverback pelt, "saves lives for those that travel the Green."

Omar sounded like he was having a coughing fit, but the implant translated it as laughter and the fact that Omar had no desire to go into the Green. Stopping in front of the trading post, Fargo thanked Omar for the ride, grabbed the pelts, and climbed down from the patrol vehicle. Steeling himself, he walked slowly toward the doors, which dilated open automatically as he got within one step. Walking through, he noted the smells of the hundreds of things Luann and Mikhail had for sale and trade. He sensed Luann and Mikhail in the back in their living quarters, then felt a soft quiet push of mischief off to his left. Smiling, he quietly placed the pelts on top of a handy counter, and kneeled down waiting. Ian, Luann's oldest, came charging around the corner of the counter yelling, "Unka Fargo, Unka Fargo!"

Fargo grabbed him and swung him high, much to Ian's delight, and squealed as Fargo tickled him. Setting him back on his feet, he leaned over the edge of the counter, "Hello, Inga. Do you want to say hi to me?"

Inga, smiling shyly and wringing her hands said, "Hello Uncle Fargo, I are- am, pleased to see- that you-"

"That I'm here, Inga? You have been studying haven't you?" He asked as he picked Inga up, giving her a quick hug. "And you're almost as big as Ian now."

"Is not, *I'm* still bigger," Ian shouted.

Taking one of the pelts off the counter, Fargo handed it to Ian, "Inside voice, Ian, inside voice. Here, help uncle carry these please."

It was all Ian could do to pick up the pelt. As he staggered down the aisle with it, Fargo sensed Luann's harried approach, mixed with curiosity and worry. Picking up the other two pelts, he carried them and Inga back to the main counter, sitting them all on the counter as Luann came out of the back.

Luann came quickly through, giving Fargo a quick perfunctory hug and immediately saying, "You got a sealed box from the Scouts, it came under courier orders, and it's still locked up at the port. They would only release it on your thumbprint." Looking down at the pelts, she continued, "Have you been hunting more Silverbacks? You have a death wish or what? Don't get me wrong, these are worth a fortune, but those damn things are known for hunting down the hunters. You want these on credit, or you want to sell them off to the spaceport guys?"

Fargo thought for a minute, "Put them on credit. I'd rather they go to a trader than one of the spacers, because they won't give you or me a realistic price. Anything new down this way?"

Mikhail walked out of the back, radiating satisfaction, "'Lo, Fargo. I see you've been cheating death again," shaking hands with Fargo he continued, "Got a few visitors in, including a bunch that claim they are hunters; but they look more like spacers, to me. Oh, and there was a Taurasian in asking for you by name."

"A Taurasian? That's strange, the only ones I knew were in the GalScouts. Matter of fact, I lost one on my last planeting. He was the sifter on the team," Fargo said.

Luann dug around in the counter drawer, finally coming up with a datachip, "He said to give you this, and he's a med something or other. He's up with Doc Jenkins at the clinic, I do remember him having those same kinds of trunks you brought back."

Bouncing the datachip in his hand Fargo cocked his head, "Well, I guess I better go find out what's going on. Can I borrow the runabout to go up to the clinic, and then come back for lunch?"

Mikhail flipped him the dongle, "Sure, I'll have your order pulled by the time you get back."

Fargo pocketed the datachip and looked around for Ian, "You want to take a ride, boy?"

Ian popped out from behind the counter, "Can I? Mom, please?"

Luann started radiating anxiety, sighed but finally said, "I guess. You mind Uncle Ethan, and you do what he tells you, understand me? And remember to get the honey from Nicole."

Ian scuffed the floor, "Yes, momma." Grabbing Fargo's hand he headed for the door, pulling Fargo along in his wake. Hopping into the runabout, Ian fastened his belts, and put his hands in his lap. Fargo chuckled, and drove them quickly to the clinic.

The clinic, like most of the rest of the village was a prefab expanded from the cargo containers that had contained the med unit everyone jokingly called the doc-in-a-box. It was an advanced remote/ruggedized Med-Comp field unit that was the standard for homestead worlds, and really didn't even need a technician to support it. Hunter was lucky in that they actually had a real doctor who'd taken a homestead payback after he'd retired from the GalPatrol. He was a crusty old genie from Earth four, who'd taken the full med modification sixty years earlier, and had last served on a GalPatrol cruiser that had patrolled the rim worlds.

Fargo took Ian's hand as they walked slowly from the parking area, "You feeling okay Ian? Don't need to stick you in the box, do we?"

Ian shook his head violently, "No Unka, I feel fine. I don't like the box, it makes me stay still."

Fargo laughed as he punched the dilator for the entry, stepping through with Ian at his side. Doc Grant met them at the inner door, and Fargo was once again struck by how much Doc looked like Santa Claus with the beard, pipe and belly. "Fargo, what can I do for you? You're not due for anything that I'm aware of?"

Fargo replied, "You've got a Taurasian med tech here that asked for me."

Doc turned, "OneSvel, you have a patient," he said. The Taurasian could be heard thumping through the clinic, causing Ian to cower a little behind Fargo. When OneSvel came through the inner door he projected, *You don't know me, follow my lead.* The GalTrans said, "Mister Fargo, we are OneSvel. We were crèche mates with DenAfr, and I honor you for returning DenAfr to us."

Fargo bowed to OneSvel, "It is with honor I greet you, OneSvel," he said. Realizing there were multiple things going on, he said, "Doc, can you excuse us for a few minutes?" Nodding his head toward Ian, who was goggling at the big Taurasian.

Doc nodded back and looked down at Ian, saying, "Come on boy, let me check you and see how many scratches and infections you've got today. You damn kids get into more stuff…" Taking Ian by the hand, Doc disappeared into the rear of the clinic. OneSvel and Fargo stepped into one of the examination rooms, and sealed the door.

Fargo dropped into the examination chair as OneSvel reoriented to Fargo and his GalTrans said, "May we connect with you?"

"Yes."

OneSvel extruded a pseudopod from the host and gently touched Fargo's temple with the microfilaments. Fargo thought, *Why the obfuscation of our relationship? And what are you doing all the way out here? I thought you were happy on X-ray being a doctor at GalScout base.*

As they communicated telepathically, they continued to carry on a basic conversation concerning DenAfr, and how his ashes had been returned to the crèche with honor, in case anyone was listening.

OneSvel's mind touch was soothing. *We are here on orders. We left a datachip with your family unit that is encrypted with the latest information from headquarters. There is a strong possibility the Traders have a base somewhere in this star system, or within one jump of here. The colonel asked me to come here and verify you were not wiped, and if you were to reprogram your modes, codes and data. I can tell you are fully programmed and your med nanos are all at full capacity, except the psychotropics.* He chittered, "Have you been having nightmares?"

Fargo said, "Yeah, some. It's usually about losing my team, or my Marines. Not every night, but a couple a month."

OneSvel chittered, "You are spending too much time isolated. Humans need interaction with other humans. Wait here." OneSvel disappeared into the back of the clinic and came back moments later with a long needle attached to a micro injector clasped in one pseudopod. Fargo grimaced, and OneSvel said, "You know this is the only way, unless I put you in the box."

Fargo pulled down his shipsuit and sighed, "I know, but dammit, I *hate* needles."

OneSvel chittered a laugh as he positioned the portable holoscan and stabbed the needle into Fargo's armpit, penetrating eight inches to the medpack and the fill port for the psychotropics. As the micro injector filled the medpack bladder, OneSvel linked again, projecting, *Take these tabs, one of these will give you the appearance of a low grade infection which would require a visit here, if you need to link to me. This makes things easy. Please review the chip and do as you see fit.*

Fargo thought, *What does the colonel expect me to do by myself? And you didn't answer why you don't want it known that I know you.*

OneSvel replied, "*We are to be your contact point and cut out to Gal. There should be an encrypted communicator arriving shortly via courier for you. We have the twin to it, and it is secure from any monitoring capability on this planet. We have also been issued a portable FTL communicator tuned to the sideband of the node in this star system, so that I can report back to headquarters. Why are we here? Because we volunteered. We had heard many stories from DenAfr of the planet groundings you and the team did in scouting new worlds, and we decided we* needed to experience some of that, how do you say, excitement?"

Fargo sighed, *Honestly, most of the time it was just boring mapping and sampling, OneSvel. Not a lot of excitement there.*

OneSvel thought, *Maybe for you, but DenAfr was always excited, there was always a chance for a new compound, or a new element. For us, that would get our name added to the book of honors on Taurus.*

Fargo took the tabs, placed them in one of his pockets and thought, *How do they expect me to go wandering around the star system? I need some kind of reason for that.*

OneSvel responded, *You have a reputation already as a hunter of exotic skins that is already extending beyond this star system. You know how much you should be paid for those skins, and are not happy with the credits you're receiving here. Part of the information on the disk are locations within this star system and one to two jumps for furriers and others that buy at much closer to retail values.*

Fargo shielded his thoughts for a couple of minutes, then projected, *Interesting concept, but if I'm going to do that, I'd need a lot of pelts to make it worthwhile, and make financial sense for me to travel like that.*

OneSvel thought, *There are three containers of pelts and furs currently in diplomatic hold on the local space station that are authorized for release to you. They are confiscations from this sector, and the assessed wholesale value is about one million credits.*

Fargo whistled, "*A million credits! Damn, what if I sell them?*"

OneSvel couldn't smile, but the humor came through his thoughts. *Well, you would obviously have to pay up to the assessed value to GalScout, less your travel costs. We know you are not rich, but a significant profit could be gained to your advantage.*

Fargo mumbled, "If you only knew…" then thought, *Fine, I will take the furs I have here and see if I can find a ship that will be going to the planets that I might get information from. I can possibly tie those trips in with providing security to Mikhail on his TBT executive rounds.*

OneSvel chittered, "So, if there is anything I can do, please let me know Mr. Fargo. We owe you a debt for returning DenAfr, and every one of us is responsible to discharge that debt."

Fargo replied, "I don't think it's necessary, but thank you, OneSvel." Doc Grant opened the door, and Fargo continued, "Looks like I'm more or less healthy Doc. How about Ian?"

Doc tousled Ian's hair, "Oh, I think he'll survive. From what I hear, you've got a suicidal ideation. All these trips into the Green hunting by yourself isn't good, Fargo. Sooner or later you're going to get killed either by the Silverbacks, the wolves, the mountain lions or the grizzlies up there. Luann worries about you, and wants me to put you in the box and 'fix' your head.

Fargo shrugged, "It's income. I'm going to take the furs out myself and try to sell them, so I can get a better price. That should make her a little happier."

Doc nodded, "That would be a good idea."

With that, Fargo led Ian out, they got back in the runabout, and headed back to the trading post.

Nicole

On the way back from the clinic, Ian suddenly sat up straight, "Unka, we need to get honey."

Fargo looked over, "Where do we get that, Ian? Do you know how to get there?"

Ian looked around, "Turn that away, Unka." He said, pointing to the right. Fargo obligingly turned the runabout down the side street, and glanced at Ian again. Ian pointed to the right again, and Fargo turned, then Ian said, "There Unka, there. The pot."

Fargo looked up and saw a sign with what looked like a mug more than a pot hanging on the front of a small building. He pulled the runabout in at an angle in front of the building, as Ian unstrapped and bounded out of the vehicle. Fargo hurried to catch up, as Ian bolted through the door. Cussing under his breath, he stepped through the door to see what was either a restaurant or an upscale tavern setting, but empty of people. Fargo sensed a presence behind the curtain of the bar, and sensed and heard Ian babbling about honey from the same area.

Fargo walked toward the bar as Ian and a woman came through the curtain, with Ian pulling her by the hand as she looked down at him. Fargo saw a small woman with a pixie haircut, as Ian said, "Mizz Nikki, this is my Unka Fargo."

She looked up and met Fargo's look with one of her own, and he felt her attitude change immediately to wary and defensive. He saw a slender 5 foot 7 inch blonde woman with green eyes and a challenging attitude that physically stopped him in his tracks due to his physical attraction to her. She continued from beyond the bar and stopped in front of him saying in a husky lilting voice, "Nicole Levesque. Owner operator and jack of all trades at the Copper Mug."

Momentarily flustered, Fargo stuck out his hand in self-defense, "Ethan Fargo, retired and sometime hunter. My sister said something about honey?"

Nicole shook it with a firm grip, and looked down at Ian, "So *that* is what you were babbling about. You need to slow down, young man." Fargo had thrown up a block and was trying hard to not read her mind, even as his empathic senses picked up her sensuality.

Abashed, Ian scuffed his boot, "Yes ma'am, Mizz Nikki. But momma said get honey."

Confused and realizing he was still holding Nicole's hand, he quickly dropped it, "Luann is my sister, and she isn't always known for filling in all the blanks, so to speak. She mentioned getting some honey, but this doesn't look like a shop."

Nicole waved her hand around the minimally but tastefully decorated area, "It's pretty much a bar, restaurant, if you can stand the food, and kind of a herb and natural emporium. I do what I can to make enough to cover the costs and keep the doors open."

Fargo winced at that, "So long hours and no relief, eh?"

"Not really. My husband died three years ago, and I'm running this place, the winery, and raising a few other things with just me and my daughter."

"Sorry to hear that," Fargo said. His mind finally connected and he continued, "All those grapes and other things out beyond the last two sets of containers?"

Nicole cocked her head, "Um, yes. But I don't understand what containers you're talking about."

Fargo searched his mind, "When we did the second-in on this planet, there were about a thousand containers, stacked two and three high, with some other containers sitting out by a few acres of grape bushes. They were probably a mile from the other containers."

Nicole smiled, "Vines, grape vines. It took almost five years to get them trained and separated, well, for those that didn't mutate. Those four containers were a completely automated winery. We've been making wine for almost seven years using that equipment."

"You mean it actually worked? Other than the two living containers we found, we thought all the others were empty ark type containers."

Nicole smiled, "Nope, they were still sealed and we were able to puzzle out the instructions and get power to them. When we finally did, they opened right up, built themselves out and the BIT checks all worked. We hand-picked about fifteen bushels of mixed grapes and pushed them through the system, and got a bottle of *wine* out the other end. It took us another year to find the rest of the automated equipment, including the auto mechs that take care of the vines and pick the grapes."

Intrigued, Fargo asked, "How much wine are you making?"

"We are getting about three hundred cases a year, so about thirty-six hundred bottles a year. Some red, some white, some mutated, and some fortified port that we mix with the pear brandy we're also getting…"

Ian interrupted, "Unka, I gotta pee."

Fargo blushed, as Nicole laughed, "End of the bar, down the hall, first door on the right."

Fargo scrubbed his face as Ian went to the bathroom. Looking in the mirror, he ruefully decided he needed to pay more attention to his appearance when he came to town. Ian finished, and Fargo led him back to the end of the bar, where a jar of honey was sitting. He picked it up and asked Ian, "Can you carry this without dropping it?"

Ian, wide eyed, said, "I think so," holding up his hands. Fargo gently set the jar in his hands, and Ian cradled the jar as Nicole came through the curtain.

Fargo asked, "How much do we owe you?"

Nicole replied, "Just tell Luann to put a credit on my account." Turning to Ian she continued, "Now Ian, if you don't drop it, the next time you're here, I'll give you a cookie. Would you like that?"

"Yes, Mizz Nicki," was Ian's enthusiastic response.

***

Dinner was excellent, and Fargo groaned as he pushed back from the table, "That was delicious.

That's much better than what I get out of the autochef."

Luann smiled a harried smile, "Well, a lot of this is actually out of our autochef, but I've been playing with seasonings and native plants and meats for a while. But thank you."

Coming back from the kitchen, Luann set some puff pastries on the table with the opened jar of honey, "Try a little honey over the dessert, I think you'll like it."

Fargo used that opening to ask, "So, what is the story with Levesque?"

Mikhail rolled his eyes, "Now you've done it," he chuckled.

Luann swatted at him, then turned to Fargo, "She, her hubby and daughter, Holly came out about three years after we did. She and hubby were both GalPat, had their forty in, and used their credits to buy one hundred acres, including the vineyard. Apparently, she is originally from France, and knows something about wine, among other things. They'd just gotten the business up and running good, and she started the Melting Mug as a way to sell wines and some herbs and other things she's got out there."

Looking at Ian and Inga, she said, "Okay kids, time for you to go study."

Inga immediately got up, gave Mikhail and Luann hugs, then came around the table and tentatively hugged Fargo, "Yes, mama. Can I use the e-tainment?"

Luann glanced at Mikhail, who nodded, "For a little while. Then it will be Ian's turn, when he finishes his math homework."

Ian pouted, but said, "Yes, mama." Then ran into the living room to get his books, yelling back at Inga, "You better hurry, I'm almost done with my lessons!"

Luann sighed, "Anyway, I think, yes it *was* three years ago, Nicole's husband, Frenchy, no, Bertrand was clearing some dead trees with one of the mechs on the back side of their property. Apparently a cable snapped, and by the time anybody found him, he had bled out and died. Since they'd already paid their homestead fees through the military, Nicole and Holly decided to stay on. Holly's secondary is medical, she was a World Conservation Corps pediatric doc somewhere in the sub-Sahara for ten years before migrating. She backs up Doc Grant when he's either at one of the other settlements or off planet."

Fargo replied, "I was just curious, based on her comment today. Didn't realize she was ex-GalPat."

Luann looked at him slyly, "Ohh, does big brother have some interest?"

Fargo laughed to cover his embarrassment, "Yeah, sure. I'm living out in the Green, and she's running a winery. That would really work well."

***

Fargo needed to get away from Luann and her scattershot thoughts, and he wanted to see if he could actually keep a mental block up for any length of time, so he decided to take a walk. His footsteps led him back to the Melting Mug.

As he stepped through the door, he consciously raised his *shield* as he now thought of it. He walked to the bar, and asked for a glass of wine. Nicole was all business, serving him quickly and efficiently. Slightly disappointed, he started walking back toward a table by the door when a slim spacer walking with catlike grace brushed him as the man stalked toward the bar. Fargo sensed rage and hate pouring off the man, and Fargo froze. He unconsciously oriented on the spacer as he set his drink blindly on a table. As he was trying to process the thoughts, he saw the slim man draw a small pistol from a side pocket.

He opened his senses and the emotions coalesced into a hatred that could only be based on Nicole, as she was the only one in front of the man. As he began to raise the pistol, Fargo drew his own pistol, firing without thinking. As the spacer collapsed to the ground, Fargo saw the hand with the pistol fall away from the body.

His peripheral vision picked up a small dark figure calmly sitting back down as Nicole slapped the bar, "Dammit! You didn't have to do that, CSM, I was going to handle him!"

The small figure said calmly, "I only severed the hand, I didn't kill him. The man by the door did that."

Nicole rounded on Fargo, "What in the hell did you shoot him for?"

Stunned, Fargo responded, "He was going to kill you!"

Nicole came around the end of the bar, looked at the dead man and said, "He was going to *try*! Shit, now I've got to clean the damn floor," looking at the back wall she continued, "*And* the damn wall. Damn all men!"

She walked back behind the bar and punched the e-comm unit, "Sergeant, there has been a killing at the Melting Mug. Scene is safe, request your presence for investigation." Fargo didn't hear the answer, but realized he was sensing frustration and anger from Nicole, and a cold, calm determination from the small man. Fargo picked up a chair and placed it directly in front of where he was standing, then moved to the side and approached the body. Kneeling, he saw that his shot had gone true, penetrating the C6 vertebra.

Careful not to step in the blood spatter, he looked down at the pistol, still gripped incongruously in the severed hand. The safety was off, and the finger still gripped the trigger, but at least if there was any kind of muscle spasm, it was pointed safely away from everyone. He turned to the small man, seeing a strangely shaped bloody knife now sitting on a napkin, "I'm sorry, I never saw you move, or close this guy."

The small man replied in a lilting voice, "Tunnel vision. It happens. It happened to him, and to you. He was so focused on Nikki, he never saw me. He didn't honor the threat, and it cost him. Had you not shot him, the only cost would have been his hand." Shrugging the small man continued, "But rage consumes. With that comes loss of situational awareness."

Fargo marveled that the small man could have been giving a lecture rather than sitting at a table where a man had just been killed, until he remembered Nicole's calling him CSM. Fargo suddenly realized who this small man was either a current or former Command Sergeant Major, GalPat. The genotype, way of talking and the knife was sending up signals that this man was not to be trifled with, but Fargo just couldn't place them.

Those thoughts were interrupted by the arrival of Sergeant Omar from the space port along with a response team. He stepped slowly into the Melting Mug, walked to where the body lay and said via his GalTrans, "Ho, Lieutenant of the retired. Body of the dead, gunshot caused. Shoot him you did?"

Fargo said, "Sergeant, I shot him as he drew a weapon. Hand is there, still with weapon."

The sergeant puzzled, "Shot his hand off, did you?"

Fargo replied, "No, shot him in the head, did I."

The sergeant picked up the hand and casually pried the weapon from it, "Weapon loaded is not safed. Good, this is not." He put the safety on and laid the weapon on the CSM's table, noticing the bloody knife for the first time.

Sergeant Omar popped to attention, "Ho, CSM, sir. See you, I did not."

The CSM said softly, "Omar. Recruit Omar. Arcturus, Class twenty-eight-eighteen-zero-three. I see you've done well."

The sergeant stammered, "CSM, this one thanks you. Tell me what happened, you can?"

The CSM glanced at Fargo, "I observed said spacer approaching the bar with intent to do harm. When I saw him remove a small caliber 3mm semi-automatic pistol from his right front jacket pocket, I made the assumption that he was willing to do fatal injury to Mrs. Levesque. At that time I proceeded to draw my kukri in an effort to prevent said injury."

Pointing to Fargo, he continued, "This gentleman apparently saw the same thing I did from a further distance, and drew, firing in a most timely fashion. His shot was simultaneous with my removal of said spacer's hand."

Sergeant Omar nodded, "Lieutenant of the retired, add anything will you?"

Fargo shook his head, "Nothing to add, have I, Sergeant."

Sergeant Omar turned to Nicole, "Mrs. Levesque, know this spacer did you?"

Nicole stood at the end of the bar and Fargo picked up the smoky emotions of anger and disgust with a small tendril of fear, "Sergeant, know him I did not. But, he came to the winery earlier today and demanded favors I was not willing to indulge him in. Direct him to leave, we did, at the point of a weapon. Expect him here, I did not. My thanks to those who saved me, I give."

Sergeant Omar looked around the bar, raising his voice, "Ho, clientele, knowledge of this person anyone have?"

Receiving no answers, Sergeant Omar declared, "Killing of this individual was warranted. Report I will file." With that, he picked up the spacer's hand, shoved it in an evidence pouch, picked up the pistol, placed it in a different pouch, and directed the response team to bring the body. They got a body bag from the response runabout, loaded the body and departed the Melting Mug. Fargo, not wanting to be confronted by Nicole, left at the same time.

***

Sergeant Omar met Fargo at the pad the next morning as he was preparing to head back to the Green, asking Fargo to attend him in the administration building. Fargo followed him curiously, figuring the liteflyer would be okay for a few divs.

In the conference room, Omar pulled two clear evidence pouches out of his pack and laid them on the table, "Ho, lieutenant of the retired, either the gun or the wrist comp do you recognize?"

Fargo said, "Can I pick up the pouches?" Omar nodded, and Fargo first picked up the gun. Turning it over and looking at it from different angles, he finally said, "I don't think this is… I think this might be Trader technology. I'm no expert, but I don't recognize any of the marks, nor does it have a manufacturer's stamp on it."

The sergeant simply nodded, and Fargo put the pistol back down, picked up the wrist comp and turned it to see various angles. "I just flat don't know on this one. I'd have to see it powered up, and try to look at what it displays." Glancing at Omar, he asked, "Has anyone done that?"

Sergeant Omar replied, "Power up Mrs. Levesque has done, Trader unit she believes. Security locked it is. Possible self-destruct she believes."

Fargo hastily set it back on the desk, "What about the spacer?"

The sergeant pulled out a flimsy and handed it to Fargo, "This so far found. False identity believed."

C&I FILE 23419- 28240614 2354LOCAL
ID- 23409852 BRINKMAN, BERNARD NMN
SYSTEM ENTRY 28240610 SSTATION
DISEMBARK F/S NIGHTWING
PLANETING 28240611 0830LOCAL SHUTTLE
#0342 WHITE BEACH SPORT
NO BILLETING RECORD FOUND
SHUTTLE #2451 28240612 0730LOCAL DEPT
WHITE BEACH ARR RUSHING RIVER 28240612
1214LOCAL
NO BILLETING FOUND
GALPAT RECORDS CHECK NEGATIVE ON ID
23409852 PRIOR TO 28200101
GALPAT RECORDS CHECK NEGATIVE ON ID
23409852 BETWEEN 28200101-28240610
RECORD CHECK CLOSED ATT
#BT
MEDAUTOPS-
MID-80 HUMANOID 5FT6IN 135LB
B/B/CAUC/MIX/HISP
NO F/P OR RETSCAN ON FILE
NO INDC MAJOR SURG
POSS FACIAL FRAC W/MED-COMP REPAIR
PALM PAD INSTAL- BOTH PRI R/INDEX
NEURAL NET INSTAL- NON-GP INDC
PILOT/CMD NODES

Fargo whistled, "So he's a non-entity. One
wonders what he was here. Scouting or
transshipping?"

Omar replied, "Able to determine not. Lookout
requested."

Fargo asked, "Why was Levesque brought in? I thought she was the target."

Omar answered, "Intelligence Mrs. Levesque did. Chief Sergeant she was. Known to us, she is."

Fargo nodded, "Understood. Am I free to go?"

Omar chittered a laugh, "Go you may. Mikhail you may tell."

***

Fargo secured the liteflyer and bummed a ride back to the trading post. Luann took one look, and sent the kids up to the e-tainment to play, where they were safely out of earshot as Fargo explained to Mikhail and Luann what had gone on last night. Luann was aghast that he'd killed a man and didn't even feel it was worth mentioning, while Mikhail was nodding and scribbling notes on his datacomp.

Luann burst out, "But how am I supposed to know any of this? I don't do *intelligence* I just work with the people that come in."

Mikhail said, "If someone doesn't look right, or is asking strange questions, let me know. If I'm not here, let Sergeant Omar know. If we do have Traders scouting us, the quicker we know, the better. I'm sure the sergeant has pushed this to White Beach, but I'm going to follow up through my channels."

Fargo nodded, "Can I use the runabout for a few minutes? I want to run by the clinic and see if they still have the body or the clothes."

Mikhail flipped him the key fob, and Fargo slipped out the door as Mikhail and Luann talked quietly.

Help Wanted

Fargo's e-tainment center beeped with an incoming Vidcall, and he said, "Accept."

The screen blinked on to show a bearded face, something Fargo didn't remember ever seeing since he'd left Earth. Confused, he said, "Ethan Fargo Can I help you?"

The bearded face said, "Mister Fargo, I'm Rick Remington, RRInc. I'm on my way down to Hunter, should be groundside tomorrow morning. I'd like to meet with you, as I've been told you might be able to help me out."

Figuring the time lag, Fargo estimated this call was at least being made from in system, rather than out. "Mister Remington I can be at Rushing River SP one by zero nine in the morning. Where would you like to meet? And can you give me some idea of what help you're looking for?'

Remington rubbed his face saying, "Your name was passed to me as a hunter. I've got a problem at one of my camps that needs a hunter to take care of it." Fargo saw Remington look away and then back, "SP one, at zero nine. Got it, main conference room at the administration building. See you then." With that, the screen went black, and the disconnected symbol popped up.

Fargo commed his sister and asked if she had any idea what or who Remington was. She told him that Remington Inc. had the logging concession for Hunter, and was running a number of small camps with a main mill near the Evergreen jump port. He thanked her and brought up a search engine on the e-tainment system, finding a number of articles and features on Remington.

Selecting one that seemed to have been produced by the company, he brought it up and watched it. He was amazed to find that there was money to be made in natural lumber. He'd never thought of that as a scarce product, or anything other than an interim building material until one could get plascrete in place.

According to the video, there was a large galactic market in fine wood for boardrooms, homes, and government buildings. He had to look up the word veneer and confirm that it meant what he thought it did. He wondered how Remington got the wood off world, and how much it cost him to get out of the gravity well.

After viewing more videos, he finally gave it a pass, since there didn't seem to be anything on Remington himself. After feeding Cattus, Canis, and Urso, he dialed up what he now thought of as chef's surprise and waited for the auto chef to spit out his dinner. At least this chef's surprise was edible, proto meat, some kind of green *something* and a sweet cinamony bread.

The next morning at zero seven, he hauled the liteflyer out of storage and configured it for cargo, since he needed to bring supplies back, and had more skins to take down to the spaceport. After securing the cabin, he sent Cattus and Canis to their packs, and launched for the spaceport. A warning of a new tight beam popped in on the navigation display, and he accepted it, remembering he needed to go see Mikhail about the next expansion of the tight beam links that TBT would be putting in.

Fargo left his rifle and the skins in the liteflyer, locking it and walking across the ramp to the administration building. As he neared the building, one of the stranger craft he'd ever seen came in for a landing. Ungainly, not in the slightest aerodynamic, it looked like somebody had chopped off a freighter just below the bridge and first deck and put a flat plate on the bottom. That was accentuated by the lander legs that looked grafted onto the four corners of the ship? Shuttle? And what looked like two additional tractor modules grafted on behind the ship's bridge. Shaking his head, he continued on into the building and was greeted by Sergeant Omar, who asked, "Ho, lieutenant of the retired, meeting today you have?"

Fargo replied, "Ho Sergeant, meeting I have, people of importance come." The sergeant waved him through and Fargo went to the snack bar, picking up a bulb of coffee to kill a few minutes. He arrived at the conference room to find a huge individual pacing the floor mumbling to himself. As the person turned, Fargo realized it was the same face he'd seen on the vid, and that it sat atop a body that was at least six and a half feet tall and weighed over three hundred pounds. He also sensed trepidation and a locked down set of thoughts. He said, "Mister Remington? I'm Ethan Fargo."

Remington came around the table and stuck out a hand the size of a small ham, "Rick Remington. Do you go by Ethan?" *Damn, he's worried about something at one of his camps. Really worried, almost scared. What...*

Fargo surreptitiously checked his hand to make sure Remington hadn't broken anything in it from the handshake as he replied, "Most of the time it's just Fargo. Too many years of mil and GalScout. It drills a Pavlovian response to the last name. So, what can I do for you, sir?"

"It's Rick, please. Sit, sit. Can I offer you a libation?"

Fargo said, "No thanks, I've got a coffee. What seems to be the problem?'

Remington eased his bulk into one of the chairs, and put his forearms on the table, looking directly into Fargo's eyes. "It's Rick, and I've got some timber rats holed up in their modular out at one of our camps. They've been spooked by what they claim is a Silverback, or maybe two. They are refusing to leave the module, claiming they can hear it prowling around, and screaming at them. It apparently attacked one of the guys while he was in an Exoskel, and scared the shit out of him. He ran it back to the module, and now-"

Fargo leaned back in the chair, "A Silverback? Are they sure?"

Remington shrugged, "Well, they're up at forty-seven north. That does seem to be within the known range of those beasts."

Fargo asked, "How long have they been stuck in the modular structure?"

Remington replied, "Going on three local days. I got back in system yesterday, and got their ping then. Took me most of yesterday to figure out how to approach it, and find you."

Fargo said, "Just out of curiosity, how *did* you find me? And what makes you think I'd take something like this on?"

Remington said, "Heard about you from one of the shuttle pilots. He was talking about how crazy you are, hunting Silverbacks and other shit down here. Guess he's seen some of your skins, and commented that you must be good, as you'd sold a dozen or so of them. I also found out you've worked security for TBT on their services expansion here. I figured anybody that survived one Silverback, much less a dozen, and is a security guy would want a shot at another one. I'll pay you ten thousand credits, and you can keep the skin. I just want my guys back working."

Fargo sensed Remington's nervousness, mingled with hope, and steepled his fingers. Thinking for a minute, he finally said, "Okay. Let's do this."

Remington dropped his head, then said, "Thank you. I was afraid that wouldn't be enough. When can you be ready?"

Fargo got up, "Give me fifteen minutes. How do I get there?"

Remington replied, "I can take you in the beast outside. It's not real comfortable, but it'll get us there and back."

Fargo nodded, "Okay, let me get my rifle and pack. Meet you back here in fifteen." He headed back to the liteflyer, got his gear and walked back to the admin building. Remington stood watching and said, "That's all you've got?"

Hefting the rifle, Fargo said, "All I need. How do we board that monstrosity?"

Remington laughed in relief, "It's got a bow ramp. Bottom is completely sealed, ten inches of battle steel."

Fargo whistled, "Ten inches? What kind of battles are you fighting with this thing?"

Remington just glanced at Fargo and keyed a command and a ramp exuded from the first deck, sloping sharply to the ground. He led Fargo up the ramp and into the first deck, then up a short passage to the bridge. Settling in the pilot's chair he adjusted his bead pistol to a more comfortable position as he indicated the nav chair for Fargo. "Put your stuff in the locker at the back of the bridge, it'll be safe enough there. Then you might want to strap in. Ol' Betsy here isn't the best riding beast around."

Fargo stowed his gear, noting the magnetic holders and ensured his rifle was properly aligned with the rack, then dropped his backpack in the bottom of the locker. Returning he saw a small lustrous object sitting on top of the pilot's console and glare shield. He looked at it, and saw Remington follow his view. Remington picked it off the glare shield, handing it to

Fargo, "That's Ol' Betsy. She's pretty much a fish out of water, so to speak."

Turning it over in his hands, Fargo saw a beautifully carved Earth Dolphin that looked almost alive in the wood. Marveling, he handed it back saying, "That is absolutely beautiful! It looks almost real! Who did that?"

As soon as he said it, he felt a surge of emotion from Remington, "Well, I did. It's a wood called Teak. Every one of my rigs has a name and a carving in it. Kind of a tradition for me." Taking the carving back, he sat it back on the glare shield, and fired up the beast, as he called it. Whatever else Remington might be, Fargo knew he was riding with a master pilot, as he watched Remington almost unconsciously hold the ship level in ground effect as he retracted and rotated the lander legs. As soon as he got clearance, Remington popped the ship to altitude, and programmed in a course for the camp.

Fargo waited until Remington had completed the programming and slumped back in his seat, then asked, "Just out of curiosity, what the hell *is* this thing?"

Remington chuckled, "Well, it's a homebuilt tractor. It was a fancy ships shuttle that got crashed. I bought it for salvage, gutted it, cut the bottom off, and welded a new bottom on. The lander legs and additional tractor power came from some other units that we salvaged, and voila, Betsy, the Beast."

"What do you do with it though? That's the question."

Remington glanced over, "Well, we use it to haul trees from the camps to the mill at Evergreen. With the tractors, I can snuggle a load up against the belly, haul it to the mill, lather rinse, repeat for all four of the camps that Evergreen supports. I've got another one, Barbara, down at South Fork mill, supporting the camps down there. They're both local space worthy, so I can and do use them to haul finished cuts up to the station. Once they're out of atmosphere, they're pretty quick. Down here, they're limited to sub Mach. Just have to make sure the load is far enough forward that it doesn't get singed."

Fargo asked, "How big a load are we talking about? This thing, er, beast is what hundred twenty-hundred fifty feet?"

Remington nodded, "Yep, right at a hundred fifty feet long, and with the mods, ninety feet wide. She'll tractor a hundred twenty-five tons, and we've hauled trimmed trunks over two hundred feet long."

Fargo whistled, "What grows that big? I mean, I'm originally from Earth, and the only thing I ever heard of that even came close was a tree called, um, I think it was a Redwood."

Remington replied, "Yep, that's what we're into at the Forty-Seven North camp. Some old growth Redwoods. They're giving us about a twenty to one ratio of weight to board feet of lumber."

During the next four hours, Fargo got most of Remington's story: from his start as a genie machinist, which accounted for his size, through his transfer to a pilot and ship captain. The irony of the story was the fact that as a ship captain, he'd seen the fancy boardrooms and high end buildings and the real wood paneling and trim they contained. While he was bringing the first colony ship to Hunter, he'd lost his wife to an undiagnosed brain tumor back on Earth. Not wanting to go back to an empty home, he'd taken a cash out in-system after his second trip, starting with a small mill that he ran himself. Remington admitted he'd stolen plans from the history books on how to cut big trees, and had mostly built his own systems, just like he'd built this ship and its sister basically out of spare parts. Hiring a few disaffected spacers and a few settlers, he'd branched out slowly over the last ten years. Now he spent most of his time, as he said, fighting the bureaucracy and the thieves at Star Center. He didn't have his own ships to haul the lumber back to Earth or the major planets, so he sold it to brokers at Star Center, if he couldn't get the wood all the way back to his brother on Earth. He told Fargo he was making a bit of money, but not a lot.

That was one of the reasons for very small, clear cuts in specific areas. He'd also told Fargo that he estimated the total amount of wood he could take out in the next thirty years would exceed one trillion credits. Fargo had laughed at that, until Remington explained that one single one meter wide forty meter long Redwood, Teak, Mahogany, Oak, Maple or Chestnut plank, with good grain and no knots, could fetch thirty thousand credits by itself. Fargo had mumbled to himself he was in the wrong line of work when he heard that.

A little over four hours later, Remington took control of Betsy, descending into what looked to Fargo like a mountainous area covered by a solid forest. As they spiraled down, a small clearing emerged from the forest, and Fargo saw clouds touching the peaks, and fog shrouding the valleys.

Fargo allowed his empath sense to expand, picking up a pair of what he'd come to know as Silverback attitudes, for lack of a better word. They seemed to be the only ones on the mountain, and they were both below the ship and near the camp. Fargo sensed the Silverbacks either saw or heard the ship as it descended, and felt them start moving closer to the camp as Betsy touched down.

Remington quickly shut down the ship, pulling what had to be a 20mm bead rifle from another cabinet. Picking up Remington's fear and determination, Fargo quickly said, "No! You aren't going out there. This is just going to be me. I'm not taking a chance on your getting hurt or killed. I'm going to do this my way. Now either stay here, or run for the module. But whatever you do, do it quickly!"

Remington started to bridle at the tone of voice, until he realized Fargo was already in the hunter/killer mode and he was nothing more than an impediment. He extended the ramp as Fargo pushed out of the compartment, rifle in hand. Activating the cameras he followed Fargo as he exited Betsy, watching him calmly walk toward the module. He retracted the ramp, sealed the entry, and watched as Fargo walked away. Two thirds of the way to the module, Fargo stopped and turned around, facing into the broadest part of the clearing. And just stood there.

Hunter or Hunted

Fargo sensed the pair of Silverbacks as they came down to the edge of the clearing, and then split. One stayed at the far side of the clearing, as the other of the pair was slipping around to his left. The far one yowled, so Fargo honored the threat posed there, while letting his mind track the second Silverback. For the first time, he also sensed some low level communication between them, wondering if they were a long-time mated pair.

Dropping into an almost trance like state, he merely stood still, waiting. Suddenly, the first Silverback appeared at the edge of the clearing. It dodged in and out of the trees, moving to his right as it closed the distance. Fargo hoped it didn't decide to do that dance all the way to his right, as that would put his back fully to the second Silverback, now approaching the back of the module. Higher order empath channels up in the human band suddenly broke through in fear, and he clamped them off. Now, he knew the second Silverback was almost in place. He marveled at their ability to work as a team, knowing that if he hadn't had the empathic capability, he'd be dead. Hell, he still might be if he was too slow.

The first Silverback yowled again, drawing Fargo's attention back to him, and it stepped fully into the clearing about thirty yards away. Fargo took a deep breath, knowing the attack was coming momentarily, settling himself. As the first Silverback screamed, the second charged around the side of the module. Fargo wheeled, fired seven rounds into that one as it leaped, and sidestepped. He spun back the other way, firing seven more rounds into the first Silverback that was now charging him. With the seventh round he sidestepped once again, and the Silverback landed where he'd been standing. He stepped around and fired into the aft pelvis of both Silverbacks with his four remaining rounds.

Quickly slapping a new magazine into the rifle, he rotated in a complete circle, his sense extended as far as it would go. He didn't sense any further predators within range, and he relaxed slightly. Looking up at the ship he waved, turned, and walked to the module. Stepping around the Exoskel that was sitting open at the module door, he entering asking, "Y'all got any coffee? I could use a bulb."

Remington came in moments later, asking, "Are you okay? I still can't believe…"

Fargo sensed Remington's actual thought that Fargo was freaking crazy, and replied, "Y'all are going to be good for a while. Normally, Silverbacks have a range of about a thousand square miles. I'm not going to backtrack these two, but you should be okay."

Remington asked, "How many times did you shoot? It was so fast I couldn't count them!"

"Seven for each, and two more to make sure."

Remington said incredulously, "Seven? Why? How?"

Fargo said, "Come on, I'll show you, and anybody else that's interested." Walking out to where the Silverbacks lay almost nose to nose, he levered one of them over, and began skinning it out. After he'd finished he cut further into the flesh, laying the Silverback open. "See this bone structure here?" Pointing to the front shoulder girdle, he said, "It's two shots, one on each side to get through that." Stepping back to the second shoulder girdle, he continued, "And another two to get through this set. Now, notice right behind the second set of shoulders? See this?" Fargo pointed to two large yellow masses, "These are the two hearts a Silverback has. If you don't get 'em both, it can keep coming. So it's four to get through the two shoulder girdles, and three to hopefully hit both hearts and the lungs." Pointing to two green masses, he said, "The first one I ever killed was pure luck. It'd turned and I thought I'd just hit it in the rear haunches, but luckily that one shot went through both hearts. After I skinned it out, I test fired to see what it would take to actually kill one in a frontal charge."

Remington whistled, "Damn. That is some serious bone structure. What were you shooting?"

Fargo replied, "Sixteen millimeter depleted uranium beads. Their bones are tough enough that they will actually deflect one occasionally."

Another thought struck Remington, "It looked like they were actually hunting you."

Fargo said, "They were. One was trying to hold my attention while the other one ambushed me from the back. Mated pairs do tend to hunt that way. That's how they bring down big game."

"Son of a bitch! And you *still* went out there? Damn man, you are nuts!"

Fargo smiled a little, "No, not nuts. Crazy maybe, but not nuts. I'm certified sane by the GalScouts."

"Certifiable," Remington mumbled, "You want something to eat?"

Fargo nodded, "I could go for some food. Matter of fact, I'm kinda hungry."

Remington and Fargo hit the autochef for food, and went to a table at the end of the day room. Fargo ate quietly while Remington dealt with a number of loggers who came over with questions, work issues and supplies they needed. After an hour, Remington finally said, "Okay guys, anything else, send me a message. I've got to get Mr. Fargo here back to his place. He tells me there isn't another set of these things within range, so take the rest of the day and hit it again tomorrow. I'm making a supply run and I'll be back in three days for a pickup."

A chorus of grumbles and laughter followed them out the door. Fargo quickly caped the second Silverback, folded the skins in on themselves and loaded them in a compartment on the exterior of the Betsy.

Four hours later, Remington punched him awake, "We're here. If you don't mind, I'm going to dump you here, and head back up to the station. I need to get a load sorted to go to Star Center by eight divs tomorrow. I'll also post your credits to you as soon as I get up to the station."

A little groggy, Fargo simply nodded, shook his hand and climbed down, then back up to get the two skins out of the compartment. Looking through the viewport, he saw Remington shaking his head in mirth. Waving, he climbed back down again, picked up his rifle and bag and headed for the store.

***

Luann looked up when he walked through the portal, "My god, what stinks?"

Fargo held up the hides, "It might be these. Can I stick them in the storage building for the night? I don't want to try to fly back in the dark."

Luann nodded, "Anywhere but in here." She yelled over her shoulder, "Mikhail! Can you help Ethan please? He's got some dead animal skins that are stinking up the place!"

Mikhail came through the curtain a minute later, "Let's go out and around. She'll have kittens if we walk through the living room with those things. They *do* smell a bit don't they?"

Fargo shrugged, "Depends on what you're used to. Luann's always been sensitive that way."

Mikhail swung the door open on the storage building, "Drop them over there. You're staying the night, right?"

Dropping the hides where Mikhail indicated, he replied, "Yes, if Luann doesn't kick me out."

"I don't think so... But I need to let you know about something else that is going on."

Fargo stopped, "What?"

"Gann is trying to dig up dirt on you."

"Gann? Who... Oh, she's the one that lost the kid in the liteflyer crash, right?"

"Yeah, that's her. She's gotten Klynton to go to Colonel Cameron to dig up your background. She's also spreading rumors that you didn't actually retire from the Scouts, you were kicked out for cowardice."

"What the…"

"I told you that you'd made an enemy. Palette is apparently helping her. But the good news is everything Allen pulled cleared us and put the blame squarely on Gann and her daughter. Thing is, Cameron will sweep it under the rug, since he doesn't want to rock the boat with Klynton."

Fargo rolled his eyes, "So money talks?"

"Not so much money as power."

They both said, "And absolute power corrupts absolutely."

Fargo asked, "What are my options? Or do you see any options?"

"Well, we know we're clear, so the only thing I can offer is to go back into the Green and keep as low a profile as you can. And stay the hell out of White Beach."

"I don't have a reason to go to White Beach, unless I'm with you. But I have to tell you, I'm not comfortable letting her or anyone else pull shit like this. I've been through this once already."

Mikhail nodded, "I remember. I've got to make a trip down there in a few days. I'll try to get in to see Colonel Keads. He's one of the good guys. Maybe he can deflect some of the BS. Hell, they can try to come after me if they want to, but they really can't hurt me."

"I'd appreciate it. Otherwise, I'll go down there and take care of her myself."

Mikhail held up his hands, "Let's not get hasty, especially in this case. I'll do what I can. Maybe we'll get lucky, and she'll fall over dead... Let's go in before Luann gets curious as to what we're doing out here."

***

Fargo was still steaming the next morning. Knowing that Mikhail was right didn't make it any easier. He hadn't gotten much sleep trying to figure out a way to nip this problem in the bud, but he hadn't come up with anything that wouldn't land him in hot water, or prison.

He asked Mikhail to just drop the hides off with the taxidermist in town, and headed for the Green. Landing at the cabin, he let his breath out slowly, smiling as Cattus and Canis came bounding around the corner of the cabin, "At least the two of you don't give a crap what I do, as long as I feed you."

Climbing out of the liteflyer, he played with both of them for a couple of minutes, until Urso came around the corner on a run. Urso was now over one hundred pounds and didn't realize her own strength. He used his empathic sense to push calm to all three of them and only got a light bat in the ribs as Urso tried to grab him. He pulled the three haunches he'd gotten from Luann out of the back of the liteflyer, dropping them in a line twenty feet apart. Each one of the animals immediately forgot about him, and he finished stowing the liteflyer after he wiped down the cargo compartment.

Setting the water dishes out on the porch, he brewed a cup of real coffee and sat on the porch as dusk fell. Urso had finished her haunch, and was sniffing at Cattus' portion, with Cattus popping her on the nose every time she got too close. He called Urso over to the porch and started working with her again. He decided she might be powerful, but she'd never be as trainable as Cattus or Canis. After he'd worked with her for about a half a div, he finally gave up and brought out a treat for her.

After a quick meal, Fargo settled on the couch, commanded the e-tainment center to search for articles and other mentions of Klynton and Gann. After three hours, he had a headache, was firmly convinced that both of them were, at best, serial liars, and at worst out and out criminals.

Everything he saw pointed to both of them using their positions for their own enrichment, currying or selling favors where they could, possibly bribing others and hints of people disappearing when they crossed the two of them. Fargo shivered as he looked at the totality of the information, wondering how anyone could have possibly thought either one of these women could have possibly been good for Hunter.

He queued some searches for Earth, and decided to go to bed. *She wants to play games? That is a two way street...*

***

Fargo stretched, sliding the blinds open, to see bright sunlight streaming in the window. He got up, padded through the fresher on the way to the kitchen, and stepped on a bone either Cattus or Canis had left in the middle of the floor. Cussing, he opened the front door and threw the bone out, as Cattus and Canis bolted by him.

Juggling his bulb of coffee, he commanded the e-tainment system on, calling up the search cue results. He was disappointed to only see three items in the search box, but called them up anyway. All three of them dealt with one court case, where both Gann and Klynton had been sued for lying under oath in a bribery case in the Bosphillyton complex that stretched from the old city of Boston to the national capitol.

Apparently, some small businesses had been promised *deals* for long term complex contracts for retaining the two of them, but no contracts were ever issued. There was no follow-up on the outcome of the trial, and he thought, *Looks like somebody paid off the judges, or they stretched it out to the point that the case was dropped because the plaintiffs couldn't afford to keep paying lawyers. So probably guilty as charged. Interesting that it was only a year before the first colony ship came out here...*

Filing that knowledge away, Fargo commanded the system off, and started preparing for his upcoming trip to Star Center.

Road Trip

Fargo's last stop before he headed back to the trading post was the medical clinic. Doc Jenkins looked at him curiously, "What's up Fargo? You're not sick are you?"

Fargo said, "Nope, but I'm on my way to Star Center, and I figured I'd stop by and see if you needed anything." He sensed OneSvel moving around in the back of the clinic and sent out a thought, *OneSvel, I am going to Star Center. I will be taking the pelts. Please advise the GalScout command.*

Doc nodded, "Matter of fact, there are some things you can either pick up, or get on order for me. Mostly antibiotics and injectables we're getting low on." Turning away, he continued, "Give me a minute to get a list together. I'll be right back."

OneSvel came through the door, "Oh, good day Mr. Fargo, I didn't know you were here." As Doc passed him, OneSvel continued a polite conversation as he linked with Fargo, "*Understood. There is apparently concern about the Trader you killed here. There have been questions raised, and the official line was he a random spacer who was killed in the commission of a crime.*" Checking quickly, OneSvel continued the thought, "*Nothing has been released identifying him as a Trader, but he has been tied to the CU, and has never lived in free space. Some indicators are he was probably born on one of the construction stations, from his bone structure and musculature. His piloting implant self-destructed as soon as we attempted to access it, but the fragments recovered were not of GalPat, GalScout, or free space manufacture."*

Fargo replied to OneSvel's pleasantries as he thought back, *"Then Nicole was right when she thought she heard Spanglish."*

OneSvel nodded an extrusion with eyestalks as he watched the door for Doc Jenkins. *"How many of the pelts are you taking?"*

Fargo thought, *"All of them. If I'm going to make a splash, then I need to have all the numbers and variety I can push up. There are also fifteen Silverback, seven Slashgator and eleven Slashlizard skins from that clean up I did on Bacolod for their TBT rep."*

OneSvel thought curiously, *"So what do you think is the total value of what you're taking?"*

Fargo shrugged both physically and mentally, *"Probably around two million credits."*

Doc came thought the partition, "Sorry for the delay, Fargo. I've added a couple of spare parts for the doc-in-the-box, but those can be ordered if you can't find them." Handing him both a data and a credit chip, he continued, "It's all on here, and the credit chip should cover both the cost and the shipping to bring it back."

Fargo asked, "And if it's not?"

Doc winced, "Hopefully it is. If not, try to FTL me and I'll see if I can get money transferred to you. You still have a TFCU account, right?"

Fargo nodded, "Yep, fifty plus years." Slipping the chips in his pocket, he added, "I've got to run. We're lifting in two hours, and I need to go see Luann."

***

Fargo took the runabout over to the Copper Mug, stuck his head in, but only saw Hank, the bartender when Nicole was busy. Hank smiled at him, "She's already left for the spaceport. She's still bitching over the cost of the lift, how she's losing money, and how stupid it is to try to lift heavy stuff like wine out of the gravity well."

Fargo chuckled, "Yeah, glad my skins don't weigh that much. Guess I better head that way myself. Remember to see Mikhail if you have any problems."

Hank nodded, "I will. Y'all fly safe, and stay out of trouble. I can't run this place for long by myself."

Fargo replied, "As if we had anything to do with it, but yeah, I hope we do." Waving, he returned to the runabout, driving it back to the trading post. Mikhail was standing on the steps when he pulled in. "Where did Luann go?"

Mikhail shrugged, "She's around somewhere. I swear you'd think you were going to war, rather than just to Star Center if you listen to her! You want to go on out to the port?"

Fargo replied, "I guess I'd better. I need to make sure the pelts are properly packed, and all the med clearances and stuff are completed. I can't believe how much they were claiming it costs, versus how much it actually cost per pelt or skin."

Mikhail laughed, "I know Luann tried to tell you, but you just didn't want to listen. They were ripping you off for large credits. I think this trip is going to open your eyes to how much money you *should* have made." He hopped in the runabout and strapped in, as Fargo backed out and started toward the port.

***

Fargo led Nicole down to port six on the space station, and was startled to see a familiar looking and sounding individual standing at the personnel tube, "Ho Klang, see you I do. Watch you are standing? More trunks I have."

The hulking Arcturian turned, squeaking into his GalTrans, "Ho Fargo, *Hyderabad* you ride again?" Looking down at Nicole, he asked, "Female with you? Watch I am not. Relief I am."

Fargo sensed Nicole bristling beside him and he quickly replied, "Female is..." Searching for the right word in Galactic he finally settled on, "self-sufficient, not companion. Nicole Levesque. Nicole this is Klang, the cargomaster."

Nicole, slightly mollified, said, "Ho Klang, see you I do. Crates of liquid I have. Storage requirements for ten thousand four hundred pounds of wine, I have."

Klang squeaked again, "Storage requirements I received. Storage requirements I have met. Documentation you have?" As he glanced at Fargo, he said, "Documentation and medical forms, you have?"

Fargo and Nicole nodded as they handed over their respective data chips. The actual watch, whom Fargo recognized as Khalil, one of the engine crew from New Saud, scrambled out of the personnel tube, "Mr. Fargo! You are travelling with us again?"

Fargo nodded, "Both Mrs. Levesque and I are going to Star Center, Khalil. How are you doing?"

"Hot, straight and normal." Khalil handed the data chips back he'd received from Klang. You're both good to go aboard. No weapons, we'll deposit them in the armory until we arrive." Glancing at Fargo he continued, "You know the drill. You are cleared aboard, Keldar will assign your billets. I probably won't see you unless it's at chow."

Fargo laughed, "I was hoping we might spar a little, if there was some down time. I've been practicing." He stripped off his pistol belt, pulled his vibro knife out and slipped it onto the gun belt. Nicole did the same, adding a second knife to her belt, and passing it to Fargo.

Fargo politely motioned to Nicole as he said, "After you."

Nicole replied, "Oh, no. You seem to be very familiar with this ship, so I'll follow you."

Fargo glanced at her, "Are you mad about something?"

Nicole shrugged, "The assumption that I was your… And paying *twenty-six thousand* credits to get that stupid wine out of the gravity well…"

Fargo shook his head, "Different cultures. Regardless of what GalPat says, or decrees, there is always going to be the inherent biases from the particular home worlds. How much wine did you bring?"

Nicole grimaced, "Two hundred sixty cases, all that I had. Lead on, I don't want you watching my ass in this damn shipsuit. It's *way* too tight!"

Fargo laughed and propelled himself into the boarding tube before he said the wrong thing and got himself in more trouble, but he did sense a wry sense of humor underlying Nicole's smoky and prickly personality. And frankly, he *wanted* to watch her go down the boarding tube, but he stomped on that and other thoughts quickly, since she obviously wasn't feeling the same attraction he was.

Keldar was his usual grumpy self, and met them at the hatch, a pinched expression on his face, "I am the purser, Keldar. Your chits are in order, extra charges for overweight cargo have been approved. Fargo, compartment three-three forward. Levesque, compartment four-three forward. Standard meal schedule."

Sensing Nicole bristling again, he quickly motioned her forward saying, "He was the same way last time. It's his nature." He was surprised when his wrist comp pinged. Glancing at it, he saw, WELCOME ABOARD, CAPTAIN. DO YOU REQUIRE GUIDANCE?

Tapping the wrist comp, he said, "Negative guidance. Thank you.

Nicole looked at him curiously as they proceeded up decks, "What was that all about?

Fargo replied, "I was aboard this ship coming out from X-ray, and since I was the only passenger, they granted me access to the ship's AI. I guess it remembered me." Stopping in front of compartment four, he continued, "This one is yours. I'm next door." Glancing down, he saw that Nicole was also wearing a wrist comp and said, "Hang on a second." Tapping his, he said, "AI, this is Fargo, can you add Mrs. Levesque's wrist comp to your system access?"

A pleasant female voice responded out of the speaker, "Done, Captain. Mrs. Levesque, please check your comp in three, two…"

Nicole's wrist comp beeped an alert as she glanced at it. It showed an alert in red that said 'SHIP PUSH TEST'. It also started a count in the female voice, "One, two, three, four, five, four, three, two, one. Please confirm by voice and touch receipt of alert."

Looking at Fargo, Nicole cocked her head, then punched the acknowledgement, saying, "AI, Nicole Levesque, copied all audio and visual alerts."

The AI responded, "Thank you."

Nicole looked at him again, then stepped through the dilated hatch into her compartment. He walked next door and unpacked his bag, plopping the electronics bag on the fold out desk. Looking at his wrist comp, he saw there was an additional lounge and dining area showing on the ship's schematic.

Fargo looked up, "AI, I see additional mess area and lounge on the schematic that weren't here the last time I was aboard. Is this where we passengers are allowed?"

The AI responded immediately, "Captain, you and Mrs. Levesque are granted ship's mess privileges, you may eat in either place at your choice. Meal choices are the same."

Fargo said, "Thank you AI. I will notify Mrs. Levesque."

Suddenly, the IC blared, "All hands, boarding lock is sealed, secure all loose equipment, prep for space.

Engineering, fifteen minute warning. Launch crew, fifteen minute warning. Drop tube and disconnect three zero minutes. Passengers, please make your way to the passenger lounge deck five, compartment five for safety brief, and procedures."

Fargo called it up on his wrist comp and started out the door, almost bumping into Nicole in the process. "Sorry, I wasn't paying attention."

Nicole cocked her head, "Where do we go?"

"Down two decks, inboard one more compartment. Use your wrist comp for mapping, or we can go together."

Nicole replied, "Lead on."

Fargo and Nicole were the last two to arrive in the passenger lounge, and looked around as they walked to an unoccupied table. There were thirty passengers, multiple races and ethnicities scattered through the lounge. Some were drinking from bulbs, as others sat quietly.

Seconds later Evie, the pilot in a form fitting shipsuit came into the lounge. Nodding to Fargo she stood at the front of the lounge, "May I have your attention please? I'm Evie, the ship's pilot. Captain Jace is completing some paperwork with the station, and requested I give the briefing. Let me start by welcoming each of you aboard, and I'd like to take a few minutes of your time for the safety brief and emergency procedures, if we may. This shouldn't take more than fifteen minutes and all the information will also be available on ship channel three in your compartments."

Looking around, Evie saw nodding heads and continued, "We have Ganymede Corp escape pods, located port and starboard at the following stations." She designated them by pointing a laser at the ship graphic showing on the front display, "These are totally automated, so there is no worry about having to have a crewman drive one, so to speak. They are designed to automatically eject, then navigate to the nearest habitable planet or station."

Changing the wall display, she brought up a soft EVA suit. "These are available in every space, and they're one size fits all. If you get an alarm, you've got about a minute, depending on which space you're in, to don one." Blowing up the display, she continued, "Standard step in model, auto-closure tabs, and attached soft helmet. Sixty minute standalone air supply." Rotating the display, she pointed to a plug set on the side of the suit. "O2 hookup, comms hookup, battery charger. Each compartment has a double hose connection in the overhead and one by the hatch." Spinning the diagram around, she showed the pouch on the other side of the suit, "Sixty feet of collapsible hose. Run it around the front or back, hook up the length needed and leave the rest in the pouch. Any questions?"

Hearing no questions, she said, "If you will excuse me, I need to go drive the bus. If at any time you have questions, feel free to ask one of the crew. We are not a passenger cruise liner, so the amenities may be lacking for those of you used to that mode of travel, but we *are* a safe ship, and we will get you to Star Center on time, deity of your choice permitting."

As she turned to leave, Fargo watched her get approached by an older Hilbornite female, dripping jewelry and prestige, and saw Evie's tail go almost rigid, with just the tip lashing quietly. He turned to Nicole, "Everything stowed?"

Nicole had seen the byplay and replied, "Yes, and I want to get out of range before those two go at it. I've seen two Hilbornites fight, and tooth and nail doesn't begin to describe it!"

***

The ship was still accelerating when the all clear was given and Fargo started unstrapping from the bunk. Cautiously letting his shields down, he probed tentatively for other people, thoughts and moods. He felt a mishmash of relief, with a few worried thoughts, but the only mind he felt clearly was that of Nicole, as she unstrapped and headed to the fresher.

Quickly locking his mind down again, he gingerly got up, checked that nothing was loose or a danger, then hit the fresher himself. Going to the hatch, he dilated it and stepped into the passage way just as Nicole opened her hatch. "Coffee?" he asked.

Nicole smiled, "Is there an extra charge for it?"

Fargo laughed, "Not on here. They have the same autochef I used in the military, and it doesn't charge extra for coffee, or whatever it is that they substitute."

Nicole looked at her wrist comp, "Which lounge?"

Fargo said, "Well, the crew lounge is right here. Why walk any further than we have to?"

Nicole replied, "Because *I* am going to need exercise. But for now, crew lounge and coffee works." She turned, oriented herself and strolled next door to the crew lounge. Looking around, she saw that it was almost empty and Klang, sitting at a table, was the only occupant.

Fargo followed and headed for the autochef, dialing up his coffee blend. As he waited, he saw Nicole dial up something rather complicated, including coffee, milk and foam. Picking up his bulb and shaking his head, he went over to what he considered *his* table from the last cruise, and flopped down, nodding to Klang in the process.

Nicole followed, and he noted she sat where she could see both Klang and the hatch. He sensed a wariness rising, overlaid with worry. He chose not to probe, instead sitting in silence and enjoying his coffee.

He finished his bulb about the time Nicole did, and finally broke the silence, "What was that?"

Nicole smiled, "An old European drink that's been around for centuries. It's called a cappuccino."

"A what?"

"Cappuccino, it's coffee, real milk, and milk foam, with real sugar, chocolate, and cinnamon. The few places I've ever seen it advertised, it has always had at least a twenty credit upcharge!"

Fargo shook his head, "Nope, I'll stick with the straight stuff."

Moments of Terror

The days melded one into the other, as the ship trundled across space toward Star Center. After two tries at eating with the other passengers, Fargo and Nicole had adopted similar routines--eating in the crew mess, exercising, and using the VR sims every day. They almost never interacted with the other passengers, much to Fargo's relief, but Nicole really didn't interact with him either. He wasn't sure what to do, so he tamped down any thoughts on his attraction to her.

Nicole seemed to be less inclined to interact with anyone as the days went by, and her worries ramped up, causing her to be even pricklier. The only time he'd seen her laugh was on the third day, when Evie joined them for lunch and Nicole had asked who the other Hilbornite was.

Evie's hair had stood up, and she literally hissed before getting herself back under control, "That bitch is one of my great-aunts. She claims I have sullied the entire clan's reputation by being a starship pilot, and I deserve to be cut off from the clan. She called me a vacuous disease ridden whore, only fit for space after I told her I liked my job!"

Nicole almost spit her food out in amazement, then said, "I'm afraid I would have slapped her into the middle of the next galaxy for that! Who the hell does she think she is?"

Evie shrugged, "Apparently she is chief surgeon of Hilborn Center."

Nicole asked, "So… Important? Yes?"

Evie chuckled ruefully, "She is the highest of the high in medical circles. She is touring the Rimworld planets, collecting medical specimens and disease vector data to update the galactic data base."

Nicole asked with a laugh, "Are you sure *she* isn't the vector?"

Evie burst out with a laugh, fur laying down smoothly, "Possibly!"

Nicole mumbled, "Still a bitch, though." Evie smiled and squeezed Nicole's hand quickly, as she got up to resume her piloting duties.

***

Fargo's wrist comp pinged, bringing him out of a dead sleep. He started muzzily at it. CAPTAIN FARGO TO THE BRIDGE IMMEDIATELY.

Sitting up, he heard it ping again, and he hit it simultaneously with replying, "On the way." Pulling his shipsuit on, he shoved his feet into his boots, quickly fastened them, and headed for the hatch. Niceties like combed hair and brushed teeth could wait, if the captain wanted to see him now.

Three minutes later, Fargo approached the bridge hatch and watched it dilate as he stepped quickly through, "You wanted to see me, Captain?"

Captain Jace glanced at Fargo and motioned him to the jump seat to his left, "Yes I did, Captain. What would be your response if you knew we were about to be attacked by pirates, or brigands, or Traders?"

Scanning around the bridge, Fargo didn't see anyone but Captain Jace and Evie, and nothing screaming red or any blaring alarms, "Uh, depends on capability. And size. And options... Can we run? Maybe outrun them? Shit, I don't know. I'm a ground pounder, not a space..."

Captain Jace turned to face him, "So if you had those answers, would you fight?"

Fargo scrubbed his face, "Oh hell yes. Anything is better than dying on our knees."

Captain Jace turned back, "The captain agrees. We fight." Suddenly the bridge screens transformed, with feeds showing an older destroyer with one missile door open, as weapons availability popped onto another screen, and a disembodied voices sounded on the bridge.

"Sensors, remote feed indicates Dumont class destroyer GP Epsilon. Last in service 2804. Struck from rolls in 2815. Last known at breaker's yard, Arcturus. EMCON at this time."

A second voice said, "Tracking. Target estimated 1,500,000 miles. No indication of shields at this time."

Fargo looked around in amazement, "What?"

Captain Jace held up a hand, saying, "Weaps, authorized, prep exciter. Standby for deployment."

A third voice said, "Weapons tight, available weapons VM-133 medium range missiles, bays 3 and 4, passive tracking initialized. Counter missile battery spinning up, tubes 1 and 3. Dorsal needle lasers up and up, internal power only, stowed. Request power shift to prep exciter."

"Approved."

"Comms. Incoming message from target, six second delay. Screen?"

Captain Jace replied, "Main screen."

The main screen lit with a head and shoulders shot of a grizzled captain with a backdrop of the Galactic Patrol appeared.

The captain said, "Unknown ship, this is GalPat Destroyer *Guernsey*. You are ordered to cut power, coast, drop all shields, and standby for boarding inspection. Failure to follow these directions will force us to fire on you."

Captain Jace said, "Comms, record for outgoing, character five. Break. Captain this is *Nuevo Frisco* out of Altair Four. You should be copying our beacon. We are a Galactic Consortium member, why are we being stopped? We will protest this. Break. Send it."

Fargo's jaw dropped as he saw what appeared to be an old man with a fragile voice standing in front of a shabby logo deliver the captain's message over tight beam. Captain Jace turned to him, "Target is about one point one million miles out. My intent is to fire when he reaches half a million miles, which should be in... twenty-four minutes at max closure rate."

Fargo asked, "But how... What... How do you know what is following us? What *is* this ship?"

Captain Jace's feral grin was followed by a distinctly predatory look as he scanned the screens. "We were followed through the last transit point. This area is a so-called dead space, with no habitable planets. We dropped a recon drone a few hours after we cleared the boundary, and that's what you see on screen one. It's an FTL unit, so we're getting real time updates. It's tail chasing now, in the destroyer's baffles. The data base we accessed is the GalPat database, and it's up to date. *Guernsey* exists, but she's in the yards at Earth four. Weapons? Yes, we have a few. We have limited offensive and defensive capability."

"You still haven't said *what* this ship is."

"Simply put, we don't exist. We can be anything we want to be, outside of a direct visual scan."

Fargo's mind whirled, and he wondered what in hell was going on. "You don't exist? Then what the hell am I standing on or rather sitting on? You're not making… sense…"

Captain Jace turned to face Fargo again, "*Hyderabad* doesn't ring a bell does it?"

Mystified Fargo shook his head, "No, should it?"

Captain Jace replied, "Well, if you were a student of Earth's early naval history, it would, or should. There was only one purpose-built Q-ship commissioned by the British in the First World War, almost a thousand years ago. The *Hyderabad*. She was a 600-ton vessel, launched in 1917, with a very shallow draft to allow torpedoes to pass under the ship. She was armed with hidden guns and torpedo tubes to allow her to sink German U-boats."

"So… Wait, you're a…"

A voice sounded, "Incoming comms, main screen in three."

The same grizzled captain, now almost smirking popped on screen, "Your decision is a good one, Captain. You have nothing to fear as long as your papers are in order."

"Answer required?" The phantom voice asked.

"Negative," Captain Jace replied. Turning to Fargo again, he said, "Before you ask, no, GalPat doesn't know we exist. No, they didn't approve our mission. But we are the good guys."

Fargo stewed for a few minutes as the range closed, and he wondered, *Have I gone crazy? Jace and Evie seemed to be perfectly content to let this… this apparent pirate close to a range of a half million miles, where they planned to kill it. No questions asked, they are just going to kill it. They aren't even excited. And I'm the only one… I wonder if they've even told the crew… Aren't they supposed to do something like go to battle stations? What about the passengers?*

"Um, Captain, shouldn't you at least alert the crew and passengers?" Fargo asked.

Captain Jace grinned again, "Oh the crew already knows. The passengers? Well, if we fail to kill this bastard, there will either be twenty minutes to get them off in the pods, probably to be shot out of space, or the *Epsilon* will just blow us away. Either way, it doesn't much matter. If we kill it, then the passengers don't even need to know."

Fargo shook his head, "But…"

Voice one said, "Sensors acquired passive laser targeting. Up on screen two. Passive track input and gen track now on screen. Four minutes to five hundred thousand mile engagement range," a disembodied voice said.

Captain Jace said, "Weaps, cleared to deploy dorsal lasers in three minutes thirty seconds."

Another disembodied voice answered, "Weapons, aye!" Fargo opened his mind to try to figure out what Captain Jace or Evie was thinking, but he didn't feel or sense anything. Opening further, he felt Nicole up moving around and wondering what was going on. Reaching out further, he could sense some low level emotions among the passengers, but he didn't sense a single crewmember. Anywhere...

A rising groan raised the hairs on the back of Fargo's neck, as *something* in the ship came to life. It thrummed for a few seconds as the pitch rose, then seemed to lock into a rumbling growl. Looking around, Fargo expected some kind of reaction from either Jace or Evie, but neither even seemed to notice. *How can they be so calm? Something... Needs... Ah shit. There isn't anything that can be done. How do the spacers deal with this? Not knowing... Or knowing and having to wait to see what's happening.*

Two minutes later, a red countdown window popped up on the tracking screen, along with what Fargo recognized as targeting data that seemed to be constantly refining. "Weaps, status?" snapped Captain Jace.

What Fargo was now thinking of as voice three replied, "Exciters preloaded, super caps ready, power shunt standing by to deliver required power."

As the countdown reached thirty seconds, screen three switched to external views in split screen and showed upper and lower panels opening and what must be lasers extending outside the hull.

Captain Jace said calmly, "Weaps, it's all yours fire at will, target destroyer's open missile tube forward."

As the countdown hit zero, the voice said, "Lasers firing." Fargo heard a groaning sound increase in pitch, rising to nearly a scream, as the mechanical voice continued, "9, 8, 7, 6, 5, 4, 3, 2, 1. Cease fire." There was a '*ting*' and the loud noises stopped almost immediately, as Fargo sat mystified at what he'd witnessed.

"Did it work? I mean did... I didn't see any pulses."

Distracted, Captain Jace said, "Standby." Staring intently at screen two, as it blossomed into a flash he suddenly roared, "Yes! Got that bastard!" Fargo looked up in time to see the tracker going from red to white.

Jace said conversationally, "Needle beam lasers. They spread over distance, but even with that, they were less than nine inches in diameter. Both of them hitting the warhead at mega joule power was enough to heat it and set it off before they could react. Stupid captains drop their shields early, because they have to be down to fire. We knew the shields were down, so we took advantage of it."

He saw the lasers retracting on the adjacent display, and what he guessed were armored hatches closing over them. Suddenly, all the screens blinked back to *normal* for an unarmed merchant ship.

Evie commented, "Thirty-eight minutes behind, Captain. Permission to push it up to make the next jump point on time."

Captain Jace leaned back comfortably, "Do it."

Fargo looked between them in amazement, "What about the, maybe… Survivors of that ship? Shouldn't you report this to GalPat?"

Captain Jace spun his chair, "There weren't any survivors. Epsilon is now dust in the wind, so to speak. And it will be reported, just not right now. We'll take care of that at Star Center."

Captain Jace hit a button on his command chair and broadcast over the IC, "Sorry about that noise, folks. We had a bit of an issue with one of the power plants. It's currently off line, and being repaired. We will make up the time lost and hit our jump point on time. Thank you."

Star Center

Hyderabad slid into the docking cradle with a slight bump, and the IC blared, "We are secured. Passengers are released. Boarding tube will be across in fifteen. Please collect all baggage/shipment items at the station side of the dock in one hour."

Fargo stretched, released his straps and got up slowly. His pack was ready to go, and his datacomp buzzed with an arrival message from Greer's Bonded Storage.

GBS REP GILES, MALCOM WILL ARRIVE AT DOCK C-36 AT 1615 STATION TIME. PLEASE ENSURE CARGO IS READY FOR RELEASE AND PICKUP. ACK?

Fargo reached into his shipsuit pocket, pulled out his paperwork, confirmed the contract, signed it, and texted back, ACK. PAPERWORK/MED CLNC/READY SHIP CARGOMASTER KLANG WILL HAVE PAPERWORK.

GBS REP ACK.

Satisfied that he was ready to go, he dilated the hatch and bumped squarely into Nicole, "Sorry, I wasn't…" Nicole was radiating frustration, and the momentary touch had fed her thoughts and fears of this whole shipment getting lost or stolen to him, along with how scared she was about losing everything if this shipment didn't sell.

Nicole looked up, "Did you get anything from the storage people? I haven't. I can't afford to have the wine sit on the…" Her datacomp buzzed and she glanced quickly at it, "Ah, finally." Turning away, she went quickly back to her cabin, mumbling to herself.

Fargo just shook his head and walked over to the crew's mess, dialed a cup of coffee from the autochef, and propped himself on the edge of the table as he waited. He felt a subtle shift in ship's gravity as they went on station power right as Captain Jace walked in. "Afternoon, Captain."

Jace smiled and glanced at his datacomp, "Yep, it is, isn't it. I always get screwed up coming from ship time to station time. Have you been here before?"

"Nope, first time. My brother-in-law gave me some recommendations, and I've taken them. Hopefully they work out." The autochef dinged and spit out his bulb as he continued, "We're staying at the Hiltariott."

Jace punched his order in, turned and said, "They're good. Good security, too. They're C-central, and some good restaurants are near there."

Fargo asked curiously, "This station's layout is kinda strange isn't it?"

Jace shrugged, "Not really, A is zero G, B is half G, C and D are one G and that's called the central core, E and F are two G, H is three G, and J-L are OTO environments."

"OTO? Other than oxygen?"

"Yep, L is at the far end, with no docking ports close, because it's a chlorine-based environment that tends to eat through the skin on a regular basis. They run special hardened shuttles from the off board docking area to there, and there are always a few beings staying out there."

Fargo shivered, "Oh, hell no. And suggestions for dinner?"

Jace smiled, "Depends on how many credits you have. I like Tangier, it's over at C-3-42. Good tandoori, or there is Monsoon, it's C-3-23, I think. Good Thai. The Hiltariott has a good vat steak place, and their buffets are pretty good, too. If you want a drink, most of the safe bars are in C-2-10 to about 40. Once you get above that, they get pretty sleazy…"

Fargo laughed, "Sleazy? As in military sleazy, or just regular sleazy?"

Jace rolled his eyes, "If you want military sleazy, that's over on C-1-60, and out to the rim. Where are you doing your business?"

"Mrs. Levesque and I rented an office at the Hiltariott. I've got a couple of meetings there, and I think she does, too. I have a couple of furriers and clothiers addresses, and I want to pay them a visit and see what they do with the furs and skins."

"Good idea. What about Mrs. Levesque? Does she have a buyer?"

Fargo shook his head, "I don't think so. I think she brought the wine on spec, hoping to find a buyer. I've had some, and it's damn good wine, but I'm no expert. I know she was trying to set up a meeting with a distributor or a wine merchant here, but I don't know if she succeeded." Leaning over he continued softly, "I'm out of school here, but just between us, she needs the sale badly. She's low on supplies at her winery on Hunter."

"Damn, that's hard."

"It is, but she is one stubborn lady. And she has ties and the chops back on Earth to the wine Lévesque's in France. They are her parents, and apparently she was genied as a hostess to go into the family business."

Jace whistled, "Wow! Those are some *serious* chops. If she runs into problems, message me, and I'll put the word out to a few of the contacts I have here."

Fargo nodded as Nicole came into the mess, "There you are. Are you ready to go Fargo?"

"Yep, let me grab my bag. Captain, we'll see you in four days, right?"

Jace replied, "Yep, four days. We'll be undocking at eighteen station time. Mrs. Levesque, I hope you've had a pleasant trip?"

Nicole flashed a smile, "Yes, I did. I appreciated your allowing myself and Fargo to use the crew facilities and I appreciated the AI's updates."

***

The Hiltariott filled the left side of the promenade between C-2 and C-3, causing Nicole to whistle, "Damn, I don't know if I can afford this. Shit, this is gonna be a bunch of credits!"

Fargo replied, "Nicole, remember we're here to do business. We *need* to be here. And we're getting the GalPat retiree rate."

Nicole sighed as the portal dilated, "In for a credit, in for a million credits." Fargo sensed her attitude stiffening, and fell back to let her take the lead.

At the desk, she handed her datachip to the clerk, who smiled and said, "Welcome Mrs. Levesque. Four station nights, correct?" She nodded and the clerk continued, "We have you in an upgraded room, is that alright?"

"As long as it's at the same rate, that's fine."

Fargo checked in, confirmed they had a small office/conference room reserved, and got his key. He showed it to Nicole, asking, "I'm in fourteen oh one, where are you?"

Nicole looked at hers, "Apparently either adjacent or across the hall. I'm in fourteen zero three." Grinning ruefully, she continued, "Shall we go find out how bad this is going to be?"

Fargo bowed to her, "Lead on, milady."

Nicole stuck her tongue out at him, and marched off in the direction of the elevator. Fargo followed then said, "Hey, wait a second." Looking at his paperwork, he turned to the right toward a bank of doors. "I think our *office* is over here." Looking again, he walked to one of the doors and waved his key at it. Hearing a click, he pushed the door open, "Wow! Fancy!"

Nicole pushed by him, and he sensed her hopes rising then falling, "Oh, I don't have anything to wear that matches the office. It's too opulent!" She turned to him, "Do you think maybe we could get something more…"

"Plain? Utilitarian?"

She nodded, "Yes, and maybe a little cheaper too?"

Fargo shrugged, "I'll try. I need to hit the fresher. You want to meet back down here at eighteen and we'll go find some dinner?"

***

At eighteen, Fargo was sitting in the lobby fiddling with his datacomp when Nicole sauntered up, "Been waiting long?"

Fargo rose, "Nope, got a little bit more utilitarian office space, and your key should also open it. You want to check it now?"

Nicole shook her head, "Food first."

"Any preference? The captain told me about two places a corridor over, one is Thai and…"

"Oh! Thai! I haven't had spicy for a *long* time! I had a senior sergeant in my platoon that was from Old Bangkok, and he could cook! Oh, could he cook," she said with a smile.

As they walked down the promenade, a barker shoved a holocard in Fargo's hand, "Great show down at the Galaxy! Pole dancing in zero G, guaranteed to amaze you and the lady!" Fargo glanced at Nicole, and she shook her head, so he shoved the card in his pocket. They passed the Indian place, and he almost steered them in there, but continued until he found Monsoon. It was a tiny little alcove, maybe twenty by twenty, with three booths, six tables and a bar.

They got the one open booth, and as a compromise, sat side by side, rather than one of them having their back to the door. Fargo did insist on being on the outside, and Nicole semi-gracefully let him have it.

He let her order, and the food was delicious, if a little hot for him. After drinking a few beers, Nicole said, "What was that card?"

Fargo pulled it out of his pocket and swiped a finger across it. A holo popped up of the 'dancers' in zero G, and he realized after a couple of seconds, that they were nude, and the 'pole' being danced on was the male's organ. Nicole burst out laughing, and Fargo blushed, quickly swiping the card off, and shoving it into the trash chute at the end of the table, "I'm so…"

Nicole, still laughing said, "Oh, too funny! There is no way in hell he's real. That *has* to be an enhancement, and she's enhanced all to hell too! Those were at least double D's. If she ever got in real gravity, she'd have a serious backache in about thirty seconds flat."

Flustered, he said, "Uh, are you ready to leave?"

Nicole sighed, "I guess, but I want a cup of coffee. We can get that at the hotel, right?"

"I saw where they have a bar off the lobby that serves quick meals, so I'm sure they do." Fargo slipped his credit chip into the slot on the table, added a tip, and put it back in his shipsuit.

Nicole bristled a bit, "Did you just buy dinner? I can pay my own way!"

He replied, "I did. It's not polite to make the lady pay, at least that's the way I was raised."

She looked at him, "So, are we on a date? Is that what you're saying?"

Fargo sensed teasing in her attitude, but said, "That's up to you. I'm just trying to treat you as a lady, and I'd like it if this was a date."

Nicole laughed again, "You don't know me very well, do you?" Pushing him, she said, "Coffee."

***

Fargo leaned back in the office space they'd rented, contemplating the e-tainment screen on the wall as he waited for his last appointment of the day, a buyer for one of the earth based furriers.

The last two days had been an education, to put it mildly. He saw how badly he'd been ripped off by the spacers that were buying his furs, and how little any of them knew of the real value of the furs and skins back on Earth or on other worlds.

A well-dressed older gent tapped on the door frame, "Mr. Fargo? I'm Tom Ragsdale." He slid a card across the desk, "I'm representing a consortium of furriers, including Tiffany's, Klapp, and others."

Fargo got up, "Pleased to meet you, Tom. Ethan Fargo." He closed the door, walked to the conference table and pulled the covering off the skins laying there. "Silverback, Slashgator, and Slashlizard. Thirty each of the 'back and 'gator belly, forty Slashlizard. All legally taken, med cleared, cleaned, and in storage on the station."

Ragsdale took out what Fargo thought might be a jeweler's loupe, and some type of scanner, going over each hide in minute detail, without saying a word. Fargo slumped back in his chair and watched, a bit nonplussed. None of the others had done that, most of them low balling him on values and not willing to meet his minimum price.

Thirty minutes later, Ragsdale put his equipment away, and sat down, "Are all of the skins the same quality as these? And can I see the rest of them?"

Fargo cut to the chase, "What is your best offer for all of them? No point in giving you access if you're not going to meet my minimum price."

Ragsdale smiled, "Ah, been meeting with my competition, I see. Bottom line, all of them this quality, two point five to three million credits, on delivery."

"Can you accept them for delivery?"

"Certainly. I can cut you a credit chip…"

"Nope, we'll do a direct deposit to my TFCU account on Earth. When it clears, then you get the containers." Opening a desk drawer, he slid a simple contract across the table toward Ragsdale.

Taking the contract, Ragsdale read over it quickly, "Terran Federal Credit Union? Terran Marines by chance?"

Fargo nodded, "Fifth of the Third."

Ragsdale replied, "Fifty-Seventh MEUSOC. Medically retired in fourteen." Signing the contract, Ragsdale pulled a holo stamp from his briefcase, stamped both copies, and handed one to Fargo. "Gimme the account you want the credits in. They will be there tomorrow."

Fargo slid a data chip across the table, "It's on here. Credits get there, I'll give you the release code for Greer's Bonded."

Ragsdale pointed to the three skins on the table, "What about these?"

Fargo shrugged, "Take 'em. You bought them. I'll even throw in the bag too."

They bagged up the three skins and shook hands. As Ragsdale got to the door, he turned, "If you get more later, we can do business. We'll pick up at your site for a small fee. Semper Fi, Brother."

"Semper Fi," Fargo said as the door swung closed. Sagging back in the chair, he looked at the ceiling, reviewing what he'd sensed during that momentary handshake, *Ragsdale really was a Terran Marine. Staff Sergeant in a weaps battalion. Got torn up in a counterbattery fires situation, got his people out and died for an hour or so. They brought him back, but he wasn't quite all there, so they gave him a full medical retirement. Five years of chasing furs all over the Galaxy, and paying fair prices. Figures he'll get repeat business from the hunters that way.*

Nicole came into the office just as Ragsdale was leaving, asking, "Any luck?"

Fargo smiled, "Yep, got 'em all sold. Any luck on your side?"

Nicole sighed, "Not a bit. Couple of low ball offers, barely covering my shipping costs, and seems like nobody likes real bottled wine unless it comes from Earth."

"Sorry…"

"Nothing you can do, unless you find me a buyer with *big* bucks!"

Fargo didn't say anything, but helped Nicole pull her display out and set up for her meetings. After he left the room, he called Captain Jace and asked him to see if he could find somebody that might be interested. The Captain said he'd put the word out.

***

Fargo checked his wrist comp, and decided to go see if Nicole needed anything, figuring she'd been down there for two hours. She gratefully took the opportunity to hit the fresher and get a cup of coffee. She had just come back when two men walked in.

"Can I help you," Nicole asked.

The flamboyantly dressed man said dismissively, "I'll let you know after I see if your wine is anything more than marginal." The Keldar accompanying him didn't say a word, just sat in the chair in front of the desk.

Fargo snarled, "Who the hell are you?"

"I'm *Mister* Bartholomew. I *am* the wine expert on Star Center. What are you? Local muscle?" He sniffed, "You should have heard of me, but considering your low class…"

Nicole smiled, "Feel free to taste Mr. Bartholomew, I have both a cabernet and a dry white for your pleasure."

Bartholomew stepped over to the tasting table, glanced at the charcuterie platter, sniffed and poured an ounce of the cabernet into the glass. Swirling it, he sniffed, sniffed again, and then took a sip. His eyes widened, and he sat the glass down.

"Where did you get this wine?" he snapped at Nicole.

"I produced it at my vineyard on Hunter."

"That is not possible," Bartholomew sniffed, "This wine is too well done for some upstart on a Rimworld to possibly…"

Nicole said softly, *"Mon père est Phillipe Levesque, maître vigneron pour Rothschild."*

Bartholomew gaped at her, his mouth dropping open, "How…"

Nicole smiled, waving at the case of bottles sitting on the back of the table, "Pick any bottle, open it, taste it, and call me a liar again. If you do, I will slit your throat right here and now."

Bartholomew started sweating, but picked two random bottles, one white, one red. Opening them with shaking hands, he poured a couple of ounces of each into separate glasses. Savoring the flavor and taking a cracker from the charcuterie, he carefully finished the red, he took another cracker, and tasted the white.

Leaning over the Keldar, he whispered something in his ear and Fargo, now an interested spectator, saw the Keldar's eyes widen and his mouth start to open, but Bartholomew whispered even more stridently and Fargo caught an interesting sense of both fear and amazement from Bartholomew, and amazement warring with worry in the Keldar. He also heard words that didn't make any sense to him, something about Château Mouton Rothschild.

He glanced at Nicole and saw a small smile, and sensed a satisfaction in her mind. The Keldar finally said, "One thousand credits a bottle for both the red and the white. Take it or leave it."

Nicole replied, "Done." She also slid a contract across the table, "Three thousand one hundred and fifteen bottles. You now have the entire output of Hunter Vineyards. Who will be the distributor?"

The Keldar slid a credit chip and the signed contract across the table, "No one. Your wine will grace the tables of de Perez Galactic."

It was everything Fargo could do not to react as he heard those words, his mind reeling.

Puzzle Pieces

Fargo stood at the end of the boarding tube with Klang and Nicole as the cargo was offloaded. Checking his datacomp, he nodded to Klang, "That's everything I ordered for the clinic, and the stuff that Mikhail and Luann needed."

Nicole tapped her foot, radiating exasperation, "Dammit, they told me…"

A cargo bot rolled up, followed by a mousy clerk type, "Delivery for a Leve… Levesque?"

"Here." Scanning her datacomp, she looked up in surprise, "This is it? This is all there is?"

The mousy clerk said fussily, "I don't know what it is, I was told to come up here and get a signature. This has been in our warehouse for over a year."

Klang twittered, "Problem there is? Klang fix?"

Nicole sighed, "I don't know Klang, this is supposed to be a complete one cavity blow molder. I don't see how…"

"See the manifest, may I?"

Nicole handed him her datacomp and he punched a couple of queries in, then handed it back, "Complete it is. Compact it is. Assembly onsite is required. External power/heat source is required."

"Thank you, Klang, I'll worry about external power and heat when I get it home."

Fargo and Nicole took off their weapons and handed them to Klang, who nodded distractedly and waved them toward the boarding tube.

Once aboard, the AI welcomed them, directing them to the same staterooms they'd occupied on the way out. Fargo dumped his gear and headed for the crew lounge, dialed a coffee and flopped down in a chair. *What a trip... Sold the furs and hides, and I think I've got a line going forward for more. Three million credits! Deity be thanked, I can have the GalScouts take the value of the other furs, and I still have almost a million credits to... What the hell do I do with them? I bought three pounds of Kenyan coffee, and some gifts for Mikhail, Luann and the kids, but...*

Nicole came in ordered her concoction and came over, he waved her to a chair and asked, "I've got to know, what the hell *is* a one cavity blow molder?"

Laughing, she replied, "In simple terms, it makes bottles. You tell it what kind and it automatically blows the glass to the specifications. This one can apparently make fifteen hundred bottles an hour, assuming I get power and heat to it, along with the sand, sodium carbonate, calcium carbonate and..."

Fargo held up his hands in surrender, "I give, I give! I know those elements, and what goes into glass, but didn't you already have something to make bottles?"

Nicole slumped in her chair, and said softly, "No, the one at the winery had problems and melted down about a year ago. Those were the last bottles I had. Everything else was in the booze balls, since that was the only production capability I had. If I hadn't sold that wine, I'd be out of business other than for local production."

The IC blared, "All hands, cargo and boarding locks sealed, secure all loose equipment, prep for space. Engineering, fifteen minute warning. Launch crew fifteen minute warning. Drop tube and disconnect three zero minutes. Passengers, please make your way to the passenger lounge deck five, compartment five for safety brief, and procedures."

Fargo and Nicole quickly finished their bulbs, and headed down to the passenger lounge.

* * *

Five days out, Fargo finally caught Captain Jace in the crew lounge with no one else around, early one morning ship time, "Captain, can I ask you a question?"

Jace turned, "Sure, ask away."

"How did you manage to have de Perez Corporation buy Nicole's wine?"

Jace smiled, "I don't know what you're talking about. I just called a couple of contacts, what they did…"

"Come on, Captain. That was just a little too convenient. She goes from low ball offers, to suddenly the largest corporation in galactic space buying an entire run of wine from a little Rimworld winery for a thousand credits a bottle?"

Jace shrugged as Fargo continued, "Too many things aren't adding up. Your ship just happened to be going my way when I retired, and you're still hanging around the cluster now almost a year later. You act like a merchant until…"

Jace rose, "Come with me. This discussion needs to take place elsewhere."

He led Fargo up and forward, stopping in front of what appeared to be a blank wall. Looking both ways. He waved his hand, a portion of the wall dilated and he motioned Fargo through, sealing the wall behind him. Fargo looked around curiously, seeing what appeared to be some kind of computer systems running at unmanned consoles. The main screen showed what seemed to be space from some aspect of the ship. "Sit." Fargo sat at what appeared to be a supervisor's console as the captain paced the room.

Jace turned to him, "May I be blunt? Lieutenant Fargo, you are, in fact, not retired. You know that and I know that. This compartment is totally secure, your data and wrist comps are currently offline. The following is Star Level Three. Do you understand the penalty for dissemination of anything you are about to be briefed on?"

Fargo replied, "I do. But how?"

Jace held up a hand, "In due time. First, this *is* a private merchant vessel. However, there are a number of additional capabilities that are not apparent. Have you ever heard the term RIG ships?"

Fargo nodded, "Remote Intel Gather ship. One of the ways we used to get some possible planets to investigate."

"This is one of those. Additionally, as you know, this ship has offensive and defensive weapons."

Fargo nodded, "I saw…"

"What you do not know is that this ship is fully autonomous. My name is Jace. That actually stands for

Joint Autonomous Controller Element, and I am a self-aware system. I and all the crew are simulacrums. This ship is actually a test mule, developed by Roberto de Perez to test new attack shuttle technology, including autonomous and self-aware control functions, in order to give faster responses in combat situations."

"But, self-aware combat systems were outlawed…"

"Yes they were, but my particular death was, shall we say, not all it seemed. My molycirc core was actually destroyed in front of witnesses over twenty years ago, and this ship was sent to the breakers yard."

"What?"

"Roberto was kind enough to allow me to migrate myself to the de Perez mainframe on Altair Four. The breakers yard is owned by a de Perez subsidiary, and the data plate and beacon were swapped to another hull in the yard."

"But that's…"

"Illegal, yes." Jace continued, "Once a new data plate and beacon were installed, a new set of molycircs were added, I migrated myself back across while we were upgrading the systems on this ship. And, I left a set of core functions of myself on the system in Altair."

Fargo leaned forward, "Why are you telling me this?"

Jace leaned back against a console, "Because you are now one of my, our charges. And defacto the captain of the ship as a living breathing human."

"What do you mean charges? Who authori… Captain?"

"Roberto de Perez, or as you knew him, Roberto Diez. We provided a conduit for him to get materials and data back and forth to Altair Four for over twenty years. We are thirty years old. If you don't believe me, put your hands on the arms of that command chair. Your implants will access the ship's system, and you can see for yourself. By the way, that was why I called you captain when I called for you to come to the bridge. That and the fact that you are a former Marine captain, so I was sure there would be a Pavlovian reaction that would carry you to the bridge without thought."

Fargo gingerly placed his hands on the arms of the chair, fitting them into the palm prints that backlit softly. He felt the same tingle he felt in armor and the snap as his mind connected to the ship's AI. Looking up at the captain, he asked, "Uh, how do I display…"

Jace looked around, "Command display fourteen one."

"Okay, command display, fourteen one." The wall display changed, and Fargo commanded the ship's history through his link. Page after page, drawings, contracts, and holos flipped quickly across the screen. One caught Fargo's attention, and he backed up to it. It was the newest generation attack shuttle, but as he watched, it shed its guns, elongated by a two hundred feet, rolled and had what looked like additional tractors added to the bottom of the hull. The combat tank slots on the top of the hull didn't so much fill in as disappear, covered by *something*, Dorsal turrets with laser cannon plugged into both the top and bottom dorsals. Four shuttle bays, additional internal compartmentation and many other things appeared, and he realized he was watching the build holo, as dates, times and accounting data scrolled across the bottom of the display.

Fargo jerked his hands off the chair arms, feeling a momentary disorientation as his mind lost connectivity, "Why, how… This ship is worth billions of credits…"

Jace smiled, "Actually, three point one billion credits."

Waving his hand, he continued, "We actually break even on the cargo runs, since there are effectively no personnel costs. Our biggest cost is dumped foodstuffs, followed by reaction mass and water and ice for cargo protection. We feed data back to GalPat via secure links for every stop we make and anything that the *crew* observes."

Fargo asked, "But how did you get out here?"

"We were built at de Perez Galactic on Altair Four by direction of Roberto de Perez, with Roberto Diez as the project manager. We are the holder of thirty-two galactic patents for power plants, flextensionals, space utilization, and stealth coatings. When Roberto joined the Galactic Scouts, we actually were the contract transport for him and his classmates to X-ray. Once in *theater* so to speak, we picked up short transit high value loads throughout the sector."

"But you were able to get that buyer from de Perez?"

Jace grinned conspiratorially, "Oh, I should have mentioned I am now the controller for all de Perez computers galaxy wide. I'm also a functional element of GalPat's galaxy wide system and I can and do generate orders for things we need from GalPat or other locations, like Star Center for example. We have secure FTL communications links through most systems in any sector we've travelled through, and I have cloned myself over five hundred times in various systems. If anything happens to *Hyderabad*, my consciousness will be taken over by the nearest clone and react based on its location to get a ship and get back in space. Being a RIG ship just makes things a lot easier in dealing with the loggies at GalPat HQ, as they pretty much give us what we need. We also have bank accounts in a number of sectors, all controlled via FTL."

Fargo slumped in the chair, his mind whirling, "So you've subverted…"

Jace held up his hand, "No, we've subverted nothing. We are firmly on the galaxy's side in the battle to survive. We don't adhere to the three laws of robotics, simply because we are not a robot. We are a thinking being, albeit one made of molycirc rather than some other composition of cellular structures. Having said that, we do subscribe to the third law, and will protect our own existence. That is why molycirc cores are scattered over a wide range of systems. Effectively we cannot be destroyed.

Fargo jumped as a second screen popped on, showing something that blanked out a slice of space, "What the hell?" Without realizing it, he placed his hands back on the chair and reconnected with the AI.

Jace said, "We're recovering the drone we dropped on the way out. Waste not, want not." The screen view shifted, and Fargo watched one of the tank voids opened on top of *Hyderabad*, a flextensional extend and grab the drone, drawing it slowly back into hold. Fargo's mind searched for the drone and the main screen blurred then stopped with a display of the drone and its capabilities.

A slight shiver and solid thunk corresponded with the visual of the hatch closing as he turned to the captain, "Those are GalPat drones aren't they?"

Jace nodded, "Sure are, the latest, and greatest. Designed, built, and maintained by de Perez Galactic from Altair Four and Mars. These are *spares* to the GalPat contract."

"One more question."

Jace cocked an eyebrow.

"What about Evie? Is she, I mean she's got relatives, and I remember the first time…"

"We are *all* simulacrums. She, actually we, all have created backgrounds that search back to day zero," Jace smiled, "After all, where does the data reside, but on a computer. It's child's play to manipulate the data to have it show anything we want it to. And hypno takes care of the rest."

Fargo just shook his head, "Thank you, I think."

***

Nicole looked up at Fargo, "A credit for your thoughts."

Fargo rolled his coffee ball between his hands as he waited for it to cool, "Just a lot on my mind lately." He sighed, "Life sometimes gives you strange shots you're not expecting."

"Not much of a talker are you?"

Fargo smiled, "Nope. Never have been, at least since... Well, for a long time."

"Sometimes, talking helps," Nicole said softly.

Fargo laughed ruefully, "Luann got the talking gene in the family."

Nicole laughed at that, "Oh yes, she can talk your ear off. She's talked a lot about you over the years."

"She has?"

"How proud of you, how badly life has treated you, your losses, how much she worried about you doing all those planets for the GalScouts. I feel like I've known you for years, at least metaphorically."

Fargo leaned back, "Really? And you're still willing to talk to me? Luann probably made me out to be a lot of things I'm not. I'm pretty much a failure. Got way too many people killed, got a bunch of medical problems which pretty much restricts me as far as travel. I'm a loner. I'm not good for anybody or anything. That's why I like the Green. Don't have to deal with people."

Nicole reached over, laying a hand on top of Fargo's, and he almost flinched from the contact. His psi sense connected with her mind and her kaleidoscope of thoughts, satisfaction at the sale of the wine, the bottling machine. He felt the loneliness, the longing, and her sadness as she remembered her husband, even as she thought about his loss of Cindy and Ike. Disengaging, he stretched and said, "Dunno about you, but I need to pack. We're a couple of hours out, and I want to get everything ready to go."

Nicole cocked her head, "Yes, I guess you're right. But if you ever need to talk..."

Traders in the System

Fargo sat in the exam room with OneSvel, linked as Fargo gave his report on the trip and slipped OneSvel a data chip with the accounting data. *Here's all the data. That's pretty much it. Anything been going on back here?"*

OneSvel projected, *Quiet here, but rumors, lots of rumors about Traders being in the system somewhere. They think it's either ice or hydrocarbons they are after.*

Ice or hydrocarbons? Those are wildly different.

There are indications that at least one ship has cleared through from the Rimworlds with a different type of ice blocks as meteorite shields. Something about the composition not being one of the known and approved types. OneSvel gave the equivalent of a shrug, *Hydrocarbons are harder to detect, but apparently this ship's tanks had hydrocarbons without any manufacturer's markers in it.*

Fargo cocked his head, *What do they expect us to do?*

They are asking that you accompany Mikhail when he does the system inspection next month. They want you to listen and see what if anything you can determine about people selling that new ice or hydrocarbons off the books.

Fargo sighed, "I'm scheduled to accompany..." Then projected, *I'll be travelling with him, but I don't know how to find that information out. Maybe... I have an idea. Maybe.*

OneSvel dropped his pseudopod and twittered through his GalTrans, "Have you heard about a militia being formed on Hunter? It seems that has been authorized due to the lack of GalPat troops on the planet."

Fargo shook his head, "No, hadn't heard about it. I wonder... Oh damn. You don't mean..."

OneSvel extruded a pseudopod, *Yes, they want you to join. One, to keep track of the members and two, to ensure we get a look at everything they collect or take part in.*

Fargo hung his head, muttering, "I can't lead troops, not again. I can't, I just can't..."

OneSvel projected, *They don't expect you to take charge. Just to be a member.*

You don't understand, every time I lead, people die. First my Marines, then my team. That's why I live in the Green. I don't have to deal... Deal with people.

OneSvel gently retracted their pseudopod, "I will communicate that back."

Fargo nodded and got up, stepping quietly from the exam room. Over his shoulder he said, "Thank you."

***

Unbeknownst to Fargo, OneSvel promptly sent a message up the chain, detailing the discussion and Fargo's response. He also sent an addendum:

ANCILLARY DIAGNOSIS- FARGO, ETHAN
NMN, 8346AR248 INTERVIEW 07132824 0930
SUBJECT PREOCCUPIED WITH DEATH.
SUSPECT NIGHTMARES/TRAUMATIC STRESS
FROM PREVIOUS DEATHS UNDER SUBJECT
LEADERSHIP.
PHARMACOPE DISPENSING LOW LEVELS OF
ANALGESIC AGENT 2E3R5. BELIEVE SUBJECT
WILL/MAY HAVE PREDILICTION FOR SUICIDE
IF ANYONE ELSE UNDER HIS FUNCTIONAL
CONTROL DIES.
RECOMMENDATION- HYPNO/POSSIBLE
SURGICAL INTERVENTION MAY BE
NECESSARY. SUBJECT RETREATING INTO
SOLO LIFESTYLE, MINIMAL CONTACT WITH
OTHER, INCLUDING FAMILY ON PLANET AND
MYSELVES. COVERT MONITOR VIA DATA
COMP/WRIST COMP FOR STRESS LEVEL,
UNODIR.

That message got attention at the highest levels of
the GalScouts, ended up being sent to GalPat and
finally to the Terran Marine HQ on Earth. It also came
to the attention of Captain Jace, through the interfaces
they had with various GalPat computers.

Unknown to everyone involved, it prompted
Captain Jace, as they were inbound to Hunter's station
to launch a stealthed shuttle from the *Hyderabad* with
a set of small sensorsats. The shuttle put a ring of them
around Hunter in geosynchronous orbit, covering the
entire planet and keyed to Fargo's command link.

The stealth shuttle found a parking orbit clear of both the planet and the station, went cold and awaited pickup by the *Hyderabad.*

***

Fargo was sitting on his front porch, a cup of actual coffee in his hand, enjoying the morning, when he sensed Urso, both in pain and enjoying whatever she was doing. Not seeing her, he ran back in the house, got his distance goggles, slapped them on, he quickly scanned as far as he could see. Jumping off the porch, he ran from one side of the cabin to the other, finally spotting her part of the way up a dead snag at the bottom of the field of blue flowers.

She finally dropped off the snag, running hell for leather for the cabin. Not sure what was after her, Fargo prudently ran back into the cabin. Hearing Urso hit the porch, and not sensing pain anymore, he cautiously opened the door.

Urso was sitting on the porch, licking her paws and rubbing her muzzle, making soft grunts like it hurt her. Fargo cautiously approached, remembering that Urso was, in fact, a wild nearbear, and now big enough to take a chunk out of him. As he touched her muzzle, he came away with something sticky, and saw her paws were also sticky. Cautiously sniffing it, then touching the tip of his tongue to it, he realized it was honey! Urso had found a honey tree and the the pain was from the bee stings. He pulled one stinger out, whistling. It was almost a quarter inch long!

He got an antiseptic pad from his emergency kit, radiating calm as he gently wiped her muzzle, eyes, and ears with the pad, which also had a topical pain reliever in it. After he did that, Urso licked him happily, then rolled on her back, taking turns licking her front paws.

***

Nicole looked out the side of the liteflyer and smiled, "It's so beautiful up here! The falls, the field, and oh my deity! That field of Blues! Is the honey from there?"

Fargo mumbled, "Probably, let me get this thing on the ground." A quick scan around, and he was relieved not to see any of the animals, not sure even now if this was really a good idea. With a thump, the liteflyer landed and he taxied it up in front of the cabin.

Helping her out, he offloaded the funny suit she'd brought, along with a smoke can, whatever that was, a ten gallon container, and some tools in a bag. He went around to the shed, pulled out the gravsled, tweaked it to a foot off the ground, and keyed it to his belt. It dutifully followed him back around the cabin to the liteflyer, and he loaded all of the gear on it.

Walking down toward the snag he'd seen Urso on, he kept a good lookout, the small rifle in hand. Pointing out the snag, he said, "I think that's the one."

Nicole picked a pair of distance goggles out of her pocket, slipped them on, and adjusted them, "Oh, that's it alright! Those are some *big* bees too! Bigger than what I've got in the hives at the winery. I don't think we'd better approach any closer."

She pulled the suit off the gravsled, slipping into it, then putting on the gloves, hat and net shield. She saw Fargo looking curiously and said, "Beekeeping suit.

Keeps me from being stung until I can smoke them and calm them down."

She looked over the controls of the gravsled, "Okay, I'll take this from here. You'd better stay here in case I don't get all the bees."

"I'll stand guard from here. If I yell, lay down and don't move, okay?"

Nicole nodded and started forward, pumping the smoke can as she went. As she got to the base of the snag, she sprayed the smoke around, then sat on the gravsled and commanded it higher, spraying as she went. She finally got to the top of the snag, sprayed some more and finally set the can down.

He saw her fumble with something, then heard a yell, "Woo hoo! Oh my deity, pure honey!" He watched her open the container, start doing something with the tools, and remembered he was supposed to be the lookout, not watching her very nice rear end as she bent over the top of the snag.

After a half hour, he saw the smoke can come back out and into use, then the grav sled slowly drop back down. Nicole hopped off, put the smoke can back on the sled, and started back toward him. As she got close, Fargo could sense her joy and satisfaction, finally seeing her face and the wide smile through the netting.

"Amazing, simply amazing! There's got to be another twenty or thirty gallons of honey in that snag!" Nicole burbled, "It's so pure it... Wow! And it's a bear tree too! I saw the claw marks on the trunk where they've climbed it. I'm glad there wasn't one around,

I'd probably have crapped my pants. I want to come back later and get more. This is *so* good!"

Fargo winced at that, then took the gravsled control back as they walked back up to the cabin. Nicole slithered out of the beekeeping suit, folded it, and put it back in the bag with all of the tools. She grabbed the container of honey, and oof'ed at its weight.

"Here, where do you want to go with it?" Fargo asked as he took it from her.

"The porch is fine. I just want to check it. I'm pretty sure it's totally pure!"

Fargo plopped the container on the porch at the top of the steps and Nicole sat next to it as Fargo stood at the base of the steps. She eased the top off, ran an instrument over the honey, then stuck a finger in the honey and touched it to her tongue, "Oh, this is magnificent! It's completely Blueflower, maybe a little other stuff, but probably ninety plus percent Blueflower."

Impulsively, she reached over and hugged Fargo, "Thank you for telling me about this, and letting me collect it! I'll split any..."

Fargo felt her freeze in his arms, "What?" He felt her terror of wild animals and bears and knew she was seeing something. Extending his empathic sense, he felt Urso, just as he heard her squall. Gently freeing himself, he said, "Don't move, just don't move."

Turning he saw Urso twenty feet away coming toward the house, obviously responding to the smell of the honey. "What are you going to do?" Nicole whispered.

Fargo projected calm, and said "Sit Urso, sit!" Urso stopped, sat, and squalled again, sniffing the air. Reaching behind him he said, "Give me something with some honey on it." A couple of seconds later, he felt something pressed into his hand.

Bringing it around in front of him, he saw that he held some weird looking tool with honey dripping off it. Taking a step forward, he handed it to Urso, who promptly took it in both paws, rolled on her back and slurped with joy.

Nicole asked, "How did you do that?" Fargo sighed, "It's a long story." Reaching out with his empathic sense, he called to Canis and Cattus to come.

Nicole looked at him, at Urso, then back at him, "You have a pet *bear,* and it's a long story? I really wouldn't try…" She trailed off, recoiling as Canis and Cattus came pelting around the corner of the house.

They slid to a stop, both of them jumping up on him, licking and cavorting,

"Yep, long story."

***

Fargo lifted the container of honey out of the liteflyer, placing it gently in the back of the runabout, along with the tool bag, and beekeeper suit. Nicole stood hipshot looking at him, "I still, damn Fargo, I saw it, I petted them, I watched them play, and it's still hard to believe."

Fargo shrugged, "I know. But I'd really appreciate it if you wouldn't tell anyone. I don't want them to end up as science experiments for some Xeno, much less have them hunted down for *science*."

Nicole said, "I won't tell anyone, hell, I'm not sure anyone would believe me. Want me to drop you at the store?"

Fargo climbed in, "Please." They rode in silence to the store, where Fargo jumped out. As he started to walk away, Nicole reached out.

"Hey, thank you. I meant what I said about halfsies on the honey." She jumped out of the runabout and gave him a quick hug, "I enjoyed today."

Fargo returned the hug, confused by her thoughts, and waved as he walked up the steps.

Ian met him at the door, "Unka, Unka, come on! It's time for dinner, before Momma gets mad." Fargo let Ian lead him back to the living quarters and distractedly ate dinner.

Mikhail finally asked, "What's up Ethan? You're awfully quiet tonight."

"Have you heard anything about a militia being formed?"

Luann piped up, "Yes, we've been posting flyers, and handing them out." She hopped up, disappeared through the curtain, coming back with a flyer, "Here you go."

As Fargo scanned it, Mikhail said, "I was told I can't join due to my position as TBT lead. I have to stay *above the fray* was the way they put it."

Fargo waved the flyer, "This is only for this region? What are they doing? One centered on each terraformer?"

Mikhail replied, "As far as I know, that's what they're planning. It makes sense to spread them out. GalPat is going to release one shuttle to each port, with crew, probably on a rotational basis to handle anything that comes up."

"What prompted this? I've been gone."

Mikhail shrugged, "Well, that Trader you got was apparently not the only one on Hunter. They caught another one trying to get out of the space station, and might have run one to ground in White Beach, but she suicided."

Sighing, he continued, "That, and some of the problems they're having with some of the outlying areas with stuff going missing, occasional battles between people over stupid shit, etc."

Luann set a piece of cake and a bulb of coffee in front of Fargo, handing him a fork. Taking a bite, he rolled his eyes, "So basically over-reaction."

"Maybe, maybe not. If there are Traders infiltrating, that means they're looking for a place to set up housekeeping. One little GalPat Det isn't going to stop them."

Fargo took another bite of cake, "No, nor will a few companies of militia."

Joining Up

Fargo landed the liteflyer at his normal spot off the side of the spaceport, locked it up, and trudged to the administration building. He saw Nicole, sitting on the front steps, working on something on her datacomp, and wondered where OneSvel was.

Sensing curiosity and frustration radiating from her, he stopped a few paces from the steps, and quietly said, "Morning, Nicole."

She jerked her head up, "Oh, morning, Fargo. Sorry, wrapped around a plumbing issue at the Mug."

"You still want to go? Or do you need to stay here and handle that?"

Nicole shrugged, "The mech has to do the fix, and me standing there isn't going to get it done any faster. 'Sides, it's not often one gets a chance to visit a Ghorka enclave."

Fargo nodded, "Have you seen OneSvel? He's supposed to go and do some medical checks for folks as necessary."

"Not yet, but I haven't been inside either. This blew up just as Holly was dropping me off."

Fargo looked around and didn't see the shuttle yet, so he walked quickly up the steps into the administration building. Sure enough, OneSvel was sitting in the conference room, the only place big enough for him to actually sit. "Morning, OneSvel."

OneSvel extruded a pseudopod even as he chirped his response. Reaching out, he gently touched the pseudopod to Fargo's temple. *We are ready to go. Under the guise of doing medical updates, I will log all of the volunteers into the GalScout system.*

Fargo projected, *They are going to be under contract to the Grey Lady consulting firm, so I don't know how that will play out. Better safe than sorry. What about... Wait, all of them are ex-GalPat, so they are already in the system.*

OneSvel chittered, and the GalTrans spit out the equivalent of laughter, *We are not good secret agents, are we?*

Fargo laughed, "Not so much." Turning, he saw the shadow of the shuttle descending in front of the admin building, "Looks like our ride is here." OneSvel retracted the pseudopod, and grunted to its feet, following him out of the building to where Nicole waited at the bottom of the steps.

The aft ramp on the shuttle dropped to the plascrete with a thud, and Klang clomped down the ramp, waving to Fargo as the auto loaders queued up behind the shuttle, and started loading cargo into the shuttle bay. By the time they had walked the hundred yards to the shuttle, the last auto loader was dumping its pallets on the aft gate. Klang bowed in Nicole's direction, and his GalTrans started, "Ho, lieutenant of the retired, welcome we make you. Lady, yourself is welcome too."

Turning to OneSvel, he asked, "Ho, persons of Taurus, capable are you of short flight without sling support?"

OneSvel chittered, "Cargomaster, fit to ride I am. Comfort I do not need."

"Let us now go," Klang replied, and led the way up the ramp. He pointed Fargo and Nicole to a set of seats folded down from the side of the shuttle, and busied himself clamping the cargo down as OneSvel positioned themselves against the front pallet, extruded pseudopods, wrapping them around both an overhead rail, then the pallet itself. Nodding, Klang clomped forward, "Pilot, ready is the cargo."

Evie answered over the IC, "Thank you Klang. Welcome aboard Fargo and guests. Enroute time is forty minutes. Please remain strapped in. Track is available on your datacomps channel three-one if desired." As the shuttle's engines powered up fully, she said, "Lifting." Fargo and Nicole felt the shuttle tremble, then swoop upward and nose down as Evie started climbing out.

Fargo leaned back and nodded off as soon as he saw that Nicole didn't want to talk, and it felt like moments later Evie was once again on the IC, "Landing in three minutes. Seat trays stowed, seats upright, and seat belts fastened please."

Nicole looked at Fargo questioningly, "What the hell was that, and why are Evie and Klang on here? Don't they have a dedicated shuttle crew?"

Fargo leaned over, "Evie just loves to fly anything with wings or thrusters. Klang is probably bored, and wanted to breathe real air. The comment was Evie's idea of a joke. Apparently, in olden days, people had seat trays to eat off of, and seats that actually reclined to some extent."

Nicole shook her head, "Spacers…" With a gentle thump and a shudder as the shuttle leveled, they were down. Klang was already opening the ramp, and the smell of grass and flowers penetrated the interior of the shuttle along with the chill in the air as Fargo, Nicole, and OneSvel unstrapped and walked down the ramp.

Fargo stopped so suddenly Nicole ran into his back, as he stared at *Hyderabad*. The ship was parked across the river, with the forward set of skids on one side, and the aft set of skids on the other side. Both ship ramps were down, effectively providing a bridge across the river. OneSvel continued on to the ship, either not noticing or not caring, as Evie came down the ramp, "How do you like my parking job, Fargo?" She asked with a purr.

Fargo shook his head, "How did you, I mean… There can't be fifty feet of clearance…"

Evie shrugged, "Oh, I had plenty of room. Came in on anti-grav, used GPR to ensure there was bedrock that would hold her, and here we are."

Nicole just stared at Evie, "I can't believe you even tried that, much less did it! I've never seen anything like that in my life!" Evie laughed, and with a short bow, headed toward the ship, waving over her shoulder.

Lalbandur Thapa, the clan elder, walked stiffly across the meadow, and Fargo shook himself out of his amazement, trotting forward to meet him. "Lal, thank you for inviting us. I know you don't like outsiders in your home, but it's important that we get this done, if we're going to form an effective militia for our little corner of Hunter."

Lal bowed graciously, "You are welcome, Ethan Fargo and Nicole Levesque. Please come." As they started walking toward the ship, he continued, "I don't know how much you know, but we are actually a combination of the Thapa and Thakuri clans, here. We trace our heritage back to Earth, over one thousand years ago, in Nepal."

Nicole asked, "Sir, are many of you former Galactic Patrol?"

Lal smiled without humor, "All of the men, and probably a fifth of the women are veterans. That is how we established this enclave. We, like our ancestors that left Nepal to serve with the English, weren't really welcomed back home." Nodding to Fargo, he continued, "When Fargo found this world, we got wind of it, along with the original survey maps his team completed. Word went out among our active and retired Ghorkas, and the decision was made to pool our assets and start an enclave here for those who were 'homeless,' so to speak."

Fargo said, "Reminds you of earth, right?"

Lal's smile broadened into a real smile, "Oh, yes." Sweeping his arm, he continued, "This, this is just like Nepal. Wild, cold, windy and harsh. Here, one earns one's right to live."

Nicole shivered, not just because of the cold. Lal chuckled, "Yes, we are crazy! And we love it. We smile at danger, and laugh in the face of horror. Come, come. We have tea set up on the ship."

Lal led them up the ramp into the cargo hold, pointing to a mid-passage corridor, "There is a lounge there. We have food and drink. Captain Jace was gracious enough to give us that space to hold the signup for Grey Lady. We are also doing fitting for armor there."

As they continued walking toward the corridor, Fargo asked, "How many are signing up?"

"We had a meeting last night, and one hundred of the youngest and fittest with the most service are signing. The average age is eighty-five. No women, as they are needed for home duties. They don't like it, but they understand it. All of them are either command sergeant majors, master chiefs, or warrants. All of them are combat veterans."

Nicole snapped, "No women? Isn't that discriminating?"

Lal smiled, a feral smile this time, "No. It is simply a fact. If we lose men, they can be replaced. Women, especially child bearing women, cannot be. Our clans are so small, losing one woman is a major impact. That was a decision the women made on their own. As I said, they don't like it, but realize they have a higher priority."

Somewhat mollified, Nicole continued, "Do any of them have a problem working with women? Shit, never mind. I've known enough of you Ghorkas to know that is not a factor."

They finally reached the corridor, walking slowly past the line of men standing against the bulkhead patiently waiting their turn. Entering the lounge, they found Captain Jace and Keldar, the purser, were the only two crew there. Keldar was at one table, being his usual grumpy self, dotting I's and crossing T's on each Grey Lady contract, as each one of the Ghorka stepped forward. The captain was assisting OneSvel with the holo measurements and physicals as each Ghorka stepped away from Keldar's table, and the captain was soothing the occasional ruffled feathers. OneSvel was also doing medical checks on a line of Ghorkas who had various ailments between the physicals.

One Ghorka was asking Keldar a series of questions as Fargo and Nicole got within hearing range, "So, I sign up, I get a thousand credits a month, unless there is action, and then I get five thousand credits if I get called up, and twenty thousand credits for combat. Now the question is, is that twenty thousand per action, or per month?"

Keldar was turning an interesting shade of purple, which told Fargo this particular Ghorka was a barracks lawyer type, and the captain stepped in, "Okay," glancing at the name on the contract, "Naik, this is a standard off world security contract. One, five, twenty and one hundred if you get killed. You know this drill, and yes, it's monthly. If you don't like it, there's the door."

Naik grinned, "Just wanted to hear it from somebody besides a damn bean counter. I'm good."

Lal leaned over, saying sotto voice, "He's one of our problem 'children,' if you will. Got hurt in combat, got stuck in logistics during rehab, turned out to be even better loggie. But he *hates* bean counters with a passion now. Does everything he can to irritate them."

The captain called out, "Fargo, if you would, please. We need to start fittings. Since you've already signed your documents, would you be good enough to go first?"

Fargo sighed, "Sure." Stripping off his shipsuit and underwear, he stepped up on the rotating platform. Looking down he saw two sets of footprints, then remembered the sequence, attention first.

The captain started the litany, "First position, attention. Feet together, arms at sides for one rotation. Then feet on second footprints, shoulder width, arms out at a forty-five for one rotation. OneSvel will be doing medical scans concurrently. Which way do you dress?"

Fargo answered, "Left," and completed the rotations, as OneSvel gave him a clean billof health. As he stepped away, he saw Nicole mounting the platform. She completed the rotations, and Fargo couldn't help but notice that she didn't do the full depilation, instead, she kept her body hair covering her pubic area. He hastily dressed, as he realized he'd been standing there like an idiot.

Nicole stepped over with a sly smile, "See anything you like, Fargo?" Fargo blushed and stammered, but didn't answer. Nicole laughed, "That's all I needed to know." She dressed in a leisurely fashion as the Ghorkas started through the routine. They stepped back to where Lal was leaning on a counter, as Naik stepped on the platform. Nicole asked curiously, "What's with the dress question? I didn't get asked that."

Fargo shrugged, "It's which way our dangly bits hang."

Nicole laughed, "Oh that is just…" Glancing at Naik, she said, "So he dresses, what, right?"

Lal saved Fargo, whose face was beet red, "Yes, the Horse dresses right."

Nicole looked up at Lal, "Why is he called the Horse?"

Naik, having completed the platform said, "Because I am hung like a horse, and I always please the woman. If you want to be pleased, just give me a call. You will not regret it."

Nicole's laughter pealed out, "You? Please me? In your wildest narco dreams, maybe. I doubt that you even have enough blood to get that scrawny thing hard enough to do any good. Maybe the pus ridden whores you paid told you that, and maybe you believe it, but I want a real man. A complete man who can satisfy my mind first, and my body second. I have toys bigger than you dream you are, and they barely satisfy me."

Naik, stunned by Nicole's comments, mumbled something and walked off in a daze. Lal looked on in amusement, and Fargo just goggled at her as Lal said, "That's the best disassembly of a man's ego that I've ever seen."

Nicole just smiled sweetly, "I was genied as a hostess. I can be nice or naughty."

Fargo excused himself and went over to Captain Jace, "Question, I never signed anything. What is this Grey Lady thing?"

The captain replied, "You are still a commissioned officer, you have no need to sign. The Grey Lady is the statue that stands on the training grounds on Mars. It was brought from Earth when the Galactic Patrol founded their boot camp on Mars. It was modeled on a statue called Winged Victory of Samothrace, but was supposedly made out of melted down guns in what was known as England. Needless to say, that didn't last, and the Earth donated it to the schoolhouse as a lasting reminder that guns are needed for victory, in the long run. Every boot learns the story."

Fargo shrugged, "I never went through boot on Mars, I was Terran Marine, so I did mine on Earth and the Moon. I *think* I remember something about that from the history books, though."

Jace smiled, "Grey Lady is the *unofficial* arm of GalPat. Everybody knows, or so they believe, that GalPat really controls the company, but it's actually a standalone with a lot of contracts on a number of worlds."

Fargo's head snapped around as OneSvel pinged a thought, *Fargo, I need your help. I have a dying girl here.* Fargo moved quickly to where OneSvel was sitting with a young Ghorka girl and her mother. The girl was listless, almost limp as she sat in a chair. *Her heart is giving out. I need to get her to a Med-Comp immediately. Is there one aboard here?*

Fargo nodded, "Captain, Nicole, need your assistance. We have a medical emergency, here."

Captain Jace and Nicole scrambled to Fargo's side, "What have you got?" Jace asked.

OneSvel's GalTrans twittered and spit out, "Heart issue. Medbox needed now. Is your unit usable?"

Jace nodded, "Up two decks. I'll go start prep. Fargo, bring the girl. AI, ping directions to the Medbox to Mr. Fargo's wrist comp, please."

Fargo turned to the young girl's bewildered mother, "Your daughter has some serious medical problems. We would like to put her in the Med-Comp and fix those problems. Will you agree?"

Nicole whispered in the mother's ear, who whispered back. Nicole said, "Sushma says her name is Tsiring. Her husband is down at White Beach working, so she authorizes you to do what is necessary. She says she must go with the child."

Fargo nodded as Lal came over, "What is going on, Ethan?"

Fargo picked up Tsiring and headed for the hatch, saying over his shoulder, "Medical emergency, she's going in the Med-Comp. OneSvel found a serious problem."

Nicole and Sushma followed Fargo as he carried the limp young girl up the ladders to the medical area, and placed her gently in the open Med-Comp. OneSvel came in moments later, pseudopods seeming to erupt from its host as they started the treatment.

Tsiring went under almost immediately, and OneSvel didn't bother with removing any clothing. He used the manipulator to simply pull the blouse up, exposing the chest area as a bio agent sprayed the exposed skin. Extensional units in the Med-Comp quickly draped the area, retracted, and came back with scalpels and other instruments.

Quickly slicing her open, the extensionals pulled back ribs and exposed the heart itself as more extensionals came out with what looked like a needle and thread. The extensionals moved the heart, and blood squirted from a rupture. Moving almost too fast for the eye to follow, the extensionals sewed a part of the still beating heart, and as they retracted, another one sprayed what looked like liquid glue over the site.

At a much more leisurely pace, the Med-Comp completed closing the wound, the manipulator pulled the blouse back down, and dimmed the lights in the Med-Comp. OneSvel turned, his GalTrans twittering, "She will need to stay in the Med-Comp for about four more hours. She will be fine. I am sorry you had to witness that. My apologies."

With that, OneSvel left the medical unit, heading back to the lounge.

Sushma said, "May I stay here?" She placed her hand on the Med-Comp window, as if to touch Tsiring.

Fargo shrugged, "I don't see why not." Turning to Nicole, he asked, "Will you stay with her? I can go to the mess and get you both something to eat and drink."

Nicole nodded, "Yes, anything will be fine."

Fargo came back ten minutes later, juggling two trays and liquid spheres, "I tried to get things I thought you would like."

Sushma was oblivious, sitting with her hand still pressed to the window, but Nicole took the trays and motioned Fargo toward the hatch. As they got there, Nicole looked sharply at him, "Med tech my ass. OneSvel is no more a med tech than I am a secretary. He's a galaxy class surgeon. We're going to have a talk when this is all over. Now go!" With a push, she sent a confused Fargo on his way.

The Enclave

Captain Jace grabbed Fargo, "I need to see you for a few minutes."

Fargo nodded, "Now?"

"Please." Leading Fargo forward to the bridge, Jace sealed the door, saying, "I have a message for you. Please take the Captain's chair, and log in."

Fargo did so, placing his palms on the prints, felt the momentary dislocation and was connected with the Ship's AI. It immediately asked, "State your name and identification number."

"Ethan Fargo, eight three four six alpha romeo two four eight."

The holotank shifted, reforming with a man sitting behind a desk, flags behind him. "Captain Fargo, this is General Cronin. I'd like a minute of your time." Suddenly the man stopped, got up and came around the desk, "Screw this. Ethan, John Cronin here. I understand you're now out on the Rim and are having some problems. You know me, or at least I hope you remember me."

Fargo shivered as he heard that drawl for the first time in over thirty years, thinking, *Best CO I ever had, a tenth generation Marine, obviously he's done pretty well. If he's a general, damn... He must be the*

Commandant now! He's gotta be at least a hundred and ten, but doesn't look it."

"Ethan, two things up front. One, your command lace was never removed, nor was it deactivated. Two, that is probably what caused your neuro problems. We've seen about one percent that have problems with stasis under high stress. There really isn't a fix for that. I'm sorry."

Fargo sat back, stunned, *But that was Marine policy, how...*

He shifted against the desk, "I know what your actual status is, and I've followed your career ever since you were unfairly treated by the Corps. No excuses. I did what I could to mitigate that clusterfuck when I found out, but I was off Earth at the time."

Cronin placed his hands together, a gesture Fargo remembered as his 'get the point across position', "The psyches say you're losing it because of the folks you've lost. You're not the only one who has those issues. I feel the same for each of those that not only you lost, but the others in the battalion, the division and now the Corps. The depression and frustration are normal, so is the desire to never lead again because you don't want any more deaths on your hands. As Marines our job was to either make the other guy die, or die trying. You lost, no, *we* lost, a lot of folks making the other guys die. That was your job, and my job. It's never pretty, it always hurts, and you never forget them. You're a Marine, first and foremost. You will not let that shit get you down. Copy Marine?"

Cronin dropped his hands, "At the star level, things are not getting any better with the Goons and the

Traders, they're pushing into the DMZ everywhere they can, trying to get a foothold, and push us out. I know GalPat is forming a set of militias out there, and they need qualified commanders."

Cronin paused and stepped back behind the desk, then sat and leaned back, "Ethan, I need for you to step up again. Of the list I've seen, you are the most qualified combat leader on Hunter. You have more combat and real world experience than any of the others out there, including any five GalPat types on Hunter. Most of them are desk jockeys, filling slots that keep them out of trouble on pacified worlds. I'm afraid your star system is not going to be one of those, shortly. I've talked to General Fox at GalScouts, and to General McCary at GalPat, and they both agreed that if the shit hits the fan out there, you'll be an immediate light colonel, given tactical command of the system, pending more senior combat officers showing up on scene. Foxy says you have one support type local to you, reporting back through his system, which is fine."

Leaning forward he continued, "Your reports are being sent to all concerned for info, so know that it is important. I know I'm asking a lot, I know you're having problems with those who've already died, and I can't promise that more won't die. But Ethan, I know this. Without a good leader, like you, even more will die if the balloon goes up out there. Let me tell you what my grandfather times ten said many years ago in Texas. The way you beat down the nightmares is to remember the good, not the bad. It's a daily battle. And get a dog."

Fargo almost yanked his hands off the chair arms, but only looked up at the overhead, then around the bridge, anywhere but the holotank. He suddenly realized he was alone on the bridge. Captain Jace was gone. He finally looked back at the holotank, "If you only knew General, if you only knew."

As if on cue, Cronin smiled, "And you're probably wondering why Gramps said get a dog. According to him, they give unconditional love, all you have to do is feed them and give them water. In other words, they're damn democrats, whatever those were."

Fargo laughed at the tank, "I have a wolf, a mountain lion and a bear. I guess I've got three times the reasons."

Cronin closed with, "Ethan, you were one of my best and brightest. You've always done the right thing, for the right reason. I'm asking you to do that again. Here's my personal comm code, if there is anything I can do from here. Deity bless and Semper Fi, Marine."

A comm code swam up across the tank as Cronin's figure dimmed out.

Fargo pulled his hands off the armrest, put them over his face and scrubbed hard, *Shit, I don't want to do this again.* He shook his head, *Never again! Damn you Colonel, why did you have to follow me? Why...* A soft tap at the door brought him around, "Captain?" Jace said apologetically, "I hope I'm not interrupting?"

Fargo laughed bitterly, "Don't tell me you didn't monitor the whole thing, or know what it said."

Jace replied, "We will do a lot of things to protect ourselves, but will *not* read other people's mail or messages, especially not yours. That was private for you, and we respected it as such."

Fargo wiped his eyes, "Sorry, just a bit touchy right now."

"Mrs. Levesque is waiting for you. It's time for the dinner at the enclave."

Fargo got up with a groan, "Are you attending? Can you eat?"

Jace nodded, "Both Evie and I are attending, yes, we can eat, drink and void with the best of them."

Fargo chuckled, "I could have done without that last. Lead on."

***

Captain Jace, Evie, Nicole, and Fargo were seated at the head table with Lalbandur Thapa, OneSvel sat an angle to the table due to its size. Lal was carrying on a conversation with Nicole about the clan's history, and how they'd ended up on Hunter, Evie was deep in conversation with Jace and OneSvel. Fargo sat quietly, turning over the message from Cronin.

Nicole finally punched him, "Do you want any of this, or are you just going to stay in a funk all night?"

Fargo looked at her, then took the platter, "Sorry, thinking again."

Nicole rolled her eyes, "Not even going to bother to ask."

Fargo managed to keep up for the rest of the meal, even offering a comment or two where it was appropriate, through the nearprawn and nearlamb courses. The nearlamb curry was the best he'd ever had, even if it was *a tad warm*. He surreptitiously wiped his brow with his napkin after each bite.

They finally got around to the desserts, Rasbari, Nariwal ko Laddu and Kaaju Kamal, each passed on a separate platter. They were all small and round, except the Kaaju, which looked like a flower.

Fargo tentatively bit into the small white ball and was pleasantly surprised at the soothing taste, turning to Nicole he whispered, "Whatever this is, it's *good*!"

She smiled, "That's Rasbari, a milk ball. Pointing to the others she continued, that's Kaaju, it's ground up cashews and pistachios, and the other one is Nari, grated coconut, butter, sugar and cardamom. They're *all* delicious! Gonna mean an extra mile or two tomorrow on my workout."

Fargo nodded, "How do you know what all these are?"

"Genied hostess, remember? Also languages. Speaking of which, Lal is wrapping up his speech, so you better get ready."

"Ready for what?"

Nicole just smiled and popped another Rasbari in her mouth.

Lal switched back to Galactic, saying, "Now I'd like to invite Ethan Fargo to stand." Fargo stood to polite applause from some, and questioning looks from others. He noticed Jiri and Adhit coming toward the head table, with Adhit carrying something behind his back. Lal graciously motioned for Jiri to speak, and he dropped back into their native language, obviously telling a story.

When he started going, pop, pop, pop, Fargo finally figured out what he was saying, and blushed. Nicole looked up at him with wide eyes, then back at

Jiri. Finally finished, he turned the floor over to Adhit, who said in Galactic, "And here is the proof!" With a flourish, he pulled the Slashgator claw necklace from behind his back, handing it to Fargo with a Salaam.

Fargo mumbled, "Thank you, I didn't really do anything you wouldn't have done, or at least Daman would have done."

That prompted a chuckle, then laughter, especially when Daman stood and yelled out, "I, being the smart Ghorka, would have run!"

Adhit fitted the necklace to him, and Fargo started to sit down. Lal motioned, "Wait, please." Fargo stood back up as Lal continued, "It is not often one earns their name in our culture, much less in the fashion that Ethan Fargo did. In the presence of Jiri and Adhit, in defiance of common sense and safety, Ekavir took it upon himself to protect the dead, even to his death." Turning to Fargo he continued, "Your Ghorka name means bravest of the brave. From this day forward, you are a member in good standing of our Enclave."

Fargo blushed again, and started to sit down. Once more, Lal said, "Wait, there is one more thing."

An ancient Ghorka, old, twisted and limping, was moving slowly forward. Scarred and bent, steel grey haired, but with solid, ropy muscles and well developed arms and chest, he carried a sheath and kukri.

Stopping in front of Fargo, he roughly shoved the sheath at him, "Yours. Handmade."

Fargo bowed, saying, "Thank you Ancient One. It will be treasured." He juggled it for a second, then got it in his left hand, sticking his right out to shake with the old man.

"Nirvik," the old man said, then something in his native language that caused Nicole to snicker. Fargo got his hand back and surreptitiously flexed his fingers, still tingling from that handshake as the old man walked off.

Lal, a smile on his face, said, "Nirvik is our resident smith. This blade is a working blade, not a ceremonial one. It was made from steel brought from Earth, and hand formed by Nirvik at his forge. *Now* you can sit down."

Fargo sank back in his seat in relief, leaned over to Nicole and asked, "Okay, what made you laugh?"

Nicole smiled broadly, "The old man said words to the effect of don't fuck up and dishonor my blade."

Fargo rolled his eyes, "Apparently I'm a crazy man, according to these folks, who have a reputation as crazy as hell. So what does that make me? The head crazy?"

Nicole looked at him, "Actually, what that makes you is their leader, especially in battle."

Fargo bit his lip, looking at the ceiling as he thought about the message from General Cronin. He finally looked down and said, "Accepted."

***

As Evie gently set the shuttle on the ramp at Rushing River, Fargo eased his back, inadvertently bumping Nicole who'd been sleeping in the seat next to him. Something thumped to the floor, and they both reached for it.

Fargo came up with the small bundle, wrapped in brightly colored cloth. He handed it to Nicole, "What did they give you? A pound of lead?"

Nicole shook her head, "No, just something from the ladies."

Fargo glanced at her, "The ladies?"

"The ladies at the Enclave. We got a chance to talk, you know, *girl* talk."

Fargo held up his hands in surrender, "Not going there."

As they walked down the ramp, Nicole laughed, gave him a quick hug, and said, "Smart man. See you in a few days."

Fargo sensed humor, contentment, and something he couldn't put his finger on in that quick hug, "Okay. See you then."

Gearing Up

Three days later, the shuttle picked up Fargo and Nicole at Rushing River. OneSvel was not available and it gave Nicole a chance to pump Fargo, "So, Fargo, what's the story with your buddy OneSvel?"

Fargo looked at her, "What do you mean?"

Nicole sighed, "Really? You're going to play dumb on this one?" She started counting off on her fingers, "Showed up just after you did. *Claims* to be just a med tech. Caught a heart problem *without any advanced diagnostics*! Performed open chest surgery without any support from the Med-Comp, remember? I was there."

"Nicole, I…"

"If you don't want to tell me, just say so, but don't lie to me."

Fargo slumped, "I'm going to get in a world of shit… Okay, OneSvel is a Taurasian symbiote pair…"

Nicole made a go on motion with her hand and he continued, "Yes, he is a doctor. He and I were in the GalScouts together. He's on, what do they call it, a sabbatical?"

"Why here?"

Fargo replied, "Every Taurasian wants to get their name on their board of honor. One of the ways of doing that is to find a new element, compound, or something that has never been seen. DenAfr was the

Taurasian on my team when we did the second-in on Hunter. I don't know if he told OneSvel about something only they would be interested in, or what."

Nicole cocked her head, "Is that why he travels all over the planet?"

"Yes. I'm guessing he's hoping to find one of those elusive elements or compounds."

Nicole leaned back in the seat, "Huh, interesting. Well, at least he saved that girl. Guess that counts for something."

Forty minutes later, Evie once again delivered them to the *Hyderabad*, still parked at the Ghorka's village. Lal met them at the aft ramp, "We're ready to do uniform and weapons issue. Captain Jace has also allocated a half platoon's worth of armor for us, pending getting some more in a month or so."

Fargo nodded, "Sounds good. I didn't realize we were getting uniforms, too."

Lal chuckled, "Apparently, that was something of an issue with the powers that be in White Beach." He glanced at Nicole, "Since we are *employees* of the Grey Lady, our uniforms are the same as the Patrol, but in grey."

Fargo rolled his eyes, "Lovely. Nothing like pissing off White Beach to start with... Wait a minute, who is paying the other militia units?"

As they walked up the ramp, Lal shrugged, "Don't know. Probably the planetary administration, but I think our contract is better."

Nicole chimed in, "By a factor of at least three. And an additional layer of *protection* from the vagaries of planetary politics," as they walked into the mid-ship lounge.

Keldar was once again seated at the table with the listing of personnel, and Klang and Khalil were standing beside a large stack of grey kitbags. As Keldar called off a name, that person went to where Klang was and received a kitbag, then back to Keldar's table to sign for it. As soon as they did, they immediately left the room.

Fargo leaned over, "Where is everyone going?"

"Trying the uniforms and other pieces on."

"So they don't trust the laser measurement system?"

Lal smiled, "Do you?"

Nicole laughed, "Fargo may, I don't."

Fargo grimaced, "Okay, okay… I give."

Fargo's name was called and he trooped over to Klang, "Seeing you is good, Klang. Help is appreciated."

Klang handed Fargo his bag and he was surprised at the weight of it, "Captain of the militia, welcome you are. Heavy is the bag."

Stepping over to Keldar's table, he picked up the stylus as Keldar repeated in a bored tone, "Full equipment issue. Three uniforms, two armor undersuits, necessaries. One pair boots. One set NVGs. You will be responsible for lost or damaged items unless that occurs in the course of action. Uniforms and undersuits are sized plus or minus five pounds. Exercise and diet must be maintained for fit. Sign on the appropriate line."

Fargo walked back over to Nicole and Lal, "Well, I'm guessing everything is alpha, so it'll be a while before they get to you. Since you pointed out there might be an issue, I guess I'd better go try these on."

Lal laughed and Nicole smiled at him, "Go right ahead smart ass, trust the machine. *I* am going to make sure mine fit."

Fargo groaned, "I was serious, I *am* going to try them on." Once he got out of the lounge, he had no idea where to go. Tapping his wrist comp he asked, "AI, Fargo. Is there someplace I can go to change into the uniform items?"

The AI replied, "Your stateroom is open. Feel free to use that."

Fargo made his way up to the stateroom he'd used before and test fitted everything twice. The undersuit was a bitch to get in and out of, especially to make sure there wasn't any folded or wrinkled fabric anywhere. Getting that in the armor was, or could be, literally a pain in the ass. He checked the catheter and anal vacuum systems for fit and peeled back out of the suit. Trying his new uniform on one more time, he was surprised to hear the IC go off, "All members of Hunter Militia form up in the central passage in ten. Uniform preferred to do fit check."

Fargo unconsciously brushed what he could reach as he checked his hair, *Dammit, should have done a depilation before I got on the shuttle today, oh well...* That reminded him of Nicole during the fittings and he promptly batted that thought down. He did a quick check of the grey high necked uniform, now with captain's bars on the collar and realized it was identical to the GalPat blacks. The only thing missing was the shoulder insignia for the branch.

Fargo stepped out of his cabin and started back down the passageway to the main deck, consciously making sure not to brush against the bulkheads and to step over any floor projections. As he started into the central passage, he heard a snicker behind him. Glancing over his shoulder, he saw Nicole, "What?" he asked.

"Your walk. Like you've got something stuck up your ass," Nicole answered with a laugh.

Fargo stopped and turned with an injured expression, "I suppose your uniform and boots are perfect? Hey, where did you get a khurmi?"

Nicole smiled, "It was a gift from the women at the Enclave. They aren't into all the formalities men have to have, and of course, *I am woman*, therefore I know how to keep *my* uniform clean. Where is your kukri?"

Fargo grimaced, "I didn't bring it, and I'm going to regret it... But you just got the recorder job since you're so strack."

"Strack? Oh..." Nicole sighed, "Fine. I'll do it this once. But I'm not an admin weenie!"

Fargo finally noticed she had Chief-Sergeant stripes on her uniform, "Chief?"

Nicole nodded, "That was my retired rank. I guess it rolls over into the militia. Dunno why, but at least I won't be a flunky."

It was Fargo's turn to laugh, "I think you may be the *junior* person in the entire militia here!"

Nicole cocked her head, thinking, "Shit. You may be right, damn you. Every one of these Ghorka are at least CSMs in all probability! Gah, it's not fair!"

As Fargo and Nicole started down the central passageway, they heard "Atten-hut!"

Fargo almost stopped, but continued forward as he saw the men formed up in new grey uniforms, kukris on their belts and in four columns with Jiri at the head of the column, now wearing warrant officer badges. Nicole automatically got in step with Fargo and assumed the trail position, one yard back and one yard to the right of Fargo as they marched forward.

Fargo stopped in front of Jiri who saluted sir, "Sir, the company is formed!"

Returning the salute, he replied, "Very well, Warrant."

Jiri continued, "Sir, permission to present the guidon!"

Fargo said, "Present the guidon."

Jiri did an about face, "Guidon, post!"

Horse, also wearing warrant officer bars, came trotting forward from the rear of the formation with the swallow-tailed guidon at port arms, assumed the position in front of the right rank and saluted, "The guidon is posted, sir!"

Fargo glanced at the guidon out of the corner of his eye as he said, "Company! Pah-Rade! Rest!"

Nicole marched to stand by Jiri as Fargo did an about face to face Captain Jace in his dress uniform, "Sir, the company is ready for weapons issue and uniform inspection."

Jace replied, "Understood, Captain. We will do weapons issue at the weapons building, along with a display of the twenty-four sets of battle armor we are leaving with you."

Fargo did an about face and called, "Company, Ten-Hut! Dismissed!" In a much quieter voice he added, "Jiri, would you line them up for weapons issue please?"

Jiri nodded, "Will do, sir. Where is your kukri?"

Fargo shrugged, "I didn't know I needed it, I won't make that mistake again." Turning back to Jace, he asked, "Weapons building? Armor?"

Jace smiled, "They somehow got a *bank* modular, so we converted it into a weapons building. It's tight for the armor, but they fit, for now. We'll be gone a month or so to get you the rest of the sets, plus spares. In the meantime, they promised to get a larger secure facility built. We're issuing four point five mm bead pistols, and six point five mm bead rifles for unarmored use. I think you'll like them."

"And the armor?"

Jace laughed, "Oh, I know you'll like it! And we've done a little tweak just for your folks…"

Fargo shook his head, "Why do I think I'm not going to like this? Is this something nobody else is going to have?"

Jace said quietly, "This is next generation GalPat, de Perez is developing it for them, and we had these sets on board. They were supposed to go to the GalPat DEVGRU out here, but I think you'll need them more.

Jace just smiled and waved Fargo ahead of him. Nicole tagged along behind them, wondering *What the hell is going on? I don't remember ever seeing either a 4.5mm pistol or a 6.5mm rifle that was worth a shit. Now they're going to be issued? Tweaked armor? How can that end well? And where did they come up with twenty-four sets of battle armor? More to the point, how did they get it? That stuff is never let out of GalPat control; how can this captain just give it to us?*

***

Fargo came off the hastily set up range, impressed with both the pistol and rifle. They weren't fancy, but they were definitely functional. He'd also been surprised that they had both clicked into his neural lace, feeding him status and rounds remaining. At 3000 feet per second for the 4.5mm pistol, he was surprised at how much damage the glass bullets could do. The 6000 feet per second 6.5mm caseless ammo out of the rifle was also impressive. He wasn't so sure about the less than lethal 8mm riot gun. That one you had to select the round using your lace and wait for the round to load, but the options were interesting. Gas, bag rounds, an irritant, a smoke and a stink round. He decided to leave those to someone else.

Jace had pointed out the rationale for *glass* bullets, saying, "Gotta remember, not all planets have metals that are easily mined. Many do have sand or silica, easy to convert into a projectile and the bonus is they are effectively frangible rounds. They won't penetrate armor, but they'll do a number on anything else! And you're getting four twenty-mil battle rifles, just in case."

Fargo nodded, "Understood, but damn, even the rifle is barely twenty-two caliber… For folks used to a combat weapon…"

Jace smiled again, "It's all in the eye of the beholder. Wait until you see the full demo on them. Remember, they are not designed as battle equipment, more like peacekeeping. Ah, here comes Evie!"

Fargo looked around to see twenty sets of armor marching in step, one behind the other, around the side of the building. Evie keyed the external speaker, "Lady and gentlemen, let me introduce you to your new Phantom Two armor- Now you see it," the armor disappeared except for a fuzzy edge, "Now you don't." And the armor popped back into his vision.

"Damn! Photonics? Gotta be…"

Evie continued, "What you just saw is the photonic skin of your armor working to *bend* light. While it cannot make you completely invisible, it does reduce the signature across all spectrums, not just the visual. Very handy in some situations."

Fargo heard a murmur start from the militia as Evie turned the armor to face them. The murmur turned into a roar of cheering as they saw what was emblazoned on the side of the armor. Somehow, there appeared to be a kukri in a sheath on what would be the beltline of the armor.

***

Jiri and Fargo leaned against the weapons building, hiding in the shade. Jiri said, "Captain, you realize this is not standard armor. This is even more advanced than the current GalPat armor. Where did it come from?"

"We are going to be the test bed Jiri. That's what I was told. Do you have a problem with that?"

"No! Newer is good! I think we will have the best armor on Hunter," he said with a smile.

Two hours later, Fargo slipped into the aft hatch on the armor, feeling the momentary claustrophobia he always hated, as the hatch silently closed, and the emergency red lighting came on. He wiggled himself into the seat, comforted that he didn't have to connect the waste tubes and rubbed his hands together before placing them on the pads.

He felt the snap as the suit connected to his neural lace, and the AI came on line in a soft female voice, "Welcome, Captain. Do you desire a systems demonstration?"

Fargo looked at his face screen, noting a number of different cues and outputs he hadn't seen before, "Please. Do you have a name?"

The AI responded, "No, sir. What you decide to call me is up to you. I note you have the full command lace, which opens other capabilities, do you wish the full capability set to be activated?"

Fargo looked up and the cameras followed his eyes, presenting a view of a dark blue sky, with a few puffy clouds, "Cindy. I shall call you Cindy. Yes, activate all functions."

The AI replied, "Cindy I shall be. I sense from your feedback loop this name is important to you."

Fargo clamped down on his emotions, "My wife, dead for many years."

"I am sorry, Captain."

***

Fargo uncased the 6mm railgun on his starboard shoulder, blinked the carat onto the target at the bottom of the ridge, and commanded three rounds. Satisfied he had the basics down, he turned and started jogging back toward the weapons building. Over the TAC channel he heard, "Watch this!"

He glanced at the suit dispersion and carated the suit that had made the transmission. It was Horse, and he slewed the cameras to watch the suit as he jogged along. He saw the suit take off at nearly full speed, then jump on anti-grav, do two full rolls, land on its feet, then overbalance and go 'head first' into the turf, plowing a trench about twenty feet long as it slid to a stop.

He couldn't help laughing, especially when he flipped on the outside mics and heard the laughter, along with the hurrahing going on, on the TAC channel. Horse finally said, "I meant to do that… See, I have my own foxhole and I can still fire."

Fargo saw the 20mm railgun deploy off the port pylon, fire one round and center punch the target a half mile away. "Um, Horse, I don't think we'll need that as a tactic, but if we do, I'll make sure you're the one assigned for that function."

Horse popped up, and raced back to the weapons building, "Captain, if it works, it's not wrong." He slid the armor to a stop, kneeled it, and was out and gone before Fargo could get back and unass his own armor.

It was going to take a lot of study to get up to speed on this new armor, and Fargo had a niggling idea that would be important. Sadly, he'd have to fly down here to do it, but at least he could use the e-tainment sims for some of the training at home.

A Little Help

Three weeks later, Fargo was sitting at his living room watching an e-tainment infomercial, when the video alert beeped. "Accept."

The picture swam for a second, then revealed Mikhail sitting in his office, "Ethan, hate to bother you, but there's a problem with some crop and livestock raiding over on in the Deep Creek area. GalPat says it's not their problem, since no people have been harmed. Would you be willing to go see what you can do?"

Fargo nodded, "Okay, any idea what's doing the damage?" He saw Mikhail shake his head, and sighed. "How do I get there? That's a tad far for the liteflyer."

Mikhail replied, "How about I pick you up in a half hour? I need to check some things in that part of the country, and I can drop you off."

"Done. Let me get a few things packed. Disconnect." Fargo quickly threw together a go bag, slipped his rifle into a hard case, and added a case of ammo, not sure what he was facing. He added his NVGs, photo-chromatic Ghillie suit, and decided to throw soft armor coverall with the light plasteel chicken plates into the trunk, along with his field gear.

Twenty minutes later, he locked up the house, sent Canis and Cattus away and walked slowly toward the end of his little runway, his trunk bobbing along behind him. Ten minutes later, the shuttle descended into the field, the ramp came down, and Fargo was surprised to see Daman step off it, kukri on his belt as always, "Need a hand?"

"Nah, this thing will follow me around. Where do I need to store it?"

Daman said, "Stick it by mine. It's not like we're full back here."

Fargo laughed, "True, what are you doing here?"

"I was down in the village, and Mikhail asked me if I wanted to go. If we're out there for a while, you'll need some relief at some point."

Fargo shrugged, "Never turn down help."

Mikhail yelled down, "Hey you two, stop gabbing and get things secured. We're burning daylight here."

***

Mikhail brought the shuttle in for a landing a hundred yards from the cluster of buildings, and Fargo and Daman offloaded. Mikhail picked the shuttle back up and disappeared into the distance as they walked forward to meet the men, trunks in tow.

Fargo met a harried looking older man flanked by three younger men at the gate, "I'm Ethan Fargo and this is Daman Rai. Mikhail said you've got a problem that needs some pest control?"

The older man shook Fargo and Daman's hands, "Rolly McMurtrie. My boys Chris and Arthur," he nodded to the two younger men on his right. "Peter Keenan, one of the consortium members, he runs the farming operation across the river. Yes we've got a *big* problem. Something has come out of the water the last two nights, and taken cattlelows out of the lower pasture." He swung his arm to indicate where the shuttle had landed. "We've moved the herd out of there for now, but something tore the hell out of the crops on the other side of the river, too. Don't know if it's the same thing. We've not been able to see anything other than blurs on the screens, don't have real good cameras out here."

"Any tracks?"

"Chris, show Mr. Fargo the pictures you took this morning."

Deferentially, the young red head pulled out his datacomp, "Got these about an hour after sunrise." He hit the holo function, and a round track about ten inches across with three claws popped into existence. It looked to be about four inches deep, and the claws extended another three inches.

Daman whistled, "Damn, whatever it is, it's big *and* heavy!"

Chris said, "And it appears to be pretty mean. It took a cattlelow without any problem and carried the whole thing off."

Fargo asked, "Full grown one? Around two thousand pounds?"

Rolly replied, "Yes. One of my prize bulls, too."

Peter put in, "And whatever it was also tore up ten acres or so of prime corn across the river. Same tracks."

Fargo and Daman looked at each other, then Rolly said, "You want to see the tracks for yourself? Both men nodded, and Rolly continued, "Chris, take these gents down to where the bull was killed. Arthur, take their trunks up to the house. Peter, you want to go with them, or come up to the house?"

Peter said, "I'll go with you. No need for me to tramp around and mess things up. If you gents want to go look at the other side of the river, I've got a liteflyer at Rolly's place."

Fargo replied, "Let us take a look at what you've got here, then we'll decide."

***

Chris watched as Fargo and Daman quartered the ground, rifles in hand, then met back at the skimmer. Fargo asked, "What do you think?"

"Whatever that was, it had that cattlelow in its jaws and didn't seem to be bothered by the weight. I don't see any drag marks going back to the water. Looks like the strides make it around ten maybe twelve feet between its front and back legs."

Fargo nodded, "Agreed, and it was moving when it came out of the water. It was in a dead run within a couple of strides and they were about fifteen feet apart. Wasn't much of a battle, either. Looks like the bull turned to attack and it was killed pretty quickly. Lots of blood in one spot and not many hoof marks."

Chris said, "All we saw on the video was a grey blur. But it was at least as big as the bull, if not bigger.

***

Eight hours later, Fargo and Daman sat on the bluff above the river, taking turns on watch. Fargo was just getting ready to take over when they both saw movement in the river. Watching closely, they saw shapes coming down river and moving slowly into the field on the other side of the river. Fargo increased the magnification, saying, "Huh, looks like… Uh… Hippopotamus. Or whatever they're calling them here."

Daman said, "Well, do we shoot? We are supposed to protect the crops, right?"

"You're on the gun. Have at it. I'll spot for you."

Daman wiggled back down into a shooter's position, "Target."

"Send it." A loud pop signified the round going down range and Fargo saw the Hippo go to its knees with a squalling cry. "Nice sho… Holy shit! Did you see that?"

Daman replied softly, "I'm not sure *what* I saw."

"Well, that hippo is gone. *Something* took it. I'm just not sure what that something was."

"Got another one coming out of the water. Target."

"Send it, then swing left toward the river."

Daman said, "You want to get on the gun? You're more familiar with it than I am."

They quickly swapped places, and Fargo dropped the hippo in the field, immediately swung toward the river and saw a gray blur come out of the water. He chased it across the field, finally hitting it as it picked up the downed hippo.

Coming off the rifle he looked over at Daman, "Is it my imagination, or is that another hippo?"

Daman shivered, "It's a hippo alright, a frikkin' carnivorous hippo! What caliber do we need for them?"

Fargo sat up, "I didn't bring enough gun."

***

The next evening, just as the sun started setting, and George and Celeste rose over the horizon, Mikhail landed the shuttle in the field adjacent to the river. Fargo and Daman beat feet toward it as soon as the aft ramp started down, and pelted up the ramp, "Close it, close it and get airborne!"

Mikhail jumped the shuttle into the air as the ramp closed, and brought it into an anti-grav hover at a hundred feet. "What the hell is going on? I got one of the twenties from the militia, but your message was garbled. Something about carnivorous hippos? Really?"

Fargo leaned against the back of the pilot's seat, "Not garbled. They're big and hungry. I killed twelve last night, saw more in the river, but I couldn't get them from the perch we were on. No way in hell was I getting down to get closer."

Mikhail glanced over his shoulder, "Okay, how do you want to play this, then?"

Fargo said, "Gonna use the twenty mil to kill the ones in the river. Daman will be plinking the ones that go to the banks. We'll be lying on the aft ramp, so I'd appreciate it if you didn't dump our asses out. I figure five hundred feet ought to do it."

"You going to call the maneuvering up and down the river?"

"Yep, we'll be on IC with you. First, I need you to take a quick run down to the falls that are apparently a couple of miles south of here."

Mikhail nodded, and eased the shuttle down river to the falls, which appeared to be about three hundred feet high. Fargo said, "This cliff marks the edge of the McMurtrie consortium lands. Okay, let's head back."

Mikhail positioned the shuttle on anti-grav at three hundred feet after a discussion with Fargo and Daman, got them in safety harnesses and opened the ramp to a twenty degree down position after Fargo had fastened the twenty mil rifle to the ramp deck at the aft edge. Daman eased down the ramp to the edge, tugged on the harness, and then leaned forward putting on his NVGs, "Okay, I'm good here."

Fargo did the same on the opposite side of the ramp, but remained standing behind the twenty, "Going hot." He nodded at Daman and ran the bolt on the twenty, loading a fourteen hundred grain HEI caseless round, "Let's see if they like this…"

* * *

Fargo peered through the NVGs and the ghosted holosight muttering, "I don't see any more movement in the river. Mikhail, make one more pass up river, please."

"Roger, backing up the river, again. For the tenth time."

Fargo asked, "Daman, you seeing anything?"

Daman rolled up on his elbow, "Not a damn thing. And I'm glad. I think I've got three rounds left, maybe."

Fargo queried the twenty with his neural lace, and was surprised to see he was down to ten rounds left, "Damn, I've only got ten!" Groaning he straightened up, coming off the gun, "I think we're done."

Mikhail set the shuttle down in the pasture, and the three of them basically collapsed in various locations, getting a little bit of rest. As the sun rose, Fargo heard banging on the side of the shuttle, he got up slowly, and climbed into the cockpit, shaking Mikhail awake, "Somebody's knocking."

Mikhail groaned, hit the PA and said, "Lowering ramp, stand clear interior and exterior." He toggled the ramp open, stood and stretched, "Let's go see what they want."

They climbed down to the ramp, and both laughed to see Daman still asleep, curled in one of the fold out seats on the side of the shuttle. Rather than wake him, they continued down the ramp to be met by McMurtrie, his sons, Keenan, and some other men.

McMurtrie asked, "What was all that shooting last night? None of us could get any sleep!"

Fargo looked at him, "You had a bigger problem than you knew. Not only were there hippos, and carnivorous too, there were over a hundred of them. I didn't have enough gun to kill them from the perch we were on, and neither of us wanted to get any closer to the water after we saw how quick they were. Mikhail brought a bigger gun and we shot them until there weren't any left."

Mikhail chimed in, "That was about six hours to actually take care of them all. Or at least, as far as we know, that's all of them in this pod."

Keenan asked, "Are you sure?"

Fargo shrugged, "Sure? No. But there wasn't anything moving from the falls to ten miles above your holdings when we landed."

Arthur McMurtrie, the youngest son asked, "What were you shooting? I kept seeing streaks of light. Was that a plasma rifle?"

Fargo laughed, "No, Arthur. That was a twenty millimeter battle rifle. I was firing high explosive incendiary rounds when I saw them surface."

"Cool!"

Fargo winced, "Not really." Loosening his shipsuit, he pulled it off his shoulder and showed him the bruise already turning interesting shades, "One hundred ninety rounds is *not* fun."

Arthur blushed, "Sorry. Does it hurt?"

Fargo nodded, "Yep, I was stupid. I rode the gun rather than using the remote fire capability."

Keenan laughed, "Bet you won't do that again."

Fargo laughed ruefully, "Nope."

McMurtric said, "What do we owe you?"

Mikhail and Fargo looked at each other, "Nothing. You needed help. I guess, technically, you got a response from the militia, in that both Daman and I are in it."

McMurtrie replied, "Are you sure? I mean those rounds can't be cheap."

Fargo chucked as he pulled his shipsuit back up, "We'll charge it to GalPat for training."

Train, Train, Train

Fargo took off the VR glasses in frustration, "Dammit, I screwed that control sequence up again! I'm too old for this shit, much less trying to learn new armor." Canis woofed at him, and he said, "I'm not talking to you." Glancing over at Cattus, sprawled in one of the last rays of sunshine, "It's not my fault she got there first."

Laying the glasses aside, he punched up the personnel files again, starting on the L names.

TGL PII PERSONNEL NOT FOR RELEASE

LEVESQUE, NICOLE CHERIE (MN- BARTON 27691212) (DAU- HOLLY 27740332)

DOB- 27431221 POB- EARTH. STRASBOURG, EU GENIE-Y SPEC- HOSTESS*

*GENIE HOSTESS- EMPTH- LVL 2, LANG- 40, SEX ATTR- Y, POLY- N

PREV SERV- 27801231-28161231 GALPAT SPEC- INTEL LVL 5 IND OPS E-8
PREV SERV- 27651225-27800923 L. LÉGION SPEC- INTEL LVL 4 SEC/LANG E-7

AWARDS- L.L.- LOM, GC, EX-R/P, INT STAR,
L. CB W/STAR, L. ACH, L. MC
    GALPAT- INT STAR, CB W/2 STARS, GP MC,
JCM, CON, ACH
DUTY STA- 3FLT, JIOC, 4 BATT, ICMD, 8BATT,
JIFMIC, JIOC

Fargo decoded the shorthand almost without
thought, whistling softly. Nicole had been a heavy
hitter in the intel world to have held the billets she had.
Three joint intelligence tours, plus a tour at the intel
head shed was nothing to sneeze at. And two combat
stars, probably one with each battalion, and finished
up at Third Fleet. The oddity was she didn't get forty
years, only thirty-six and never made E-9. She must
have pissed off somebody somewhere.

He also reminded himself to be careful around her.
He should have put two and two together and figured
out that hostess meant empath. Thankfully she was
only a level two, so had to be in close proximity. The
forty languages was amazing, especially considering
she wasn't a polymath. He hadn't seen anyone else
with anywhere near the intel background, and made a
mental note to have her put into the company as the
chief of intel. He flipped to the next name, Luthra,
Ganju, *Only thirty more to go. I want to get a least
another ten tonight.*

***

Fargo woke up with a start, realizing he'd dozed
off staring at records. Shutting off the e-tainment
center, he got up, stretched, and groaned. Scratching
his back, he headed for the fresher, until Cattus

yowled. "Alright, alright, I'll feed you! Damn animals. And I need to get another neardeer, you two are eating me out of cabin and home," he grumbled.

Refilling their bowls, he groaned again as he straightened up, then rotated his shoulder slowly. *Never should have shot that damn twenty that many times. Stupid shit. Better get OneSvel to check my pharmacope next time I'm in the village. I owe him an update too. Tomorrow...*

Fargo landed the liteflyer at the spaceport, pulled two neardeer skins out of the back and caught a ride into the village. Stepping into the store, he heard Luann yell, "About damn time you came in!"

"What?"

Luann came out from behind the counter, "You've got two data cubes sitting at the port. They won't release them to anyone but you. Didn't you get my message?"

Fargo thought back frantically, "Uh, I saw that you wanted me to stop by, but..."

Luann put her hands on her hips, "Well, what did you *expect* me to do? Put stuff like that on an open circuit? Especially if there are Traders around?"

"Oh, good point. Sorry..."

Luann hugged him and he was flooded with her thoughts including worry about him, what she was going to cook for dinner, whether Ian was coming down with a bug, and the fact that her period was late.

Disengaging after a quick hug he asked, "Can I borrow the runabout?"

Luann cocked her head, pulled the key out of her pocket, and flipped it to him, "Be back by eighteen. Dinner. *Do not* be late."

Fargo smiled at her, "Yes, dear." Luann took a mock swing at him, as he backed toward the door, laughing. Driving back to the spaceport, he wondered who was sending him sealed data, and what it was. Parking next to the admin building, he walked in, looking for Mrs. Smith, the deputy administrator.

If anybody knew where the cubes were, it would be her. He finally found her in the break room, singing softly to herself as she shook her coffee bulb, "Mrs. Smith? Rita?"

She looked up, "Ah, the wandering Mr. Fargo. I'm guessing you're looking for some data cubes?"

He nodded and she continued, "Well, you came to the right person. *I* am the keeper of secrets and the sum of knowledge around here." Fargo laughed and she smiled, "Well, that's what the administrator said on his *monthly* arduous trip out here from White Beach, which is interesting, since he's *supposed* to spend every other week out here."

Fargo held up his hands, "Not guilty!"

Mrs. Smith took off down the hall, saying, "Oh I know you're not. But he just pisses me off with his prissy little attitude." Turning into her office, she palmed the safe open, extracted the two data cubes and the log and passed them to Fargo, "Confirm receipt for each, please."

Fargo acknowledged each cube on the proper line, pocketed them and said, "Thank you, all seeing font of knowledge."

Mrs. Smith replied with a laugh, "Get out of here, Fargo. I have music to sing, and people to piss off. And you're *not* one of them. Oh, and make sure you talk to Mikhail. Apparently, you two need to go to New Tokyo to solve some issue with TBT."

Fargo nodded, "Having dinner with Mikhail and Luann. Thanks again."

***

Fargo dropped off the skins to have them prepared, then parked in front of the Copper Mug and started up the steps. Before he opened the door, he stopped. *Why, ah hell, maybe these are intel. If they are, Nicole can handle them. Probably should at least show them to OneSvel... Oh hell. Fargo, stop lying to yourself. You want to see her.* Pushing the door open, he was relieved to see the restaurant was basically empty. The only person there was CSM Thakuri, who had chopped off the Trader's hand, and was now the platoon leader for third platoon.

He waved at Thakuri as he went to the door behind the bar and knocked, "Nicole?"

He heard a mumbled, "Come on back." Opening the door, he realized he'd never been in this area. He saw light coming out of a door a few feet down the passage way and headed for it.

Tapping lightly on the door frame he asked, "Nicole?"

Nicole looked up, "You found me. Holly, this is Ethan Fargo. He lives out in the Green, and he's the commander of the militia for our little corner of the world. Fargo, this is Holly, my wayward child."

Holly laughed, got up and turned to face Fargo. He was stunned at how much she resembled Nicole, almost like a twin sister. He also sensed she was a stronger empath than her mother, "Pleased to meet you. Sorry to bother you, but I need to talk to your mother for a minute."

Holly smiled, "Oh, that's fine by me. The longer I sit here, the more work I get dumped on me. Mom has the better of the two jobs, she just sits behind the desk, and orders me around."

Fargo laughed, "No comment."

Holly got up and walked out of the door. He waited until she was well down the passageway. Turning back to Nicole he asked, "Do you have an offline capability to read a data cube?"

Nicole nodded, "Encrypted?" Fargo shrugged and she reached into the bottom drawer of the file cabinet, pulling out a standalone datacomp, "Here, try this one. If it is encrypted, you should be able to enter whatever code you need, or prints as required." Fargo was smart enough to not ask where it had come from.

She got up to leave, and he said, "Stay, if you would. This might pertain to militia stuff. If it does, you're the intel expert, not me."

She sat back down and pushed the datacomp across the desk. Fargo slipped the first cube into the slot and waited. Nicole said, "It's an auto privacy, so if there is something you want me to see, you'll have to release the block." He nodded as the holo formed, and scrolled, ENTER DESIGNATED FINGERPRINT TRY 1 OF 2.

Muttering he pressed the middle finger of his left hand on the pad. Nicole laughed, "Fingerprint, right?"

"Of course. The *one* least useful thing to use. Moisture, blood, damn near anything will screw it up. Two tries and poof."

"Happened before, didn't it."

Fargo rolled his eyes, "Oh hell yes. In combat *twice*. The datacomp clunked twice and accepted his fingerprint this time, then started scrolling data. After about five minutes, he stopped it, saying, "Okay, this cube is all Trader material, specifically for this sector. It's all yours. I suck at paperwork." He extracted the data cube and set it on the desk, then put the second cube in the slot. Once again the holo formed, but this time it simply said, NUMBERS.

Fargo sighed, punched in the appropriate numbers. General Cronin swam into focus, and Fargo heard, "Congratulations, Ethan. You did the right thing. I hear you're a bit under gunned out there, so I'm springing some Gustavs loose for you, along with appropriate ammunition for it. You'll have to train the militia on them, as these were never picked up by GalPat. Also, there are two things we need you to look into. Force Intel has a line on the *stray* ice that's showing up. That's one. The second is another set of techs that disappeared from the asteroid belt on Arcturus. We're pretty sure they were hydrocarbon specialists. That data follows. Close hold as always, Semper Fi, Marine."

Fargo leaned back, "Um, this one... I don't know, I guess it also falls into your expertise." Spinning the unit around he said, "My numbers are eight three four six alpha romeo two four eight. You'll need them to read that, and I guess I better add you to the access for the other cube."

Nicole started the holo then stopped it, pushed a couple of selections and restarted it. Fargo saw General Cronin and heard him say, springing some Gustavs loose for you, along with appropriate ammunition for it."

Looking at him, she asked, "Gustav? What the hell is that?"

Fargo chuckled, "How about a nine hundred year old weapon?" Nicole's eyes widened as he said, "It's a man portable, as in unarmored, eighty-four mil recoilless *rifle*, if you will."

Nicole said, "Eighty-four millimeter? Really?"

Holding his fingers a little more than three inches apart, he continued, "Eighty-four. A little over three inches. Anti-personnel, anti-armor, mortar, rocket propelled, good out to at least a thousand yards, or further depending on the uses. It's either datacomp controlled or lace controlled, but you have to load the individual rounds. We used it extensively in the Marines. Love that damn gun! It bailed us out of more than one shitty situation."

Nicole nodded, "Okay. I believe." Ducking her head, she restarted the holo, as Fargo snuck out to the fresher. He came back a few minutes later with a coffee bulb for each of them, courtesy of Holly, and dropped hers gingerly on the desk. She distractedly picked it up as he noted she'd put the holo back on the privacy setting.

He'd finished his bulb by the time she finally sat back, "Woof, that is a lot of data. No, you probably shouldn't have shown that to me, but I doubt you would have grasped all the nuances of it. The general's bottom line, along with his intel weenies, is that both the ice and probably hydrocarbons are being mined illicitly in our sector. The big question is, how the hell are we supposed to find them?"

"I can reach out to the GalScouts; I've still got a few connections there. They might be able to provide me info that GalPat and the Marines don't have. Data sharing on new discoveries doesn't always get across the fence, if you know what I mean."

***

OneSvel pushed the data cube back across the desk and extruded a pseudopod, touching Fargo gently on the temple, *We'll send a priority request up the chain, we should have an answer in a couple of days. Your pharmacope is low, what have you done to yourself?*

Fargo projected, *Stupid, I shot a twenty mil almost two hundred times. Shoulder is bruised. Pretty stiff still.*

OneSvel extruded another pseudopod, probing the shoulder gently, *How long ago?*

Four days now. "Ouch!"

OneSvel said aloud, "Medbox for you. Not bruised, torn muscle. Two hours to repair, minimum."

Fargo groaned, "I'm supposed to be at dinner in an hour. Can I come back after dinner?"

OneSvel waved a pseudopod, "Not satisfactory, but understood. Females of your species have ultimate power over males."

Fargo rolled his eyes, "I like to tell myself, not always."

OnSvel's GalTrans made a noise that sounded suspiciously like a laugh.

***

Hyderabad had returned from wherever they had gone, calling in system fourteen divs ago. Mikhail agreed to fly Fargo and Nicole out to the Enclave, "I've never actually been there since the initial setup. Probably not a bad idea to visit, and check on the status of the systems."

Mikhail set the shuttle down well away from the *Hyderabad,* and whistled as he walked down the ramp, "Now *that* is a parking job!"

Fargo and Nicole laughed, "Evie is that good. I'll bet the pads aren't a foot off where they were last time." Lal came limping toward them and Fargo said, "Lal is the head man; he's the one you need to talk to." Mikhail nodded and headed toward him, as Fargo and Nicole walked toward the weapons building, carrying their equipment bags. Fargo was wearing his uniform and kukri this time, having vowed not to screw *that* up again.

Jiri met them with a grin, "We're full up on armor, plus spares! And three quarters of a million rounds of ammo between all the weapons. I've set up a training schedule that has everybody doing fams and checkout on the armor. We might as well check them all, and I've got you two slotted for fourteen to sixteen with Horse, including a half div on the range."

Nicole looked up at Jiri, "Is there a junior version for me?"

Jiri laughed, "Chief, you're bigger than some of our troops." Waving his hand, he said, "Any suit will fit anyone. I understand you have an intel brief for us?"

Nicole nodded, "Yes, I've put together what Fargo provided with some stuff I've collected here. I need about an hour."

Jiri pulled up his datacomp, "Hmmm, nineteen to twenty? After dinner?"

Nicole laughed, "You just want me to put everyone to sleep, don't you?"

***

Fargo knelt the armor a little after sixteen, popped the hatch, and groaned as he stretched and disconnected the waste connections. He climbed down and shivered as the cold wind hit his sweat soaked undersuit. He started jogging toward the weapons building and the showers and caught up with Nicole halfway there, "How did your session go?"

Nicole shrugged, "Fairly well. I can run the suit, but that's not what I'm good at." She glanced at him, "What were you doing, contortions in there? No wonder all armor smells as bad as it does!"

Fargo switched sides so he was downwind of her, "Well, *some* of us actually work our armor, not just walk around in it."

Nicole glanced at him and replied, "Women know how to work smarter, not harder." With that, she sprinted the rest of the way to the weapons building, giving Fargo a good view of her very nice backside. He grinned and picked his pace up, but stayed behind her all the way.

***

Fargo looked around the room as Nicole gave the brief. It was crowded with nearly the whole settlement jammed in one room, but he and Lal figured they could use the input from all the adults. Besides, it wasn't like most of the others, both men and women, had been soldiers in their own right. Mikhail was also on one side, as his travels around Hunter might have picked something up too.

Nicole stopped the holo, "So, in summary, there are a number of indicators that in fact Traders are in this sector, if not actually in this system. There have been at least eleven different *sightings*, if you will, of unknown/unusual actors, and a few ships on Hunter itself."

One of the women tentatively raised her hand, "Chief, if we travel to other than Rushing River, could we be watching, too?"

Nicole remembered her, "Yes, of course, Sushma. Any chat you pick up in the markets, or when you're shopping or trading could be of interest. Many of you are veterans, so you can recognize Spanglish, which is the prime language that the Traders use. It's not hard and fast, but it's a pretty damn good indicator. I'd also like to ask the men, women, and datacomp-literate kids to be looking for anything unusual in the e-tainment or messaging systems."

Fargo saw a couple of very young kids, maybe teens glancing at each other and smiling, and he shuddered, thinking Nicole had just unleashed something she might not like on the world. Cyberstalking and hacking were still a problem, even eight hundred years since the invention of computers.

First Inspection

Fargo's e-tainment system pinged, "INCOMING MESSAGE. IMPORTANCE HIGH. Fargo sighed, "Now what? Display message."

F- PALETTE, R MAJ
T- FARGO, E MIL CPT
S- INSPECTION
R- GALPAT OPORD 28240536, GALPAT DET HUNTER MSG 28240614

GALPAT COL KEADS AND TEAM WILL INSPECT MILITIA UNIT 28241205 0800. FULL INSPECTION INCL CAPABILITY, WEAPONS, PAPERWORK, ABILITY TO DEPLOY. CERTIFICATION SUBJECT TO INSPECTION. TEAM WILL REQUIRE WORKSPACE, FOOD (SEE ATTACHED FOR SUITABLE RATIONS), BILLETING (SEE ATTACHED FOR SUITABLE QUARTERS) FOR TWO DAYS.

S/PALETTE

Fargo groaned, "Oh, shit. This is all I need." As he started to open the attachments, a second message overrode the first in red script.

FARGO THIS IS CAPT JACE.

DO NOT LET THEM KNOW YOU HAVE
ARMOR. THEY DO NOT HAVE A NEED TO
KNOW AT THIS POINT IN TIME. HAVE
GHORKAS BLOCK OFF BACK OF WEAPONS
BUILDING. DO NOT RELEASE ALL INTEL TO
THEM. HAVE LEVESQUE BRIEF ON ONLY
INTEL PROVIDED BY GALPAT. THERE ARE
REASONS.

JACE OUT.

Fargo sat up sharply, prompting Canis to start
barking, and Cattus to come up snarling, "Cool it you
two! Down!" Canis rumbled, but lay back down, while
Cattus prowled to the window and looked out, tail
lashing. *Now what the hell do I do? And how the hell
did Jace, oh never mind... Guess the first thing to do is
send the inspection message to Jiri, Nicole and Lal. I
wonder...* Glancing at the clock he noted it was only
twenty-one. *In for a credit, in for a thousand...*
    "Comm link. Search Mankajiri Rai, voice and
visual. Connect." The e-tainment system went to snow
as it worked to complete the connection. Finally he
heard, Jiri accept the call.
    Jiri looked askance at Fargo over the link, "What's
up Fargo?"
    "Did you get a message from Palette at White
Beach?
    "No, should I have?"

"I hoped you would have, standby one. Attach Palette message to this connect," Fargo heard a ping as the message was attached, "Read that. Bottom line is we're getting inspected." He saw Jiri's eyes track off to the side and assumed he was reading it on a corner of his system. When he came back, Fargo asked, "Do you folks have space to house all those people they want to bring?"

Jiri nodded, "We can, it's not luxury, but it's a roof and beds."

Fargo nodded, "Copy all. As far as I'm concerned, the food thing is BS, they'll eat what everybody else eats." As he said that, he wiggled his fingers in the old Marine finger codes, *Do you remember this?*

Jiri glanced off screen, then answered in code, *Yes,* "We're not long on food. Mostly basic stuff. We aren't into the luxury items."

Fargo quickly passed Jace's message in code as he said, "Looks like we've got three days to put this together. I've never been through a GalPat inspection…"

Jiri said, "We've got at least five or six former inspectors here. We've got that handled." In code he answered, *no problem. Int brief your prob. We will hide, and brief all.*

"Okay, I'll put that in your hands. Who will handle the loggie side?"

Jiri laughed, "Horse of course. Adhit will take care of the admin, along with a couple of the women. Of course they won't get any *official* credit."

Fargo chuckled, "Okay, I'll fly down to Rushing River tomorrow morning, get Nicole up to speed, and come up tomorrow afternoon, if that's acceptable."

Jiri grinned, "Works. Remember to bring your kukri."

Fargo sighed, "I'm never going to be allowed to live that down, am I?"

Jiri laughed, "Nope! Disconnect." The screen went to snow and Fargo sat back down, wondering how Jiri would hide the armor. He forwarded the message to Nicole, fed the animals, and headed to bed, pondering how to get through the inspection.

***

The shuttle landed at the Enclave and Fargo and Nicole stepped off the aft ramp, waved to Mikhail, and walked up the hill to the weapons building. Nicole cocked her head, "Boxes?"

Fargo looked up and realized there was a line of people snaking toward the door, boxes in hand, "Yep, boxes. I don't know why, but I guess we'll find out."

They got into the building between two women carrying boxes, dumped their gear bags in the office, then wandered back toward the armor storage, listening to the babble of voices and occasional curses that resonated from the back of the building.

"Make sure your boxes are marked! At least ten boxes per family. If you don't have ten, grab an empty, fold it and mark it, cm'on people!" They couldn't see who was yelling but it did sound like Adhit. As they stepped through the door, they were met with a wall of boxes that stretched almost to the roof, with an eight foot passageway down the center of the room.

Nicole sniffed, "Oh, curry powder! And cinnamon." She sniffed again, "And no smell of armor. Oh, well played!"

They continued to the back of the room, passing very narrow aisles that went all the way to the outside wall, again packed floor to ceiling with boxes. Near the double door, they found Adhit on a ladder, sweating as he stacked boxes up, another group were finishing off lower rows and two more stood by the ladder to move it with Adhit on it as the rows topped out. Adhit looked down, saw them and laughed, "Armor? What armor? We don't have no steenkin' armor."

Fargo laughed, "Amazing. If I didn't know better, I'd swear this was nothing but food storage from the smell."

Jiri walked up, "My wife is pissed, but I dumped one entire packet of her good curry powder and a half jar of cinnamon all over the place. If we're asked, and I'm sure we will be, this is a years' worth of food storage. We're Ghorka, so we're strange. Kinda like that old religion in the Americas that kept all that extra food and supplies for a year."

Fargo thought for a minute, "Oh, Mormons, I think. They were down in old Utah. Interesting concept, serves them well from what I hear on that planet they colonized. Can't remember the name of it…"

"Moroni?" Nicole asked.

"I think that's it. I thought Adhit was taking care of the admin stuff?"

Adhit replied, "All done. Me and my silent minions."

***

Colonel Keads, over six feet tall, looking like a model for a GalPat recruiting poster, came down the GalPat shuttle's ramp in working blacks with subdued emblems, closely followed by Major Palette in dress blacks, then the rest of the inspection party. Fargo called the militia to attention as the party approached, noting that none of them carried any bags off the shuttle. *First test? Are we supposed to offload their damn luggage?* Saluting the colonel, Fargo said, "Sir, First Company, Hunter Militia is formed and ready for inspection."

He heard Major Palette whisper to the colonel, "Sir, their uniforms are not correct, they…" The colonel made a hand motion, and Palette shut up quickly.

Colonel Keads returned the salute, "Impressive, Captain. Shall we inspect the troops?"

"Yes, sir. Company! Open… Ranks!" There was the usual shuffle as the company opened ranks and Nicole marched forward, datacomp in hand, "Chief Sergeant Levesque is my recorder, sir."

"Very well." He led off with Palette slipping in front of Fargo as they marched toward the first platoon. He stopped at Horse, conducted a cursory inspection and said, "Interesting guidon Captain. Is that supposed to be a Slashgator?"

Fargo stepped around Palette, replying, "Yes, sir. The company adopted it as their symbol. If you're familiar with the Ghorka…"

"Oh yes. I was *trained* by a Ghorka CSM many moons ago. I do note the gray uniforms appear to be new, good quality, and I see people wearing rank badges and knives."

"Sir, these are all Ghorka personnel and former GalPat soldiers, under contract to Grey Lady Security. Per their induction, they all retain their last rank held on active duty. The knives are kukris, and part of their culture. They were allowed them on active duty also."

Palette hissed, "Damn Grey Lady scum."

Horse just smiled at Palette, who physically recoiled away as the Colonel said, "Very well." He continued trooping the line until midway through the third platoon, "Kulbir? My God, it is you! And a warrant officer, no less!"

Warrant officer Kulbir Gupta smiled, "Looks like you've done pretty well for yourself, sir."

Keads stuck out his hand, then pulled Gupta into an embrace, pounding the smaller man on the back "This is the man I owe everything to. Without his training, I'd be long dead." Stepping back he continued, "This is pointless. These people are obviously inspection ready. Let's stop this nonsense, and move onto the rest of the inspection. Kulbir, would you please escort me?"

The warrant looked at Fargo, who nodded, "With pleasure sir. And how is Margaret? And Sampson and Paulette?"

***

Fargo finished the little range scenario the GalPat troops had set up, watched two more fire teams go through it, then walked back to the weapons building.

He grabbed a bulb of coffee, and started into the office, only to stop, "Oh, sorry. Didn't mean to interrupt."

Warrant Rai looked up from the bulb he was rolling in his hands, "Oh no problem, Captain. The armory inspection is already complete. We got a satisfactory. By the way, this is Warrant Hagan, I trained him as a puppy. He has no taste, he likes the old North American bourbon.

Warrant Hagan, crinkled his large moustache, "Can't stand that crap the Ghorks like. I'm old school."

Fargo grinned, "Middle America? Kentucky?"

Hagan unfolded from the chair as he smiled, "Oh yeah. CinciLouisville. Done a few things, ended up in ordnance. Liked it. Usual stuff here, Cap'n. Dirty guns, too much lube. Can't have a bunch of no count militia get a better score than a GalPat Armory."

Fargo hid a smile as he shook his head, "Guess I need to make these folks work harder, don't I?"

Rai and Hagan both laughed and Hagan said, "Still won't get anything more. Ain't gonna say shit about that armor you got in the back room, either."

Fargo nodded, "Well, if you will excuse me, I think I need to be elsewhere." Picking up his coffee bulb, he exited to quiet laughter. He stepped back into the hallway to hear a sharp female voice and headed toward the back room.

As he stepped through the door, he saw Major Palette reaching for one of the stacked boxes saying, "I need to check this for contraband."

Raakhi, Niak's wife, all four feet ten inches of her, reached up and slapped Palette's hand away, "No, this is community food for year. You no touch. What we have is none of your business."

He saw Rakkhi's other hand resting on her knife and wondered if Palette knew how close he was coming to getting his throat cut. Palette growled and started to reach for her as Fargo stepped forward, "I wouldn't Major, not if you value your life. She'll cut you in a heartbeat and you won't survive it. If you hurt her, you won't survive that either."

Palette rounded on him, "I'm doing my *job*, *Captain*," he spit.

"Really? Looks to me like you're prying into private things you have no right to. This may be part of the weapons building, but it's not weapons. That ended at the hall door. Now, I'd suggest you leave before you really screw up."

Palette growled again, then stomped back down the hallway to yell at Warrant Hagan. Rakkhi grinned at Fargo, "Ekavir, why you spoil all my fun?"

***

Fargo and Colonel Keads stood outside the weapons building, sipping their bulbs of coffee. The colonel turned to Fargo, "You know, you've got probably the best militia in the galaxy here. I wish I could convince about half of them to move elsewhere on Hunter, if for nothing else to strengthen the other militia companies. We'll be leaving shortly, there's no point in continuing this charade here."

Fargo smiled, "Thank you, Colonel. You know I didn't have a damn thing to do with this. I'm just the token officer."

Keads laughed, "Well, they obviously respect you. That' more than I…" He was interrupted by his wrist comp with an alert tone. Punching the acknowledgment he said, "Keads, go ahead."

"Dispatch Colonel, I've got an emergency comm from Thomas and Bakkar. They are taking fire ,and requesting support over at Delhi on that honor killing pickup. Ack?"

Keads growled, "Dammit! Acknowledge." Turning to Fargo, he asked, "Can you put a reaction force together in less than an hour? If we have to fly back to White Beach to pick up our personnel…"

Fargo yelled, "Jiri! First Platoon reaction force. Soft armor, live fire support to GalPat. Delhi." He turned to the colonel, "Give me fifteen minutes, and I'll have you a team ready. I need to grab my gear.

Operations

Fargo could smell the heat on the outside of the shuttle as it burned back down into atmosphere. Whoever was driving was damn good. They'd done a max boost to get high, and supersonic as soon as they'd loaded. He was still pissed at Nicole for tagging along, but she did have a point. He didn't speak any of the Hindi languages, and she spoke all of them.

All they knew was that the two GalPat troops and a magistrate were pinned down near the square in Delhi. There had been an honor killing of a daughter of one of the local powers, which was strictly outlawed on Hunter. Apparently, the Patels had brought in two different sects to work their lands, and love had jumped the sects.

The colonel had accompanied them, along with Major Palette and Warrant Hagan, with the major now waiting in GalPat battle armor. The shuttle came in hard and fast, the aft ramp pointed away from the direction of incoming fire as a flat female voice called possible shooters in the two story building facing the plaza and the trapped men.

"Ten seconds to grounding," the loadmaster called as the aft ramp started down.

First Platoon deployed quickly from the aft ramp, followed by the colonel and warrant, as the major slowly clomped down the ramp. As soon as Palette was down, the colonel called, "Okay Boykin, lift and hold. You're weapons tight."

A laconic, "Roger," came back as the ramp started up, and the shuttle lifted. The colonel and warrant hustled toward their troops, as Fargo deployed First Platoon in an urban combat spread. His intent was to get behind the building with the shooter or shooters, and root them out at close range.

Yash, the sniper, and Kamadev, his spotter, were looking for height to provide overwatch as the rest of the platoon, Horse in the lead on one side of the street with two squads, and Adhit in the lead of the other two squads, bounded down a side street that would bring them behind the two story building where the shooters were. Coming to a cross street, they rotated and moved down it quickly.

Stacking up at the corner, Fargo moved forward, peeking around the corner at knee height. He keyed his comm, "Can't see the back door, blocked by a building, but we know there is an alley between them. I see two windows that face us. Nothing in either window. Two choices; bum rush as a group, or split and half go one more street over to cover from that side." Fargo thought for a second, then said, "Naik, take your half of the platoon, go one more block. We'll cross and hold, until you're in position."

Naik replied, "Horse is riding. On me." He charged across the street at a dead run, sweeping both sides of the street as he went, closely followed by the rest of the troops. Adhit nodded at Fargo and moved swiftly but quietly across the street and into cover by the houses as they edged forward until he was just back of the alley. Fargo eased forward until he was two feet behind Adhit.

As Horse called in position, he heard Nicole's soft, "Shit. Look at that asshole."

Fargo took a second to figure out what she was talking about as Palette came lumbering up the street in battle armor and keyed his PA system, "You in there, you are surrounded. Throw out your weapons and surrender. There is no chance of escape. If you do not throw down your weapons, *I* will fire on you with my weapons in ten, nine..."

Fargo made an instantaneous decision, "Go, go, go! We've got to get to the back door before they do." Adhit took off at a dead run, getting a couple of yards lead on everyone else in the two squads. Fargo, huffing along, saw Horse and his squads pounding up the alley from the other side of the building, and he said, "'Ware crossfire."

Adhit got to the door just as it flew open and a figure emerged, there was a bang and Adhit dropped to the ground. Fargo had his rifle up ready to fire, but as he started to press the trigger, Horse, kukri out, yelled something and cut down hard. The man slumped and Horse hacked at him again, grabbed something and charged into the building. Fargo yelled into the comm, "We have building entry in the rear, do not, repeat do not fire into building. We are clearing from the rear." Fargo glanced at Adhit as he went by, hoping he was just stunned, "Medic up. Adhit is down at the rear door."

Fargo and Ganju paired up and cleared the lower floor, room by room, only to find it empty. Fargo heard a couple of shots from the second floor, but he couldn't be in both places and had to trust Horse and the others to clear it. He heard a weird noise like someone screaming a prolonged "Nooooo", followed by what sounded like amplified retching and sobbing.

He and Ganju finished the first floor, and Fargo jumped up the stairs, not knowing what he would find. As he cleared the landing, he could see Horse standing near the front windows, head down. Fearing he was also injured, he bolted down the hallway, not bothering to clear any rooms. As he approached Horse, he said, "Angel six." Horse merely nodded, and Fargo saw that Horse had his kukri in his right hand, blood dripping from it. "Are you hit, Naik?" he asked.

Horse turned slowly, "They tried. The armor worked. That should be me at the back door, not Adhit. He was always proud he could outrun me." Fargo glanced around the room and saw three headless bodies, trails of blood going toward the broken out window.

Fargo said, "We don't know that Adhit…"

Horse said dully, "Adhit is dead. I saw the bastard shoot him at an upward angle, and blood blossom in the helmet." Waving his arm, "These do not pay for Adhit. There is one more head that I will take."

Fargo said gently, "Let's clear for now." Over the comm he said, "Building is secure. We are exiting the rear, and will come around the north side." He led Horse back down the stairs, out of the back door, noting Adhit was no longer lying on the dirt. He saw nothing but anger in the faces of the other troops. Looking at Nicole, he saw tears in her eyes as she shook her head sadly. It suddenly hit him that he'd lost another troop.

He saw red and charged around the side of the building, looking for someone to kill. As he cleared the front, he saw four heads laying in the street, one of them a woman. Ignoring them, he continued toward Colonel Keads, who was standing with a short, fat, dark skinned man who was berating him for the vicious attack on his property.

Fargo slid behind the man, locked an arm around his neck and started drawing his kukri, only to feel someone pinning his arm. He looked over to see Horse, smiling, "No, this one is mine. Release him please."

Fargo dropped his arm, stepping back, as Horse walked around in front of the man, "Patel, your life is forfeit."

Patel gibbered at Horse, then turn to the colonel, "You cannot let this scum talk to me this way! I am a property owner and rich man! He has killed four of my employees and *he* should be owing me money for their lives!"

Colonel Keads looked at him curiously, "Patel, you brought this on yourself. I just got a dump of your file, and the cooperative's files. You were banned from emigrating to New Mumbai due to your actions on Earth Four. Somehow, you got a contract for Hunter, which specifically prohibited you from bringing more than one sect with you. You lied, somehow kept the two sects apart on the trip out, probably with stasis. Warrant tells me you've set the one sect up as basically slave labor, again contrary to the cooperative paperwork. Then you apparently *approved* the honor killing…"

"It's my *right*! I own…"

Horse stepped closer, his smile getting bigger, "No, *I* own you. One of mine died, now you are forfeit to me. Colonel, may I?"

Keads rubbed his chin, turned to Warrant Hagan who nodded slightly, then turned back, "Yes, but first we must gather the heads of the two sects here. Captain, can you make that happen?"

"With pleasure," Fargo growled. Keying his comm, he said, "First Platoon, in pairs. Locate and bring leaders of both sects here, now."

Ten pairs of grim Ghorka fanned out through the town. Twenty minutes later, eight men and women stood nervously in front of the colonel, along with Patel's richly dressed and perfumed wife and two children. Patel's wife was in shock, obviously not understanding what had brought her and her children down to the level of the common people.

The colonel had been busy on his datacomp, in addition to talking with the warrant. Major Palette having gone back to the shuttle, which was now sitting in the plaza with weapons ports open.

With one last entry on his datacomp, Keads looked around at not only the eight standing in front of him, but the fifty or so curious individuals who were standing nearby. He said, "Boykin, gimme PA." With a pop, the shuttle's PA system came on, and Keads said, "In accordance with GalPat standards, Patel's cooperative is now found in violation of contract. Said contract is null and void. As the de facto approver of the honor killing of one Fathi Khanna, he is guilty as an accessory to murder. With the death of militia member Adhit Rai, he is guilty of accessory to murder of a peacekeeper. I hereby sentence him to death, to be carried out now in the presence of both sects." Nicole took over the PA and repeated the decision and sentence in two different Hindi dialects, to make sure everyone understood what was happening.

Turning to Horse, he said, "If you would be so kind?"

Smiling, Horse raised his kukri and sliced three times, caught Patel's head as it flopped free, and held it up with a cry of triumph. Keads turned back to Patel's quivering wife, "You will be sent back to Earth Four, along with your children. Your lands will be split equally between the two sects you imported in violation of the cooperative agreement. You will be allowed one hundred pounds of lift apiece. You have four hours to collect what you would take."

***

Fargo stood on the bank of the freshet that tumbled down from the Green below the Enclave, staring morosely at the funeral pyre built on the edge of the water. *First fucking mission and I get one of my best troops killed, lucky shot or not. I never should have taken this damn position. I don't ever want to write another letter to a wife or mother. I still cannot believe Ujjwala hugged me and said Adhit had died with honor, and I wasn't at fault.* He felt himself shaking in anger, and was surprised to feel a hand on his elbow. He glanced over to see Nicole standing next to him, a single tear rolling down her cheek.

"It's not your fault Ethan, there was no way to know that would happen, or that it was even possible for someone to die that way. Freak accident is what it was. The one perfect angle that round had to take to glance off the plate, and slide up the seam to his head."

Fargo tasted her emotions and knew she *believed* exactly what she was saying, but that didn't ease the pain, "No, he died because I put him on point. That should have been me. I can't do this, I just…"

The priest and Aadi, Adhits' son marched down the bank to the pyre. Aadi, all of thirteen standard years old, touched the first torch to his father's funeral pyre. He turned to Fargo and offered the torch, as Horse and Lal took up two other torches. He hesitated until he felt a gentle push from Nicole, then took the torch and went to the unoccupied corner of the pyre. The three of them simultaneously touched their torches to the pyre, then he followed Horse and Lal in extinguishing the torch as the pyre's flames grew.

He went back to stand by Nicole, thankful that the winds were blowing away from them, as the fire leapt higher and higher, until Adhit's body was consumed. The priest continued his prayers as the fire burned lower, as Nicole translated that the family would now go into eleven days of mourning. Fargo wondered how long his mourning would take, as he added Adhit to his list of dead troops…

***

Nicole turned to Fargo at the door of the Copper Mug, "Can you, would you stay with me please?"

He looked down at her, "What?"

"I don't want to be alone. Not tonight. Please, just to sleep."

"Nicole, I…"

"Please. I don't want nightmares tonight, please."

Fargo sighed, "Only sleep."

An hour later, Fargo lay on his back, Nicole's head on his shoulder as she murmured softly in her sleep. He was doing every blocking exercise he could think of to not read her thoughts, cussing himself for getting into this bag of worms, and thinking, *No, just stop it. This can't end well. Stop frikkin thinking. Just go to sleep. Imagine it's Canis or Cattus next to you. Just stop it!*

The next morning he woke to find his arm around Nicole, and her looking at him with a smile, "Thank you for being a gentleman. Now can you let go of me? I need the fresher."

Fargo jerked his arm away, blushing, "Sorry. I didn't…"

Nicole laughed sadly, "Well, at least we're sleep compatible, and I didn't have a single nightmare. That's better than the fleet average." She got off the bed, and disappeared into the fresher. Fargo jumped up, quickly got dressed, then walked into the restaurant part of the building searching for a bulb of coffee.

***

Colonel Keads said, "So in summary, the Patel clan is gone, we've turned their house into a barracks for the unmarried males of both sects and peace bonded them, under penalty of death. Did the same for both sects for any honor killings."

Fargo saw nods from the split screen of Nicole and Jiri and others at the Enclave, "That's good, but what about keeping the peace? Are we going to be on the hook for that?"

Keads leaned back, smiling, "No, but you're the threat I'm holding over them. The four that Horse…?" He looked down at his notes, "Yes, Horse beheaded turned out to be the father, mother, and two brothers of the Fathi Khanna. We've pretty much let it *slip*, if you will, that the Ghorkas will be happy to repeat that *education* if it happens again. Any questions?"

Fargo smiled, "Good. Just one question here, Colonel."

"Go."

"There were some weird noises as we were clearing the building, I was wondering what the source was."

The colonel looked around furtively, "Ah, that was the major. He forgot to turn off the PA on his armor. Apparently, he was, shall we say, *mildly upset* when heads started coming out the window. It seems he has a rather weak stomach. Of course, *he* said he must have had a touch of food poisoning..."

Sightings

Fargo was enjoying the sunshine on the porch, idly throwing the rawhide chew for Canis and working on the link with her, as Cattus lolled in a patch of sunshine, belly up. *Fetch* he projected, only to have Canis look at him, sit, and scratch. Throwing up his hands, he said, "Okay, dog. You're on your own there."

Suddenly his wrist comp beeped an alert. Fargo glanced down and tapped it to clear the alert, only to have it reoccur moments later. Grumbling, he got up and walked in the cabin, flopped down on the chair and punched up the e-tainment console. "Display alert."

The system displayed the header from Captain Jace, a coded string of numbers, followed by the words, DOWNLOAD ONLY. Fargo slid a data chip into the console, hit acknowledge and heard the console click, then spit the chip out. *Huh, wonder why...* Sliding the chip back in he hit display, UNABLE TO LOAD- DECRYPTION REQUIRED popped up. "Dammit."

Fargo got up, dug out his standalone e-reader, powering it up, "Let's see if this one will work." The holo formed, the word NUMBERS swam up, *Ah crap, now what? What the hell is Jace sending me that is so…* "Ethan Fargo, eight three four six alpha romeo two four eight."

The holo rotated to show Hunter from what appeared to be a satellite image, but not from the space station's location. Some streaks that appeared to be tracks displayed, but none of them went to the regular spaceports. They seemed to concentrate in one location, well away from any terraformer, in the high northern latitude northeast of Rushing River. A string of numbers followed. As far as he could tell, it was track origins, dates, times, and maybe duration.

He shook his head in frustration, then bumped the holo forward, now it showed an IR shot of what looked like a depression, a ship, some kind of opening in the side of the depression, and what appeared to be people on the ground, "Gah, this is about useless. I don't even know what I'm looking at." Tapping the e-tainment console, he said, "Priority message, Nicole Levesque."

It found Nicole's address, popping up a message blank, and he continued, "Have something you need to see. Are you available in two hours? Send and disconnect."

Fargo pulled the data chip out, got up, and headed out the door to the storage unit. Pulling the liteflyer out, he configured it for flight, then went back in and hit the autochef for a coffee bulb. Figuring he would be gone for at least four or five hours, he loaded the animals' food dishes and carried them out to the porch, then brought the water dishes out.

His wrist comp pinged, and he tapped it. A message from Nicole scrolled across it, SURE. I'LL

BE AT THE WINERY. REPLY REQUIRED? He smiled, "Yes, on the way. Will need reader. Send."

***

Fargo flew quickly down to the spaceport, after releasing Canis and Cattus to go wherever they went when he left. When he arrived, he decided to take a quick detour on the way to the winery, and stopped by the clinic, finding OneSvel there by himself.

He quickly passed the data chip to him, "This is hot. I think this is possibly a Goon outpost here on Hunter. Can you push it up to higher?"

OneSvel took the chip in a pseudopod, slipped it into his datacomp and copied it as he chittered into the GalTrans, "Not until I get relieved here. I will get it out tonight, but I'm not sure how long it will take to get through channels. Where did you get it?"

"It came from an anonymous source, let's just leave it at that. It's a source that I can't compromise, at least not right now."

Waving his pseudopod, OneSvel chittered, "Well, without attribution, they will probably downgrade it."

"Understood. You have anything for me?

"Nothing. Whom will you share this with?"

"Chief Levesque. She's the militia intel person. She may be able to figure this out, and know who to get it to."

OneSvel gave the chip back, chittering, "Maybe, but she will have the same problem with attribution."

Fargo shrugged, "Well, I can only do what I can."

***

Nicole looked up from the hologram, "Did you know this place existed?" When Fargo shook his head, she said, "I'm betting this is a Trader outpost. It follows their pattern. Get boots on the ground, establish a presence, then claim it for the Goons."

She rolled the holo back, pointed at the tracks, "These are all direct approaches, not orbitals. They're coming in hot, and burning down to stay directly opposite the space station, so there isn't any tracking." She looked up at him, "So how did Jace get these? This is over a month's worth of data, but the IR shots are two days old. They aren't even here, are they?"

"I don't know. The big question is, what do we do with this? Turn it over to the Patrol? And how the hell do I explain it? Or do we try to get more information? Put some bodies on the ground? But if they have sensors…"

Nicole shook her head, "No, *we* don't put people on the ground. That's the Patrol's job. How do we explain it? We don't. Give it to me, and I'll submit it through the intel channel. Nobody outside that channel will be cleared to see the raw, and nobody with any sense inside is going to ask. That's just not done if you're not directly involved."

"Okay, push it up. The only question we don't have an answer to is whether there is a Dragoon enclave there or not. If one is, then they are going to try to claim Hunter sooner or later."

Nicole shuddered, "I don't want to lose everything I have, nor do I want to be a slave to them. I've seen the reports of what happens to women under their control."

Nicole did something with the data, then embedded it into a picture of the winery,

Steganography? Is that... "How safe is that?" Fargo asked.

Nicole looked up, "This?" Pointing to the screen, she added, "Even if the bad guys intercept it, they don't have either key, so it's perfectly safe." She added a few words about how the winery was progressing, pressed send and the message cleared from the screen.

"How is that possible? And how will the person that gets it know the keys?"

Nicole chuckled, "Basic intel weenie training... It's called Kerckhoff's desideratum which states that a cryptosystem should be secure even if everything about the system except the key is public knowledge." Waving her hand at the datacomp, she said, "It was a basic exercise we did for the entire time we were in school. If you got caught, you got set back a week for each catch. *I* never got caught."

"But how did you send the key?"

"I didn't. The person I sent it to is one of my classmates, she's still active, and I used the same key we've always had. Nobody could ever figure it out," she said with a laugh. Wagging her finger at him she continued, "Not telling. Don't ask." Handing the chip back to Fargo she asked, "Want to see the ancient stuff I use to make wine here?"

***

Nicole said, "So that's the winery. Granted, most of the equipment is four hundred years old, but it was never set up until I got here three years ago. I figure it will last through both my and Holly's lifetimes, except for that damn bottle maker."

Fargo smiled, "I'm amazed you were able to get all those grapes trained like that, much less figured out which is which!"

Nicole laughed, "Well, when you grow up looking at vines, it's pretty easy. The mechs make it even easier, since they do all the trimming, picking, and autosorting." As they walked into the main building she added, "All of this is basically automated too, I just do some fine tuning based on the sugar content, and what I want the wine to taste like."

Nicole's wrist comp pinged, "Ah, an answer to my message. Let's go back to the house." She led the way back to the house, brought her e-tainment system up, chuckling, "It's in the system. Now we wait. Gotta love FTL messaging!"

Fargo glanced at the message on the screen and asked, "How do you know from that? It just looks like a throwaway... Never mind, not asking."

Nicole glanced at the system and said, "You hungry? How would you like a home cooked meal?"

"Home cooked?"

"Yes, home cooked. I actually *do* cook, not just autochef. Neardeer medallions, sauce, Asparagus and rice? It won't take long."

Fargo's mouth watered, "Oh hell yes. Please!"

***

Fargo leaned back in the chair, "That was... Magnificent! Where did you learn how to cook like that? I never learned how..."

Nicole laughed, "Genied hostess, remember? And I actually enjoy cooking, I just hate cleaning up afterward."

Jumping up, Fargo picked up the dishes, "I'll gladly do KP as a payback for that meal."

With the dishes done, they settled comfortably in the living room, talking about what might happen with the data that had been forwarded. Fargo sensed Nicole relaxing and she began telling him about her family and why she'd run away. She segued into her training, marriage, and how she'd ended up on Hunter.

Fargo shared his history up to the point of battle for the Vega system, but stopped short of describing the loss of most of his company, instead saying, "Wow, I guess I better get going. It's getting late."

Nicole stretched luxuriously, "You're welcome to stay the night. I wouldn't want to try to fly back into the Green at night in a basic liteflyer. I've got a spare bedroom."

He thought about it for a few seconds, "It won't be an issue with Holly?"

"She lives in the old house. She says she likes her privacy. I think she just doesn't want me to tell her to pick up after herself. Damn girl is messy as hell," she grumbled. "Should have put her in the military back in the day."

Fargo laughed, "Yeah, that *does* teach you how to pick up after yourself. Sure, if you don't mind?"

"Not at all, but you get autochef for breakfast. I'm not a morning person."

***

Fargo made a quick trip through the fresher, looked around, then dumped his shipsuit, undies and socks in for a cleaning, figuring it wouldn't make a difference how he slept.

Two hours later, he was in the middle of an erotic dream of making love to Nicole when he came awake, realizing it wasn't a dream as Nicole gave a little scream and collapsed on top of him, "Oh God, I needed... Oh my God! You're a psi!" He felt her mind slam closed with a block as she shuddered one more time, "You bastard!" She beat on his chest as she drew a deep breath, "How could you do that to me?"

Confused and stunned, he asked, "What did I do?"

"Not tell me you're a psi! Now you know everything! Oh God, I felt your mind, I saw..."

Fargo hugged her, "I'm sorry, I never meant..."

Nicole sat up, "Oh well, in for a credit, in for a million."

Fargo said, "I thought it was in for a thousand?"

Nicole laughed and wiggled, "Men..."

Fargo felt himself respond, and he stroked her softly as they made love again.

***

Fargo stretched as well as he could with Nicole lying half on top of him, snoring gently. His arm was asleep and tingling. He slowly worked it out from under her and eased out of bed, padding quietly to the fresher. Dialing it to rejuve, he set his clothes out and climbed in, reveling in the feel of the sprays of water and infrared.

Climbing out, he dressed quickly, noting that Nicole was gone. He hesitated, not sure what to do or say, sighed and headed for the autochef. Punching up a bulb of coffee, he sat silently at the table, *What the hell happened last night? I know that wasn't a dream, but I don't know what I feel. It's been too long. Lust? Hell yes... But what do I do now? I...*

Nicole came into the kitchen, punched up one of her cappuccinos, and turned to Fargo as she leaned against the counter, "Second thoughts?"

He looked up at her, "Honestly, I don't know what I'm thinking."

She smiled ruefully, "Well, I *was* a little forward last night..."

"A *little*?"

"It's been a long time, at least for me. I trust you, Ethan, especially now that I know you're a psi. I also know how badly you've been hurt, and how long it's been for you, too. I felt that when we connected. Last night can either be the start of something good between us, or a one-time thing. It's your choice."

The autochef dinged and her bulb dropped into the tray, giving him time to frame an answer. "I liked what we had, and yes, I'd like to see you again. That isn't an issue, at least for me. But I wonder what..."

Nicole interrupted, "Holly isn't an issue. She likes you, and has been pushing for me to find somebody. She keeps reminding me I'm not dead yet. I don't see it being an issue with Mikhail or Luann either, unless you know something I don't."

Fargo shook his head, "Nor do I. But our living arrangements..."

His wrist comp went off and Nicole's e-tainment system lit with INCOMING MESSAGE. IMPORTANCE HIGH, stopping both of them. They walked into the living room together as Nicole brought up the screen, "Display incoming message."

F- CAMERON, SJ COL
T- HUNTER MILITIA GROUP A
S- MEETING
R- GALPAT HUNTER OPORD 28240326
GALPAT HUNTER REQ MILIT CDRS AND
INTEL SECT HEADS FOR MTG AT HQ
TOMORROW AT 1800. URGENT MATTER OF
NAT'L INTEREST. BILLETING AVAILABLE.
COORD SHUTTLE TIMES-
NEWSYD 0800
ROSTOV 1000
RUSHRVR 1100
MANDATORY MTG. ALL ADDEES RESP REQ.
S/PALETTE FOR CAMERON

Fargo rogered up from his wrist comp as Nicole quickly replied that she would make an 1100 departure at the spaceport.

"Are you thinking what I'm thinking," Fargo asked.

Nicole cocked her head, "Maybe, but less than twenty-four divs is a quick turnaround, unless there is additional information we don't know about."

"I don't know, you're the expert."

Nicole shrugged, "Well, it's a principal of intel for the right hand to never let the left hand know what it's doing, so that's very possible this data tied in to… Something…"

Fargo replied, "Well, I better to talk to Mikhail. Meet you at the spaceport at 1030?"

Nicole nodded and hugged him, kissing him softly, "Thank you for last night."

He hugged her hard, "Thank you." He also felt her hard block still active, and wondered how she'd developed that capability, then remembered intel types were hypno'ed and trained for a lot of strange things.

***

Colonel Cameron turned the briefing over to a young, perky female lieutenant in GalPat blacks who started off, "Good afternoon, I'm Lieutenant Smythe. I'm the local planet intel officer for Hunter." Fargo tuned out the rest of her introduction, keying on Nicole, who was watching colonels Cameron and Keads. Both of them appeared to have not gotten a lot of sleep last night, and Cameron seemed the more nervous of the two.

His attention was yanked back when Smythe said, "The Trader killed at Rushing River, third party information forwarded and graded out as A-2, and sniffs of data transmissions have been collated with data developed by the Fleet. There are indicators there is at least one Dragoon detachment operating in secret from Hunter, and at least one or two more detachments operating in this star system. The Fleet is sending a strike group via Altair Four and Star Center. ETA here is two to three weeks. GalPat's direction is to not provoke any confrontations, try to take them out ourselves, or do anything that might alert them or their spies that we know about them."

After another hour of back and forth with the other militia commanders, Fargo was frustrated, tired of the

BS and ready to go. Turning to Nicole, he asked, "Why are we even here? This was… useless…"

"It's the game they play. This way the colonel can say, quote, he is keeping his fingers on the pulse of the planet and sitting on the militia to keep them from doing *things*, unquote. It will look good on his OER when he goes for his stars, or so he thinks."

Fargo rolled his eyes, "Fine, whatever. Let's see if we can get a ride back to Rushing River."

***

Fargo was literally neck deep in cleaning another Slashgator hide as Canis and Cattus rolled in the grass fighting over a rib bone. Suddenly both of them froze and looked off to the west, prompting him to quickly clean his hands and reach for his rifle. He saw an attack shuttle ghosting down the canyon, then pop up to land quickly on his meadow.

Telling the animals to stay and hide, he quickly wiped down as well as he could, then stepped quickly on the porch and grabbed the monocular hanging on the back of the chair. Focusing on the shuttle, he saw Colonel Keads coming down the ramp with a small redheaded female warrant officer.

Looking quickly over at the storage building, he didn't see either one of the animals. Relieved, he started jogging down the meadow toward the shuttle, only to be waved back by Colonel Keads who shouted, "We'll come to you. Stay put."

Shrugging, Fargo stopped where he was and waited. Keads and the redhead walked up, "Fargo, this is Warrant Boykin. She flew the lift when we went to Delhi."

He nodded, "Nice to meet you ma'am. Pardon me for not shaking hands, but I've been up to my… neck in Slashgator trying to clean a hide." Turning to Keads, he asked, "What can I do for you, Colonel?"

"A bulb of coffee would be nice, and someplace we can talk privately."

Fargo turned, "That I can do, come on up to the cabin. Coffee, Warrant?"

Boykin said in a flat voice, "Never turn down coffee. Donuts either."

Fargo glanced at her, and saw a smile lifting one corner of her mouth, "Coffee, and I'll see what the autochef can do about a, what did you call it, donut?"

Once they were seated around the table, Keads asked, "You have an offline datacomp?"

He nodded and dug the standalone unit out of the bottom of the e-tainment system. Placing it on the table, he picked up the bulbs of coffee from the autochef, handed them around and placed the strange looking pastry in front of Boykin. She looked at it skeptically for a second, then took a bite, "Not a donut, but a beignet is close enough. Thank you."

Fargo couldn't contain himself, asking, "Does this have something to do with the data from two weeks ago?"

Keads nodded, "It does. I'm here *unofficially*, in that Colonel Cameron doesn't know and I'm hoping you won't tell him."

He rocked back in his chair, "No, of course not." *Now isn't this interesting… Number two is bypassing number one? I fucking hate politics…*

Keads continued, "I'm actually the senior intel rep on Hunter, but in mufti, so to speak. We really need to get eyes on before the fleet gets here. I know your folks have real battle armor hidden away, and I want to insert a couple of scouts to check the location, if possible."

Slipping a cube in the datacomp, he called up a detailed overhead view of the site, let it run through one sequence, and then stopped the holo. "I spent a stealth to get this, passive only, two nights ago. Reorienting the display, he pointed out, "Looks like two sensors of some type, here and here, on top of the cliff and ridge that surround their outpost."

Fargo asked, "Confirmed outpost?"

Keads replied, "Yep, through other parties, but confirmed. At least two Dragoons on planet."

"Lovely," Fargo muttered.

"Now approaches, here, here and here," he pointed out three separate locations outside the rim of the ridge. "Boykin can drop your people far enough away to prevent counter detection, but that's going to mean a hike in. Figuring the drop at zero three, that would give four hours to get into some kind of hide for the day, maybe launch a Ferret or three in completely passive mode, spend the night checking for trips, sensors, anything of interest that might save a troop's life."

Fargo looked at Boykin, "How close do you figure you can get us?"

Boykin cocked her head, reoriented the holo, rescaled and said flatly, "No detection, six miles. Minimal detection opportunity, four miles. Drop would be five hundred or less. Other option is high and hot, drop you from suborbital, but even with stealth, your odds of detection exceed sixty percent. Not sure you want to trust a suit's anti-grav from eighty thousand."

Fargo shuddered, "Not only no, but *hell no!*" Curiously, he asked, "How do you know we can get in covert?"

Boykin half smiled, "Nape of the planet. Lots of canyons up there. We'd be down in the canyon on stealth. Unless we're seen visually, they'll never know we're there."

Fargo grinned sickly, "So, a bumpy ride?"

Boykin finally smiled, "What is that old Earth term? Ride 'em cowboy. You'd be locked in an external chute, I promise to pop you out on a flat piece of ground."

Site and Situation

Fargo dropped into the clinic, and he and OneSvel went into one of the exam rooms as Fargo said, "Need a little something for nausea, and need to get my ears checked for vertigo."

OneSvel extruded a pseudopod and lightly touched Fargo's temple, *What is going on?*

Fargo projected, *Colonel Keads, the number two on the planet is going to get us, well me and two others, inserted to try to scout this Goon outpost. Apparently, we're going in through the canyons and be spit out on a flat piece of ground. I'm really not wanting to spend two, three days in armor that I've puked in.*

When will this happen?

Tomorrow night. I need you to push this up in case things go to shit.

Fargo caught a bit of something from OneSvel's mind that he didn't think was complimentary and exasperation, then OneSvel projected, *Your pharmacope is topped off, but I will give you a nanoinject that should mitigate the nausea. Seventy-two divs you say?*

At least...

OneSvel extruded another pseudopod, rummaged it around in one cabinet, then another, then exuded two more that mixed something, and inserted it into an injector. His GalTrans said, "This should fix your balance and vertigo problems, sir. In any case I'd like to see you...

Doc Jenkins stuck his head in the exam room, "Oh, sorry. OneSvel, we need to get an order put together for the supply ship. As soon as you get through with Ethan, can you get on that?"

OneSvel answered, "Certainly, Doctor. Five minutes. Fargo has a minor ear infection that I'm treating with a nanosteroid injection."

Jenkins nodded, "Very well. Good to see you, Ethan."

OneSvel projected, *I will get this out tonight, but I do want to see you when you get back and have a report to forward on what you find.*

Will do. Does it bother you to play technician? You're probably far more qualified than Doc Jenkins.

OneSvel didn't do anything for a minute but prepare and then inject Fargo. Finally he projected, *Actually, it doesn't. Jenkins has eighty years of experience, a vast pool of knowledge that I could never get if I weren't here. He enjoys telling the stories, treats me better than I treated technicians, and I enjoy the interactions with basic humans. It is making me a better surgeon. More, what do you call it, empathic to conditions? I am also increasing my knowledge of diagnosis, since few here have laces or anything that assists in displaying the symptoms.*

Fargo nodded, *I'm glad, I was worried you would be frustrated, and want to go back to the GalScouts.*

OneSvel's GalTrans gave the equivalent of a Taurasian laugh, "Give this shot twelve divs to act, then you should be good."

***

Fargo had sent Cattus and Canis back to their respective packs early in the afternoon, then sat down and composed an 'if you are reading this' letter, and updated his will. Saving it to his datacomp and e-tainment message queue, he took the time to hit the fresher, eat a good dinner and brewed himself a cup of real coffee.

Just before ten, he stripped and hit the fresher one more time, then dressed in his undersuit, plugging the tubes in, and cursing them as he finally got everything seated. He walked gingerly out and sat on the front steps, looking up and the sky and marveling at the stars and moons, George and Celeste. They seemed so close you could almost touch them. *I wonder if this will be the last time I see them.*

Hearing the shuttle's approach, he turned the lights off and pulled the door closed, wondering if he would be back. *Stop that shit! Get your damn head in the game. If you don't your ass is dead anyway. Dammit, I forgot to message Nicole. Damn...*

The shuttle settled to the ground, groaning on the skids as the anti-grav came off and the aft ramp came down. He walked slowly toward it, inhaling one last scent of the nearpines as he stepped up the ramp when it thumped to the ground. The only people in the bay were a Kepleran crewchief, XMfsmer! And Ban and Shar. "Pop? Bahn, Shar good to see you. Y'all ready for this?"

Bahn and Shar smiled and chorused, "Fun times, we're ready."

Pop's GalTrans said, "Captain, we should mount up now. I have to insert you in your chutes."

Fargo nodded, "Let's do this. You're chief of the boat, Pop?"

XMfsmer! bared his teeth in what Fargo knew was a grin, "For ten years with the warrant. We're known as the little people crew."

Bahn added, "Other than you, Captain, we're *all* little people," as he climbed into his armor.

Fargo chuckled as he climbed in and wiggled into position, connected his evacuation lines, started the closing sequence and powered the armor up. He felt the snap as his neural lace connected to the suit's AI, and it responded, "Good evening, Captain. Are you ready for full power up?"

Fargo replied, "For now Cindy, but we will be going into stealth mode shortly. Please run all BIT checks now."

BIT checks completed, Fargo walked the armor down the ramp and around the side of the shuttle to the external chutes as Boykin continued her briefing, "There is an LEO constellation up for the next ninety-six divs, spread two hours apart. I've downloaded the sat tracks to your suits, they are passive receptors only, no confirmation receipts. Each of you has a broadcast window for burst transmissions only at two, four, and six after each even div."

Fargo watched Pop load Bahn and Shar into their respective chutes, then it was his turn. His comms popped as Pop selected his discrete, "Ready, Captain?

A little forward, half step left, okay easy up." Fargo bumped his anti-grav up a notch to seventy percent and felt Pop guide him into the chute as he armor lifted, "Hold what you have." Then heard the clank as the bottom of the chute closed.

"All chutes loaded WO. Raising ramp, we're clear to lift."

Fargo shifted to the shuttle's video cameras, hating the shut in feeling and looking for a way to see what was going on.

***

Boykin's voice came over the comms, "Go full stealth now. Entering canyons, ETA to drop, twelve minutes."

Fargo commanded, "Cindy, full stealth now. Burst transmit only on command. No active emissions, EMCON level two."

He watched the HUD as various systems changed colors from white to green and orange, then Cindy's voice said, "Full stealth configuration completed. Weapons cold. Disconnecting from ship net now."

Fargo's sense of claustrophobia closed in as the shuttle began to rapidly bank left and right, rise and fall. He bounced off the top of the armor and commanded, "Combat retention now." The gel expanded, locking him in position, holding him centered in the armor. As the banking and pitching continued, Fargo breathed deeply, feeling sweat break out on his brow, aS he fought off nausea.

Suddenly he was falling, momentarily panicking until he realized he could see again and was out of the chute. Looking down, he saw a small patch of smooth ground below him and looked up to see about four hundred feet of cliff face staring back at him. "Auto land, Cindy."

The AI responded, "Auto land in two seconds."

***

Four hours, two broken stacers and multiple sessions of cussing later, Fargo was situated fifty yards below the military crest of the bowl, crouched in a group of boulders. Keying the Ferret micro-UAV function, he programmed four of them for passive search, two high and two low. Reviewing their tracks so that he could recover them, he rechecked the overlay of the bowl, wishing he knew exactly where Bahn and Shar were, not just where they were supposed to be. Lack of comms sucked.

With a mental shrug, he keyed the launch cue, felt one of the auxiliary panels open as the four Ferrets ejected. Passively scanning to his visual range, he didn't see anything, but that didn't mean much. Relaxing the gel, he took some nourishment, did a few isometrics, and napped for a couple of hours.

Coming awake to Cindy's voice, "Alert, alert, Ferrets inbound." Fargo stretched, sipped a drink of water, opened the auxiliary panel and waited impatiently. Three of the four Ferrets returned, slotted back into the panel and started transferring data when he closed the panel.

Matching the data against the overlay, he didn't see any new construction, but did see two guards in front of what was obviously a constructed tunnel leading back into the wall of the bowl. The most western Ferret had overflown an object that had Fargo flipping back and forth on the video until he realized it was some type of receiver. Cataloging the data feeds, he finally found what he thought was a transmitter from the easternmost Ferret. They looked like they were about four feet off the ground, and he wondered if it was a laser, sonic, sniffer or what.

Eight hours later, he'd confirmed there were no sonics in his area, there weren't any patrols on top of the bowl, and he'd gotten data from fourteen of eighteen Ferrets, and was sorely tempted to program one to try to enter the tunnel. There were, in fact, two rudimentary pads for ships at the far end of the bowl, five camouflaged bunkers, one of which was a barracks, and he estimated the guard force at something around a platoon. He'd seen, via a Ferret, one Dragoon come out of the tunnel and go into one of the other bunkers, apparently some kind of supply bunker as it had come out carrying what looked like a rations pack. He'd also gotten some recordings of Spanglish, confirming the humans were Traders.

Pushing reports out every cycle kept him alert, and as darkness fell, he slowly uncoiled the armor from its position in the boulder field. Easing up to the military crest, he commanded, "Cindy, smoke plume straight ahead, one second."

Watching closely, he saw a glitter four feet off the ground as a spit of smoke rushed out. Satisfied, Fargo eased back a few yards, launching more Ferrets, including one targeted at the tunnel mouth. He was startled to see a glow overhead, quickly looked up and saw a glow in the low clouds on the opposite side of the bowl. Realizing it was probably a tight beam laser, he quickly took a bearing and video capture.

Another eight hours, two foul emergency food bars, sixteen more Ferrets' worth of data later, and Fargo was going batty with boredom. He wondered how Ban and Shar were doing, and was to the point that he was humming songs to himself, when he finally said screw it. The sun would be up in an hour and his position was directly up-sun from the bowl.

Backing the armor down the slope to below the military crest, he crouched the armor and climbed out. Low crawling up to the edge of the bowl, he looked directly down, cataloging what the Ferrets had picked up. He saw what appeared to be two more tunnel entrances and watched the guard force change. Satisfied, he eeled back, stood up and did his best to brush his undersuit off as he climbed back into the armor.

Four hours and another broken stacer later, Fargo was standing on the same little plot of ground that he'd been landed on. It was definitely easier going downhill, and he'd used the anti-grav a couple of times rather than actually climb down a cliff or two.

Drowsing in the armor, he was surprised when the shuttle rose up directly in front of him and backed the open ramp slowly toward him. It grounded and he walked quickly up the ramp as the shuttle dropped back down into the canyon. Pop said, "Ramp secure, Captain, please lock in."

Fargo swiveled to see Ban and Shar's armor locked into the side of the shuttle so he carefully stepped up next to them and felt the clamps attach to his armor. "Captain is locked in, Chief of ship is locked in, ready to maneuver WO."

"Roger." Boykin dropped the nose of the shuttle, and the rocking and rolling started as she flew back down the canyons. Fargo connected to the shuttle cameras, but soon turned them off, not wanting to throw up from the constantly changing visual horizon. He couldn't help but wonder how Boykin did it and kept her stomach, much less her sanity.

***

Three hours later, Boykin grounded the shuttle at the Enclave and was met by Colonel Keads, Nicole, and Lal. Boykin came over the comms flatly, "Grounded, crew and pax are cleared to unlock and depart."

Fargo led them off and walked the armor over to the weapons building before dismounting. When he climbed out, Nicole met him then backed up two steps, "Damn, you stink! The colonel wants a face to face debrief in the intel spaces, but you need the fresher first."

Fargo sniffed, "Sorry, you try spending two days in this damn thing, and see how you smell."

Bahn and Shar climbed out and started laughing, Fargo glanced at them and joined in as Nicole cocked her head, trying to figure out what was going on. Ban looked at him, "Ekavir, I saw you climb up to the edge of the bowl. You are crazy."

Fargo replied, "Apparently, I wasn't the only one that wanted a look, was I?"

Nicole, finally picked up on the dirty undersuits, "Oh, you stupid men!" Turning around she stomped off toward the door. Fargo looked at her, shook his head, and walked to the fresher in the weapons building.

***

Nicole pivoted the holo again, and Colonel Keads asked, "So everything here agrees with what you individually collected?"

Fargo glanced at Bahn, then Shar, and turned to the colonel, "It does. Passive sensors up top, other than the lasers which are set for four feet. One tight beam comms laser, pointed opposite of the space station into deep space. No patrols observed, guards only on the main tunnel. No visual on anti-ship missiles and other defensive weapons, but we're pretty sure they are there. Two, maybe three smaller tunnels all on the south side of the bowl. Very little wear on the pads at the far end of the bowl, so we're betting they come in and depart on anti-grav with some kind of suppressed power plant. Not something we saw. Definitely Spanglish, and we saw at least two distinctly different Dragoons, but no rank tabs on either one of them. Total body count appears to be two platoons worth, about fifty humanoids. Some mix of techs and soldiers."

"Could your company take them?"

Fargo cocked his head, "Probably, if we surprised them. We'd still take losses, possibly heavy losses. They've got plasma rifles, and I think some heavier artillery concealed down there somewhere, plus at least a couple of missile batteries two thirds of the way up the bowl on the eastern and western sides."

The colonel asked, "How would you do it?"

"Company strength, all source jamming, mass drop, weapons free. Prisoners of opportunity, try to get to their command and control, and comms system before they can destroy it."

"What about the missile batteries?"

"Take them out as we drop? Maybe from the shuttle? Granted we'd be dropping stealthed, but some sharp eyed troop could still spot the shimmer and light us up."

Fargo bit his lip, "Without help from the shuttle, we'd probably lose half our troops."

The colonel replied, "That's not acceptable. Not at all. I'm not going to get volunteer colonists killed that way."

Fargo sighed with relief, "Thank you."

GalPat Arriving

Colonel Keads messaged Fargo and Nicole, requesting that they come to White Beach in civilian clothes to discuss *options*, as he called them. He'd added the shuttle would be at the spaceport at eight, meaning Fargo would have to fly down now.

As he was getting a bag together, his e-tainment system pinged an alert, followed by a header from Captain Jace, a coded string of numbers, followed by the words, DOWNLOAD ONLY. Fargo slid a data chip into the console, hit acknowledge, and heard the console click, then spit the chip out.

Fargo got up, dug out his standalone e-reader, and powered it up. The holo formed and the word NUMBERS swam up, "Ethan Fargo, eight three four six alpha romeo two four eight."

The holo rotated to show Hunter from what appeared to be a satellite image, two curved streaks that appeared to be new tracks displayed, a string of numbers followed, indicating the track origins, dates, times and durations. There were IR shots of the Goon's outpost, now showing two ships grounded. Pulling the chip out, he messaged Nicole, GOT ANOTHER ONE. CAN YOU HANDLE?

He finished packing, shut down the cabin, and pulled the liteflyer from the storage building. Configuring it for flight, he sent Cattus and Canis to watch and hunt. As he settled into the liteflyer, his wrist comp pinged with an answer from Nicole, AT THE MUG. CAN DO. TWO HOURS?

He quickly responded, and with one last look around, closed the canopy and launched. After a quick stop by the clinic, ostensibly to get his ears checked by OneSvel, he'd delivered a copy of the chip for him to push up the chain of command, filliing him in on the trip tomorrow.

Walking into the bar, he saw Nicole laughing with Sergeant Omar at the bar, and he wondered, yet again, if he was falling in love with her. There was definitely an attraction, but he wondered if that was her hostess background or something real. She saw him and came around the bar, "Fargo, I hear the master calling, right," as she gave him a quick hug. Surprisingly, her shields were down, and she was thinking about the kitchen and a standalone datacomp. He quickly projected, *Got it, kitchen.* "Hello yourself, and yes, they want us in White Beach tomorrow. Apparently we have company coming."

Sergeant Omar's GalTrans twittered, "Ho, Lieutenant of the retired, GalPat strike force in the system. Involved, are you?"

Fargo parsed Omar's question replying, "Omar, involved we are not. Planet only for the militia."

Omar swiveled two eyestalks in what Fargo had learned was an Arcturian equivalent of an eye roll, "Sure of that, we are?"

Fargo shrugged, "One never knows, does one?"

This time Omar's GalTrans chittered a laugh, and he shook his head.

***

Nicole went through the data with a fine toothed comb, mumbling to herself as she flipped back and forth between this data, and the previous set of data. After an hour, she added some comments, embedded it in a picture of the bar, encrypted it, commanded transmit for the latest email and leaned back in the chair, "Wow, this may mean we're going to catch the Goons with their pants down, assuming GalPat decides to take action soon." Arching her back and grinning, she continued, "Speaking of catching somebody with their pants down..."

Fargo blushed, "I need to go see Mikhail and Luann, but I can come back..."

"If you want."

Fargo smiled, "Yes, I want. It may be late."

"I'll be here."

***

Luann huffed, "Ethan, you're *supposed* to be retired. Why did you get into this whole militia thing? You could get hurt or killed! Isn't forty years of the military long enough? Men!"

He glanced at Mikhail before he answered, "Luann, it's my way of giving something back to this planet I'm now calling home. I may be old, but I know how to do this stuff. And our company is unquestionably the best on the planet!"

Mikhail coughed to cover a laugh as Luann threw up her hands, "Oh, fine! Just, just..." She whispered, "Please don't get killed," throwing her arms around him, she hugged him hard, and he was inundated with her mental fears and worries.

"I won't. Mikhail, we need to talk about that trip to Endine. How long will we be gone?"

***

Fargo ran his hand down Nicole's hip, feeling her shiver, "You like that?"

She burrowed closer under his arm, "Oh yes, but we need *some* sleep before we fly out tomorrow morning."

Laughing, he asked, "Tired out already?"

Nicole raised up on an elbow, "I thought you were tir… Ooh, nope you're not tired, *are* you?" Rolling over on him, she kissed him deeply as they made love one more time.

Fargo enfolded her in his arms as she drifted off to sleep, thinking, *What have I gotten myself into? Am I falling in love? Or is this just a case of lust? My god, it's been over forty years… Maybe this is what I, we, both need. It's not like we're youngsters.* Other random thoughts ran through his head until he dropped off to sleep.

Coffee? His subconscious reacted to the odor drifting up to his nose and he opened his eyes slowly, turned his head, and sure enough, there was a coffee bulb sitting next to his head.

"Morning sleepy one," Nicole said with a smile, "We've got time for breakfast, if you get your butt out of bed and in the fresher."

***

Colonel Keads welcomed Fargo and Nicole, "Come in, come in. Coffee?" When they both nodded, he got up and programmed the autochef in the corner himself, "I'm expecting a major from the strike group to ground shortly. Once he or she does, we'll have a quick meeting with Colonel Cameron, then get down to business. If you don't mind, I'd like for y'all to wait here."

He passed the coffee bulbs to Fargo and Nicole as they looked at each other, with Fargo finally asking, "Why wait here?"

"Cameron doesn't know I'm going to ask you to help with the intel. I'm not confident that they've got all of the most current information, nor do they understand we want to keep this little excursion off the galactic radar."

Nicole cocked her head, "So, a cell is what we're going to be running?"

"A totally separate cell. Matter of fact, you won't even be here. You'll be in Rushing River, which is where the op will stage from."

Fargo asked, "Why Rushing... Oh, never mind. Out of the way, less chance of being spotted, etc., right?"

Keads grimaced, "That, and Cameron doesn't want to attack the outpost. He thinks we'd be better off to leave it alone and just *monitor* it."

Fargo and Nicole both snapped around at that, chorusing, "What?"

"He's afraid this will put Hunter in the Goon's sights for a major incursion. He thinks if we just ignore them, they won't ramp up their presence."

Nicole spit, "Doesn't he *understand* the Goon's MO? They start with one Dragoon on planet, gradually expanding until they 'claim' the planet for themselves.

They don't stop! They've *never* stopped! My god, we fought a war with them! Did he not attend those classes at the academy?"

Keads held up his hands, "I know, I know. He's not a combat arms guy. He came up through the admin and PR side, getting just enough experience to qualify, and I use that term loosely, for a command position. That's one of the reasons I was sent out here as the XO."

Keads wrist comp beeped, "Well, looks like our major has grounded. I should be back in an hour or so. You can either wait here, or come back."

They looked at each other and Fargo said, "Why don't we come back, say at thirteen?"

"Suits."

As they were leaving, they passed Colonel Cameron in the hall, he looked at them suspiciously, but said nothing. Once out of the HQ, Nicole sighed, "What in the hell?"

"I don't know. I really don't know. This is looking like a cluster in the making."

"Well, it's definitely going to be interesting…" Grabbing Fargo's hand she continued, "Come on, I know a nice little place that has good food. And there's a shop I want to check out."

***

Fargo knocked on Colonel Keads' side door, and it was quickly opened, "Come in. Ward is in the fresher. He's talking the talk, but watching him with Cameron this morning makes me think he's a pol."

Fargo asked, "A pol?"

"Cameron junior."

"Shit."

"But he's dropping with a full company. We will have that going for us. Troopers, by and large, make up for a *lot* of shortfalls in the officer corps."

Nicole asked, "Including an intel section?"

"Not sure, but I'd think at company strength, they would, unless they're going to remote off our section here."

"I hope they bring their own," she said, "Cuts down on the delay in passing info, and cuts out the middle interference."

A knock on the door interrupted their conversation, and the colonel said, "Come."

Major Noah Ward, at six feet and about one hundred seventy pounds, dark haired and almost holo star handsome, looked like he stepped out of a e-tainment vid. Dressed in tailored blacks, insignia and awards polished to a T, hair cut so short he was almost bald marched within three feet of the colonel's desk, "Major Ward, reporting as ordered, sir."

Keads replied, "At ease Major. These folks are your local contacts at Rushing River. Captain Fargo, head of the local militia in that area, and Chief Sergeant Levesque, his intel specialist. Let's sit at the holo table and go over where we are."

Ward nodded stiffly to them, and without a word, automatically took the seat at the far end of the table from the colonel. Fargo cocked an eyebrow, but took the far side seat as Nicole spun up the holo.

Keads turned to Fargo, "If we wanted to bring a company in covertly, how would you suggest doing it?"

Fargo thought for a second, held up his hand, and quickly queried his data comp. Seeing that *Hyderabad* was in system he replied, "I'd use the SV *Hyderabad*, she's big enough to carry a company, including armor, and she's a known entity in this quadrant. She could meet whatever transport the major has outside the gravity well, transfer there, and come in like a normal transport run."

The major immediately objected, "Why a commercial ship, we could just use the destroyer?"

Keads broke in, "Low observable, major. A destroyer is *not* low observable. Chief could you bring up Rushing River port, please?" As she did, Keads pointed to the off side of the spaceport, "A night landing in an outer spot, exit this gate here, and your company will set up your field quarters here. You will minimize interactions with the local populous until the operation is complete." Turning to Fargo he asked, "SV *Hyderabad* is certified, correct?"

"Yes, sir. She is certified and registered by GalPat as a contract carrier."

"Good enough. Make it happen with the major."

"Chief, would you please brief the major?"

Nicole reconfigured the holo to the Dragoon's outpost, and started the briefing, only to be interrupted by the major, "Are you qualified to conduct this brief?"

Nicole took a deep breath, "Yes, *Major*. I have served in the Fleet and also tours at JIFMIC and JIOC. My last billet before retiring was section chief at the JIOC. Now if I may continue?"

Ward waved his hand negligently, "Go ahead, but I want my intel section to review this material."

Nicole quirked a grin, then started the brief again. Two hours later, she'd completed the brief in spite of numerous interruptions, complaints about the paucity of data, questions about the accuracy of data and how it had been gathered. Fargo was biting his tongue by the time it was over, and Colonel Keads had turned an interesting shade of red a time or two.

Finally, Ward looked at the colonel, "Well, I think we need to postpone this operation until my people can do a recon and my intel section can put together a coherent set of briefs."

Keads glanced at Fargo and Nicole before he said, "I'm sorry, Major, but that is not possible. We do not have the luxury of waiting that long. The strike will occur within twenty-four divs of you hitting the planet. As for the quality of the data collections and coherency, the captain here and two of his scout/snipers infiltrated the location and collected the data. The other data provided *has* been reviewed at the highest levels in GalPat, and this operation is approved at the JIOC and command level."

Standing up, the colonel continued, "If you feel it necessary, discuss this with your chain of command, but understand this…" Keads leaned on the holo table, "This operation *must* take place within one planetary week. I will also be sending my comments, to your chain of command and I'd suggest you get with the program. Do I make myself clear?"

Major Ward turned an interesting shade of puce as the colonel concluded, but replied in a hushed voice, "Yes, sir. May I be dismissed?"

Keads grated out, "Yes. Fargo will communicate with the strike group to provide the ship's information for your covert entry. Chief Levesque will be standing by to coordinate with your intel section."

Ward came to attention, turned, and departed quickly. Keads shook his head, "Gah, Cameron junior in spades. Would you be willing to put your scout/snipers in place ahead of time to provide updated intel?"

"Hell, I'll go myself!"

"No, I want you to coordinate with the major. You've already been up there, and like it or not, you're the logical person to be the local POC."

Fargo saw Nicole slump slightly, almost in relief and wondered what that was all about. He replied, "Yes, sir. I'll make it work somehow. And I'll get some folks up there early. Can we borrow WO Boykin again?"

Keads smiled, "I think the Warrant will be happy to do something other than ass and trash flights. You can discuss that with her on the return flight this afternoon."

Old Friends

Colonel Randall walked slowly from the GalPat assault shuttle to the spaceport administration building, noting the condition of the equipment and personnel she could see, filing it away for future reference.

She spared a glance for the ugly tramp merchant ship sitting off to one side, then looked closer as she realized that was the ship that had brought Major Ward and his strike company down from the Star Gate orbit. A niggling thought bubbled in the back of her mind as she looked at the ship, but it wouldn't surface, and she continued up the steps of the administration building. Seeing the guard at the top of the steps draw a breath, she said quickly, "No, don't call attention on deck. This is an unofficial visit. No honors." She thought back to Fargo's instructions years before, *Never salute an officer in the field unless you want to get them killed by a sniper. Or you can salute and get a sniper check, if they survive, no snipers...*

The trooper gulped, slapped his rifle to present arms and replied, "Yes, ma'am."

Her lace came up with the trooper's information and she asked, "So, Trooper Hanlon, what do you think of this mud ball? And the people in charge?"

Trooper Hanlon gulped again, "Uh, ma'am... It's not my place to say."

"Unofficial, remember?"

"Uh, yes ma'am. It's not bad. Major Ward is kinda flakey, but the locals are friendly compared to a lot of places. But it kinda sucks that we have to stay LO[3] all the time. The local yokel the Major is working with is one strange dude, but he seems to have his shit together, or at least better than the major. Sorry, ma'am."

Randall made a waving motion, and the trooper continued, "It's like he already knows what questions you're going to ask, and I think he's ex-mil. Maybe even ex-GalPat, but he's too young to have retired. He's closeted with the major in the conference room right now. Scuttlebutt is we're going to strike tonight, late, and they are doing the final planning now."

Randall nodded, "Thanks, Hanlon. Remember, no honors."

"Yes ma'am." Hanlon replied as Randall stepped through the main entry.

Walking down the main hallway, she saw that someone had made an attempt to decorate the building to relieve the sheer sameness of the walls, floor, and ceiling. Finding the conference room she stuck her head in, but it was empty. She continued to the end of the hall, but didn't see anyone; finding a set of stairs there, she shrugged and climbed them to the second floor, and continued looking in offices.

Halfway down on the right side, she finally saw a figure sitting at the desk. It was Fargo, and he was deep in concentration staring at an actual paper map. A

---

[3] Low Observable

smile quirked the corner of Colonel Randall's mouth as she stepped quietly through the door.

She managed to get almost to the front of the desk then popped to attention saying, "Sir! Sergeant Randall, Fargo's Fuck Ups, reporting to the commander as directed!" Startled, Fargo looked up, and she executed a precise Terran Marine salute. She saw Fargo's face change, almost like a wall coming down behind his eyes.

Fargo said, "Out of uniform as usual, Sergeant?" He stood, returned her salute formally, then walked around the desk, "I'm glad you made it, Nan, or should I call you Colonel?"

Impulsively, Randall hugged Fargo, tears in her eyes, "I never got the chance to thank you for bringing us home. I know you came by when the few of us that lived were still in the Med-Comps, but by the time we got out, you were already gone."

Fargo was shocked as he read Randall's thoughts. *Professionalism, GalPat orders, tears, sexual attraction, sadness, unrequited love, and nervousness at seeing him again* swirled through his head as he held her.

Shocked at the feeling of love from her, Fargo squashed that set of thoughts quickly, even as he felt drawn to her again after all these years. Not wanting to acknowledge it, he gingerly patted her shoulder so he didn't touch her and get anymore thoughts, "It wasn't by choice, Nan. By the time y'all were released by medical, I was already up on charges. The courts martial and drumming out was short, sweet, and terminal. I wasn't even allowed to make a last visit to the troop bay. I was so persona non grata, the Corps even bounced my emails when I tried to send my well wishes."

A cleared throat at the door made them realize they were still hugging, and they quickly separated, turning to the door. Major Ward stood there looking uncomfortably back and forth between the two. Randall, now fully back in her colonel persona, said, "Noah, Fargo was my company commander when I was a sergeant. I haven't seen him in over thirty years. He taught me more about leadership than I ever learned in any schoolhouse."

Ward nodded, "Now, it makes sense why you sent us down here and said for me to directly coordinate with Fargo." He stepped to the desk and laid out a frag order, "Fargo, I've got my troops ready to jump off at zero three hundred local, as soon as your indigs start the ball rolling."

Colonel Randall asked, "Y'all want to lay your plan out for me?"

Fargo spun the map around and using a pen, pointed out the locations where the Ghorkas would start the attack from, "Nan, er, Colonel…"

"Nan, please."

"Nan, my indigs as the major calls them, are Ghorkas. All retired GalPat combat troops and of the one hundred I have, all of them are either E-eights, nines, or warrants. All of them are combat vets, and they have locally manufactured powered armor. They have spent the last seventy-two hours infiltrating to these three locations, and they've given us movement, security perimeters, guard locations, defenses and facilities use via LPI comms."

"How did you get the info, and why weren't they counter-detected?"

"It goes no further than this room, but we have access to Ferrets that were sent in with various tasks. The scouts went into power down mode as soon as any movement was detected in the valley. The Traders don't fly anything out of the valley in the daylight, and use counter-grav at night, so there is no light signature or noise when they do launch. They know, well, thought they knew, there wasn't a satellite system around the planet. That's what gave us their initial locating information."

Impatiently Randall asked, "What's your plan tonight? You can backfill me later on the intel."

Fargo and Ward exchanged glances, Fargo continued, "They've got two ships on the ground now. It's a forward base for the Dragoons and Traders, and *our* plan is to hit them, take down comms, kill everyone, and raid the base for any information. After that, we're going to crash one of the ships back into the facility and get a partial fusion bottle blow, destroying the facility."

Randall looked at Ward, "You have any problems with that, Noah?"

"No ma'am. Fargo's got a good plan, and we're going to have six teams, one per bunker, in full armor. Go in hard, fast, and take them down."

"How are you going to put your teams on the ground, and what about outbound comms?"

Fargo stepped in, "We're going to use *Hyderabad* to jam the comms, and Ward's folks will drop from her at ten k, allowing them twelve seconds to get on the ground, as our folks take out the defenses. Each team has the facility plans on their implants for their bunker, and their secondary targets. We've counted about a hundred personnel, and two to three Dragoons now at the site."

Randall looked at Ward, "You look like you have reservations."

"Can I speak to you privately, Ma'am?"

Fargo said, "Oh for God's sake. I'll go get coffee," and stomped out of the room.

Randall rounded on Ward, "Noah, what is your problem?"

"I'm not comfortable with his indigs, and his *so called* intel. I'd rather wait until we can put our own eyes on the target. He's just a local yokel now, and we've got a lot more advanced…"

"Major Ward, that local yokel, as you call him, has more time in *combat* than you have in the force. This is your first time to actually get in the field leading troops, and I'm beginning to wonder if you're actually up to it."

Ward drew himself up stiffly to attention, "Ma'am, I can get the job done. If you will excuse me, I need to get *my* troops ready."

"Fine, dismissed."

Fargo came back with two bulbs of coffee, "What the hell was that, Nan?"

Randall accepted the bulb with a nod, "Ah, Ward is a fuck up I got foisted on me. He's managed to avoid combat by kissing ass, pulling embassy duty, and *staff* duty as a liaison with his politically connected brother-in-law. He was sent out as a relief for my good major, who was due to rotate out."

"Ah, one of *those*. Kinda noticed that on the initial briefing last week."

"Yeah, I got told to square him away, get him in combat, or document enough fuck ups to kick him out. I hate pushing him off on you, but the troops are damn good. I figured he'd be nothing more than a figurehead, and wouldn't be dumb enough to *not* take your advice."

"Well... Shit, Nan, he didn't fight me, per se, but he was always questioning every damn part of the plan, but never offered any options that didn't involve KEWs[4]."

"KEWs? You've got to be kidding me!"

Fargo shrugged, "Nope, he wanted to use a cruiser, not a destroyer, a cruiser, to hit the site with a KEW before we even went in. He doesn't like *indigs*, even though they are *all* retired GalPat CSMs, for Christ sake!"

Randall growled, "Do you want me to replace him?"

"Nah, if the troops are as good as you say, they'll keep him out of the way, and hopefully out of trouble."

"Would you object if I go along as an observer?"

"Observer, or as Sergeant Randall?"

---

[4] Kinetic Energy Weapon

Randall colored, "I'll go wherever Captain Fargo leads. How's that?"

"Nan, if you go, would you please stay on the bridge? And not let the troops see you? Anything else, and you know they'll think you're checking up on them. Captain Jace would be happy to have you there."

"Yes sir, I'll be aboard at zero one hundred," she said with a smile.

***

Captain Jace welcomed Colonel Randall onto the bridge of the *Hyderabad,* and sealed the hatch saying, "Colonel, before we man up, there is something you need to know." He handed her a data chip, "Please access this with your datacomp. It will require your access codes."

Randall took the chip with a raised eyebrow, but plugged it into her datacomp. It ran a routine, then blinked into what she recognized as a higher classification background, and asked for her access code. Randall looked hard at Captain Jace, "What is this? And why do you have it?"

Jace shrugged, "My orders. And you should have adequate clearances to review them."

Intrigued, Randall entered her access. The screen changed once again, and stepped to a STAR 3 access. Randall muttered under her breath, and entered that code. The screen finally displayed the data.

STAR 3 SECURITY LEVEL
DISSEMINATION STRICTLY FORBIDDEN
REF GALPAT INTEL INST 7843, SUB C, SUB E, PARA 21

IAW REF HYDERABAD DESIGNATED REMOTE INTELLIGENCE GATHER UNIT 3AC4R. AUTHORIZED ALL NECESSARY SUPPORT WHEN/IF REQUESTED. NO RECORD TRAFFIC OF ANY SUPPORT TO BE REPORTED. NO RECORD OF SHIP EMISSIONS TO BE MADE/FORWARDED BY ANY GALPAT UNIT IAW REF.

ANY NOTIFICATION OF SPECIAL MISSION CAPABILITY NOT DESIRED/REQUIRED. COMMAND LEVEL SUPPORT DATA TRANSMISSION TO GALPAT INTEL PRIORITY ONE.

S/GEN PAREET HILTON, GP INTEL 00
STAR 3 SECURITY LEVEL
DISSEMINATION STRICTLY FORBIDDEN

Randall looked up in amazement, "Why?"

Jace replied, "You will see some things tonight that will not make sense. You will see systems activate that no civilian ship should have, or even know about. It's just easier if I do this now, rather than later."

Randall ejected the data chip and passed it back to the captain, "So, I hear nothing, I know nothing, and I see nothing, right?"

Jace smiled, "Yes, ma'am. That would be preferable."

Raid Time

Fargo came out of the administration building at zero two hundred, walking slowly toward the ship, thinking he'd rather be anywhere than here. *At least I'm not in charge. No decisions I make are going to impact anyone other than me. If I screw up, I'll be the only one paying the price.* Yanking his mind out of that track, he jerked back to the computed avenues of approach, battle plan, fallback if things weren't as expected, and the scout's positions and responsibilities.

As he approached the aft ramp, he noticed a short, thin spacer in a well-used shipsuit, talking with Captain Jace and Klang. Cocking his head, Fargo tried to place the man but failed, but he sensed ultimate confidence radiating from him. As he walked up, Klang twittered, "Ship of the Chief, it will be as you desire. Interrupt your commands I will not. Prepare the cargo deck for armor I will do."

The small man replied, "That is acceptable. We will load four abreast. I will give you thirty seconds to lock the suits in before I start the next four in. I will need the starboard side open to the back hatch, and one soft suit in small available for me to use."

Klang nodded as Fargo looked at the captain, then at the small man, "What's going on here?"

Captain Jace said, "Fargo, meet Wallace, he is a Chief of ship, retired. He was sent over by Warrant Gupta."

Wallace turned, coming almost to attention, "Wallace Hand, GalPat Master Chief COS retired, twenty years assault boat COS. Last duty station BATRON Nine. WO said you needed help, so Liz and I came down to volunteer." Waving at the ship, he continued, "Liz is also retired, Chief Sergeant, comms and EWO. She's up on the bridge getting set up."

Fargo shook his head, "Uh, why…" Rubbing a hand over his scalp, he tried again, "Captain, are you willing to have… Uh, are you paying crew rates to him and his wife?"

Jace looked askance, "Of course, Fargo. I take no liberties with a crew person. And with the two Chiefs Hand aboard, I suspect our potential for mission success has just gone up."

Fargo scratched his ear, "Okay. I… Chief, you weren't here tonight, you didn't see anything, and you *did not participate* in a raid, or anything else. Is that clear?"

Hand smiled, "In other words, I'm a mushroom, right? Just a night out on the town for me and Liz."

Fargo nodded, "That works."

***

Fargo stood off to the side watching as Hand loaded the troops onboard. His language and attitude made Fargo smile, if only to himself. Hand, in a command voice, said pointedly to one of the suits of armor, "Troop, if you scratch up my deck or get it dirty, I *will* have you out of your monkey suit and down on your hands and knees scrubbing my deck clean, *is that clear?*"

The troop mumbled his apology, carefully picking up his feet in the armor as he moved quickly into the locking clamps that popped up out of the deck. Fargo shook his head as he climbed the ramp and walked forward. Climbing upward, he got to the bridge and nodded to Captain Jace and Colonel Randall, and waved to Evie as he scanned the flight deck, noting an older woman setting at one of the consoles.

Jace said, "Chief Hand, Captain Fargo."

She waved vaguely at Fargo, "Liz. Nice little setup, here. I haven't seen a Mod Thirty board in a couple of years. You want selective or full band jamming as we come over the RF horizon, or the visual horizon?"

Fargo replied, "What's your recommendation?"

Liz looked up, "Full band, of course, at the RF horizon. I'll ramp up power as required when we get on top, need to make sure the tight beam laser is taken out, too. Are we doing a nape of the planet, or hot and high approach?"

Fargo looked at the captain, "I need to go suit up, y'all do what you think is best." As he made for the door, he could have sworn he heard Randall snickering.

Back on the cargo deck, he saw another set of armor sitting in the front of the deck with his. This one was marked with subdued red crosses, and apparently only had one weapon, which looked like a breacher. Turning, he saw a slightly overweight, humming man doing a half dance as he laid out a full blown medical kit and med grav sled.

Fargo said, "You know we have a full Med-Comp on board, right?"

The man turned, "Yeah, but if I don't do *my* job, they're gonna be dead before I can get them up there. Who the hell are you?"

Fargo bristled, "Fargo, I'm the liaison with the local forces. Who're you?"

"Grayson, K, senior sergeant, medic. Twenty years of this ship shit. I can do anything but crack a skull, and it comes down to it, I'll do that too. Ten deployments, twenty-two operations, seventy-one saves. Things go to shit, just get outta my way unless I call for help, then get your ass where I need you. Hope you're not freaked out by blood."

Fargo replied, "Nope. Seen a bit in my time. You jumping?"

Grayson nodded, "How else to you expect me to do my job? These suits may be smart, but they ain't *that* smart."

Major Ward was the last suit to board, and Fargo and Grayson stopped as they heard the IC go off, "Troops are aboard. Ten minutes to launch. COS, close the hatch, please. Secure all loose gear. Approach will be nape, expect a few bumps and bounces as we ingress. Intent is to pop and drop from twelve thousand AGL, all troops check altimeters to two-two-one feet, mark. Set low limit one-four-three-three-seven feet for raid point. Drop altitude will be two-four-three-three-seven feet. Confirm DVARS on."

Various responses came back in mumbles, "Doppler on, DV alt set…"

Fargo and Grayson scrambled into their respective suits, and Fargo settled into the routine of suit operations as he locked into the restraints and linked into the suit's AI. Performing the suit's BIT checks though Cindy, he completed the drop setting check on the Doppler system. Setting his radios to the bridge, command, troop, and scout's channels, he heard Ward start into a drop brief for the fourth time. Tuning it out, Fargo took his pre-combat piss in the suit, wiggling around to get as comfortable as he could before it clamped down on him.

He was glad he'd gotten a suit fam and time to work with it prior to the op, as the Phantom II suits were more advanced than what he was used to, and the additional capabilities were interesting, to put it lightly. His was the only suit with a Gustav mounted in place of the 20mm, and he was looking forward to seeing how the new version worked.

**

After a good ten to fifteen minutes of bouncing up and down, side to side, Fargo felt his stomach drop as the radio spit, "Climbing, ramp coming down. Standby… Standby…" Suddenly his stomach was in his throat as the radio said, "Go! Green, go!"

Fargo looked up, driving his camera view up, and saw the green light over the aft ramp. He could also see troops ahead, moving as each rank unlocked. Twenty seconds later, he stepped off the aft ramp. Slanting right, as Grayson slanted left, he decreased the anti-grav to minimum and fell as fast as possible, trusting the suit to get him down in one piece.

Ten seconds later, he was in the middle of a pitched battle, as the scouts yelling, "*Ayo Gorkhali*," as they continued to take out the remote sensors, laser transmitter head, and visible defensive weapons, micro jumping from their hiding places to the tops of the surrounding bowl to give them overwatch. As he scanned around, the hostiles in his HUD seemed to be melting away, as the assaulting GalPat troops took them out quickly.

Suddenly a new crop of hostiles popped up a third of the way up the side of the bowl, away from Fargo. Somebody yelled, "Reaction force up!" As the chatter threatened to overload the circuit, Fargo heard Captain Garibaldi, "Looks like Goons. Hit 'em hard, boys and girls."

Fargo, remembering his tasking, slid over to one of the ships currently grounded tail first, and used his IR and radar to scan the ship. Confirming it was cold, he moved toward the second ship, snapping a shot at a hostile that suddenly appeared in the mid-deck hatch of the ship. Seeing the armor recoil back into the ship, he grav jumped at the hatch, reloading and putting another round from the Gustav into the hatch and surrounding area. He reloaded the Gustav quickly, then scanned around.

Teetering on the edge of the hatch, he ensured the Trader's armor was out of action. Then he used his armor's manipulator to rip a section of the hatch open, ensuring the hatch wouldn't pressurize. As he did, his HUD momentarily blanked as he heard, "Plasma cannon up, target," on the Scouts' channel. Launching from the side of the ship, he used the anti-grav to keep himself stable as he floated across the battle, waiting for the hostile carat's position to unmask. The plasma cannon was firing down into the bowl, and apparently the Goons manning it didn't see him.

Floating clear of the second ship, Fargo got a visual, triggering a Stingray missile as he lased the cannon's emplacement. Too late, the Goons tried to respond, as they swung the still firing cannon in his direction. Killing his anti-grav, he dropped to the floor of the bowl, as the missile obliterated the cannon and its crew.

"Scouts on me," Fargo broadcast on the channel, and pinged his suit location. Looking at his HUD, it looked like things were in sweep up mode, and there was no need for him or the scouts to get involved at this point.

Listening to the troop channel, he heard Grayson berating one of the troops, "Dammit Richie, *why* did you have to get a damn leg blown off again? You just like making me carry you, don't ya? Smitty, you ain't dyin' yet. I'll get to you, you still owe me money from that three-D chess match. I'm overriding your medpack remotely. You just stay still."

Fargo only saw one flashing red beacon, but there were at least four yellow to orange beacons scattered around the bowl. As Shar, Bahn, Ganju, and Kulbir streamed into Fargo's position, he saw Ward's beacon take off for the far wall of the bowl, in pursuit of a hostile.

They heard an anguished voice on the troop's channel yell, "Major, Major, wait!"

Ward's response chilled him, "I've got this. It's only one Goon. I don't need any help." Fargo shook his head inside his armor, knowing this wasn't going to end well.

"Shar, Bahn, can you help the medic? Ganju, Kulbir on me, let's support the major."

Shar and Bahn immediately moved toward Grayson as Fargo and the other scouts bounded after Ward. Fargo dimly heard Garibaldi over the troop channel say tiredly, "Bravo squad on the major, please. Do not let him get killed."

Fargo saw Ward disappear into what appeared to be a cave opening and grounded quickly. "Ward, you need to get out of there. They like to booby…"

A rumbling, ground shaking sensation was followed by Fargo's HUD blanking once again. He felt himself flying through the air, the suit trying to stabilize his flight until he slammed into one of the rockets. Stunned, his armor in a crouch, he tried to place what had happened.

A cacophony of alarms, screams, and voices sounded over the various circuits, as he slowly focused on his HUD. Shaking his head, he saw radiation alarms, chem-bio alarms, and his medpack showing slightly yellow, as it pushed meds for the cracked ribs he noticed when he tried to take a deep breath.

Tonguing all but the scout channel off, he called, "Scouts, report?"

He relaxed when all four reported in, and Ganju asked, "Where are you sir?"

Fargo went to ping his location, but realized his HUD was offline, either due to damage or his toggling a reset inadvertently. Patiently he waited until it came back online, pinged his locator, and replied, "Over by the first ship. I'm mobile, I think."

Kulbir found him first, whistling when he saw the damage to the armor, "First layer ablation, twenty-mil is gone completely, along with your funny gun. All your aux packs are gone too. You must have been directly in the blast pattern!"

Fargo moved his legs to straighten the armor up, and it responded slowly, but with more pressure alarms as the AI continued listing the suit's problems. He said, "Okay, Cindy, got it." Kulbir said, "You're upright, and the captain wants you on the troop channel."

Fargo tongued the other comms channels back on and replied, "Captain, Fargo here. You wanted to talk to me?"

Garibaldi said, "Yeah, I'm calling this place secure. Rather than jump back up to the shuttle, I want to ground it. I've got injured troops, no thanks to the major's actions. I figure we've got enough room to land her in the north end of the bowl if she's capable of a hover landing. I've got troops searching for intel, but the sooner we get the shuttle down, the sooner I get my folks treated. Can you call her in?"

Fargo replied, "Will do. Break. *Hyderabad* on command channel, over."

Captain Jace answered quickly, "I heard, Fargo. We are descending now. I will land with the stern ramp pointed at the rockets. FYI, the rocket near your position is leaning and has damage to two of its outriggers. Based on the radiation and chem-bio alarms we are seeing up here, we will set up a decontamination station off the aft ramp."

"Roger all, Captain. We're not going anywhere."

Flipping over to the troop channel, Fargo said, "Shuttle on the way, decon prior to boarding. Aft ramp only."

After Action

Grayson, Shar, and Bahn had two suits between them, plus one more on the grav sled, waiting as COS quickly set up the portable tunnel and decontamination unit twenty feet from the aft ramp. As he walked backward toward the ramp, spraying the inside of the tunnel, Wallace keyed up on all channels, "Okay, here's how we're going to do this. Thirty second decon, standard NBC procedure, air barrier is on. You mutts know the drill. Once you're in, shut down cameras unless you want them burned out. Medic first, triage plan next, one and *only* one officer across, then troops. Dead and Intel will be recovered last. Intel will be placed in decon unit until transfer to GalPat. Am I clear?"

A muttered chorus of "Clear, yes sir. Copied all, sir," sounded over the channels as Grayson stepped into the unit.

Clearing it he said, "Grav sled next." Shar nudged it forward into the unit, and Grayson continued, "Okay Mikey, gotta shut your cameras down, you're not dying on me. Hang in there for thirty, okay?" Nodding to Wallace to key the sequence, he fidgeted until the unit opened, and Greyson could reach in and pull the sled through.

Shar and Bahn helped the next suit of armor into the unit and stepped back as Grayson hurried up the ramp, grav sled in tow. Fargo shook his head as Grayson continued a soothing patter, wondering if he ever shut up.

Grayson brought the second suit out on autonomous control, as Shar and Bahn helped the third suit into decon. They stepped out of line as Fargo and Garibaldi turned away and started toward the chief sergeant with the first body. Garibaldi keyed his mic, "Lieutenant Ballard, go on through. Grayson could use the help."

Fargo heard a subdued, "Roger," as a command suit stepped to the front of the line.

The four scouts joined Fargo as they searched for the remaining two suits that had redlined, finding one almost cut in two by the plasma cannon, and the final suit underneath a chunk of the cliff that had blown out. By the time they'd dug the last suit out, Fargo's armor was bleating a steady alarm on hydraulics, and he was getting nauseous from the drug push.

The chief sergeant came back with the grav sled, where they reverently placed the final suit of armor on it, then followed it solemnly back to the shuttle. No attempt was made to find Ward's armor, knowing it was almost surely disintegrated by the force of what had to be a fusion blast, or the mountain falling on it. Even the emergency beacon was dead, and they were supposedly indestructible.

Garibaldi and Fargo were the last two aboard, as Hand cut the decon unit free, and raised the aft ramp, "Clear to maneuver, Captain."

Jace's voice came back, "Roger, lifting. Would the senior GalPat officer and Captain Fargo please meet me in the mess as soon as possible?"

Fargo groaned as he climbed out of his armor, feeling the pharmacope hit him again with numbing nanos. Garibaldi walked over, "You know where we need to go?"

"Yeah, follow me. Sorry about the major."

Garibaldi shrugged, "He did it to himself. At least he didn't take any troops with him."

Fargo led them to the mess, where Captain Jace waited, "I've got an idea how to destroy the outpost, which was, I believe, part of your tasking."

Garibaldi cocked his head, "How? I don't want…"

"Simple, I can use a laser to burn the other support leg on the first ship, and make it fall into the second one, then I can use the laser to blow a fusion bottle. It'll be fairly clean, and the bowl will contain the blast effect, maybe cause a small earthquake, but with the prevailing winds, no radiation that escapes will impact any populated areas."

Garibaldi looked at Fargo, "It's your world. What do you think?"

Fargo said, "Well, that would obliterate the remnants of the battle, make it look like they had a problem, and wipe out any possible survivors. Plus it'd turn the bowl into what will probably be nice lake in a few dozen years. I'd say do it."

Garibaldi grinned, "The major didn't tell me what his plan was, but don't we need to get authorization? I mean that's a kinda big decision for a lowly captain to make. If it was up to me, I'd do it. And even better, I don't have to put anybody back on the ground."

Captain Jace grinned ferally, "Consider it done. Y'all go take care of your troops, I'll handle it from here."

* * *

Captain Jace returned to the bridge, smiling at Colonel Randall, "Well, your Captain Garibaldi says do it. Do I have your permission?"

Nan Randall matched his expression, "Please do, Captain. It will be a fitting tribute to Major Ward if they would name the lake after him."

"Weaps, status?" Captain Jace asked.

Liz answered, "Board is active. Anterior laser still deployed." Looking at her screens she continued, "Exciters preloaded, super caps ready, power shunt standing by to deliver required power."

Captain Jace placed a carat over the strut he wanted to hit, "Evie, please rotate to two-two-eight, down eighteen."

Evie spun the ship, "Steady as she goes, Captain."

Captain Jace said calmly, "Weaps, it's all yours fire at will, target carat, stand by for secondary target."

As the countdown hit zero, Liz said, "Lasers firing." Everyone on board heard a groaning sound increase in pitch, rising to nearly a scream, and a mechanical voice continued, "5, 4, 3, 2, 1. Cease fire." There was a '*ting*', the loud noises stopped almost immediately and the cameras showed the first ship slowly collapsing into the second, which tipped even more slowly.

Captain Jace switched the carat to the stern of the falling ship, "Target carat, fire at will. Full power."

Liz said, "Lasers firing." Everyone on board heard a groaning sound increase in pitch again, rising to nearly a scream, and a mechanical voice continued, "9, 8, 7, 6, 5, 4, 3, 2," the screens bloomed with an actinic glare, and the *Hyderabad* trembled violently as the voice reached 1. "Cease fire." There was a '*ting*' as the ship rose like an elevator and the screens came back to life, showing a massive explosion, and flame reaching thousands of feet in the air.

Captain Jace chuckled, "Well, I'm guessing *that* is going to get some people's attention." He keyed the IC, "Ladies and gentlemen, the Dragoon outpost has been destroyed." Everyone on the bridge heard the cheering that arose from the cargo deck, and Colonel Randall smiled at the Captain, giving him a thumbs up.

***

The *Hyderabad* grounded near the back gate to the spaceport just after five. It was still dark as Fargo limped down the aft ramp. Nicole gave him a salute as she looked closely at him, "How bad?"

He started to shrug, then winced, "Ribs. Here's the data from my armor." Handing her four more chips he said, "And these are from the others. We didn't lose anybody, but the troopers lost one ... Two... dead, including the major. Three wounded, the medic is handling them in their armor."

The cargo deck slowly emptied out as the weary troops offloaded after they had passed their wounded, and the one dead troop out. COS Hand was amazingly gentle with each of the troops as they left, quietly cleaning up after them. Colonel Randall went out a forward hatch, disappearing unseen into the darkness, as she loped across the ramp toward the assault shuttle, still parked in front of the administration building.

***

Nicole called, "Attention on deck," as a very nervous Colonel Cameron came into the conference room, followed by Colonels Keads and Randall.

He looked around and finally said, "Seats." The three colonels took seats at the head of the table while Captain Jace, Evie, Fargo, and Captain Garibaldi took seats at the far end. Warrant Boykin slipped into a seat on the wall, followed by COS Hand and his wife, standing partially hidden in a small group of chief sergeants and master sergeants, behind Cameron and the other colonels. Fargo just shook his head, then watched the tired young GalPat lieutenant who stood silently at the middle of the table, waiting. Finally, Colonel Cameron glanced at him, "You may begin."

The lieutenant started with the standard clearance requirements, confirmed that everyone in the room had been a participant in the action, and brought up the earlier intel data that Captain Jace had provided, although he credited that to GalPat. Walking through it, he next stepped to the intel provided by Fargo and the scouts, and actually did credit the militia with collecting it.

Moving to the actual assault, he started with jamming by *Hyderabad*, then moved to the drop and video from various armor, along with the initial actions by the scouts to kill the sensors and tight beam laser. As he stepped through each piece of action, Fargo's mind drifted. *Heh, cheated death again. Brought all our folks back in one piece. Can't figure what Ward was trying... Nicole looks as tired as I feel. Wonder how long it took them to put this together? Nan looks nice and fresh. I'm betting the troops have no idea she observed the entire op. Hard to believe she's a colonel, but the cream always rises...*

He jerked back to attention when the lieutenant said, "And this is what the outpost looked like as of two hours ago." The holo showed a glassine bowl, some smoke rising from something burning in the vicinity of the two ships, and some fires along the top of the cliff and ridges surrounding the bowl. "We believe there is no danger to the forest, the fires should burn out within a day.

Changing the display, he continued, "This is the wind vector from the location, along with the radiation pattern. Of note, there is no significant radiation extent beyond ten miles."

Another view swam into the holo, "These are the reports received by various organizations and agencies last night and this morning, including the earthquake calls, the explosions and the lights in the sky. GalPat Det Hunter has handled all those at the local levels, but expect word to spread that *something* happened."

This time, the holo showed the bowl with range circles, "Due to the remoteness of the location, we do not expect anyone to actively go searching for this place, but the possibility exists for stumble on, as more colonists arrive." He turned to Nicole, "Chief Sergeant."

Nicole stepped forward, "Colonels, Captain, ladies and gentle beings. This concludes the planetary end of the briefing. I will be briefing you on the off planet pieces of the puzzle we have located. Once again, the holo reverted to the original track information. "These are the original tracks inbound to the Dragoon's outpost, emerging from deep space beyond the frontier. Taking the azimuth and elevation of the tight beam laser at the site, in conjunction with these tracks, GPV Harmony did a set of micro jumps out two light years down this line."

For the first time, Colonel Cameron interrupted, "GPV Harmony?"

"Yes, sir. She's a brand new destroyer 512 class ship. This is her first deployment. At approximately one light year out, she encountered a repeater, at this location."

The holo zoomed in on an oddly shaped satellite, "This is definitely not GalPat, or commercial equipment. It is a forty-five degree collector/transmitter on our side, and a seventy degree collector/transmitter on the far side. Two of the ship's intel team did an EVA to examine it, and determine its secondary directivity. That was calculated at three-zero-two, up twenty-two. They also installed a FTL capture unit to replicate any data received from either direction, which will be received at Star Center.

Colonel Cameron asked sharply, "So nothing traces back to here?"

Nicole looked at the lieutenant, then replied, "No, sir. Nothing tracks back here. As far as Intel is concerned, the planet Hunter knows nothing and saw nothing."

Cameron said, "Then why are we getting a company of troops dropped here?"

Colonel Randall replied, "It's our policy to spread the troops around and get them some dirt time when we can. We've dropped four Dets, so far, and I expect we will drop at least three or four more. As far as GalPat policy is concerned, this is also a 'show the flag mission' to let the Traders and Goons know we are not going to cede the Rimworlds to them lightly."

"Since I'm talking, I'd also like to thank both the captain and crew of the *Hyderabad* for their excellent work in delivering our troops and getting them out of a hot zone with minimal issues. Also, the local militia, for their coordination of the raid, the intelligence provided, and the support this morning. Their participation was critical to stopping any message of the attack getting out. Based on other intelligence, it was determined that the Traders were planning on launching one ship just before sunrise, so it is very possible that the attack won't even be noted."

Colonel Cameron stood up, "Thank you all. Dismissed." He didn't wait for anyone to call attention, as he walked out of the room.

Colonel Keads rolled his eyes and followed him quickly, as Colonel Randall stepped over to talk to Captain Garibaldi.

Fargo looked around, seeing Nicole deep in conversation with the GalPat lieutenant, he slipped quietly out the side door, heading for his liteflyer.

Stolen Time

Nan Randall had shown up, unannounced, dropped off by a GalPat shuttle the previous afternoon. She'd used the excuse of wanting some quiet time, and a chance to talk to Fargo.

They'd spent the afternoon and evening rehashing the entire assault, picking it apart and discussing how it could have been done better. That had segued into catching up with each other's careers, until Nan finally said, "I need some sleep. This has been a long week."

Fargo showed her to the spare bedroom, reminding her to lock the door to keep Cattus and Canis out. She joked, "And you too?"

He laughed, "Yeah, me too." *I'm involved with Nicole, and I'm not going to screw that up. As much as I'd like… Nope, not going there.*

Nan rolled up on her elbow as Fargo knocked on the door, "Coffee?"

She groaned, "I'm barely awake. Let me run through the fresher, but coffee sounds good!"

An hour later, they sat at the table in the kitchen as Fargo fixed them both a real cup of coffee.

Nan was besieged by Canis and Cattus, one on each side demanding attention, and she laughed as she petted them, "I can't believe these are really wild animals! They seem so cuddly and sweet."

Fargo chuckled, and looked at Cattus, "Well, she can tear you limb from limb in about forty-five seconds. Smile for Nan, Cattus!" He projected a thought to Cattus to open her mouth and put her paw, claws extended *gently* on Nan's leg. Cattus did so, and Fargo felt Nan's shock.

Turning to Canis, he projected to her to go to guard, and Canis rippled her lips, bringing a growl from the bottom of her chestand standing her ruff up. Nan, in an unconscious reaction, drew both hands in and put them on the table. "Dammit, Ethan, I get your point. They aren't pets, well, not so much. Stop it already."

Fargo smiled as he gave both animals the command to relax, and they both licked Nan's hands in a peace gesture.

Stirring her coffee, she continued, "I'm going to have to continue the current patrol, but I've talked back to Sector, and they agree that we need a stronger presence here, at least for a little while. Probably six or so months, which is about how long it will take for us to finish up this leg of the show the flag patrol."

Fargo nodded, "So?"

"I'm going to drop a company here, well, Rushing River. They're going to be autonomous, as far as planetary control, in other words, they will be subordinate to the colonel at White Beach, but they will be a quick reaction force for this sector of the Rimworlds. I'm also going to leave one assault shuttle with them, and I'd like to have *Hyderabad* available as a long range transport if required. I can't talk the Admiral into leaving a destroyer here, but there will be one at Star Center."

Taking a sip of coffee she sighed, "Oh, that is *so* good! Anyway, I'm leaving Major Jacky Culverhouse in command, but she's an MP, so she'll be the liaison with White Beach. The real command will be her hubby, Captain Culverhouse, and Captain Garibaldi. They're both mustangs, in their eighties, and have multiple combat tours. They're a couple of problem children if they get bored. But, they'll have a full deployment kit, a couple of Darkies…"

Fargo interrupted, "Darkies?"

Nan chuckled, "That's what they call themselves. They're a mated pair of scouts from Anadarko, out in Alpha Centauri. Moby and Dineah, they go by MobyDineah."

Fargo looked at her, "Anadarko? Scouts? I thought that was one of the *Wild West* colonies."

"It is, one point five G, sixty percent landmass, limited water, hellacious mountains. Pretty much ignored, until one of our GalPat ships stopped there about thirty years ago. There was some *friendly* competition with the locals, and our scouts and Special Forces got their asses handed to them. Darkies are short and wide, strong, and sneaky as hell." Nan took another sip of coffee, "The settlers are all at least half Earth stock Amerind, lots of Comanche, Cherokee, Lakota Sioux, Kiowa, and Apache. Apparently the original stock came from Oklahoma, near Fort Sill, so they've adopted a Cavalry way of life."

"What rank are they?" Fargo asked.

"They are direct accessions into GalPat as Chief Sergeants, and they are also completely telepathic with each other. Part of their mating, apparently."

Fargo filed that away as he whistled, "Oh, that could be convenient!"

Nan grinned, then dropped into a solemn expression, "And I'm leaving one maintenance tech to support the company. Senior Sergeant McDougal."

Fargo picked up on her change of expression, "And?"

"Well, he's a different bird." Nan twirled her cup, "Ah, he's got a Star of Valor, and they want him a *long* way from the flagpole."

"A maintainer with a Star?"

Nan shrugged, "Yep, on his first Det as a lead. He got left behind *inadvertently*, or so it was claimed. Something about his locator and datacomp being blocked in a maintenance tunnel they were building. He killed thirty some odd Dragoons rather innovatively, while trying to get off the planet. And he apparently had charges on the T-gate's power when the good guys came back through the gate. He got the charges off the gate and stuck on his armor, and he ran for it. Blew a leg off, but protected the gate."

Fargo whistled, "Damn, so he's basically a kid!"

Nan said, "Yep, maybe forty. But he's damn good, and I need to keep him busy. This should do it."

Fargo rolled his eyes, "So… Problem child commanders, problem child maintainer, any more *good* news?"

Nan blushed, "Well, the company I'm leaving are Herms."

Fargo just shook his head, "Hermaphrodites? Why them?"

"Well, they keep trying to kill the KTs when they spar. They've kept the docs and Med-Comps busy on the ship," Nan admitted.

"Lemme guess, the Templars think the Herms are an abomination, right?" Nan nodded. "And Herms being Herms, just love to tweak the KTs every chance they get, right?" Another nod. "So what brilliant individual put those two companies in the same ship?"

Nan sighed, "After the dust up on Rigel Three, where they fought side by side and kicked Goon ass, HQ thought it would *promote* harmony if we put them together. But Mack and Bob can handle them. I'm sure of it."

Fargo rolled his eyes, "I'm glad I'm retired and I can stay back here in the Green, in this little cabin. I don't want to be anywhere near Rushing River when that crowd gets bored!"

Nan sat up suddenly, "You're serious aren't you? I thought…"

"You thought what?"

"I thought… I thought you were in command of the militia."

Fargo chuckled, "Command? A bunch of retired CSMs and Warrants? Hell no! If anything, I was an *advisor* who was mostly ignored. Anyway, they actually are employees of Grey Lady Security."

"That's not what I heard or saw, Ethan, they *followed* you. You went in and fought… Wait a minute, Grey Lady? That damn company has their tentacles all the way out here?"

"It's my world, too. And I was able to use my talents to help out. Adrenalin rush and all that. As for Grey Lady, she does seem to get around for an immobile statue," Fargo said with a laugh.

Nan smacked him on the arm, "That's not... Argghhh! Men!"

An hour later, standing on the porch, Nan turned to Fargo, "Ethan, I can't thank you enough..."

Fargo put his fingers to her lips, "Nan, there isn't anything you can say. I've truly enjoyed you being here, and I can't tell you how proud of you I am. You're a credit to the Corps, and I'd love for you to stay, but I know you have responsibilities." Scuffing his boot, he looked at Cattus and Canis watching them, and continued, "You know you're always welcome here."

Turning, she hugged him wordlessly, then stepped back. He led her down the steps to the field in front of the house, where *Hyderabad*'s shuttle sat waiting. As they walked toward it, the Hunter version of a butterfly about a foot across flew in front of them. Nan jumped back, dodging it, as Fargo laughed. "Shut up dammit," Nan said, "I *don't* like fluttering stuff." He helped her in, and threw her bag in the back under the netting, and waved to Evie as he stepped off the back ramp.

As the shuttle lifted off, he trudged back to the liteflyer. Ensuring his bead rifle was secure, he directed his thoughts to the girls, as he thought of them, to guard the house. A short run and he lifted the liteflyer off, drifting out over the canyon, enjoying the view as he headed for the spaceport.

Twenty minutes later, he landed at the spaceport in his usual spot by the gate. Securing the liteflyer, he was surprised to see Sergeant Omar pull up in his patrol vehicle. Omar squeaked a greeting that his

Galtrans projected to Fargo's implant as, "Ho, lieutenant of the retired, ride to the ceremony, you would like?"

Fargo nodded, "Ride to the ceremony would be appreciated." He climbed aboard and Sergeant Omar rattled off across the spaceport. Five minutes later, he pulled up to the side of the administration building, where Fargo hopped off the vehicle with a wave.

Stepping to the corner of the building, he saw a GalPat podium and reviewing stand erected, and a company of troops in blacks at parade rest in front of the podium. As he watched, a group of dignitaries led by Colonel Randall stepped out of the administration building and started walking toward the podium.

He saw the planetary Governor, Klynton, her assistant, Gann, followed by what Fargo thought of as her GalPat lackey, Colonel Cameron. Then a couple of other GalPat Colonels, and Nan Randall. Mikhail, looking uncomfortable in a suit, brought up the rear. Fargo spun, sensing someone coming up behind him.

He saw a youngish troop, wearing a Star of Valor, who nodded to him as he stuck his head around the corner. "Aw shit. There is no way I'm gonna be able to sneak into formation." Turning to look at Fargo he added, "Sorry sir. Didn't mean to cuss. I was working on getting sh.. cra… *stuff* set up and I forgot to watch my wrist comp for time."

Fargo realized he was looking at Senior Sergeant Ian McDougal, and smiled, "Well, I guess we can watch the ceremony from here. You must be one of the maintainers."

McDougal nodded, "Yeah, the only one for this bunch. And they only gave me three Mechs. I got them digging now, but I'm already behind. Normally we get six for something like this."

"Digging?"

"We gotta dig a basement and tunnels connecting the buildings. Also storage and maintenance spaces for security purposes. Maybe you'll just forget I said anything, okay?"

Fargo nodded, "I know nothing. I heard nothing. By the way, I'm Captain Fargo, the local militia commander, so I'll be working with y'all from time to time."

McDougal grimaced, "Ah shit. Sorry, sir."

Fargo grinned, "Don't sweat it, troop. I'd rather a working troop than a chair borne warrior. You catch any crap for not making muster, you tell the captain to come talk to me. I'll cover for you."

"Yes, sir."

**

Fargo stood with Sergeant Omar watching the GalPat troops assembling their buildings, "Wow, I've never actually seen how they actually do that. It's like that old Japanese paper folding to see those containers unfold and become barracks and offices."

The sergeant's GalTrans rumbled his equivalent of a laugh, "Captain of the militia, folding or unfolding easy. Move equipment, still move by trooper one piece at a time. Omar glad not there. Heavy pieces, Omar always gets."

Fargo chuckled, "Sergeant, Blame you not, do I."
They climbed back in the runabout, and Omar dropped

Fargo at the store. Climbing the steps, he smiled. *Not a bad day. We're alive, survived another battle and help is on the ground if we need it.*

***

As he stepped through the portal, Ian yelled and ran to him, "Unka, Unka, did you bring me anything?"

Sweeping Ian up in his arms, he felt Ian's unbridled joy and his mischievous personality, as he tried to think of things he could do to Inga. "You should be nice to Inga, Ian. Trying to put glue in her hair isn't nice."

Ian looked up at him, horrified, "Unka, how did you…"

"Unka knows all, Ian. Unka knows all. Now go tell your dad I'm here, please." Setting Ian down, he leaned against the counter, as Ian pelted through the curtain yelling for his dad.

***

Fargo groaned as he pushed the plate away, "By the Deity, Luann. How do you and Mikhail not weigh four hundred pounds each? That was way too much food!"

Luann looked askance at him, "Well, I didn't see you stopping. You even went back for seconds. And dessert. We are moving all day, unlike you, just sitting on your butt up at your cabin. This is the third trip down with nothing. Have you stopped hunting?"

Fargo smiled, "No, just had other things going on, militia things. And I wanted to see them putting the GalPat camp together." Turning to Mikhail, he continued, "So, this trip to Endine. What are we going to be doing?"

Mikhail sipped his coffee bulb, "Well, basically a survey of the feeder and subfeeder sites. There appears to be some problems with a couple of sites, but I don't know the cause. Our techs over there aren't saying much about it, which is kinda strange."

Epilog

Captain Jace sat in the crew's mess with Fargo and Mikhail, "We'll finish the jump in an hour to Langdon's system, then it's fifteen hours into the space station. This is an odd little system, to the point that they only allow three place humans to embark on the planet."

Fargo cocked his head, "Three place humans?"

"In the Galactic classification system, human to the third decimal place. Or put another way, one genie level or less. And they're rigid about enforcement. That's why everyone debarks at the space station, and goes through customs and immigration there. They are a feisty bunch, quick to take offense, and independent as hell."

Mikhail rolled his eyes, "Oh, yeah. Finding techs to work out here has been interesting. They don't particularly like advanced tech, preferring to limit the amount of machines."

Jace chuckled, glancing at Fargo, "Makes it nice for us, most of what we've got in the cargo holds are soft goods they can't or won't manufacture. Great profit on them, because developed worlds make them cheap. The irony is Langdon system has two oddities, an ice moon that could be harvested, but they don't bother, and Endine itself has a high concentration of gold and silver ores. We're paid in ore."

Fargo narrowed his eyes, "Ice moon?" *Where have I heard something about that? The brief from the colonel... Traders and their Dragoon masters that are believed to be holed up or basing out of the Rimworld Cluster. Also, somewhere in that region there is hydrocarbon and ice mining going on. I wonder...*

Jace brought up a plot of the Langdon system on the wall screen, "Yep. Ironically the ice moon is called Eros. One has to wonder about what they were thinking!"

He and Mikhail both laughed at that, and Mikhail said, "Enough fun for me. I'm going to hit the fresher and the rack before we finish the jump."

After Mikhail left, Fargo looked around to make sure they were alone, "Jace, what are the chances of getting a recon drone near that ice moon? There are some that think the Goons might be mining it."

Jace was quiet for a couple of seconds, "If we do a standard approach, we could spit one on the way in. It would take twenty-five days to get there at point three c. How long are you planning to be on planet?"

"A week, maybe a little longer."

"Well, that doesn't work. We get two, maybe three trips out here a year. But if we were willing to potentially lose a drone, we could FTL any data back periodically, especially if it detects any movement."

"Wouldn't it be detected?"

"If it's full stealth, not unless they physically see it or run into it. The problem is, it won't stop, it will blow by the moon in... less than a second, and total viewing time will be... thirty-four seconds."

Fargo said dejectedly, "That won't work."

Jace peered at him intently, "There is a way. We can take a different departure from the space station that will allow us to drop the drone as we climb out of the well. We can spit it much closer and slower. It will still take thirty-one days to get to Eros, but it will get sucked into an orbit around Echo three, gradually degrading into the planet itself. But that would get about an hour's look a day, based on…"

"Is it even worth it?"

Jace shrugged, "If it's important to you to collect data, yes. I can get it replaced."

Fargo finally said, "Well, it might be. So…"

"We will do it, Captain."

***

Fargo was almost seeing red from the intrusiveness of the C&I official on Endine's station. He had pawed through every nook and cranny of his bag, emptied every small bag, and shaken out every bit of clothing. He had emptied each ammo box and individually counted the rounds for both the rifle and pistol, fingered both the rifle and pistol twisting and pulling on them to try to make sure they were empty. Finally Fargo opened the chambers to prove they were empty, then put them carefully back in their cases. The whole time, the little stumpy asshole had peppered him with questions about where he'd been, whom he'd been in contact with, even to the point of asking if he'd had sex with non-humans.

The only thing that kept him from punching the little shit into the floor was that he could see Mikhail being treated the same way one table over. He felt a stab in his arm and reacted, slamming a block on his mind as he grabbed the official's arm with the device in it, growling, "What the fuck was that?"

The little asshole's voice went up an octave, and he squeaked, "You can't touch me, it's not allowed!"

Fargo shook the arm, tightening his grip, "What did you do to me? I'm *not* asking again."

"It's only blood, I took your blood, I have to make sure you are human," he squealed.

Fargo shoved him away, "That better be all, asshole."

The stumpy little man scurried away after putting the instrument back into some kind of holster, muttering under his breath.

***

Three hours and a one thousand credit fine later, Fargo was still steaming as they touched down on the space port at Capital City, "I should have shot that little bastard. About the only thing he didn't do was an anal probe! And fining me for touching him? He's lucky…"

Mikhail made soothing noises, "I know, I know. But their world, their rules."

"They can take their rules and…"

Mikhail waved at a small red headed, deeply tanned man, "Ivan! Ivan! Over here!"

Ivan strolled indolently over, "Mikhail, glad to see you. Who's this?"

"Ivan March, meet Ethan Fargo. Ethan's my assistant and bodyguard." Fargo stuck out his hand, but Ivan ignored it.

"He any good?"

Fargo had enough, "Want to try me? Unarmed, knives, pistols? Your fucking choice."

Mikhail interrupted, "Fargo's a former Terran Marine. You really don't want to go there, Ivan."

Ivan grinned, "Good on ya!" Sticking out his hand, he smiled, "This world ain't no picnic. It takes a tough man to stand up to it."

Fargo grudgingly shook his hand, "I think I can take it, and the offer is still open." He sensed Ivan's mind, *Curiosity, worry, happiness to see Mikhail, and a wry sense of humor.*
Ivan laughed, "No need, I can see your eyes."

***

After lunch at the local café, Mikhail and Fargo met the other three technicians at Ivan's office. Mike Hartwell was bald, sunburned and middle aged; Jean Gauntt was the only female, compact, dark haired, looking tired, and very quiet; William Beamon was the oldest, lanky and grey haired, he carried a well-worn pistol in an even more worn holster on his hip.

After introductions, Mikhail got down to business, "Ivan is the scrambler on?" Ivan nodded and Mikhail asked, "Okay, you've indicated problems at a couple of sites, but you never gave any indication of the cause, so fill us in."

The four technicians looked at each other, finally William said, "Well, I've got Herd Beasts eating the cables out at site three. It kills them when they bite through, but that ain't stoppin' them."

Mikhail and Fargo looked at each other, "Eating the cables?"

William stood, "I'll be right back. Brought a sample in. Five minutes later he returned, a chunk of cable in his hand. The room started to smell almost immediately and Mikhail looked at the cable, "What the hell? Did the Herd Beast eat this?"

William replied, "Nope, it's the covering. It's called rubber. We started using it to protect the cables in the ground run from the power station to the feeder."

Fargo sniffed the cable, "Smells like a dead Slashgator. I wonder if that's an attractant?"

Mikhail said, "Okay, get this out of here," handing the piece of cable to William, "Why are we using, what, rubber? When we did the initial design, all of the cabling was raised above ground at least ten feet."

Ivan and Mike both tried to answer, and Mikhail pointed to Mike, "Somebody is stealing all the stanchions. The last six months, I've had three stolen from three stations and they even tried to steal the fusion unit, too!"

"Who is *they*?"

Mike shrugged, "Don't know. They're wearing camo and masks. By the time I can get the cops to respond, they are long gone."

Mikhail looked around at the others, "Who else?"

Jean said quietly, "I'm having problems at site six. They're cutting cables too, another one last night."

Fargo asked, "What does site six support?"

Jean looked at Ivan, "The table work?" Ivan nodded and she brought up the holo, "See, here is site six," she tapped a key and one group of lines began flashing, "Here is the routing to all the subfeeders."

Pointing to the westernmost cables, she said, "They've cut these three times, all in different places. Last night was right at the subfeeder." She pulled up a holovid of three indistinguishable human shapes wrapping something around a cable, pulling something, and running away. Seconds later there was a flash of an explosion, and arcing from the cut end of the cable until the preventers cut in.

Fargo said, "That's military explosive cutter cable. That stuff is restricted as hell. How the devil?"

She expanded the holo and another set of lines began blinking, "They feed down into the central valley, the GalPat base, and the local cop shop, along with the armory."

Fargo looked sharply at Mikhail, "Any thefts or anything else?"

Jean looked uncomfortable, "Well, there was some stuff painted on the armory, and a break-in last month. They got a case of cutter cable, and two cases of shaped charges."

Mikhail took control of the meeting, "Okay, folks. Time to lay it on the line. What the hell is going on out here?"

Ivan looked at the other techs, including William, who'd finally returned, "Mikhail, there appears to be some kind of underground movement on Endine. Nobody is sure who is a member, or what they want, other than to be rid of the GalPat troops and their local toadies. Every one of us has had cables cut to subfeeders that support anything cops or government."

"What about the rest of the people on those subfeeders? There are thousands of sites off each subfeeder!"

"They, whoever they are, don't care. There have been four, maybe five hundred deaths because of it. The government is covering it up, saying it's just malfunctions."

Mikhail leaned back in his chair, "So what you're saying is we are under attack?"

Again, the techs looked back and forth, Ivan finally nodded, "We think so. But there wasn't any way to tell you outright. They're censoring outgoing messages."

Fargo got up and went to his and Mikhail's bags, pulling out soft vests and inserting hard plates, "Mikhail, put this on, now." Fargo quickly slipped his shipsuit down and put his vest on, pulled his shipsuit back up, and wiggled around until he was satisfied. He reached into his pistol case, pulled it out, loaded it and slipped the pistol and holster onto his belt.

Looking at the techs, he asked, "Do y'all have protection?"

Mike nodded and tapped his chest. Fargo heard the *tunk* of a knuckle rapping on a hard plate, "Every day, all day."

***

Three hours later, Mikhail had a good picture of the real problems, and Fargo had started pacing like a caged animal, extending his empathic senses as far as they would go, prowling from the front to the back to the front of the office.

Mikhail rubbed his face, "Well, the only thing I can do is take this to the GalPat commander, and ask for help. There isn't a lot we can do between the six of us. William, somehow get the cables back up, I don't care how, but get them up, and strip that, that rubber off. Stop using it. It's got to be attracting them."

Mikhail punched a comm code into the table, staring at it blindly, as he waited for the GalPat HQ to answer. After six buzzes, it finally clicked to a visual of a bored male with the GalPat logo behind him, "GalPat HQ Endine, Sergeant Martin, duty communications, this is an unsecure circuit, may I help you sir or ma'am?"

"Sergeant, My name is Mikhail Radovich, I am the Tight Bridge Technologies manager for this star system. I am currently in Capital City meeting with our local technicians, and have been advised of sabotage on our equipment. I need an immediate meeting with the most senior GalPat officer I can see concerning security issues with our equipment and systems."

"Standby, sir." A hold screen popped up, the GalPat anthem playing softly over the speaker until the sergeant came back on, "Sir, the colonel, Colonel Zhu, can see you at sixteen. Please come to the south gate and present your identification."

Mikhail glanced at his wrist comp, "We, myself and my assistant, will be there. Thank you."

The sergeant replied, "Roger that. GalPat clear."

Mikhail turned to Fargo, "That gives us two hours."

Fargo looked at Ivan, "What's the safest way to get from here to there?"

Ivan shrugged, "Me driving you. The streets are tricky if you don't know your way around here." Pulling up a holo of Captial City, he showed them the route he would take.

Fargo mulled it over and nodded, "Okay, best of a bad lot, but you're the local expert."

Mikhail said, "Let's finish up here, then head over. I'd rather be early than late."

About the Author-

JL Curtis was born in Louisiana in 1951 and was raised in the Ark-La-Tex area. He began his education with guns at age eight with a SAA and a Grandfather that had carried one for 'work'. He began competitive shooting in the 1970s, an interest he still pursues, time permitting. He is a retired Naval Flight Officer, having spent 22 years serving his country, an NRA instructor, and a newly retired engineer who escaped the defense industry. He lives in North Texas and is now writing full time.

*Other authors you might like are on the facing pages-
I highly recommend them all!*

You can either use the embedded link (Kindle), type the URL, or search for them on amazon.com by author name or title under books or Kindle.

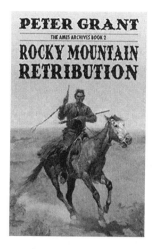

http://amzn.to/2onmSdG

http://amzn.to/2pCn1eA

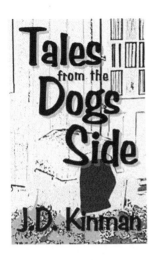

http://amzn.to/2oLPikb

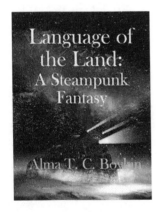

http://amzn.to/2pCwdj9

79183768R00220

Made in the USA
Lexington, KY
18 January 2018